My Sister's Child

KAREN CLARKE

ONE PLACE. MANY STORIES

HQ
An imprint of HarperCollins*Publishers* Ltd
1 London Bridge Street
London SE1 9GF

www.harpercollins.co.uk

HarperCollins*Publishers*
1st Floor, Watermarque Building, Ringsend Road
Dublin 4, Ireland

This paperback edition 2022

1
First published in Great Britain by
HQ, an imprint of HarperCollins*Publishers* Ltd 2021

ISBN: 9780008525507

MIX
Paper from
responsible sources
FSC
www.fsc.org
FSC™ C007454

For my family, with love

'Very often, all the activity of the human mind is directed not in revealing the truth, but in hiding it.'

Leo Tolstoy

Prologue

She was so light these days, bony wrists protruding from her jacket cuffs, her cheekbones too pronounced. There was barely a sound as she hit the water. Only a tiny ripple disturbed the surface.

I stared at the canal as if she might burst upwards any minute, hand outstretched. She'd been drinking before we met. I smelt it on her. So much for giving up. Another of her lies.

I shouldn't have pushed her so hard, but she came at me fast, and the things she said … her words like knives in my heart. She wouldn't listen.

I shivered as the wind picked up, my breathing ragged. How had it come to this? I wasn't a bad person. She brought out the worst in me.

My pulse raced as I trained my eyes on the water. How long had it been? Too long. I let out a groan, cold creeping around the back of my neck, settling in my heart.

I recalled the cruel curl of her lips, the way her eyes had gleamed, caught in a streetlight, before she tipped backwards. A flash of surprise across her pale face, as though she couldn't believe it.

Emotion exploded across my chest. Turning, I pushed my hands in my coat pockets to stop them shaking and half-ran from under the bridge, up the steps to the road, crashing shoulders with someone coming the other way.

'Watch where you're going,' I muttered, keeping my head down, resisting the urge to glance over my shoulder as I hurried on.

A fox screamed, tearing the silence. Hard to believe I was in the city. Life, carrying on. The blare of a car horn made my pulse fly. I snapped my chin lower and tried to breathe evenly. Could I continue as though nothing had happened? I had to, or it would all be for nothing, and I couldn't live with that.

It was for the best.

Chapter 1

'Jess, I'm so sorry about your sister.'

I nodded at the woman who had spoken. Caroline, a neighbour and so-called friend of my mother's from when we lived in London. A memory of her in our kitchen after Mum died jumped into my head, her lips clamped to Dad's.

'Thanks,' I murmured.

Voices ebbed and flowed in the pub around me. Dad was at the bar looking like a wreck, talking quietly to Uncle Denny. Not a real uncle – Dad didn't have siblings – but a childhood friend, and frequent visitor to our home over the years.

I should go to Dad but felt incapable of leaving the leather chair where Adam had settled me, handing me a measure of 'medicinal' brandy before taking Noah into the garden.

'He doesn't like everyone being sad.' Adam's dark eyes had searched mine from behind his black-framed glasses. 'Will you be all right?'

I'd nodded, feeling oddly detached.

Now, I craned my head and looked through the window to where Adam had created goalposts using his jacket and Noah's red jumper. He'd adopted a goalkeeper's crouch, arms spread as he waited for Noah to kick a scruffy football.

3

Noah would be 6 in a couple of months – a November baby. Watching my robust boy, his brown curly hair a little too long, I felt tears burning my eyes. He was too young for this. *She* was too young. I flashed back to my sister's email two weeks before she died.

Can I come and see you? We need to talk. Rachel.

No context, but that was typical. My heart had leapt, questions flooding my mind. Filled with an unnamed dread, I replied, *Yes. When?* She hadn't responded.

It was the last time I heard from her.

Dragging my gaze back, I scanned the bar of the bland London pub where we'd gathered for refreshments, chosen for its proximity to the crematorium.

'She must have been what … 27?' Caroline had settled in the chair opposite, knees jutting from the hem of her black skirt. She knew all about my sister's lifestyle; probably thought she'd got what she deserved. 'Far too young,' she went on when I didn't answer. Her heavy blonde fringe moved as she shook her head. 'I know she put your parents through a lot, but even so—'

'Why are you here?' My voice was even. 'You didn't like Rachel.'

Caroline's head jerked back. 'I'm here for you and your dad.' She flicked a look at him at the bar. 'We've known each other a long time.' Her gaze softened. 'Maybe it's as well your mother's not here.'

I placed the tumbler of brandy on the table in front of us. My hand trembled and I bit back the words I wanted to say. *Don't you remember that day? The day you tried it on with my dad. Some friend you were.* 'It's been a difficult time,' I said instead.

Caroline rested a hand on my trouser-clad thigh. 'I know you all did everything you could for your sister.' I studied the web of veins beneath her skin. 'An accident, the coroner said?'

'I'm sure Dad's told you that was their verdict.'

Caroline's hand pulled away. 'Alcohol does terrible things to a person.'

In that moment, I hated Caroline. She didn't remember the little girl I'd read stories to when she was ill, who would allow only me to wash her hair at bath time – the girl who had so much potential. 'We thought she'd given up drinking.'

Caroline absorbed this for a moment. 'Was it seven, or eight years between you?'

Was it. Past tense. 'Eight.' Mum had thought she couldn't have any more children after me, so Rachel had been a surprise. A *nice* surprise, she stressed, with no idea of the heartache that lay ahead.

I'd assumed that when we were older, my sister and I would establish a relationship that worked, just as my parents had prayed they would reconcile with their youngest child, but Mum's illness had taken hold, and after the final seizure she'd died without seeing Rachel again.

'Your dad did well at the service.' Caroline seemed determined to prolong our exchange.

I nodded, though in truth, I'd barely heard his well-scripted tribute to Rachel that glossed over all the ways she'd let our parents down. Not that there had been many people to listen apart from Caroline and her husband, and someone from the art gallery where Rachel had been working. Rachel had never been good at making friends. In a fog of disbelief I had kept looking at the shiny wooden coffin thinking, *How can she be in there?* while keeping half an eye on Noah, restlessly kicking his heels.

'I still can't believe you upped sticks and moved so far away.' Caroline gave a light laugh.

'It was always on the cards once Dad retired.' My smile felt thin. 'You probably remember we used to holiday in the Lake District.'

Caroline nodded, eyes glossy with tears. 'You scattered your mum's ashes at Windermere,' she said softly. 'Will you do the same with your sister's?'

I swallowed a hard lump of grief. 'I don't know.'

Caroline seemed to gather herself. 'You didn't mind giving up your job in the city?'

'Not really.' Finance was the career path I'd followed to live up to my role as 'the good daughter'. When Noah arrived it was an easy decision to follow Dad to the Lakes and be closer to Adam's mum. 'I didn't enjoy it.'

'Your dad still teaching?'

He'd been a professor at the London College of Music until he retired.

'He gives private piano lessons and goes fishing a lot.' I sipped my drink and tried not to shudder as it burnt my throat.

'He always was sociable.'

I glanced over and caught Uncle Denny's eye. He gave a solemn nod and rested a hand on Dad's shoulder as if to say, *I've got this. Don't worry.* Denny had long since retired from the police force, but still had an air of quiet authority.

Caroline seemed about to say more, then rose and moved to the window. 'He's such a handsome boy.' I looked out to see Noah doing a victory lap around the play area. 'He looks so like you.'

It was a throwaway comment, but I felt a tremor of nerves. 'Thanks.' I removed myself from the sweaty clasp of the leather chair, willing Caroline to go back to her husband.

'Well, I'll leave you to it.' As if reading my mind, Caroline summoned a smile. 'Take care of yourself.'

'Thank you for coming.'

As she hurried to the bar, a man materialized as though he'd been waiting for her to leave. I recognized him from the service as the owner of the gallery: Will something-or-other.

'Jess?' I had a vague impression of a teenager wearing his dad's suit. 'Sorry to bother you,' he said, blocking my view of Noah. 'It's about your sister.'

I stiffened. 'What about her?'

'It's just ...' He rubbed a hand round his jaw. 'There's something I think you should know.'

6

My heart missed a beat. 'Go on.'

Behind him, Dad peeled away from the bar, eyes seeking mine. His movements were unsteady as he made his way over, closely followed by Denny.

'I have to go,' I said as I watched Dad stumble. 'Tell me.'

Will turned, tracking my gaze. 'It's nothing.' He held up his hands. 'Forget it,' he said quietly. 'I'm sorry for your loss.' He moved away quickly, nodding to Dad as he passed.

'Who was that?' Dad said, as the door swung closed. He was steadier now, Denny's hand on his arm.

'A friend of Rachel's paying his respects.' I pulled out a chair for Dad to sit down. 'We should make a move.'

He nodded, eyes on the table.

'I'll fetch Adam,' Denny said, a smile on his weathered face. I let him go, knowing he wanted an excuse to kick a ball with Noah as Caroline's words came floating back. She was right: Noah *did* look like me, but it was Rachel I saw in his profile. He had the same long-lashed dark eyes as those in the photograph of her at the service, one of only a handful we could find, but the thing Caroline didn't know – that virtually no one knew – was that Noah wasn't biologically mine. He was Rachel's child.

Chapter 2

'How are you feeling?'

It was the third time Adam had asked. The first had been during the long drive from London back to the Lakes. I'd murmured *fine*, too drained to say more, keen for Noah to sleep during the journey. He was worn out after our 'trip', which had included a night in a Premier Inn he'd loved. Dad had slept at Denny's and was staying another night. *He'll drive me home tomorrow.*

I pretended to be dozing the second time Adam asked, and continued until we were back in Ulverston and he'd stopped the car outside our converted farmhouse.

Now, I looked at him over the mug of hot chocolate he'd made while I settled Noah into bed, recalling the awful moment when I'd heard that Rachel had drowned in the canal in Camden, close to where she was living. She'd been drinking heavily when she slipped and fell in, according to the coroner's report, though it didn't explain why she'd been there after midnight. A row with her flatmate Hannah perhaps. She hadn't been at the funeral, so I couldn't ask.

'I keep thinking about that email Rachel sent.' I needed to get the words out. 'Why did she want to visit after all this time? Nothing but the odd message for years, letting us know she was alive, and suddenly she wants to talk to me.'

'It was strange,' Adam conceded, as if we hadn't gone over it many times since the police turned up at Dad's with the bad news.

'We didn't even know she was living in London.'

'Maybe she wanted to reconcile, but …' Adam ran a hand through his crop of dark hair, which was starting to grey at the temples. For a moment, he didn't look like himself, but I supposed I didn't look like me either. Catching my reflection in the kitchen window, I appeared older than 35, my shoulders rounded, skin loosened, as if disbelief had burrowed beneath it. The fear I hadn't voiced to Adam, or my dad, was that Rachel had wanted Noah back, despite her insistence that it would never happen. If only she'd said more in her email, or I'd been brave enough to ask the simple – most obvious – question. *Is it about him?* But I couldn't bring myself to do it, scared of the answer, of what might lie ahead if she'd said *yes*. My and Adam's names were on the birth certificate, but nothing was set in law, despite Rachel's signature on the note she left with Noah, giving us custody of her baby. A DNA test would have confirmed she was his birth mother – that she had every right to be in his life.

'You think she'd changed her mind about Noah, don't you?'

Hearing Adam say it so baldly gave me a jolt. Putting my mug down, I glanced at the doorway to check Noah hadn't appeared, but Adam had kept his voice low.

'People change their minds.'

My mind flew back to that morning, nearly six years ago, to the email waiting in my inbox; an announcement from Rachel that she was nearly five months pregnant. She had only just found out and was panicking.

I'm not drinking. I've been working, saving to go back to Thailand. There's no way I'm being saddled with a baby, I wouldn't cope. Do you want it? If not, I'll put it up for adoption. Due in November. Let me know ASAP. R.

Just like that, as though offering a piece of furniture she was considering getting rid of. No context, or update about her life

9

in general. When I shakily replied with a request for her to call, to come home, followed by a barrage of questions, she only responded to one.

The father's out of the picture. He doesn't know and it's best it stays that way. He's no good. Yes or no? R.

I immediately called Adam, who'd left for work. He came straight home, his friendly face compressed into an expression I didn't recognize when I told him Rachel's bombshell.

'Isn't it typical that we're struggling to have a baby, that we want a family more than anything, and your sister, she ...' Words appeared to fail him, but in spite of his initial shock, a glint of brightness had entered his eyes, a look that said, *Here's an opportunity*; to have the baby we'd assumed would come easily, but still hadn't, with doctors failing to find a reason why. I'd watched Adam grow more silent, less sure of himself, had mooted the idea of IVF, despite not wanting to fill my body with hormones. I'd even suggested we start the adoption process but this ... this was the perfect solution. A baby that would have my family's genes.

'Don't you care that it won't biologically be yours?' I'd barely believed we were even discussing it when an hour earlier Adam had been quietly showering, trying not to wake me before slipping out of the house, an argument about the hours he was working lingering from the night before.

'A baby, Jess.' He came over and pulled me against him. He'd trembled with excitement. 'No gruelling hormone treatment, and newborn babies rarely come up for adoption.'

'Rachel's hormonal right now.' I was trying to be realistic, but already my mind and my heart were adjusting, making room for this unwanted child – imagining the feel of him or her in my arms. 'She might change her mind.'

Holding me tighter, his voice a rumble in his chest, Adam had said, 'Have you honestly ever known your sister to change her mind about anything?'

I emailed, *Yes. 100% YES!* And Rachel replied that she would

10

let us know when the baby was born and leave it with us. Just like that.

We told my dad, but not Adam's mum, Jennifer, in case she didn't approve. At Adam's insistence, we invented a pregnancy I'd been unaware of until I was almost five months along as I'd had no symptoms, then developed 'complications' necessitating leaving work for complete bed rest. I hadn't liked the deception, or lying low, putting off Adam's mum when she wanted to visit, but spent my time reading everything about pregnancy and babies until I felt as if I really were pregnant. Dad had been angry at first that Rachel 'typically' wasn't taking responsibility, fretting about the father, suspecting it was *you know who*.

I don't think it is, Dad. I think she would have wanted his baby, don't you?

The only update she sent came a month before Noah was born, on a windy October day. We were painting the tiny spare room in our apartment, turning it into a nursery, when I received a selfie of Rachel with her top rolled up, revealing her distended stomach with its popped-out bellybutton.

Had a scan, all good. It's a boy, so you'd better start thinking of names. I've been playing him classical music, so he has half a chance of coming out cultured, ha ha. R.

In the scan picture attached, *Jess Sanderson* was visible in the corner. She had given them my name. I printed it out and wept, an outpouring of grief for the pregnancy I would probably never have as long as I was with Adam, and for the little pot-bellied little sister I used to bathe. When I emailed back a plea to come home, for us to go through the birth together, she didn't reply.

'I guess we'll never know now.' Adam's words landed me back in the moment.

'I guess not.'

'Maybe it's for the best.'

I caught Adam's apologetic wince. His normally clean-shaven

jaw was stubbled, and there were grey troughs of tiredness under his eyes. 'Sorry,' he said, sweeping crumbs off the breakfast bar.

'It's OK.' I knew he wasn't being cruel, but voicing a thought I'd already dismissed, ashamed it had crept in. That Rachel wouldn't be coming to reclaim Noah one day.

Chapter 3

'Jess! I wasn't expecting you back so soon.'

I hung up my jacket and smoothed my hair before turning to smile at Kristin. 'It's been three days. I can't sit at home doing nothing.'

The sight of my desk was like greeting an old friend. I wanted to run my hands over its shiny surface, but Kristin was watching me, as well-groomed as ever in a fitted dress patterned with tiny flowers. Her mahogany, blunt-cut bob gleamed under the downlighters which picked out the rose-coloured tint along her cheekbones. My usual outfit – white shirt, plain skirt – felt dowdy, though I'd made an effort with my make-up and washed my fine brown hair before tying it up in a ponytail.

'How are things here?'

'Great.' She came over to envelop me in a fragrant hug before pulling back, concern in her warm, brown eyes. 'How are you really, Jess?'

For a second, I wished she didn't know so much about me, but with only the two of us at Cumbrian Cottages most of the time, we'd become close. I'd taken over management when the owner retired six months ago, and interviewing Kristin for my old job I'd felt an instant connection, despite her being several years younger. She made a refreshing change from Moira, who worked part-time and was lovely, but preferred a businesslike relationship. With an air of maturity, and an expressive smile that drew people in, Kirstin was a hit with clients, securing sales even when they seemed unlikely, making our little agency – tucked down a side road off the main street – surprisingly successful.

'I'll feel better when I've had some coffee,' I said.

'Sit down, I'll get it.'

When Kristin returned with two steaming mugs, I was settled at my desk.

'I expect Adam has stepped up.'

'He's been great.' My reserve faded as I inhaled the steam from my mug, shoulders loosening for the first time in days. 'He never really approved of Rachel, but forgave her a lot when she gave us Noah …' I paused, remembering the night I'd poured it all out to Kristin after a few drinks at the local pub on her birthday, once everyone had gone home. I'd been unusually tipsy, struggling with my coat. Kristin had been telling me how cute Noah was when I blurted out the truth. To her credit, she hadn't expressed surprise, was merely thoughtful as she helped me with my coat and handed me my bag.

'It sounds as though Noah is exactly where he's meant to be,' she'd said, and I hugged her drunkenly and said something about providence bringing her into my life.

'Well, actually, it was a friend of mine who told me you were looking to take someone on, but thanks,' she replied with a trace of her Essex accent – she'd grown up there, before relocating to the Lakes – smiling as she linked arms with me, leading me out of the pub, and driving me home. I rarely drank that much and the next day vowed to be more careful, but Kristin had never once alluded to my confession, or hinted that she saw Noah as anything but my child.

'The funeral must have been hard, especially after not seeing your sister for so long.' She slid gracefully into the leather swivel chair at her desk.

I took a sip of coffee before answering, sifting through my emotions, something I'd been doing a lot since the phone call from Dad three weeks ago, asking me to come over. Seeing the police car outside his cottage, I'd known in my gut it was about Rachel.

'I think, in a way, we'd been expecting it for a long time,' I admitted. 'It was as if there was a void inside her, waiting for—' I didn't want to utter his name. The boyfriend who'd been Rachel's undoing: *Lucian West.* Bored, rich, living off his parents' money, looking for thrills and someone to idolize him. 'Something to fill it,' I finished. 'Nothing we ever did was enough.'

'Poor you.' Kristin's eyes shone with sympathy.

Deciding to head her off, I said, 'Anyway, yes, the funeral was awful, more so for Dad.' I pushed away an image of his grief-ravaged face, thinner as sorrow ate at him. He'd already lost Mum – the love of his life – and now his youngest daughter.

'And she drowned because she'd been drinking.' Kristin gave a grimace of horror. 'No wonder you don't like alcohol.'

I tried not to imagine my sister's last moments. Whenever I did, it was like seeing it happen to someone on-screen – horrific but not quite real. 'I don't mind a glass of wine now and then.'

As if sensing my reluctance to discuss it further, Kristin said brightly, 'Anyway, everything here is fine. We've a couple of viewings lined up …' She paused as the door opened, letting in a waft of September air. A middle-aged couple entered, enquiring about a property on our website, and while Kristin answered their questions, I switched on my computer and checked my emails, grateful to slip into the familiar routine.

Adam hadn't been able to hide his relief when I said I was going back to work after dropping Noah at school. He'd been treating me like a delicate piece of china since the funeral, adding to my sense of unreality. It was easier when Noah was there, demanding our attention, but once in bed the atmosphere became fraught, as if something unresolved hung in the air.

When the couple had left, Kristin said with a smile, 'I've got a good one for you.'

'Oh?' I stopped midway through typing a reply to a client who was concerned her house sale was dragging on too long.

'A woman came in yesterday and asked about Tarn Cottage.'

'Really?' The property in nearby Broughton Beck had been on the market for a while as the owners were holding out for the full asking price. 'Did you offer to show her round?'

'Yes, but she didn't have time. I've booked a viewing for tomorrow afternoon if you'd like to do it.'

I was relieved to feel a buzz of adrenaline. 'I would.'

'I got the feeling that money's not an issue for Mrs …' Kristin consulted her screen. 'Vanessa Blake. She sounded as though she's already made up her mind.'

'Brilliant.' I brought up the details of Tarn Cottage on my screen as the phone on Kristin's desk started ringing.

'Oh, and a letter came for you,' she said. 'It's in your tray.'

While Kristin answered the call, I picked up the slim, white envelope, bearing my name and the agency address. There was a stamp, but no postmark. I stared at it for a moment, a tingling awareness at the back of my neck. I ripped it open, pulled out a sheet of paper, and read the two sentences printed in tiny font:

He's not your son. Tell him who his father is, or I will.

Chapter 4

Rachel

Before

From: RBeresford@gmail.com
To: JessSanderson11@gmail.com
Subject: Getting things off my chest

I saw a counsellor once, Jess. Do you remember? It was a condition of me being allowed back to school after I was suspended. I only went once. I hate talking about myself and 'opening up' (you might have noticed). I kept pretending to fall asleep and she got angry, and I suggested she might need to see a counsellor, which didn't go down well. Always the joker, me. Always the joke.

She suggested one thing though, before it all went downhill, and that was to write things down, as though I was addressing the words to someone.

'But don't show them. It's to get things off your chest.'

Or words to that effect. I wasn't listening too closely,

but since being sober because of the baby (and it's not easy believe me) I need something to do with my hands that doesn't involve tipping vodka into a glass. It's tricky, typing on my phone, but that's good in a way as it keeps me occupied for longer.

Funny, but I visualise you as if you're still 16, all long hair and big worried brown eyes. Poor Jess. The Good One, saddled with the family from hell. Even your email address is pure. I'll bet all the money I don't have any more that the number 11 is a reference to Mum's birthday.

Anyway, what to write? Well, for a start, here's a list of all the things you haven't missed by not being pregnant.

1. Being sick on a regular basis
2. Heartburn
3. Stretch marks
4. Piles
5. A craving for fish paste sandwiches. What's that all about? I thought making fish paste was a criminal offence, but I found some. Disgusting. And amazing. I couldn't get enough of the vile stuff.

So, yeah, I took one (more than one) for the team.

I was in Spain by the way, while pregnant. It felt as much like home as anywhere did without Lucian, so I thought I'd stay until closer to Birthing Day, which couldn't come soon enough, to be honest. I wasn't looking forward to it one bit. Then I headed back to Blighty to do the deed.

Talking of Lucian, which I still love to do, even though we've officially 'parted' for a while … actually, I'm not going to talk about him. You always hated him, didn't you? Couldn't see what I saw in him. I have a strong feeling we'll be together again one day (he's the only person I feel 'romantic' about) and maybe then you'll understand. That's *my plan, anyway. It's why I'm back in London, being a Good Girl. Mostly.*

OK, that's enough. My thumbs are aching, and I feel a fish paste sandwich coming on. Only kidding. Time to delete.

Bye, Sis x

Chapter 5

I managed to shove the letter in my bag by the time Kristin finished her call.

'Who was that from?'

I swallowed. 'A grateful buyer, thanking me for helping them find their "forever home".'

'That's so sweet,' she said, while my cheeks flamed, and my hands trembled.

Ten minutes later, I called Adam from the tiny bathroom at the back of the building to tell him what had happened. 'It must be from him,' I said, voice shaking. 'Noah's father.' I would never normally come out with it like that. Adam hated any reminders that Noah wasn't biologically his. 'Rachel must have told him. Maybe that's why she wanted to talk – to warn me.'

'You think he's coming for Noah?' Adam sounded calmer than I'd have expected. 'Why not go through normal channels and approach us like a decent human being?'

'I don't know, Adam. Because he's deranged?' My voice rose. 'Rachel said he was no good, remember?'

'Why would she have told him now, after all this time?' He sounded bewildered.

'I've no idea, but I think we should call the police.'

A slight hesitation told me how deeply Adam didn't want this to be happening. Then again, neither did I. 'Do you want me to do it?'

'No, it's fine. I will.'

Claiming an early lunch break, I hurried to my car and spoke on the phone to an officer at the local police station, only to be told the letter in itself wasn't evidence of a crime.

'There isn't a threat to life and I'm afraid one letter isn't considered harassment,' the officer explained, sympathetically. 'If you get any more or feel that you or your son are in danger, call 999.'

I could barely focus on work for the rest of the afternoon, relieved that Kristin was out with potential buyers for most of it. As soon as I got home, I called Denny from the bedroom where I wouldn't be overheard.

'Someone out there wants Noah.' I could barely hold back tears. 'Can you come up and keep an eye out?'

He agreed immediately, as I knew he would. He missed the force and kept his hand in some private work – insurance fraud and cheating spouses – and in addition to that, he would do anything for our family.

'I don't want Dad to know. He's got enough to cope with.'

'You won't know I'm there,' he promised in the gravelly voice that had scared me a bit as a child. 'If anyone so much as looks at Noah, they'll wish they hadn't.'

I came off the phone reassured, but it was hard not to worry. *Tell him who his father is, or I will.* Every time I replayed the words, a shockwave ran through me. Adam was putting on a brave face for Noah's sake and didn't want to discuss it once I told him I'd spoken to Denny, but I could hardly sleep that night, mind and stomach churning while Adam fidgeted beside me, hogging the duvet.

'I wish I didn't have to go to Berlin,' he said the following morning, stuffing a shirt in his holdall without folding it. 'I can't get out of it.'

The trip had been booked for a while, but I'd forgotten about it. 'It's fine,' I said, though in truth, it would have been nice to have him at home while things were so unsettled.

'Are you sure you'll be OK?' He threw me a concerned look. 'You know that nothing bad will happen with Denny on the case.'

'I hope not.'

'Maybe whoever it is wants money,' he said. 'A friend of Rachel's making a blackmail attempt.'

The idea was weirdly reassuring, though wouldn't a friend of Rachel's have been at her funeral? 'Some friend,' I said. 'So, what, we might get a demand for cash?'

'I don't know, Jess.'

'We'll pay it though. Won't we?'

'Daddy, I don't want you to go burling.' On cue, Noah shot into the room and dive-bombed the bed, where he began pulling out everything Adam had packed.

'Hey, little monkey.' A grin transforming his tired face, Adam grabbed Noah and hoisted him in the air. 'It's Berlin, not burling.'

'Daddy will be back on Saturday night.' I brightened my tone as I scooped Adam's clothing back into his holdall. He'd taken an overnight trip a month earlier to meet a potential client who had invited him back, with the intention of offering him a contract, we hoped. 'We can make his favourite cake for when he comes home.'

'Yay!' Noah executed a wobbly spin on the rug by the bed, arms punching the air. 'Chocolate chips!'

'That's *your* favourite.' Adam zipped his bag shut. 'Mine is a unicorn cake made with Smarties.' He wiggled his eyebrows at me. 'Think you can manage that?'

'I'm afraid you'll have to make do with a Victoria sponge.' I tried to match his smile, sensing him struggling as much as I was to be upbeat for Noah.

'Time to get ready for school,' Adam said to Noah, checking the clock.

'Can we do my dinosaur jigsaw?'

'Again?'

'Please, Daddy?'

'Get dressed and brush your teeth first,' I said, moving to the window to look outside. *What if he was out there now, waiting?* How was I supposed to let Noah out of my sight?

'Do as Mummy says, little man.'

'OK, Daddy.'

Adam shot me a look of concern as he led Noah out to the bathroom. 'Try not to worry, Jess.'

'I'm not,' I lied, catching my reflection in the mirror. I was a mess, eyes pink-rimmed from lack of sleep, and I'd lost weight, my stomach too knotted to eat much. I'd caught Adam staring a couple of times lately, as if searching for signs of the woman he'd met in Greece, ten years ago. Back then, on my first holiday in ages, not long after Mum had died, I'd found myself nudging out of my grief and away from my sensible persona.

Maybe it was being with my girlfriends Sasha and Jo, in blazing sunshine, the cerulean skies, and lapping ocean, or the sense of new beginnings, but I'd thrown myself into everything the island had to offer; windsurfing, scuba-diving, hiking, and skydiving, which had left me breathless with adrenalin. One evening, I let Sasha and Jo talk me into a karaoke session at a bar near our hotel in Crete, and while belting out 'You're the One That I Want', I started aiming the words at a solidly attractive man, drinking alone at the bar. Emboldened by a couple of sangrias, I made my way over and asked his name, something I'd never have done back in England. I assumed, because of his tanned skin, black hair, and dark eyes he must be Greek, but he introduced himself as Adam Sanderson, a fellow Brit from London. Putting on a pair of tortoiseshell-framed glasses, as if to see me more clearly, he told me I had an amazing voice and asked where I'd learned to sing. I admitted, red-cheeked, I'd belonged to a choir at school, and he confessed he was supposed to be on holiday with his fiancée, but she'd dumped him a week before they were due to fly out.

'We'd already rebooked the trip twice, because of a last-minute emergency at work, and she decided she'd had enough of me putting my job first. She said only heart surgeons and the Prime Minister are allowed to cancel holidays, not IT consultants.' He gave a self-deprecating shrug that endeared him to me. 'Anyway, I decided to come on my own.'

'Are you having fun?'

His gaze warmed up. 'Not yet.'

We hung out for the rest of the week with my friends' approval, taking in the sights, exchanging life stories, and enjoying sunset walks on the beach, Adam slowing his pace as I struggled to match his six-foot-two stride. I remember laughing a lot, comparing him with my last boyfriend, who had taken himself too seriously.

At 30 – six years older than I was – Adam had seemed mature, a fully grown adult who knew what he wanted from life; to get married and have children. I liked him being so open and loved his geeky passion as he explained that he worked in partnership with clients, advising them how to use information technology to meet their business objectives. 'I want to go freelance so I can set my own hours.'

There'd been an adjustment back in drizzly London, me still living in Barnes with my dad, working in finance for an insurance company, and Adam in his hotel-like, Canary Wharf apartment, a bag always half-unpacked as he prepared to fly to some European city, but once the awkwardness of meeting our everyday selves wore off, we'd become enmeshed in each other's lives. For a while, I'd imagined travelling with Adam, exploring new cities when my job allowed, but although I joined him on a couple of trips, it hadn't been as much fun going around on my own. Adam had made it clear that what he wanted was something stable to come home to. Between us, we earned decent money and I had some that Mum had left me put aside, but we still couldn't afford our own place in London. I'd split my time between Dad's house and Adam's apartment while we planned our wedding, finally moving in with him after our honeymoon in Greece, where we discussed buying a place in the countryside to raise our children. Eighteen months later, we were still in his apartment, I still hated my job, and despite timetabling sex to coincide with ovulation, there was still no sign of a baby. Then Dad retired and moved to the Lakes, and six months later I got the email from Rachel that changed our lives.

I put the breakfast bowls in the dishwasher once Adam had left the house with Noah, who was excited his daddy was dropping him at school on his way to the airport. Then I showered and dressed on autopilot, standing for a moment at the landing window overlooking the hills. *He's not yours. Tell him who his father is, or I will.* My stomach tightened, nausea rising as I scoured the landscape, as if the sender of the letter might reveal themselves. For a moment, I yearned for the sounds of life I'd grown used to living in London. We'd fallen in love with our house, with its mix of old and new, the double-glazed windows in traditional wood frames, the Rayburn that warmed the kitchen, and the original stonework, but occasionally, I found it too quiet.

I realized I was shivering. On impulse, I phoned the school to check that Noah had arrived safely.

'He's here,' the head teacher told me. 'Is everything all right, Mrs Sanderson?'

I made up something about there being a problem with the car, jittery with nerves as I rang off, picturing a faceless person snatching Noah away.

Unless Adam was right, and it was about money. Someone under the illusion – fed to him by Rachel – that Adam and I were well-off.

It was a relief when my phone buzzed with a text from Denny.
I'm in Ulverston. Try not to worry. D
Thank you

I took a deep breath and wondered whether there was time to check in on Dad before heading to work. He wasn't answering his phone, but his house was a twenty-minute drive. Maybe I could persuade him to come round for dinner this evening. It would be a nice distraction.

As I picked up my car keys and kicked off my slippers, my phone rang, making me jump.

'Hello?'

'Is that Jess?' The voice was male, a London accent.

'Who is this?'

'Will Taylor.' A pause. 'We met at your sister's funeral.'

'Of course.' I had a memory of his navy suit, hands raised as he backed away. 'How did you get my number?'

'Rachel had you down as her emergency contact.'

His words landed like a blow. 'But we hadn't spoken for years.'

'Listen, do you have a minute to talk?'

'About what?' My pulse rocketed.

'I'm still trying to get my head around what happened to Rachel.'

'Me too.' I wondered whether Will had been more than a friend, but he sounded too nice, too well-spoken and educated. Not Rachel's type. 'Look, I don't think—'

'The thing is,' he cut in, 'I think your sister was murdered.'

Chapter 6

I forced a breath into my lungs. 'Rachel's death was an accident. The police said there was no evidence of foul play.' It sounded like a line from a crime show.

'No evidence only means they had no proof.'

Wasn't that the same thing? 'Why are you saying this? Don't you think we've gone through enough? My father is in pieces.' I struggled to regain my composure. 'Do you have any proof?'

'Of course not, or I would have gone to the police.'

'So it's only a theory?' I wasn't normally rude, but I wanted this man off the line, to stop giving shape to the whisper of worry I'd had about Rachel's last message and what it meant. 'She drank a lot,' I went on, not giving him time to respond. 'You must know that. She fell off a balcony once and shattered her pelvis.' Lucian West had vanished after that episode, probably worried he'd be implicated. They'd been partying at his parents' villa in Portugal at the time. 'A few months later, she nearly died from alcohol poisoning. It was a miracle she wasn't run over when she collapsed in the middle of a busy road.' *Shut up.* I rarely talked about Rachel. Hadn't for a long time. Nearly every memory contained a version of her in hospital somewhere, snarling at us to get out, leave her alone, stop ruining her life.

'I know she'd had problems' – I barely suppressed a snort of disbelief at Will's understatement. Maybe he hadn't known her that well – 'but she'd been good for a while, and then … she wasn't.'

I couldn't listen any more. 'If you've any concerns, I suggest you take it up with the police,' I said coldly. 'Nothing will bring her back.'

'Jess, hear me out. I think—'

I cut him off and threw my phone into my bag. My neck muscles were tight. I tried to massage the tension away, furious that Will – a stranger – had me so rattled.

As though magnetized, my eyes moved to the gallery of photos along the wall; me cradling Noah as a tiny baby, his eyes shut tight, my face suffused with wonder. From the second I held him, Noah had been mine, as surely as if I'd given birth to him. In the photo next to it, Noah was in his bathtub, Adam cradling his downy head, and above that was one of Noah swaddled in a blanket in my father's arms. Dad was smiling at his grandson – a real smile, like the one he used to reserve for Mum.

Without Rachel, there would be no Noah.

Dread settled in my stomach. With effort, I pushed my feet into my shoes and looked at my watch. Time for work. Visiting Dad would have to wait.

For the next few hours, I managed to push everything else out of my mind. If Kristin noticed I wasn't my usual self, she didn't comment, taking my cue by sticking to work topics. There had been a spurt of interest in a cottage overlooking Morecambe Bay and Kristin had booked a couple of viewings. 'I'll be back before lunch, and don't forget you're showing Mrs Blake around Tarn Cottage at three o'clock this afternoon. She'll meet you there.'

My stomach lurched. I'd completely forgotten. Just as well Noah was going to his friend Ben's after school. I'd wanted to cancel but Adam thought we should carry on as normal, for Noah's sake.

'No worries.' I made a point of checking the online diary. 'Maybe we'll both have offers on the table by the end of the day.'

Kristin and I had a healthy rivalry when it came to selling, though she had the edge on me when it came to closing. At her previous job at a high-end clothing store, she had honed a way of being persuasive without being pushy, whereas I tended to back down.

'I've a feeling they'll be fighting over this one.' There was a faint flush of anticipation on her cheeks that matched her poppy-patterned dress. 'I might put in an offer myself,' she said, dimpling into a smile.

'What would your mum say about that?'

When her smile dimmed, I regretted my throwaway comment. Kristin lived with her mother in Lancaster – an agoraphobe who hadn't left their house in years. Her brother was a ski instructor, living in Switzerland, so their mother depended on Kristin. 'Sorry,' I said. 'I wasn't thinking.'

'Don't be silly, it's fine.' Kristin gave a little shake of her head. 'Are you OK?'

For a second, I considered telling her what Will had said, and about the letter – still crumpled in my bag – but it seemed too big for sharing. I went cold as a thought struck. *Could Will's claim about Rachel, and the letter be connected?* 'I didn't sleep too well last night,' I said, aware Kristin was waiting for an answer. 'I never do when I know Adam's going to be away for a few days.' Especially since the last time he was on a trip, seeing a potential client in Buckinghamshire, when I'd become convinced that someone had been in the house. It had taken a while to notice a photo missing, and I'd sensed a disturbance in the bedroom, but there had been no sign of a forced entry. When he got back that night, Adam had been doubtful anything had happened, but I was unsettled for days. I couldn't help wondering if there was a link with what was happening now.

'I thought he didn't travel for work any more.' I'd told her about the long hours Adam had put in before Noah, building up a client base in order to go freelance, while working for the company that had employed him out of university. Often, I wouldn't see him for days and just when we'd relaxed into each other's company, it was time for him to fly off again. Looking back, neither of us had been particularly happy then, but after Noah, everything changed. Adam wanted to be at home, to be part of the family he'd longed for, but lately work had begun to take over once more.

'Things have been a bit tough,' I admitted. 'Big companies are cutting back so he's taking jobs where he can.' We were lucky to not have to worry too much about money. We still had savings from the sale of Adam's apartment, but it was important to him to provide for his family. His father had walked out when he was a toddler and money had been tight. 'It's only Berlin,' I added. 'And he'll be home on Saturday.'

Kristin's smile returned. 'You're so lucky,' she said, not for the first time. 'Shame he doesn't have a twin.'

I widened my eyes. 'How weird would that be?'

Kristin's spurt of laughter made me smile in spite of myself. 'A friend with a twin personality, then.'

'Adam hasn't really stayed in touch with friends.' I thought of Simon, one of his old university buddies – the one he'd considered his closest friend. Then again, neither had I, only occasionally swapping messages with Sasha and Jo since we'd moved out of London. 'You'll meet someone when the time is right.' I caught an odd expression on Kristin's face, gone so swiftly, I wondered whether I'd imagined it. Had I touched a nerve? Maybe I wasn't as focused on what I was doing and saying as I'd thought. My mind veered to the letter, and Will's phone call, and when the postman came in with the day's mail, my heart drummed as I riffled through it, half-expecting to see another envelope addressed to me.

'Looking for anything in particular?' Kristin's face was puckered with curiosity.

'Not really. Catching up, that's all.'

Kristin glanced at her phone and got up from her desk, gathering her bag and jacket in a graceful movement. 'I'd better make a move,' she said. 'See you later, alligator.'

By the time she returned with an update, brandishing a bag of our favourite pastries from the bakery across the street, I'd booked a couple of property valuations, arranged to photograph a cottage for our website, and negotiated an offer for a client wanting a quick sale. Nearly two hours had passed.

'I haven't got time for lunch.' I rose from my chair, stretching to ease an ache in my lower back before checking I had everything I needed for my meeting with Vanessa Blake. 'I'll head off now in case traffic's bad.'

'Take this with you.' Kristin shook the bag at me. 'You need to eat.'

It wasn't a long drive to Tarn Cottage and the roads were less busy now the holiday season was over. In the height of summer, it was necessary to add at least fifteen minutes to every journey. I slowed as I passed the sign for Broughton Beck and the road narrowed. Dry-stone walls and fields of grazing sheep gave way to a row of whitewashed houses, green hills rising beyond. The sky had darkened to gunmetal, hanging low over the landscape, giving it a gothic feel. Goose bumps bristled my arms. I preferred showing houses when the weather was bright. Everything was better under blue skies and sunshine, and clients tended to be in a better mood.

I couldn't get Will's words out of my head. *I think your sister was murdered.* He must have had a reason for saying it. Why hadn't I heard him out?

On edge, I looked for Tarn Cottage. It was tucked into the hillside at the end of a winding road and my heart dropped at the sight of a small white Honda parked by the gate at the front of the building. Vanessa Blake had arrived already, even though I was early. I'd hoped to have a walk around, empty my head, and get a fresh feel for the place. I'd also wanted to finish the pastry I'd absentmindedly started, scattering crumbs down my front.

Pushing everything else out of my head for now, I brushed myself down and checked my appearance in the rear-view mirror before getting out. It wasn't uncommon for a viewer to sneak a look around if they knew the owner wasn't present.

I locked my Mini and smoothed my skirt, wishing I'd thought to bring a coat. A cool breeze had sprung up, working its way through the thin material of my shirt. Taking a breath, I began walking towards the gate, jumping when the door of the Honda sprang open. A woman stepped out, blocking my way.

'Jessica Sanderson?'

For a second, I had a dizzying sense of déjà vu, as though I knew her and had heard her voice before. 'Please, call me Jess,' I said.

She smiled and held out a hand. 'I'm Vanessa Blake.'

Chapter 7

'Have we met before?' As soon as I said it, the feeling I knew her dissolved and I wished I hadn't asked. 'You looked familiar for a moment.'

'I have that kind of face.' She didn't smile back as she tightened her grip on my hand. Somewhere in her late fifties, she was small and slender with a mass of curly brown hair in a bun, tendrils framing a finely featured face. Faint lines shadowed her pale-blue eyes, which swept over my features as though memorizing them.

I pulled my hand away. 'Have you been waiting long?'

'I wasn't sure exactly where the place was and didn't want to keep you waiting.'

I hoisted my bag onto my shoulder and turned to open the gate. 'Have you visited the Lake District before?'

'Not for a long time.' Her voice was soft, her accent hard to place. *Posh*, Kristin would say. She was wearing a baggy grey linen dress with tan leather sandals and a fringed shawl wrapped around her shoulders, and holding a leather tote bag with a designer tag. Around the strap, her knuckles were white, and a frown marred her forehead as she scanned the grey-stone cottage. Maybe it wasn't what she'd been expecting. 'It's a beautiful area,' she added. 'A nice place to live.'

'Will it be a second home?'

'I'm actually looking for my daughter.'

Confusion scrambled my brain. 'Your daughter?'

Her frown intensified. 'My daughter is relocating here. She doesn't have time for viewings.'

I smiled again and shook my head. 'Sorry.'

'Don't worry about it.' Her tone was remote as she dug a hand into her bag and pulled out her phone, peered at the screen, and put it back again. 'Shall we go inside?'

'Of course.' The key jammed in the front door, and I jiggled it, face flushing. No doubt Vanessa Blake was judging my performance and finding it lacking. *What was wrong with me?* The letter, and Will's call were making me jittery, but something felt off. The effect was heightened by the overcast sky and a distant rumble of thunder. 'Looks as though the weather is about to break.'

She didn't reply.

Finally, I had the door open and gestured for Vanessa to enter. I followed, catching a trace of her clean, elegant scent.

'The photos online don't do it justice,' I said, keen to get her out of the hallway. It was darker than I remembered. 'The owners have spent a lot of money on improvements, which is reflected in the price. There's a lovely view of the fells from the lounge and we're not far from the Cumbria Way if you are ... if your daughter is into walking. It goes all the way to Carlisle, but it's seventy-two miles so not for the faint-hearted.' Aware I was babbling like a tour guide, I led the way, glad I'd familiarized myself with the floor plan of the old cottage. 'Does your daughter have children?'

I turned to see Vanessa framed in the doorway, casting her eyes around the super-sleek kitchen, the open living-and-dining room, and the huge sliding doors leading onto a paved patio. Perhaps she was imagining her family there once the place was furnished, the polished floorboards warmed with rugs, the white-painted walls filled with artwork and photos.

She moved with poise, trailing her fingers on the wall as she crossed over to the doors, the soles of her sandals barely making a sound. 'It's incredibly quiet.'

'It is peaceful,' I agreed, aware that she hadn't answered my question. 'There are no neighbours for a few miles, but it's a short drive to Ulverston—'

'Is that where you live?'

'I … yes.' I spoke to her back, shifting my bag to my other shoulder. 'There's plenty to do there actually. It's a market town with a canal, the world's shortest and deepest …' *Why had I mentioned the canal?* An image of Rachel being pulled from the water slid into my head, and my father's face when he returned from London after identifying her body. I had offered to do it, though I hadn't wanted to. Adam did too, grey-faced with horror. *Are they sure it's her, your sister? Maybe they've got it wrong.* In the end, Dad insisted on going alone, wouldn't even let us drive him to London. He took the train while I sat at home, unable to face work, wishing I'd gone with him, snapping at Adam when he suggested taking Noah to his mother's for the night. *I want him here. I have to tell him his … that his auntie has died.* That had been the arrangement, Rachel's instruction, left in a note the night she dropped Noah off at Dad's, all cloak-and-dagger, none of us present. We were to tell Noah that she was his auntie if we mentioned her at all, but he wasn't to know the truth. It hadn't been too hard in the end to decide we wouldn't tell him. Until she emailed me, I hadn't considered she might change her mind. *Because once your sister makes up her mind about something, that's it,* Mum always said, with the sad little smile that accompanied any mention of Rachel.

He's not yours. Tell him who his father is, or I will.

'There's also the Laurel and Hardy Museum,' I continued, pasting my smile back on. Vanessa was still staring at the garden. 'Ulverston is known for its festivals and its independent shops and the Roxy cinema, and the National Park isn't far, though you probably know all this if you've researched the area.' I swallowed, wishing she would turn around so I could see her face. 'We get a lot of rain,' I continued, as the sun punched through the clouds and illuminated the room, almost blinding me with its brilliance. 'But we've had a great summer this year. Lake Windermere's only fifteen minutes away—'

'Wordsworth, Beatrix Potter, Arthur Ransome.'

'Pardon?'

'Famous people associated with the Lake District.'

I couldn't tell whether she was mocking me. One hand rested on the sliding door, and she traced a heart on the glass with her finger.

'The place has inspired a lot of writers,' I said.

I moved to unlock the door. As I slid it back, Vanessa stepped onto the patio, staring at the wrought-iron table and chairs left by the owners.

'Schools?'

I was thrown for a second, then realized she must be asking for her daughter's children. *Had she mentioned them?* 'Several.' I angled myself out of the sun to look at her, shocked to see a shimmer of tears in her eyes. 'My son goes to Sir John Barrow, the primary school.'

'You have a son?' She swung to face me, her extraordinary eyes completely dry. Maybe I'd imagined the tears, or it was a trick of the light.

'A son. He's 5, nearly 6.' Smiling instinctively, I hooked a strand of hair behind my ears, adding, 'He loves living here, though he's never known anywhere else.' *He'll never remember those early months in London before we uprooted our lives.*

'What's his name?'

'Noah.' We'd been so happy to use the name we'd chosen for the son we hoped to have one day. 'There are two other Noahs in his class, which can be a bit confusing.'

Vanessa drew her shawl closer. 'Do you have a picture?'

'Oh.' Showing clients family photos was unusual, but I found myself wanting to make a good impression. 'Only about a thousand.' I rooted through my bag for my phone and showed her the screensaver: Noah leaping through a spray of water from a hosepipe, the droplets creating a rainbow of colours. He was laughing, his curly hair haloed by the light.

Vanessa craned her neck, a smile hovering at the corners of her mouth. 'He doesn't look like you.' It was an oddly personal comment. I switched to my photo gallery and brought up another image, of Noah in his school uniform, head tilted like a robin's. 'Maybe he takes after his father?' she said.

'He looks like both of us.' I tucked my phone away, a sense of dread returning. It was the sort of thing people said. Like Adam, drawing Noah into his world of computers and comic books to create a father-and-son bond, and exclaiming when Noah developed a fascination for insects, *He's like me when I was that age*, reddening when he realized it could only be a coincidence.

'How many grandchildren do you have?' I said, changing tack.

Vanessa didn't seem inclined to exchange personal details. She moved inside, and I followed, watching as she slid the door shut and retreated to the kitchen area.

I joined her, opening and closing one of the empty units to demonstrate their glide. She didn't seem interested, absently stroking the walnut worktop instead.

'The garden's large but well-maintained. A gardener comes once a fortnight.' There was a hint of desperation in my tone. 'There's a studio at the bottom that would make a good office or playhouse.'

When she turned, her expression was bland. The sun gave her eyes an almost translucent quality, like glass. 'How long have you lived around here?'

'About four and a half years. We love it, though it took a while to get used to how quiet it is.' I had the feeling I was doing the opposite of selling this house.

'Where did you live before?'

For some reason, I hesitated before saying, 'London.' She was looking past me now, and I realized with a thump of relief that she was making polite conversation and not really interested in me at all. 'Shall we look upstairs?'

Her attention snapped back. 'Sure.' She straightened her shoulders as though throwing off something heavy. 'After you.'

Going through the motions, I kept a professional smile in place as I showed her the en suite bedrooms and family bathroom and talked about proportions and lighting. I pointed out the apple trees in the garden and storage space in the attic and mentioned that travel links weren't great. 'Most people moving here aren't expecting a long commute to work.'

Occasionally, Vanessa nodded as she peered around a door, but she didn't ask any more questions. Once we were back in the hallway, she glanced at the slim gold watch on her wrist. 'I should get going.' Her lips twitched into a smile. 'Lovely to meet you, Jessica.'

'Jess, please.' Only my mother had ever called me Jessica. 'Good to meet you too,' I lied. There was something unnerving about Vanessa Blake. I sensed she was wasting my time and couldn't hide a bolt of surprise when she said, 'It's perfect.'

'It is? I mean, that's great.' Relief washed through me. I'd clearly got her all wrong. 'Do you want to come back to the office before you return to …' I had no idea where she'd come from. 'Before you go home.'

'I'm staying nearby for a few days.' She didn't elaborate. 'Do you have a business card?'

'Of course.' I took one from my bag and handed it to her.

'I'll be in touch,' she said, and exited through the front door without looking back.

Chapter 8

'It was weird,' I said back at the office when I'd explained the viewing to Kristin. 'Did you get a feel for her over the phone?'

Kristin pursed her lips. 'Only that she sounded keen.'

'Did she say where she was staying?'

'No.' Her gaze softened. 'I doubt it's personal,' she said with a smile. 'You're the least offensive person I know.'

'I didn't think it was personal, just odd.' I sat back in my chair, rubbing at the knots in my neck. 'I suppose I'm used to viewings going a certain way and she was … different. I couldn't read her at all.'

'Everyone's got their own stuff going on.' Kristin's mouth pulled down briefly, before her smile bounced back. 'Hey, weren't you going to visit your dad?'

The reminder made my heart clench. 'I need to pick up Noah first. Are you sure you don't mind closing up?'

'No problem. I've got some paperwork to finish.'

'At least your couple made an offer.'

'It hasn't been accepted yet, but I think it will be.'

On impulse, I hugged Kristin before leaving. She returned the gesture, hands gentle on my shoulders. Breathing in her vanilla-scented hair it struck me that Kristin was the closest thing I had to a sister now.

When we arrived, Dad was in the garden, on the wooden bench by the fish pond, legs outstretched, head tipped up to the late afternoon sun. The sight of his untidy grey hair and the salty flecks in his stubble gave me an ache around my heart. In my mind's eye, he was still the father of my childhood, when Mum was well and he was teaching music, filled with passion for his job, always smiling as he ploughed a hand through his thick, dark hair. *Charismatic* was the word people used to describe him. Students developed crushes. One turned up at our house once and spoke to Mum, then cried outside on the pavement. I watched from my bedroom window, feeling sorry for her. It was obvious to anyone who knew him that my father had eyes only for Mum, whom he'd met at university where they'd played in the orchestra.

Grief had taken its toll on Dad's appearance, but after he moved to the Lakes – before the news about Rachel – he was more like the man he'd once been. Now, he looked older than his sixty-seven years, a greyish tinge beneath the tan he'd acquired during the summer.

'Grandpa!'

As Noah raced to the bench my father turned, a smile lightening his face.

'Hey, big fella. I thought I saw a crocodile in the pond. Can you have a look?'

Noah's laugh was like music. 'Crocodiles are too big to be in there.' He went to look anyway, crouching to peer in with a frown of concentration. 'Maybe it was a toad.' He'd seen one a couple of weeks ago and lived in hope of spotting another.

'Maybe it was,' Dad conceded, straightening as I sat beside him and running a hand around his bristly jaw. 'I wasn't expecting you, was I?'

'I know, but you don't pick up when I call. I wanted to see how you were.'

'Still in one piece.' It was his usual response, accompanied by a raised eyebrow. 'As you can see.'

'Dad, you know what I mean.'

'I do,' he said quietly.

After years of being the two of us, we'd developed a shorthand way of communicating that didn't always need words. When Mum died, he'd retreated for a while, finding solace in his job at the university, but we grew close again as we supported each other. Now though, I struggled with what to say, relying on Noah's innocent chatter and sunny smiles to ease the way, and on comments about the garden. It looked wild, the hedges heavy with brambles.

'How was your day?' he said, clearly trying to sound interested.

'Busy.' I was about to tell him about Vanessa Blake when he looked over his shoulder at the house. Music was drifting out, something by Ella Fitzgerald. A movement at the kitchen window caught my eye and seconds later, a woman appeared at the patio door.

'I'm going now, Jon.' Her flame-red hair was piled high, bright lipstick clashing with her sunflower-yellow top. From a distance, she could have been 30 or 60, and the way she spoke – as though hoping Dad would ask her to stay – reminded me suddenly of Caroline 'popping round' after Mum died, until the day I walked in to see him pushing her away, tears leaking from her downcast eyes as she muttered an apology and left.

'I'll see you at book group on Friday, Ruth.' Dad raised his hand in a wave, the wedding ring he still wore catching the light. His feet were bare, one of his trouser cuffs turned up as though he'd dressed in a hurry.

'Who was that?'

'Ruth Duncan.' His tone was disinterested as he watched Noah poking a stick through the fronds by the pond. 'I'm giving her piano lessons.'

'You never said.'

'I'm sure I mentioned it.'

It wasn't unusual for people to turn up wanting lessons, once they knew he'd taught music at undergraduate level, and especially when they laid eyes on the beautiful Steinway he'd inherited from his grandfather. He'd quickly become the talk of the village when he moved to Rosside, somehow exotic in his tweed jacket and silk cravat, driving an old Aston Martin – like a character in *Midsomer Murders*. He'd grabbed the opportunity to reinvent himself from a grieving widower with an estranged daughter to a dashing newcomer with a fondness for literature, jazz, and fine wine, a loving father and grandad. I'd assumed it was only a matter of time before he started dating – had encouraged it – but he hadn't shown much interest. Maybe Ruth was an escape from his circling grief. 'I'd like to meet her.' I glanced back, but she'd gone.

'You're welcome to join the fell-walking club.'

'She walks as well?'

'That's where we met.' He folded his arms. 'She's divorced, lives near Windermere, has two grown-up sons, and has completed Wainwright's. Twice.' A ghost of a smile flitted over his face. 'That enough information?'

I nudged him with my elbow. 'Maybe she can do them all again with you.' One of Dad's goals had been to do the thirty-six circular walks covering all the peaks in Alfred Wainwright's *Pictorial Guides to the Lakeland Fells* but had so far done only twelve.

'Maybe.'

'Are you eating?'

'Jess.' He said my name on a sigh. 'You mustn't worry about me, love. I'm fine, or at least … I will be.' A nerve twitched in his temple, a sign of tension. I thought about the letter in my bag, the phone call that morning from Will, and my shoulders tensed.

'Careful, Noah,' I warned as he leaned further over the pond.

'The fishes are swimming all the same way.' He smiled at

me over his shoulder, wrinkling his nose. 'Like this.' He made a wiggly motion with his arm, but my smile faded as an image bubbled up: Rachel, face down in the canal, dark hair floating like seaweed on the water.

'Dad, do you really think Rachel's death was an accident?'

I didn't look at him as I said it. He was quiet for so long, I thought he wasn't going to reply. Risking a glance, I saw a brightness in his eyes. 'Oh, Dad. I'm sorry. I shouldn't have said that.'

'That was the coroner's conclusion.' He leaned forward suddenly, dropping his head into his hands. 'It's not so surprising, is it?'

I wondered whether he wanted me to say, *No, it's not surprising, knowing Rachel*, but Will's words were loud in my head. *I think your sister was murdered.*

'If it wasn't, though … I know there was no evidence but—' I stopped, not knowing how to continue.

'Jess, what's brought this on?' He turned to meet my gaze. The anguish in his eyes was hard to look at.

'I was just thinking,' I said feebly. 'I don't really know.' I couldn't tell him about the phone call, about the warning to tell Noah the truth about his father. It wouldn't be fair when he'd already gone through so much.

'She's gone,' Dad said bleakly. 'Nothing will bring her back.'

A long breath escaped my lips. 'I'm sorry.'

'You have nothing to be sorry for, kitten.' He took my hand in his and squeezed. His palm was warm and dry, reassuring like it had always been. 'Let it go, sweetheart.'

I knew that I should, but what if Will was right? 'What are you going to do with her ashes?'

'Same as your mum's, I suppose.'

We had travelled up to the Lakes throw Mum's ashes on Coniston Water with a scattering of rose petals, walking around her favourite places, arm in arm, until the memories became too much.

My phone signalled a text, startling me from my thoughts. As I pulled it out of my bag, Dad pushed to his feet. 'By the way, Denny's up this way,' he said. 'Fancied some fresh air and fishing, though I reckon he'll be coming here to check on me.' He beckoned to Noah before I could respond. 'Shall we find some chocolate cake?'

'Yes, please!'

'A small piece or you won't want dinner,' I cautioned, hoping Dad wouldn't ask me why my face had gone red.

I was expecting to see a message from Adam, though he'd sent one earlier to let me know he'd arrived in Berlin and would call tonight, but it was an unknown number.

I'm sorry about this morning. If you want to talk, call me. If not, I won't bother you again. I have some things that belonged to your sister. If you'd like me to send them on, let me know. Will Taylor.

An oily feeling wound through my stomach as I read the message again. Denny had collected Rachel's belongings from her flat as Dad couldn't face it. A single cardboard box containing her worldly goods: clothes and boots that looked worn and faded, some paperback novels, several pairs of cheap earrings, a couple of abstract prints, and – bizarrely – a mug shaped like a cat, its tail forming the handle. Rachel hadn't acquired stuff the way most people did, so what could Will Taylor have of hers and how did he come to have it? There was only one way to find out.

Chapter 9

Rachel

Before

From: RBeresford@gmail.com
To: JessSanderson11@gmail.com
Subject: Getting things off my chest

Me again, you'll be thrilled to (never) know.

I was thinking about Thailand – the first time I went, with Lucian, after I dropped out of college (oops!). It was, not to put too fine a point on it, AMAZING!! We blew Lucian's allowance, mostly on booze and maybe a few tiny drugs, nothing serious. I always preferred alcohol, since drinking a bottle of port one New Year's Eve. One of Dad's friends brought it round, maybe it was Uncle Denny. I was 13, you were out with your boyfriend, a hairy bloke called Mack who looked like he hadn't evolved – not that it lasted because Mum was having a bad phase and you spent all your spare time helping to look after her (Saint Jessica), but anyway, I was bored because I was supposed to go to my friend Daisy's and she bailed, but that's when I discovered I didn't love the taste of port, but I LOVED how it made me feel – sort of soft and floaty and clever, a better version of myself. Though I got the impression no one else saw that side of me and definitely not you. It made me very sick once. Didn't I nearly get run over by a lorry or something? Waking up in hospital wasn't fun. Oh, and I remember falling off a balcony in Portugal at Lucian's folks' villa. You all went ballistic when you found out. God, it was painful, but only when I came round. Mostly though, drinking makes me feel great. I wish it didn't, but there you go. I thought I might have kicked the habit after stopping for the best part of a year, but back in Thailand on my own, I needed something to get by and it's a great way to meet new people and make friends. I tried to drink 'in moderation', as they say. You should have travelled more, Jess, but I suppose it's my fault you didn't get to go away more. Remember those holidays at Windermere? SO boring, though I didn't mind swimming in the lake. Imagine living somewhere like that though. Ugh. I remember our parents going on about getting a place there one day, and you going along with it like you were 50 instead of 15.

Where was I? Oh yes, Thailand the first time with Lucian … things I loved … mangroves, the rainforest, Khao Sok National Park, elephants, a bright green tree snake, and monkeys – long-tailed macaques – following along in the branches right above our boat, watching us. At least I think they were. I might have dreamt it, thinking back. If I did, it was a nice dream.

Happy times. R x

Chapter 10

'There isn't much, but I thought you might want it.'

'What sort of things?' I couldn't hide a note of suspicion. 'All her stuff was collected from the flat.'

'A few personal items from when she stayed on my boat.'

A flash of curiosity. 'Boat?'

'I have a houseboat.'

'Where she fell in?'

'No, no. I'm moored further along, near Regent's Park. And I wasn't there that night.' After a pause, he added, 'Look, like I said in my text, I didn't intend to upset you. If you're happy with the verdict, I'll leave well alone.'

'Happy is hardly the right word.'

'If you're comfortable giving me your address, I'll post Rachel's things and that will be the last you'll hear from me.'

'I'm not,' I said. 'Comfortable giving you my address.'

'Right.' His voice was flat. 'So, you're saying you don't want her things?'

'I'm saying, I'll come down.' I pressed a hand to my throat. 'I'll need to make arrangements.' It sounded melodramatic, but I couldn't just take off. What would Adam say, and Dad, who had told me to let it drop? Five years ago, I would have said I owed

47

Rachel nothing, that I had tried every way I could think of to help her, but now there was Noah. Rachel was his biological mother and she'd reached out to me. I owed it to her to find out what Will Taylor had to say.

'Of course.' Will's tone had changed, a hint of surprise. 'Let me know when.'

'It won't be this week.'

'That's fine.'

My mind was littered with questions, but Noah was calling me from the house. I'd kicked off my shoes while talking to Dad, the grass damp beneath my soles. 'I'd better go.' I rose, slipping my shoes back on. 'I'll be in touch.'

I went to join Noah and Dad in the cluttered kitchen, where the washing machine was reaching its spin cycle and his ginger cat, Tiger, was sitting on the windowsill licking his paws. 'Sorry about that.' My gaze circled around, taking in the array of pot plants, the family photos on the dresser, and the heap of cook-books – not so different from our old kitchen in Barnes, though Dad had claimed to want a fresh start. He wiped his fingers on a tea towel and passed me a mug of tea. 'Adam?'

I nodded vaguely, not wanting to lie outright, or invoke his disapproval. He seemed annoyed about Adam working away from home, though he hadn't objected to it when we were first together, had even admired his drive.

'I hope you haven't got Ruth doing your washing.'

'She offered and I didn't like to say no.' He winked at Noah, who was kneeling on a chair at the old oak table. He had chocolate around his mouth and was stabbing the crumbs on his plate with his finger. 'Another slice?'

'No, Dad,' I said, as Noah nodded enthusiastically. 'Did Ruth make that cake?'

'She knows I have a sweet tooth.' He said it wistfully, as if remembering Mum's famous apple and cinnamon cake. 'I'm not hungry right now, though.'

'Come back to ours for dinner.' I had a desperate urge to make him feel better. 'Or I can cook something here.'

'I'll get something later. I promise,' he said, when I gave him a sceptical look. 'Jethro and Brian are coming round later to play cards.'

Relief loosened my shoulders. I wasn't sure how much he'd told people here about his past, about Rachel, but assumed they knew he had another daughter. 'That's good,' I said, glad they were looking out for him. 'And you know where I am if you need anything.'

'What does Grandpa need?' Noah tuned in sometimes when we thought he wasn't listening.

'A great big hug.' Dad held out his arms to catch Noah, swinging him up in an arc, the way he used to swing Rachel and me when we were little.

Back home, I focused my attention on Noah, grilling fish fingers for dinner, letting him splash in the bath for longer than usual, and reading two extra stories as we cuddled up on his bed.

'Can I say night-night to Daddy 'fore I go to sleep?' he said drowsily as I eased away and pulled his duvet up. Normally, Adam would call to say goodnight, but he'd explained he was dining out with his client this evening and it wouldn't be possible.

'Daddy said to give you a big cuddle from him, and he'll call you tomorrow,' I whispered. I pressed my lips to Noah's cheek, closing my eyes when his skinny arms wrapped around my neck. 'Love you to the moon and back.'

'Love you to all the planets and back again.'

He was almost asleep as I backed out, leaving his nightlight on and the door ajar.

Downstairs, silence loomed. I put the TV on while I tidied up, missing the low rumble of Adam's voice, and the familiar sounds he made moving around the house. I liked knowing he was there, even if he was in his study, catching up on work before joining me on the sofa for a couple of episodes of whichever show we were watching on Netflix.

Outside, rain began spattering against the windows, followed by a crack of thunder. I ran upstairs to check on Noah, but he was sleeping, one arm thrown out. I watched him for a moment as the storm gathered pace, before returning downstairs.

I couldn't settle and ate a bowl of cereal standing at the kitchen island, waiting for Adam's call. When my phone rang a minute before ten, my heart leapt into my throat. I felt oddly unprepared for the sight of my husband's face on my phone screen.

'You OK?' He leaned closer, brow gathered in a frown. He was wearing his contact lenses and although I loved how he looked in glasses, I liked being able to see his eyes, how deep, and dark they were. It reminded me of the first time I'd seen him in the bar in Greece. A couple of his shirt buttons were undone, his hair mussed.

'Have you been drinking?'

'Had to be polite,' he said with a grin, dropping down on the bed in his hotel room, which looked as neutral as all the rooms he'd called me from over the years. 'Dinner went well. I got the contract.'

'Adam, that's great.' I tried to sound enthusiastic. 'I knew you would.'

'Naturally.' He bowed his head and flourished his hand like a magician. He was more than a bit tipsy. 'How's Noah? Is everything OK? Have you heard from Denny?'

'Woah,' I said. 'Yes, Denny's up here, everything's OK, Noah's fine but missing you. We went to Dad's after school.'

'How was the old man?'

'Not so much of the old.' Dad hated being reminded of his age. 'There was a woman in the cottage. Ruth Duncan. I think they're more than friends.'

'Good for him.' I detected a touch of acid in Adam's voice.

'Maybe he'll get off my back about work if he's got himself a girlfriend.'

'So, how's Berlin?' I didn't want to end up in an argument about my father. He and Adam had got on well until Adam's second – or maybe it was his third – trip away last year. 'Will you get to see much while you're there?'

'Doubt it.' He raked his fingers through his hair. 'Hey,' he sat forward again, 'I've been thinking. Maybe it's time we had another baby.'

My stomach plummeted. We hadn't discussed it for ages, but I knew, deep down, he wasn't going to let it go. He loved Noah with all his heart, but didn't want him to be an only child, like he was, while I was happy with how we were, for now at least.

'It's hardly the right time to be thinking about another baby, Adam.' I picked up the remote and switched off the TV, my hearing attuned to sounds from Noah's room. The storm had passed, and he rarely woke before morning, but my senses were on high alert. 'How can you even mention it, when Noah's fath … someone's out there, threatening us?'

'C'mon, babe.' I might as well have not spoken. 'We can afford a couple of rounds of IVF.' *Babe?* He was slurring his words.

'How much have you had to drink?'

'Hey, I was celebrating!' Wagging a finger, he slumped against the headboard and gave a bleary smile. 'Wish you were here.'

'I wish you were here,' I said with a rush of emotion. 'I can't relax for worrying—'

'Wouldn't you like to have a little baby?'

'Adam, I've already had a little baby.'

'Yeah, but not—' *Don't say it, don't say it.* Even with him drunk, I couldn't bear it if he chose now to point out that I hadn't *really* had a baby, as in given birth. 'Not a baby that I put in your tummy.'

'Adam, for God's sake!' I tried to laugh, though my heart was hammering and my mouth had dried. 'I thought you weren't bothered about that.'

'I'm not. I just wish sometimes …' He blew out a breath, drawing a hand down one side of his face so it looked lopsided.

'Adam, listen,' I said to stop him, hiding a queasy panic. 'I spoke to that guy Rachel worked for today. He has some of her things.'

'What?' Confusion contorted his face as he tried to grasp the change of topic. 'Who?'

Impatience sharpened my voice. 'She worked at his gallery.'

'And he called *you*?'

'Rachel had my number as her emergency contact.'

He took a moment to digest this. 'I thought he was her boss.'

'Yes, but it sounds like they were friends, too. He was at the pub, after the service. He wanted to tell me something, but didn't get a chance … Adam?' He'd risen, dropping the phone on the bed, treating me to a view of his sleeve, a flash of beige wall, and part of a curtain. 'Where are you going?'

'Sorry, felt a bit dizzy.' More snapshots of the room as he retrieved his phone. His face reappeared. 'Didn't Denny pick up her things?' The light was behind him, creating deep shadows under his eyes.

'Apparently she left some stuff with this guy … Will.'

Adam was shaking his head. 'What would she have that's important?'

'Probably nothing but …' I wanted to tell him Will's theory, about Rachel being murdered, but the words stuck in my chest. 'You're right,' I said. 'It can't be anything important.'

'So, leave it.' He looked back, gaze burning through the screen. 'I'm glad she's gone.'

'*What?*'

'You heard me.' Suddenly, he didn't sound drunk at all. 'I'm glad she's gone, Jess. We can finally stop worrying she'll come for Noah.'

Chapter 11

I went to bed with Adam's words ricocheting through my head. *I'm glad she's gone.* Rachel's death had released something in him I hadn't guessed was there. Or, maybe, it was the alcohol talking. Did I have any right to argue when I'd worried about the same thing – that my sister might return for Noah one day? It didn't mean I was glad she was dead, though.

Suspecting he wouldn't remember our conversation in the morning, I said I was tired and rang off, ignoring him when he called back. Seconds later, a text had arrived. *Sorry, J. Love you. Kiss Noah for me XX*

I was drifting in and out of a restless sleep when something disturbed me. I sat up in bed, heart thumping, and glanced at the time on my phone. 2 a.m.

Noah. Instantly, I was out of bed and crossing the landing. Ambushed by a wave of dizziness, I stumbled, hand flying out to the wall.

Noah's battery-powered nightlight barely made an impact through his half-open door. I felt along the landing wall for the light switch but when I flicked it down, nothing happened. I tried again. Still nothing. The bulb must have blown.

I shivered in my thin pyjamas as a draught licked my arms and legs. Had I left the bathroom window open after Noah's bath? I was rigorous about locking up, especially when Adam was away, but had been distracted.

I poked my head around Noah's bedroom door. Seeing the window open, my eyes flew to the bed. The woodland animal–patterned duvet was pushed back in a heap, and I could just make out a small dent in the pillow where Noah had lain hours earlier.

'Noah?' Fear leapt into my throat. 'Noah!'

He'd sleepwalked for the first time a couple of months ago, terrifying Adam and me when we found him standing in the bath, staring glassily at nothing, before coming to and bursting into tears. We fitted his window with a latch after that, which prevented it opening wide enough for him to climb out. Thankfully, it hadn't happened again. *Until now?*

I ran to the window and looked out anyway. The garden was mostly shrouded in darkness, only a sliver of light from a crescent moon picking out the shed's roof.

'*Noah!*' In my head it was a scream but came out as a frightened bleat. 'Where are you?'

I checked the bathroom was empty, eyes straining through the darkness, before crashing downstairs, almost falling at the bottom, slapping the light switch by the front door. Still no light. Was there a power cut, or …?

He's not yours. Tell him who his father is, or I will.

Whimpering with fear, I fumbled with the latch, tore open the door, and ran out onto the drive, barely noticing the gravel cutting into my feet. Down the side of the house and round the back, into the long, wet grass. '*Noah!*' My voice was swallowed by the night. The plum tree swayed in the breeze, and in the distance an owl gave a plaintive hoot.

'Noah, where are you?' I spun around, straining my eyes, but all I could hear was dripping water from the earlier rain. I should have brought a torch. There was one in the kitchen, but I didn't want to waste time going back inside. 'Noah!'

I should have asked Denny to watch the house. I called his name in case he was there, but no one answered. A rustle of movement made me spin round again.

'Noah? Is that you?'

My gaze blindly sought his shape in the blackness. 'Noah?' Fear gathered in my chest. 'Come out now, love. You'll catch a cold.'

A dog. Why didn't we have a dog? Thoughts circling crazily, I careered back into the house, pyjama bottoms clinging to my legs. *Call the police, call Adam.* Noah. My little boy.

Sobbing, I tried the light in the kitchen, a desperate yelp escaping when nothing happened. *Had the man who sent the letter cut the power and stolen Noah?*

Will's voice in my head. *I think Rachel was murdered.*

'Oh my God.' Panting with terror, I blundered to the cupboard under the sink. Why hadn't I brought my phone down? I could have used the torch, as well as phoned the police.

When my hand met hard plastic, I yanked out the torch, almost dropping it in my haste to turn it on. The landline phone was nearest. No time to run upstairs for my mobile. Heart thrashing, I finally found the torch's switch and flooded the kitchen with a pool of yellow light.

What was that? A noise behind me, from the hallway. A terrifying scenario sprang up – Noah's father had him hostage, was here to demand a ransom to let him go before confessing he'd killed Rachel.

'Who are you?' I yelled, the torch shaking in my hand. With my other, I scrabbled along the worktop for the knife block, the beam of light shuddering towards the doorway and blackness beyond.

'Mummy?' Noah materialized like a ghost, clutching his battered teddy Blinky that had once belonged to Adam. 'What are you doing?'

'Noah!' Dropping the torch, I hurtled towards him, fell to my knees, and gathered him against me. 'Oh, sweetheart, where were you?' I picked him up. I used to love the weight of him on my hip when he was a baby, keeping me anchored. 'Are you OK?' My eyes scanned the darkness behind, looking for a shadowy figure. 'Are you hurt?'

'Mummy, you're all cold and wet.' He wriggled and I reluctantly set him down as the kitchen flooded with brightness, and the light came on in the hall. Instantly, everything shrank to normality; the stairs winding up to the landing, my cereal bowl on the kitchen island, the coats on their hooks in the hallway. 'I went for a wee, but it was dark, and I dropped Blinky' – he held up his threadbare teddy,– 'and I couldn't find him for ages, so I looked for him.'

'Why didn't you come and get me?' I crouched, surreptitiously wiping my tears away with my fingertips, not wanting to frighten him. Of course someone hadn't snatched him, and he wouldn't have left the house; he couldn't reach the locks. Overwhelmed with relief, I pulled him close once more, and this time he relaxed against me, unprotesting when I kissed his hair and breathed him in, cursing myself for not hearing him go to the toilet, for flying into a panic and tearing around the house like a madwoman – for thinking someone had deliberately cut the power. It wasn't unusual to lose electricity, especially after a storm. 'Didn't you hear me calling you?'

He shook his head. 'Only just now. I hided in my wardrobe with Blinky.'

'Oh, Noah.' I scoured his face for signs of trauma but found only sleepy confusion. Had he got up because he was sleepwalking and became disorientated? 'You don't normally need a wee in the night.' I tried to sound light-hearted. 'You must have had too much orange juice.'

'I woked up because of the light.'

I stiffened. 'Light?'

'It was shining on the ceiling, like that.' Shifting, he pointed a finger to the torch I'd dropped, its light barely visible on the tiles.

'There was a light on your ceiling?'

Noah nodded, rubbing his eyes with his fist. 'I looked out of the window to see.'

'Did you open the window?'

He nodded, sticking his bottom lip out. 'I wanted to look, Mummy.'

'It's OK.' I stroked his hair off his forehead, a curl of fear in my stomach. 'Did you see anything?'

He nodded, leaning back in my arms, and making Blinky's arm move up and down. 'I waved to the monster.'

'Monster?' My breathing quickened.

'It waved back.' He tilted his head. 'You don't have to be scared, Mummy,' he said kindly. 'It was only a dream.'

'How do you know it was a monster?'

His forehead furrowed. 'Because monsters only come out at night.'

'Sweetheart, you know that monsters aren't real.' *So why was my heart racing, and my forehead clammy?* 'Let's get you back to bed or you'll be too tired for school in the morning.'

Once I'd tucked him in and closed the window, and Noah was sleeping once more, I double-checked the house was secure before sliding back into bed. As I stared unblinking into the darkness, I couldn't banish the image of someone outside the house, waving at my son.

Chapter 12

'You look tired.'

'I didn't sleep well.' I tried to avoid Kristin's sympathetic gaze. 'Noah had a nightmare,' I said, deciding not to mention that I'd thought someone had snatched him and had run around outside in my pyjamas.

'Was he sleepwalking again?'

'Maybe.' Perhaps he only came to when he realized I was scrabbling around downstairs. He'd been his usual cheerful self at breakfast, chattering as he ate his Weetabix, and I hadn't wanted to remind him of the 'monster'. In the bright light of day it seemed impossible, though I'd hunted around the garden looking for flattened patches of grass where someone might have stood. I even checked the shed but there was nothing to indicate anyone had been lurking about. I messaged Denny, who replied he would have a scout around and watch the house while I was at work.

I'm on it Jess. We'll get to the bottom of it. D

'I used to sleepwalk,' Kristin said. 'Scared Mum silly, but I grew out of it in my teens.'

'There was a power cut,' I said. 'It must have been the storm.'

'I know, I was reading. My bedside light went off.'

Relieved, I said, 'That was late, to be reading.'

Kristin flushed. 'I don't like thunder,' she said. 'Sounds babyish, but I couldn't sleep in case it started again.'

'You don't look tired at all.' I took in her clear eyes and smooth skin. 'I can't get away with less than eight hours without looking as if I've been dug up.'

'Rubbish,' Kristin said loyally. 'You look a bit sleepy, that's all. You must be missing Adam.'

'We had a bit of an argument,' I admitted.

'Oh?' When Kristin's eyes widened, I wanted to snatch the words back. 'It was nothing serious,' I added. 'Listen, is it okay if I take the day off on Friday?'

Her eyebrows rose. 'You never take time off.'

'I want to go into London and look for a gift for Adam's fortieth.' The lie brought heat to the back of my neck. I couldn't tell her I'd decided to visit Will Taylor without explaining why. I'd already called my mother-in-law to ask if she would look after Noah. Jennifer relished time alone with her grandson and didn't hesitate to say yes. I desperately wanted to take him with me, but it would disrupt his routine, and I trusted that under his grandmother's watch – and Denny's – he would be safe.

'Still no call from Vanessa Blake?' I went on, before Kristin could ask for more details.

She shook her head. 'Maybe she's still consulting with her daughter.'

A text arrived from Adam half an hour later. *I'm sorry if I upset you last night, J. That's why I don't drink whisky xx*

Don't worry about it xx. I was certain he wouldn't want to discuss what he'd said about Rachel any more than I did. It would mean unpicking complicated feelings, reassessing our view of each other.

I meant what I said though, Jess – my pulse ticked faster – *I know it sounds harsh, but our lives will be better now, admit it.*

Not while his biological father is out there making threats. It was if Adam had forgotten – or didn't want to face it.

Sorry, you know what I mean. Have you heard anything else?

No. I didn't add kisses. Perhaps being far from home meant Adam could pretend that everything was rosy – that I was sitting around, pleased to be free of my sister and contemplating us having another child. Something shifted inside me. *Let's talk when you get home.*

I half-expected him to call and wondered what I would say – whether to mention Noah's disturbed night – but my phone stayed silent. Then, another text arrived.

Stay safe. Love you xx

I didn't reply.

While Kristin was busy with a customer, I brought up Facebook on my computer and typed in *Will Taylor*. There were too many. Narrowing them down by adding *London* resulted in some possibilities, but I couldn't remember what he looked like.

After a moment's hesitation, I typed in *Rachel Beresford* and clicked the link to a news article.

A woman who died in Regent's Canal last month has been named as 27-year-old Rachel Beresford from Camden. The post-mortem revealed a high proportion of alcohol in the victim's blood. It was concluded that Ms Beresford had been drinking heavily before falling into the canal. An inquest at St Pancras Coroner's Court has returned a verdict of accidental death.

I could have been reading about a stranger. Rachel no longer seemed real to me, and undoubtedly hadn't to whoever carried out the post-mortem. She was a drunk, another dead body, discovered by a passing cyclist, who might have needed counselling afterwards. Had the police even investigated once they knew Rachel had alcohol in her blood?

Camden. Less than an hour from where we grew up. We knew she'd gone to Thailand after leaving Noah with us, because she emailed me some photos. *Had she returned as part of a plan to reclaim him?* That was my first thought on receiving her final message, though I had no idea she'd been back for a while by then, working and living in London. *How was Noah's biological father involved?*

My mind felt full of sharp edges and once Moira came in, all smiles and brisk efficiency, I gave up pretending to work and gathered my things. 'I'm going to photograph that house on Laverty Street before I collect Noah from school.'

Kristin, busy with a call, cast me a worried look and nodded. I turned away, eager to get out, stifled by the proximity to other people, the overheated office. I needed space to think.

The Laverty Street property was empty, making it easy to snap shots that showed the interior at its best, but I was on autopilot.

When I'd finished, I headed to Noah's school. I was early and managed to find a parking space halfway down Argyle Street. I looked around for Denny, but wherever he was, he would be inconspicuous. On cue, my phone buzzed.

Nothing to report, at school or home. D

I wondered where he was staying, and whether he'd been to see Dad. I hoped he was true to his word and didn't tell Dad the real reason he was here, but I suspected Denny was good at keeping secrets. He'd worked undercover during his time with the force and even his wife hadn't known the details.

Reassured, I got out of the car, breathing deeply. It had started raining. As I reached inside my bag for my umbrella, I spotted a familiar figure hurrying up the road. *Vanessa Blake.*

'Hello.' She slowed, seeming unsurprised to bump into me. Her light-coloured coat was open over another billowing dress – navy blue this time – and her mass of hair was loose around her shoulders. 'Are you going to pick up your son?'

'I am.' I stuffed the umbrella back in my bag. The rain wasn't heavy. 'Are you staying around here?'

She gestured vaguely over her shoulder. 'I thought I'd check out the school,' she said, falling into step beside me as I began to walk.

'For your daughter?'

61

'That's right.' Her tone was light and airy, a bounce in her step. 'It looks nice.'

As we reached the gates, passing the hand-painted sign that read, *Don't park on the zigzags*, Vanessa strained to look past the sea of parents, their eyes trained on the doors as they opened, releasing a stream of children in dark blue sweatshirts bearing the school's initials.

'Like I said, it's a good school.'

Vanessa's hands were in her coat pockets, her pale gaze more intense than the day before.

'You should make an appointment to talk to the head teacher,' I said.

'I might do that.' A smile hovered at the corners of her mouth.

'The deputy head won an award a few years ago.' Compelled to keep talking, as if selling her the school was part of my job, I added, 'The pupils get invited to perform in the South Cumbria Music Festival every year. It's good for their confidence.'

'Which one is yours?'

My gaze scanned the children. I instantly spotted Noah with his friend Jasmine, their dark heads close together as they chatted. I caught the eye of Jasmine's mum and we exchanged smiles. Their friendship was new, and I didn't know the family very well, but resolved to invite Jasmine round for a playdate. 'That's him.' I pointed and Noah caught sight of me, breaking into a run, his smile reaching his ears.

'Mummy!'

'Hi, sweetheart.' I bent to catch him in a hug and adjusted the straps of his rucksack, praying he hadn't seen any more monsters. 'Have you had a lovely day?'

He nodded. 'Who's that lady?' Screwing up his eyes he observed Vanessa beside me.

'I'm having a look at your school because my family is moving here,' she said before I could speak. 'I want to check it's a nice place to live.'

'You can't live in a school,' he said earnestly.

She pouted her pale lips, clearly attempting to be playful. 'I meant the town, silly.'

'It's nice, isn't it, Mummy?'

I nodded, wishing Vanessa wasn't standing so close. I hadn't expected her to follow me into the playground. Was she going to do as I suggested and seek out the head teacher?

'What do you like to do?' Vanessa crouched low so she was eye to eye with Noah. 'Do you play football?'

Suddenly shy, he pressed close to me and pushed his thumb in his mouth, a baby habit he hadn't quite grown out of.

'Bye, Noah!'

I looked over to see Jasmine waving, but Noah buried his head in my skirt and didn't return her wave. Annoyance at Vanessa rippled through me.

'We'd better get going,' I said. 'Good to see you again.'

She straightened, keeping her gaze on Noah. 'Nice to meet you.' Her smile was friendly, a tinge of pink on her cheekbones. It was raining steadily now, and the shoulders of her coat had darkened, raindrops clinging to her curls. My fringe was dripping, and I fumbled my umbrella out of my bag and shook it open.

'Come on, Noah.' Hustling him away, I nodded to Vanessa with what I hoped was a pleasant smile. 'Good luck.'

She didn't reply and made no move to leave. All the way back to the car, I was certain her eyes were burning into my back, but when I turned to look, she'd gone.

Chapter 13

'Make sure you buy something nice for yourself.' My mother-in-law parked her car outside Ulverston Station and leaned over to the passenger seat to hug me. 'You deserve a treat.'

I returned her hug, burning with shame. I'd fed her the same lie I'd told Kristin – that I was going to London to look for a gift for Adam's fortieth birthday, adding that I was going to meet my friend Sasha for dinner. Like Kristin, she hadn't questioned it. Why would she? Jennifer – a retired nurse – had been like a mother to me from the moment we met, thanking me for *making my son happy*. She was the embodiment of kindness, her smile wide and sunny, her dark, intelligent eyes framed by laughter lines.

'Be a good boy for Nanna,' I said to Noah. He was in the back of the car, watching a Paddington Bear film on his tablet, but shuffled forward to plant a kiss on my cheek. 'What are you going to do today?'

'Make cupcakes with Nanna,' he said. 'Chocolate ones with Smarties on top.'

'Of course we are.' Smiling, Jennifer turned to ruffle his hair, her expression identical to the one I'd seen in countless photos of her with Adam, from when he was a baby, to his graduation, to our wedding day. 'It was a good idea to stay overnight,' she said to me. 'You can see your friends while you're there.'

After buying my train ticket and realizing I wouldn't get home the same day until after Noah was in bed, and that Jennifer would be staying over anyway, I'd reserved a last-minute room and guiltily packed a small bag. 'Thanks again for this.' My smile wobbled at the memory of Noah's empty bed the night before, and the letter in my bag. 'You will lock up properly, won't you, and don't let him outside without you?' *What if she wasn't strong enough to fight off someone determined to take Noah?* I'd messaged Denny to tell him I was taking a shopping trip and would be back tomorrow.

Noah's safer here, don't worry. D

'Of course I'll look after him.' Jennifer's eyes were understanding. 'He's precious to me too.'

'I've put the baby monitor in the living room.' I lowered my voice. 'So you can hear if he wakes up and needs the loo.'

'Don't worry, Jess, we'll be fine.'

'Go, Mummy, or you'll be late,' Noah instructed.

'Sounds like he can't wait to get rid of me.' I rolled my eyes at Jennifer.

She grinned. 'I'll keep him busy. Now, go and enjoy yourself.'

I switched trains at Lancaster, but once on my way to Euston my guilt and worry increased. It was ages since I'd been away from home, and it seemed like terrible timing. But I had to know what Will Taylor had to say before I spoke to Adam about it. If I could reassure myself that my sister's death was nothing more than a tragic accident, I would look for a gift for Adam's birthday, as I'd said I would, and get in touch with Sasha too.

Placing the tea I'd bought at the station in the cup holder, I brought up her number on my phone, careful not to nudge the man furiously tapping at his laptop next to me.

Hey, stranger! I'm in town for the day. Do you have time to meet this afternoon? Jess X

Her reply came quickly. *Hey! Would love to see you, Jess. Let me know what time X*

I thought of the text I'd sent Will the night before, after chatting with Adam – sticking to safe topics, avoiding the subject of Rachel and the previous night's escapade with Noah – informing him that I would be arriving in Euston at 12.30.

He'd replied quickly. *I can meet you at the Quaker café opposite the station. Will.* I spent a while trying to decipher the tone, wondering what I'd expected. A gushing reply, saying how much he was looking forward to seeing me, how grateful he was that I was taking the time to visit? Hardly, considering I'd cut him off at the pub, and accused him of trying to stir up trouble when he called.

I texted Sasha, *3 p.m. at the Three Crowns? X* That should give me enough time to talk to Will.

Perfect, see you then X

I hoped Adam wouldn't decide to call his mum. I doubted he would buy my story about a secret gift-finding mission in London, knowing how frightened I'd been by the anonymous letter. Would he make the connection between my trip and the call from Will? How would I explain having Rachel's things?

Uneasiness swirled in my stomach. I was making a habit of hiding things from Adam, and I didn't like it. *So, call him.* I ignored the voice in my head and opened the Kindle app on my phone so I could read, pausing to buy a chocolate bar and some coffee when the refreshment cart came round. After that, I stared out mindlessly at the scenery, a blurred watercolour through the rain-speckled window, trying not to worry about Noah. I attempted to picture Will Taylor and brought up the art gallery on my phone to see if he was mentioned. He wasn't. Nothing about Rachel's role there either, but I had no idea what that role had been, or whether it was usual to mention the loss of a staff member on the website. How long had she even worked there? It was so hard to imagine her holding down a job, especially one in an art gallery. She didn't even like art, as far as I knew.

It was a relief when the train slowed on its approach into Euston. I switched my phone to selfie mode and checked my appearance, rubbing colour into my pale cheeks with my fingertips. I'd tidied my hair, but my concealer hadn't disguised the shadows under my eyes, the irises darkened to charcoal. *My sister's eyes.* One of our physical similarities, the other being the tiny gap between our two front teeth we'd inherited from Mum. I swept my fringe aside, revealing the scattering of freckles on my forehead, remembering a time when Rachel had hacked her fringe so short with kitchen scissors, Mum cried. Rachel was 9 at the time, and swore she hadn't meant to do it, but I'd caught her studying her reflection in the mirror, looking pleased with herself.

When the train shuddered to a stop, I pulled my jacket on over my jumper and jeans, a rush of nerves tightening my chest. I waited until the carriage was empty before stepping onto the platform, trying to regulate my breathing.

Heading for the ticket barriers, I was overwhelmed by a feeling of familiarity, but the slower pace of life I'd got used to in Ulverston meant I had to stand still for a moment and gather myself before heading out of the station.

As I waited on the rain-slicked pavement for the lights to turn green, I realized I didn't miss the sound of police sirens, or the smell of traffic and scented gusts from shops and cafés. At least the rain had stopped, the sun slicing through fast-scudding clouds. I wished I really was here to shop, or meet old friends, with nothing else to worry about. After checking into the towering Travelodge hotel and dropping off my holdall, I headed straight back out.

The Quaker Centre Bookshop and Café was housed inside a four-storey brick-and-stone building with impressive columns at the entrance. Inside, I paused to get my bearings. The bookshop area seemed quiet, but the café was busy. Should I text Will to let him know I was here? I jumped when my phone buzzed.

In the courtyard. Will.

I made my way through the airy café, enveloped in the rich aroma of coffee, my stomach growling as I caught sight of the cakes and pastries at the counter. I'd eaten nothing but the chocolate bar on the train since dinner last night; a microwaved jacket potato after Noah had gone to bed, which had sat like a stone in my stomach as I lay awake half the night, listening to the sounds of the house.

The courtyard was mostly empty thanks to the recent rain, the silvery paving stones drying in the sun. Shielding my eyes, I scanned the area, taking in the array of plants, and grey mesh tables and chairs. At a table in the farthest corner was a man, holding a mug in one hand, his head bent over his phone. As if sensing my presence, he glanced up and got to his feet. My heart gave a hard kick as he walked between the tables, and all I could hear was my rapid breathing. He stopped in front of me and held out his hand. 'Hi, Jess. Good to see you again.'

Chapter 14

Will's hand closed around mine, warm and strong, sending a surge of blood through my body.

'Nice to see you too.' I hadn't noticed last time how direct his gaze was, or that his eyes were blue like patches of sky. 'Have you been waiting long?'

'Only a few minutes,' he said, while I took in the rest of him: dark-blonde hair cut short at the sides, a soft beard, and a friendly smile. He was a bit shorter than Adam, slighter, yet somehow solid, a man with his feet firmly on the ground. 'Thanks for coming.' He let go of my hand. 'I know it wasn't an easy decision.'

'Well, I'm here now.'

He seemed to weigh up my tone before asking pleasantly, 'Good journey?'

'Long.' I shaped my lips into a smile to make up for sounding defensive. In my mind, Will Taylor had morphed into a faceless character, needling me with words that had wormed their way into my thoughts, but now he was real and he seemed ... ordinary. Nice. Attractive, even. I wondered again whether he and Rachel had been more than friends, but the thought wouldn't stick. Lucian was the only man she'd ever wanted.

'The Lake District, isn't it?'

He obviously knew already, must have got it from Rachel – unless he'd spoken to Caroline after the service.

'That's right.' I lifted my tone to match his. 'Ulverston.' I thrust my hands in my jacket pockets and took them out again, aware of my pallor, my hair hanging limply around my shoulders, the trainers I'd put on for comfort that had seen better days. Casually dressed in jeans and an open shirt over a white T-shirt, Will looked well put-together, though his boots were worn, the laces coming apart. 'I managed to doze on the train.' It sounded as though I hadn't a care in the world, so I added, 'Not much sleep last night' then felt stupid for overexplaining. 'Do you have my sister's things?' It came out more brusquely than I'd intended.

Will's eyebrows rose a fraction. 'Why don't we order something to eat?' He gestured to the table behind him. 'I don't know about you, but I'm starving and the food here is good. Vegetarian, if that's OK.'

'It's fine.' I deflated slightly. 'I'm hungry too.'

Silence fell as we sat down and looked at our menus. I could hardly take anything in, too aware of him opposite – his furrowed brow, the sun glinting off a thin gold bracelet around his wrist. How long had it been since I'd eaten out with a man other than Adam? I twisted my wedding ring round and round, wishing I was at work.

When Will said, 'The vegetable lasagne's good,' I nodded, annoyed that I was acting like a teenager on a first date. He pushed his chair back. 'I'll go and order.'

As he went inside, I let out a breath and rolled my shoulders to ease the tension. I took out my phone and texted Jennifer. *Arrived safely, hope all's well* and she replied straight away, *Fine, stop worrying and spend some money!*

Nothing from Adam, but that wasn't unusual when he was busy. No point sending Dad a message as he rarely looked at his mobile. He'd said he was going to tidy up the garden today, which

I'd read as a good sign. I wondered whether he would invite Ruth Duncan round to help him.

I rubbed my arms, wishing I'd worn a thick coat. It was chilly, despite the sun. Perhaps Will was used to being outdoors, though there was a waterproof jacket draped over the back of his chair. He didn't appear to have brought anything else. I bent to look under the table, to see if there was a bag or box that I'd missed. Nothing.

'Lost something?'

I jerked upright, catching my head on the side of the table.

'Sorry.' He looked mildly amused as he sat down. 'I didn't mean to startle you.'

'I was looking for my sister's things.' Resisting the urge to rub my head, I folded my arms on the table. 'You have brought them?'

Mirroring my pose, he leaned forward. 'You're not at all like her,' he said, unexpectedly. 'I mean, your eyes are the same colour, but …' He shook his head. 'You're completely different.'

I wondered whether he was comparing our features and finding me lacking. 'She was beautiful,' I said honestly. Rachel had possessed the type of looks that made people stare, a quality hard to define that wasn't about her long, dark hair, full lips, and big smoky eyes. There had been a wildness about her, licking at the surface, desperate to break free; a sense that any second, she might do or say something unpredictable. Combined with the restless energy that seemed to jump off her, her boyish limbs always in motion, she tended to draw attention. She would have been a brilliant athlete, according to her sports teacher, a champion swimmer if she had put in the effort, but all Rachel wanted was Lucian, and to get drunk as often as possible. 'At least she used to be,' I added. Alcohol had taken a toll, her cheeks becoming sunken, but that was before she fell pregnant and cleaned up her act. 'We didn't know she was here,' I added when Will didn't reply. 'Not until … We assumed she was still in Thailand.'

'You only knew she was in London when you heard she was dead?'

When I nodded, Will let out a low whistle. 'That's awful.'

'That was Rachel.'

'I always assumed something bad had happened in her past that set her on the path to—'

'I'll tell you what happened,' I broke in on a surge of emotion. 'Rachel came along eight years after me, but my parents couldn't have been happier when she was born. We all loved her, so, so much, and our grandparents doted on her. She couldn't have been more loved, but nothing we ever did was enough.' My throat was suddenly tight with tears, my voice strained. 'She always seemed to be looking for something she couldn't find. She started smoking, drinking, staying out late, skipping school before she turned 14. It didn't matter what our parents did or said, she wanted to break the rules. At 15, she snuck out of the house to a party she'd been invited to by someone who was very bad for her. Our lives were hell after that.' A reel of memories scrolled by: the swirling lights of a police car outside the house, Rachel tumbling out of the back seat and vomiting all over the drive; picking her up from the police station, her bag full of shoplifted make-up; empty vodka bottles under her bed; suspension from school; a call from the rehab centre to say she'd run off, another from her counsellor to say she hadn't seen Rachel for a month; Mum crying on her bed, Dad pacing the house, face drawn, trying to think of a way to remove her from Lucian's corrosive influence, though of course it made no difference. Whenever he reappeared, she'd relapse and when he didn't, she was worse. 'She only got in touch when she wanted money, but my parents never turned her away, ever. They told her she would always have a home, that they would always stand by her. Even when my mother was too ill to leave her room and hadn't seen Rachel for months, she never stopped loving her.' My heart was racing, my breathing shallow, the backs of my eyes burning with tears. It was like going back in time, to when a boiling fury at my sister had begun to outweigh the love – fury at her inability to get help, to stay sober, to give Mum and Dad a break from worrying, fury at her addiction to Lucian. I would have done anything to help her but grew to understand that nothing would. Then, I'd longed for her to stop involving us, stop turning up in a dreadful state, stop demanding money and trashing the house when she didn't get it, stop seeing Lucian – stop ruining our lives as well as her own. 'Before she went to Thailand the first time, with her so-called boyfriend, I begged her to stay in touch, to email, to let us know she was alive, and she did.' I gave a strangled laugh. 'Every now and then I'd get a message, literally saying, *I'm alive!*' I did jazz hands. 'Nothing else, no details about what she was doing, how she was, but I was grateful I could at least report back to my parents that their daughter wasn't dead. How about that? She was 17. Mum died soon after. Rachel didn't come home for her funeral. When I emailed to let her know about Mum, she replied, "At least you can get on with your life now."' I stopped, closer to crying than I'd been in a long time. Her words had cut deeply. Right up until the end, Mum had hoped Rachel would come home. *What is wrong with you?* I'd typed back with shaking hands, tears raining down my face, while Dad sat in the car outside the hospital, dry-eyed and numb. She hadn't responded. 'She didn't come back for my wedding either,' I said, after taking a breath. 'I kept up the email contact, letting her know stuff even though she didn't deserve it or care, and she did email back sometimes, but always the same thing, "I'm alive!!" and occasionally a snapshot of wherever she was in the world, on a beach, in a club, or a sunset, as if it would get me off her back. But she never came home.'

Will was silent for a moment, letting my words sink in. 'I'm sorry,' he said at last, his expression sober. 'I honestly had no idea.' He reached out, rested his hand on mine. I pulled away, embarrassed.

'What did she tell you about us?'

'That's just it.' He paused as our lunch arrived, waiting until the waiter had gone before saying, 'Rachel told me her parents were dead and she was adopted.'

Chapter 15

Rachel

Before

From: RBeresford@gmail.com
To: JessSanderson11@gmail.com
Subject: Getting things off my chest

This one is a shocker, Jess. I will delete it even more quickly than the others but thought I would get it 'out there' in writing because I have never said it aloud to anyone, not even Lucian. Isn't that weird? I don't know why. Maybe I didn't want to ruin his image of me, though I sometimes don't know how he saw me in the first place. That'll be the drink, I suppose. All I know is the minute we crashed his 18th party at that massive house in Little Venice, I knew we were destined to be together. God. Sounds like a line from Frozen and not very Independent Woman, but I'm not independent. I'm very Dependant. On booze. On Lucian. My twin crutches.

Anyway, I might have blurted it out once, this shocker, in rehab – that ill-fated holiday Dad paid for, which sadly wasn't meant to be – but I retracted it straight away because I didn't want it getting back to him, and then I ran away.

Right, brace yourself. Or not, as you'll never read this.

DAD IS NOT MY DAD. Gasp!! I told you it was a shocker. Poor Mum ... Turned out she'd had enough of his 'dalliances' (love that word, a bit regency romance, but sums it up), at least the ones with students almost young enough to be his daughter. One came to the house, do you remember? I think you were in your bedroom. I was about 8 and we were due to go on holiday. I was sitting in the cupboard under the stairs, waiting for mousey to come out so I could give him some cheese, and I heard this girl's voice saying she loved him, and Mum said, 'you don't know the meaning of the word' in this really sad voice, like she felt sorry for the girl. I didn't really get what was happening, wasn't interested to be honest, but that's when I knew that Dad was officially A Shit. Years later, I was 16 I think, Lucian had started seeing another girl to make me jealous, so I was waiting for him to get fed up with her and came home for a couple of days, and I was snooping about looking for booze (they didn't keep it in the house by then, but it never stopped me looking) and I heard the parents arguing upstairs. Mum was crying because I didn't want her to take a photo of me in the garden because I was so hungover, and they were in the bedroom and Mum said, 'I suppose this is payback for what I did' which made me stop and listen, and then she said, 'You must hate me', which was weird because despite being A Shit, it was obvious Dad was mad about her, and he said of course he didn't hate her, he'd forgiven her a long time ago and loved me as though I was his own child – liar – and he reminded her that her 'fling' had made him realize how much he had to lose and that's why he hadn't been unfaithful again and if she couldn't see that, he was sorry. Huh. Maybe he was, I don't know and could care less, but I was glad I overheard it because it made sense of a lot of stuff for me. I never said anything to Mum. She was really ill by then, and what was the point in making her feel even worse? She loved me, I know that, but I kind of … liked her a lot less after that, I can't explain why, but even so I wasn't about to confront her. I didn't tell anyone. Maybe I like secrets – knowledge is power and all that. Maybe I didn't want to ruin your rosy view of their marriage. It wasn't your fault, was it? And you had enough on your plate, goody-two-shoes Jess, homework in on time, always home on time … I could never be as good as you. Oh, and I didn't bother trying to find out who he was either, the man who spawned me, though it explained why I felt different. Do you remember me saying I was adopted, once? Now I knew why. That there was someone out there, like me. If I'd found him, things might have been different, or could have been worse. He might be dead. I liked pretending I could call him any time I wanted. I chose not to. And I couldn't ask Mum. I just couldn't. It might have killed her sooner.

Phew. That was intense. I might have to take up drinking again.

Time to delete.

Chapter 16

As Will's words settled around me, I realized I wasn't surprised. I'd stopped being shocked by Rachel a long time ago, but I ached for my parents, for how they would have reacted to hearing themselves cruelly killed by their daughter. 'She asked me once, whether I thought she was adopted.' I poked at the food on my plate. It smelt delicious, but my stomach churned. 'She said she felt different.'

'Why do you think that was?' Will seemed to be having trouble eating too, holding his fork but not touching his lasagne.

'I don't know. She wasn't treated any differently to me growing up and she definitely wasn't adopted. I was there when she was born. My mother went into labour early. I'd just got home from school when her waters broke. I called Dad and he rushed home, but there was no time to get her to hospital. By the time the ambulance arrived, Rachel had too.' I vividly recalled Dad's muted panic as he alternately encouraged Mum to breathe as she lay panting and groaning on the kitchen floor, refusing to go up to bed, and flipped through a book about home births, which was what Mum had wanted, but not like that. I'd been told to watch for the ambulance, and then to go across the road and get Maggie Marshall, who was training to be a midwife, but she wasn't home.

Mum's cries had frightened me. I'd hated seeing her helpless, at the mercy of the mysterious force that had taken over her body, compelling her to push my sister out onto the cold tiles as the ambulance appeared at the corner of the street. I would never forget the look of tenderness that flooded her face as Dad – on his knees, shirtsleeves rolled up – awkwardly placed the purple, bloodied bundle in her arms, or the breathless silence that seemed to stretch forever before a plaintive cry erupted and Mum, all traces of pain wiped from her features, said softly, *Come and meet your little sister, Jess.*

'Rachel hated me telling that story,' I said. 'It didn't fit with her theory about not belonging.' The atmosphere between Will and me had eased, my flow of words seeming to bridge the distance – words I hadn't spoken for a long time.

Spotting the waiter returning with an enquiring expression, I ate a forkful of lasagne. 'It's delicious,' I said truthfully and quickly ate some more. 'What was Rachel like?' I dabbed my mouth with the edge of a napkin, wanting to put off the moment of truth.

He leaned forward once more, pushing his plate aside. 'I'm trying to take in everything you've told me.' He gave a slight shake of his head. 'It's as if you've brought a completely different person to life, someone I didn't know at all.'

I tried to read the look in his eyes. 'Were you and she …?' I waved my fork between us and let the words hang.

His gaze snapped back to mine. 'God, no.' He spoke in a heartfelt way that reminded me of the first time Adam saw a photo of Rachel when I took him home to introduce him to Dad. While Dad was making tea in the kitchen, Adam crossed over to the bookshelf to look at the row of framed pictures on top; my parents' wedding photo in the centre, kissing outside St Mary's Church in Barnes, Mum's lustrous dark hair – inherited by Rachel – pinned in an intricate coil, Dad's hand pressing hers to the chest of his Eighties-style velvet suit jacket.

Bypassing a school picture of me grinning self-consciously

with my newly straightened teeth, Adam had picked up a photo of Rachel aged 16, taken surreptitiously on a rare occasion she was home because Lucian had dumped her, and she'd run out of money. She was in the garden wearing tiny denim shorts and an orange bikini top of mine, looking as if she'd been disturbed sunbathing, though I knew she was sleeping off a hangover. She was propped on one elbow, her other arm raised as she pushed a pair of sunglasses into her glossy hair, long legs stretched in front of her on the grass. Her eyes were narrowed, her lips slightly parted as though on the verge of a smile, but a second later she'd sworn at Mum for disturbing her and told us all to piss off and leave her alone. Mum had looked devastated, passing the camera to me – reading in a deckchair – before going back in the house, leaning heavily on the stick she used sometimes. *Gorgeous, isn't she?* I'd said to Adam as he continued to stare at the photo. I'd said it lightly, not jealous, because I knew the Rachel he didn't, but flushed with relief when he looked at me startled, and said, *I was thinking how different you are, that's all.*

Will picked up his mug and swallowed some coffee, his gaze steadier. 'I could see that Rachel didn't like getting close to people, unless it was on her own terms,' he said. 'She was a tough nut to crack, but it was obvious sometimes that she needed a friend, even if she didn't show it.'

'She liked you?'

'As much as she liked anyone, I guess.' He raised a shoulder. 'I think she trusted me.'

'How did she end up at the gallery?'

'She marched in one day back in January, said she needed a job and would do anything, even cleaning.'

'Wow.' I thought of the state of Rachel's room at home, how she seemed to revel in the mess, a sign on her door that read, *Keep Out or I'll Kill You.* 'She must have been desperate.'

'I got the impression she'd asked around a lot of places and been turned away, but as it happened, one of our part-time staff had left.'

'I don't think she ever had a regular job.'

'No.' Will smiled. 'She was honest about that. Admitted she couldn't provide references because she'd been abroad for a while, mostly working in bars' – *the worst possible place for someone with a drink problem* – 'and she was upfront about being a recovering alcoholic looking for a break.'

My heart skipped a beat. Had I been right then, about her wanting Noah back? Why else return after so long, desperate for a job and not drinking? Had she contacted Noah's father and enlisted his help?

'I spoke to my mother,' Will continued. 'She owns the gallery, I'm not there all the time, and we agreed to take Rachel on.'

'Was she reliable?'

'She was, for months. Kept her head down. Not chatty, but that didn't matter as long as she turned up and did her job.'

Curiosity stirred. This man had helped my sister, for no other reason than he could sense she needed it. 'What else do you do?' I poured some tea from the pot Will had ordered. 'You said you're not there all the time.'

'I repair boats, essentially.' He gave a self-deprecating smile. 'There's plenty of demand on the canal.'

'How did you get into that?'

'I was into fixing things, from when I was young. I used to help my grandfather. He was a boatbuilder back in the day, had his own boatyard in Scotland. I stayed with my grandparents in the summer holidays and learned a lot from him.'

'Sounds interesting. No, really,' I said, when he raised an eyebrow. 'Being outdoors, working with your hands.' I glanced at them, saw something like oil ingrained in his fingertips.

'My wife and I were going to move up there. I was going to specialize in narrow boats.'

'But?'

'She met someone else.' His gaze dipped to the congealing food on his plate. 'We're divorced. It seemed easier to stay here, keep an eye on the gallery for my mother, live on the boat, pick up jobs when I can.'

'I'm sorry,' I said. 'About the divorce.'

'It's been a couple of years. I'm pretty much over it now.' He raised his eyes. 'I'm sorry your mum died,' he said. 'That must have been tough.'

Unexpectedly, tears rushed to my eyes. 'Thanks.' I cleared my throat. 'She had Addison's disease. It's rare. She was often fine but deteriorated quickly towards the end, started having seizures.'

'You must miss her.'

'Every day, though part of me is actually glad she's not here right now. She always hoped Rachel would come home one day.'

'How old were you when you lost her?'

'It was ten years ago. I was 25. Rachel hadn't been living at home for a while by then.' I swallowed and turned away.

'She didn't say *you* were dead.'

My head jerked up. 'Sorry?'

'What Rachel told me about being adopted. She told me her parents were dead, not her sister.'

'But she didn't mention me either.'

His mouth twisted. 'No,' he admitted.

I looked into my cup of cooling tea, at my distorted reflection. 'I'm mostly sorry Mum didn't get to meet her grandson,' I said. 'She would have loved being a grandma.'

'You have a son?'

I checked his face, saw only kindness and curiosity. Rachel really hadn't told him anything. Even drunk, she had managed to hold onto her secrets.

'He's called Noah.' I took out my phone and showed him the screensaver. 'He's 5.'

Will's smile was warm. 'He looks like you.' *The opposite of what Vanessa Blake had said.*

81

'You don't have children?'

He shook his head. 'We never got that far.'

I pushed my phone back in my bag, hoping I hadn't stirred something unwelcome in his mind. I used to resent it when people asked when Adam and I were going to start a family. I didn't know Will, had no idea of the life that had shaped him. 'I should go.'

He looked alarmed. 'Already?'

'I've arranged to meet a friend, someone I used to work with. If you could give me Rachel's things.'

As I made to stand up, Will's hand shot out and circled my wrist. 'Jess, wait. We haven't talked about what I said on the phone.'

I sank down, heart thudding. I wanted to clamp my hands over my ears. 'You still believe it then?'

He let go of me. 'That Rachel was murdered?' He nodded. 'Yes, I do.'

With a rush of clarity, I realized what I'd really wanted was to hear about my sister from someone who knew her, someone who could tell me she'd loved and missed her family – not this.

'Why do you think it wasn't an accident?' I picked up my bag, braced to leave. It was clear he hadn't brought Rachel's things if there were any. Had it been a ruse to get me here?

'A man came looking for her.'

'A man?' He had my attention now. 'Who?'

'I don't know.' Will's tone became urgent. 'She wasn't at work when he turned up and I couldn't get hold of her.' In the pause that followed, everything around us receded. 'He said he'd come to talk to Rachel about their son.'

Chapter 17

I was running. Through the café, onto the street, bag thumping my hip, feet pounding the pavement as I tried to pull air into my lungs.

'Jess, wait!'

I pushed past pedestrians and veered onto the road, leaping back when a black cab swerved past, horn blaring. I stopped abruptly and doubled over, heart banging in my chest.

'What's going on?' Will had caught up with me. 'Are you OK?'

I glanced at him, perspiration prickling my forehead. 'Do I look it?'

Concern etched his features. 'What happened?'

I straightened, face pulsing with heat. 'I'm sorry.' I pushed my hair back with shaking hands. 'I didn't pay for lunch.'

Will shook his head, brow knitted, jacket hanging from one hand. 'It's fine,' he said. 'I paid when I ordered.'

'I owe you my share.' I began fiddling with my bag, his words still ringing in my ears. *He'd come to talk to Rachel about their son.*

'What I said back there.' Will stepped closer. 'It obviously meant something bad.'

Catching my breath, I said, 'This man … He didn't give you his name?'

'No.' Will raised a hand as I took a twenty-pound note from my purse. 'Honestly, you don't have to,' he said as I shoved the note at him. He took it and thrust it in his jeans pocket. 'You know who he was?'

'What did he look like?'

'Oh God, I don't know …' Glancing round, he cupped my elbow and steered me to the low stone wall outside the building I'd fled, away from a group of tourists. 'Tall, surfer hair,' he made a sweeping motion over his head, 'light-coloured eyes, maybe blue.'

My heart dropped. It had to be Lucian West. At the time, I'd prayed so hard he wasn't Noah's father but had concluded he couldn't be, not only because, as far as we knew, he was off the scene by then, but because Rachel would never have given up her baby if he was Lucian's. A baby would have roped them together for life. She would have done everything in her power to make that happen, I was sure of it. Even if he'd told her to get rid of it, she wouldn't have. She would have used the baby to try to win him over, bring him back to her. Plus, she'd been insistent in her email that the father wasn't involved, didn't even know about the baby, stating that it was better that way. Yet Will's description fitted the boy … man … I'd met only twice before and had hated for the hold he had over my sister.

'Did he have a tattoo on the back of his hand?'

Will frowned. 'He did, now you mention it. A spider's web, I think.'

I shuddered at the memory of seeing it for the first time, how apt it had seemed. My sister, the spider, caught in his web of … who knew? It had been impossible to see the attraction, beyond his obvious good looks. 'I know who he is.' I couldn't help a note of bitterness, even as shame began to sink through me that my reaction had been to flee from Will, as if I could outrun his words and leave them behind.

'Was he drunk?' That was my abiding memory of Lucian West. A sneering smile, glazed eyes, bare-chested, and skinny-jeaned, one sinewy arm slung around my sister's neck as though anchoring her to his side while I pleaded with her to come home, to sit her exams. *What does she need exams for? We don't need that shit,* he'd drawled. *We're going to Thailand for the summer, that's a proper education. Real life.* Real life. They'd been drinking so heavily, reality had lost its meaning.

'Drunk?' Will was shaking his head. 'No, he was … articulate, soft-spoken. Calm. That's what struck me. He didn't push it when I told him I didn't know where Rachel was.'

That didn't sound like the Lucian I remembered, but I hadn't set eyes on him for years. Maybe he'd finally grown up. *Maybe he was ready to be a father.* The thought pushed my heart rate up, and I thought of the letter in my bag. 'So, where was Rachel?'

'She'd gone to run some errands, but I didn't tell him that. He left a number for her to call him.' Will paused. 'I'd never seen her look so happy when I told her.'

My head was spinning. 'What happened?'

'I honestly don't know. Like I said, she didn't like people knowing her business. She was on a high for a bit and must have met up with him because she went downhill suddenly, drinking a lot and missing work. I found her passed out in the bathroom one morning. She shared the flat above the art gallery with a student, Hannah.' He rubbed his brow. 'Hannah was worried because she couldn't wake her up. I asked Rachel what was wrong, but she wouldn't tell me. She said she was going to make it work, sort everything out, that she'd made a big mistake and she wanted to put things right.'

'I knew it. She wanted Noah back.'

'What?'

Too late, I realized what I'd said. 'Oh, God.' I buried my face in my hands. 'Why is this happening?'

'Jess?' I caught Will's scent, coffee, and oil, felt his hand on my shoulder. 'Are you saying that *Rachel* is Noah's mother?'

'She *wasn't* his mother.' I jolted away from him. 'She didn't want

85

him. She asked me to have him. *I'm* his mother. *Me.*' I jabbed my chest, fury coursing through me. 'I've taken care of Noah since he was born.' I remembered his breathing, fast and shallow as I held him against my chest. 'She left him on the doorstep at Dad's, would you believe? She wouldn't even come in, couldn't bear to see us. She dropped him off like a parcel and ran away, like she always did.' I pictured her, fleeing like a butterfly leaving its cocoon, free to fly unburdened wherever she chose. 'She left a note saying she didn't want anything more to do with us and we didn't hear from her again until a week or so before she died.' I ran out of steam, my body sagging. 'She wanted to visit me, said we needed to talk. I had a nasty feeling she was going to ask for Noah back, as though she'd only lent him.'

Will dropped onto the wall beside me, though I couldn't recall sitting down. I felt dislocated, my real life a million miles away.

'I can't believe I had no idea about any of this.' He raised his voice over the rattle of a passing truck. 'She never mentioned a child, even in the form of a nephew.'

'Why would she if we were dead to her?' My cheeks were damp. I wiped them with my fingers. 'She put it out of her mind until it suited her.'

'Until this Lucian turned up?'

I tried to think. 'I don't understand why, if he was the father, she didn't tell him she was pregnant in the first place.'

'Maybe she did, and he wasn't interested back then?'

I looked at Will. 'And nearly six years later, he is?'

Will raised his eyebrows. 'Maybe something had changed, he was ready to take on the responsibility.' *Rachel too.* He didn't say it, probably wasn't even thinking it, but the thought that she might have wanted Noah purely on the basis that Lucian was ready to be involved made me want to be sick. Bile burnt the back of my throat.

I swallowed a couple of times before saying, 'Why didn't he contact us, especially after she died? He didn't come to the funeral, so he can't have cared that much.' I had no idea what I would have done if I'd seen him there. Dad definitely wouldn't have coped, would most likely have punched him – or got Denny to do it. 'Then again, he'd have known he wasn't welcome. Or maybe he didn't know she was dead.'

'Or, he had something to do with her death.'

I stared. 'You think he killed her?'

Will blew out a breath. 'I know she was going to meet someone that night.' His face set in a frown. 'Hannah mentioned that Rachel seemed hyped up about seeing whoever it was.'

'It doesn't mean it was Lucian ...' A thought crashed into my head. I scrabbled for my bag and pulled out the crumpled envelope, thrusting it at Will.

'This came for me at work the other day.'

He took out the sheet of paper and scanned it. 'You think it's from him?'

A worried gaze whipped between us.

'I don't know what to think.'

'It's an odd coincidence, don't you think? Not long after he showed up at the gallery, Rachel goes off to see someone late at night and doesn't come back and then you get this letter.' Will studied the envelope. 'No postmark.'

I was struggling to put it together, work out what could have gone wrong. 'She could have been meeting someone else and they didn't turn up.' It felt surreal to be having this conversation, though Will didn't seem shocked at discovering that, not only had Rachel given birth, but had given the baby to a sister she'd never mentioned. 'If she'd been drinking, it makes sense she could have slipped and fallen in the canal. And the police interviewed everyone who knew her, the people she'd been in contact with.' That was the information the police had relayed to Dad. 'They didn't mention Lucian.' *No CCTV*, they said. *No suspicious circumstances.*

'I was the only one who knew about him.' Will shook his head. 'But I didn't know his name, only that she'd had a visit from a man who left his number, which I gave to Rachel. They couldn't find her phone afterwards. It wasn't on her, or at the flat.' I felt a curl of shame that I hadn't known. 'Obviously, I didn't know about you, or I would have been in touch sooner.'

'You did try to talk to me at the pub.'

'Yes, but it was badly timed, and I admit, I was confused and not very happy that Rachel had lied to me about her family.'

'Did you talk to anyone else?'

'A woman called Caroline asked me how I knew Rachel. I told her she'd worked for me. She said something about what a hard time she'd given you all, that it was no wonder you'd moved to the Lake District to get away.' That's how Will had known where I lived. Of course Rachel hadn't told him. She hadn't said a word, about any of us.

Will handed the letter back and I folded it into my pocket. He dropped his jacket by his feet and looked at his boots, and I wondered what he would normally be doing on a Friday afternoon. 'You should tell the police about Lucian, his connection to Rachel,' he said. 'They could reopen the investigation.'

'How, with no proof?'

He hesitated. 'It's not proof, but …'

I waited a beat, feeling on the edge of a precipice. 'Go on.'

'There was a witness.'

'A witness?' Ice ran down my spine. 'But the police said—'

'It wasn't official,' Will cut in. 'I took a walk down there one evening, to the stretch of canal where she fell in. Not in a ghoulish way.' He shot me a look. 'I suppose I was trying to process it all. I thought if I walked around where she'd been that night, it might make more sense.'

'More sense than her being drunk and falling in?'

'You don't want to believe it, I get that. But what if that guy, the baby's father, what if he killed her because … I don't know why, but he's out there now and he intends to find his son. It fits with the anonymous letter.'

I wanted him to stop speaking. 'It sounds so far-fetched.'

'Now I know Rachel had a baby it seems plausible it's linked to what happened to her,' Will continued. 'What if Rachel told the father that *you* had Noah?'

'So, what, he pushed her into the water and let her drown then sent me a warning letter instead of talking to me?' Desperation made my voice shake. 'It doesn't make any sense.' But neither did anything else.

'A moment of madness?' Will shrugged. 'He panicked and ran away but wants you to know he's not giving up.'

That sounded like the Lucian I remembered. But he had changed, according to Will's impression. If it *had* been Lucian ... but the tattoo was a giveaway. It couldn't be anyone else.

My head throbbed with questions. 'Who was this witness?'

'A homeless guy. He sometimes sleeps under the bridge and that night—'

'A *homeless* guy?' A strange relief took hold. 'For God's sake, Will. Hardly a credible witness.'

'Hear me out.' Will raised a hand. 'He told me someone had drowned there, where I was walking.'

My breathing faltered. 'He saw it happen?'

'No, but he did see someone hurrying towards the main road around that time. He'd been moved on earlier by the police and was making his way to the bridge because he wanted somewhere to shelter.'

'Didn't he tell the police all this?'

'He did but couldn't give them a clear description. He told me it was obvious they didn't believe him because he'd been drinking, but he knows what he saw.'

'And you do believe him?'

'I don't see why he would lie.'

My temples pounded as I absorbed the information. 'But he didn't see them clearly?'

'Only a figure with their head down. He bumped into whoever

it was, and they told him to watch it, or something, and he thought he could smell perfume. He didn't think anything of it until he heard a body had been found and realized she'd drowned the night he was under the bridge.'

'But he was drunk.'

'Maybe,' Will conceded. 'But that doesn't mean he was imagining things.'

Tension tightened my chest. 'Oh God,' I said. 'I don't know what to do.'

'Look, I'm sorry for bringing it up, but I thought you would want to know.'

I didn't. 'It's OK,' I lied. 'Rachel was lucky to have you on her side.' I glanced at my watch, startled to see how much time had passed. 'I should go,' I said, when a moment's silence had lapsed. My temples throbbed. 'I appreciate everything you've told me. I'll take it from here.' *Too formal.* 'I take it there isn't anything of Rachel's you wanted to give me?'

'Oh, I almost forgot.' Reaching down, he picked up his jacket. He dug his hand in an inside pocket and pulled out an A4 padded envelope. 'Here.'

'That's it?' I took it, testing its weight. 'There isn't much.'

'No, but I thought you should have it.'

'Thanks.' Pushing the envelope awkwardly into my bag, I tried to smile. 'I'm sorry you've been dragged into this mess.'

He didn't smile back. 'I dragged myself into it,' he said. 'I'm just the messenger.' We rose and faced each other. 'Are you staying in London?'

'For tonight. I'm meeting a friend and might try to squeeze in a bit of shopping.' It sounded ridiculous to be talking about shopping after discussing the possibility that my sister had been murdered, but I needed to get away, to think.

Will took a breath. 'Listen, if you want some company this evening or to talk some more, call me.'

I backed away, a defensive feeling constricting my shoulders. 'Thanks, but I'm not sure that's a good idea.'

He gave a tight nod. 'You have my number if you change your mind.'

I won't. I rushed away, feeling the shape of the A4 envelope through my bag, the letter rustling in my pocket, wishing suddenly that I'd never heard of Will Taylor.

Chapter 18

Rachel

Before

From: RBeresford@gmail.com
To: JessSanderson11@gmail.com
Subject: Getting things off my chest

I thought I'd better double-check I didn't send you that email about Mum. I dreamt I had and woke up in a cold sweat. Maybe it's because you're a mum yourself now and the truth ... so many truths ... would break you. Or not. You're strong, that's obvious. In a good way. In the way a mother should be. That's why I'll never be a good parent. I'm not strong. But hey, I'm me. Let me be me.

Can't stand this flat with its miserable view of the street, not even a tree to look at. I do push-ups sometimes, go for long, long walks when I'm not working. Work. Hah! Cleaning, that's all I'm good for. That and bar work. Trying to stay away from that though. The gallery's nice. Will's nice. Could *be worse. Got to keep my head down. I miss Lucian so much. I still wear his favourite perfume and remember how it used to drive him wild. Hopefully, I won't have to miss him for much longer.*

That's it. Just wanted to check I hadn't sent that email about Mum. PHEW!!

Better delete this one now.

Chapter 19

When I arrived at the pub on the corner of Brunswick Place, Sasha was already there, sitting in the high-ceilinged bar at a table by the window, eyes trained on the door.

'There you are!' Smiling broadly, she wiggled round to clutch me as I reached the table. 'I thought you weren't coming.'

'Sorry I'm a bit late.' Aware of heat in my armpits as I hugged her narrow frame, I wished I'd had time to shower and change before getting the subway. Luckily, Sasha's floral scent was strong enough for us both.

'I ordered you an orange juice,' she said, sitting down and crossing her slim legs, her dark gaze appraising. 'Unless you've taken up drinking.' She nodded to her glass, which I knew without asking contained her favourite tipple, gin and tonic. 'Naughty, but I've finished work for the day.'

'This is great, thanks.' Keeping my jacket on, I settled opposite and took a few thirsty sips. After my exchange with Will, I could have done with something strong and alcoholic to numb my feelings and dull my churning thoughts but couldn't face explaining why to Sasha. I put my glass down and glanced through the window at the quiet, bollard-lined pavement and, further down, the chunky brick-and-glass building where I'd worked for several years. Everything felt strange, even the busy pub where we'd gathered so many times for functions and parties in the past, with its chandeliers and mahogany-style panelling.

'You look good,' I said, returning my attention to Sasha. She was glancing at her phone screen, no doubt checking work emails. She hadn't changed; still whippet-thin and high-cheekboned, wearing flawless make-up, her shiny blonde hair swishing around her shoulders. I looked like a country mouse in my jeans and jumper next to her corporate suit, a slippery blouse beneath her navy jacket. Turnbull and Fraser didn't believe in dress-down Fridays – another reason I'd been more than happy to leave.

'You too,' she said unconvincingly, dragging her eyes from her phone. 'Country living obviously suits you.'

'You're not tempted to try it?' She'd never visited, despite my invitations. Looking at her now, it was hard to visualise her in Ulverston, hiking across the fells with a rucksack on her back.

'Definitely not. All that fresh air and mud, no Nando's or Pret?' She gave an exaggerated shudder. 'Nothing to do in the evenings.'

'We're not a million miles from civilization.' I smiled to take out the sting. 'We have plenty of nice restaurants and cafés that know how to serve an espresso.'

'Ooh, you've been converted,' she teased, eyes sparkling over the rim of her glass. 'Don't you miss the city at all?'

'Not really,' I said, trying and failing to push Will out of my mind, to forget our conversation – to squash the suspicion that Lucian had met with Rachel the night she died. 'I was ready for the change.'

'Hey, I'm sorry about your sister.' Sasha's pale pink lips pulled down. 'I know you weren't in touch, but what happened to her was awful.'

'Thanks,' I said shortly. I hadn't talked much to friends about my family, but on holiday in Greece with Sasha and Jo, I'd let my guard down and told them a bit about what life had been like with Rachel. 'My dad's taken it badly.'

'I can imagine. Especially after losing your mum.' Her eyes were pools of pity and I had to look away. 'You know, we would have come to the funeral. For moral support. You could have stayed at mine overnight.'

'I know.' I'd relayed to her and Jo what had happened in one of our infrequent catch-up sessions on WhatsApp, but despite their concerned *Let us know if there's anything we can do*, I hadn't crossed my mind to see them while I was in London. 'I don't think we would all have fitted into your flat,' I added, to remind her I had a family. Sasha rarely asked about Noah in anything other than a perfunctory way. From the moment I told her Adam and I were trying for a baby, to revealing I was 'pregnant', to Noah coming into our lives, her interest had only skimmed the surface. She didn't want children and found it hard to relate to people who did, and while at first it had been refreshing to keep up with the gossip at Turnbull and Fraser, it soon wore thin. My priorities had shifted, and I bit back a yawn as Sasha brought me up to date with the latest work goings-on.

'So, how's lovely Adam?' she said when I'd failed to respond in the way she'd hoped. 'Being a rock, no doubt.'

'He is.'

Having been there when Adam and I met, both Sasha and Jo still tended to speak as though they were the ones who had brought us together in Greece by playing matchmaker. 'He's in Berlin at the moment on business.'

'And while the cat's away …' Sasha wiggled her neatly groomed eyebrows.

'What's that supposed to mean?'

Her head pulled back at my tone. 'Sorry, I was teasing.' Her eyes narrowed. 'Is everything OK, Jess?'

I tried to smile. 'I've got a headache.' At least that was true. 'I was up early this morning, and the train journey in … you know what it's like.'

Her face relaxed. She didn't really want to know that my life was far from perfect. 'So, what brings you to London again?'

'Adam's fortieth next month,' I lied. 'I wanted to look for a gift.'

'Any luck?'

'Not yet.' Her gaze had drifted past me to the door. Not sure why I was bothering to regain her attention when I wanted, suddenly, to go back to my hotel room, I said, 'Are you still seeing Simon?'

Adam had introduced his best friend to Sasha after we got together. Although neither were keen to settle down they'd been seeing each other on and off ever since.

Her eyes returned to mine. 'I think he's planning to propose.' Smiling, she leaned forward and said in a confidential tone, 'I'm going to say yes.'

'That's … amazing.' I hadn't hit the right note of enthusiasm and her forehead crumpled. 'I thought you weren't the marrying type, that's all.'

'I'm allowed to change my mind.' Her voice cooled. 'Simon's a good guy and I've dated enough bad ones to know I'm lucky to have him.'

'Adam will be pleased.' I forced a smile. 'He hasn't heard from Simon in a while.'

'Works both ways.' Sasha cocked her head, slightly combative. 'He was never the same with Simon after that stag do in Spain.'

I sighed inwardly. 'So you've said.' Adam hadn't wanted to go, busy with a project and working long hours, but a mutual friend was getting married, and in the end, he'd agreed. I'd got my period after a barrage of tests had shown there was no reason for me not getting pregnant, and I suspected he'd been happy to have an excuse to escape, but when he came back he was moody, snapping when I asked what was wrong, until I'd suggested that maybe we needed some time apart. Full of self-recrimination, he'd begged me to stay, as close to tears as I'd ever seen him. I stayed and things got better. I hadn't thought about it in ages. 'I told you, it wasn't personal,' I said. 'He's busy.'

'Too busy to text?' Sasha looked sceptical. She opened her mouth as if to say more, then closed it again.

'What?'

'Nothing.' When I didn't push, she continued, 'I didn't say anything at the time because I know you were having a tough time with the baby stuff, but Simon told me they didn't see much of Adam on that trip. He kept wanting to go off on his own.'

'I know, he told me that too.' Why was she saying this? 'He wasn't in the right frame of mind for partying. It's not his cup of tea.'

'That's not how he was at university, according to Simon.'

'Well, he's an adult now. Like you said, people change.' Why were we having a conversation about a stag do that happened years ago? 'Sounds as though you've been saving that up.' My tone was caustic.

'I didn't know you knew.' Sasha looked hurt. 'I didn't tell you at the time because I didn't want to upset you.'

'Why would I be upset that Adam went off on his own?' My brow pulled into a frown. 'It's ancient history.'

She shifted, seeming uncomfortable. At work, she'd relished a rumour more than anyone else. 'I shouldn't have brought it up.' She glanced at her polished nails. 'I'm sorry.'

'Don't worry about it.' Annoyance pierced the shroud of nervy unease I'd carried around all day. 'I'd better make a move.' I reached for my bag. 'It was good to see you.'

She looked at my barely touched drink, not bothering to stop me, and I realized how far apart we'd grown. 'I'll tell Simon you said hi, shall I?' Her face was set, her mouth a straight line. 'You haven't even asked after Jo.'

'Actually, she messaged to say she was going on holiday this week and she's coming to visit soon. And, by the way, Noah's fine. Thank you for asking.' It was a childish parting shot. Tears hovered as I walked away and I wondered whether she too was recalling that happy holiday in Greece together, and the evenings we'd spent watching films on the mustard-yellow sofa in her flat, drinking wine. It seemed like a lifetime ago.

As I exited the café, I knew we wouldn't meet again.

Chapter 20

After catching a train to Knightsbridge, my mind in turmoil, I forced myself into Harrods and wandered around the menswear department, knowing there was nothing I wanted to buy. Guilt swirling in my stomach, I sent a photo of some ornate cufflinks to Jennifer.

Do you think Adam would like these? I was salving my conscience, trying to prove I really was shopping for a birthday gift. Waiting for her reply, I checked out a selection of overpriced watches, even though Adam hadn't worn one since losing the watch his mother had bought him for his thirtieth on one of his business trips.

They're lovely, but does he wear cufflinks? X

Good point! I'll keep looking X

Maybe I should have told Jennifer the real reason I was in London. I'd talked to her about Rachel in the past and she'd been sympathetic. I was sure she would have understood. *But Adam wouldn't.*

Reluctant to buy a gift for the sake of it, I gave up and made my way back to the hotel, wincing at my ghostly reflection in the train window, replaying my conversation with Sasha. Maybe she had a point about Adam not staying in touch with Simon. Their friendship went back a long way, not like Sasha and me, who'd met at work and didn't have much else in common. Unlike Adam, I hadn't held on to friendships from school and university – home life had always taken precedence – glad to make new friends after we moved from London.

On impulse, I messaged Kristin. *Hope you've had a good day. Any news from Vanessa Blake? X* She didn't reply but tended not to check her phone when she was working.

It was nearly six when I arrived at the hotel and the evening stretched ahead with nothing to do but worry. Should I call the police and tell them about Lucian's connection to Rachel? But with no proof she'd met him that night, they wouldn't be interested. I knew from Denny that evidence was everything. Without it, there was no case.

It wasn't too late to get the last train home. There was no reason to stay in London now I'd spoken to Will. But I couldn't face another long journey right now. I thought of Noah, yearning to hear his voice and rang home, sinking onto the bed as he chattered excitedly about the cakes he'd made with Nanna, and his fishing trip to Eden Lacy with my dad tomorrow.

'Nanna's coming too.'

'You're going fishing?' I said when Jennifer came on the line. 'That's brave.'

'It'll be nice.' There was a smile in her voice. 'The weather forecast is good so I thought we could take a picnic. I can always read a book while they do their thing.'

My heart was beating fast. 'You will keep a close eye on Noah, won't you? Don't let anyone into the house.'

'Of course I won't.' She seemed unsurprised by my vehemence. 'I promise you, Jess, no harm will come to Noah while I'm here.'

'I'm worried he might sleepwalk.'

'I'll sleep in his room. I don't mind.'

'Maybe take the baby monitor when you go to bed. It's in the living room.'

101

'Are you sure you're OK, Jess?'

No. I shouldn't have left Noah. What was I thinking? 'I'm fine. I don't like being away from him, that's all.'

'I get it.' Her voice was gentle. 'I promise I'll call if there's any problem.'

We chatted a bit longer until Noah called her away and, twenty minutes later, as I stepped out of a steamy shower wrapped in towels, my phone rang. When I saw Adam's number, my stomach clenched.

'You're in London,' he said the second I answered.

'You've spoken to your mum.'

'I rang to speak to Noah, and she answered the phone.'

My heart had picked up speed. 'What did she say?'

'That you were on a shopping trip, and it was a surprise, so I shouldn't say anything.'

'There you are then.' I said it lightly, trying to defuse the tension.

'You didn't mention going when we spoke last night.'

'You do understand the meaning of "surprise"? I want to get you something special for your fortieth.'

'And you happened to choose today?'

'Why not?' I adjusted my towel. 'You know your mum loves spending time with Noah, especially without us breathing down her neck.'

'I get that, but … after everything that's happened? I thought you were worried about Noah.'

'You were the one who said we had to carry on as normal.' Guilt sharpened my voice. 'He's safe with your mum.'

'Is that the only reason you're there?'

'I met Sasha for a drink.'

'Sasha?' There was surprise now, and a hint of wariness. 'How is she?'

'Actually, it was a bit uncomfortable.' I was relieved to be honest about something. 'She's still seeing Simon. I think it's serious.'

'Really? He never said.'

'Because you're not in touch,' I reminded him. 'Maybe you should give him a call.' It was on the tip of my tongue to mention the stag weekend and relay what Sasha had said, but it was so long ago. It seemed pointless to bring it up now. And if he contacted Simon, I didn't want there to be any awkwardness between them. 'She thinks he's planning to propose.'

'Well, good luck to them.' He liked Sasha, as far as I knew, or he wouldn't have introduced her to his famously single friend, but perhaps he hadn't pictured them being together for life. 'So, how's London?' he said grudgingly.

'I'd forgotten how big it is.' *Tell him that Rachel was murdered.* But I couldn't. Not without proof.

'Same here.' He gave a small laugh, a sound I hadn't heard in a while. 'I always knew I wasn't cut out for city life. I wished I'd realized sooner.'

'We wouldn't have met if you had.' I imagined, as I did sometimes, all the tiny factors that had led us to being on holiday at the same time, how different our lives might be with the smallest variation.

I rubbed my hair with the towel. 'I can't wait to get home.'

'Me too.' Adam's words were heartfelt. I had half-expected him to mention Noah's 'monster', the power cut, me waving a torch in the kitchen, certain Noah would have said something, but it clearly hadn't come up. 'What are you doing this evening?'

'I'll probably order room service, watch TV, and have an early night.' I glanced out the window where the sky was beginning to darken. 'I'm shattered.'

'And you've picked up Rachel's stuff?'

For a wild second, I wondered whether I'd told him and forgotten. 'Sorry?'

'Come on, Jess.' His voice grew strained. 'Isn't that why you're really there?'

'I told you—'

'I know what you told me, and I'm sure you've engineered a

103

shopping trip, but it's too much of a coincidence that you decided to go right after that phone call from her boss.'

Her boss. Now I'd met him, it was impossible to see Will as someone authoritative, in charge of Rachel. My stomach plunged as I tried to marshal my thoughts. There was so much Adam didn't know. 'OK, I admit I wanted to pick up her things,' I said. 'I know you don't approve, but Dad might want them.'

'I doubt that.' Now his tone reminded me of Sasha's, cooling on hearing something he didn't like. 'Didn't he shove that box from the flat into the shed because he couldn't bear to look at it?'

It was true that when I'd picked through Rachel's paltry items in his kitchen, Dad had left me to it, going out to sit in the garden while he waited for me to finish. When I asked later what he was going to do with them, he stared at his trembling hands. 'Throw them away, I suppose.'

'You can't do that,' I protested, even though there was nothing worth keeping. Nothing with any sentimental value, just a motley collection of belongings I suspected hadn't meant much even to Rachel, yet the thought of binning them felt wrong. In the end, Dad had put the box out of sight, where I supposed it would remain.

'It's difficult to explain,' I said to Adam, catching sight of myself in the wall mirror, hair dripping onto bare shoulders, brow furrowed as I tried to find the right words. 'The thing is, Adam—'

'It's fine, I get it,' he cut in, as if wanting to be finished with the topic. 'It's closure. Once it's done you can come home and put it behind you, yes?'

He sounded so hopeful I couldn't disagree. 'Yes,' I said faintly. 'I'll be home tomorrow.'

'Can't wait to see you.' His voice warmed up again. 'I gather your dad's taking Noah fishing in the morning.'

'Your mum too,' I managed. 'I hope she won't be bored.'

'They've never been alone together, have they?'

'Maybe it'll be good for them.' I tried to picture them making conversation and found that I couldn't. 'They have Noah in common so that should break the ice.'

'I'm sure your dad will work hard to win her over,' Adam said dryly. 'He can't help himself.'

I told myself he was basing his opinion on a past version of my father, the man he'd been before Rachel's death, then pictured Ruth Duncan baking cakes in his kitchen, and realized Adam had a point. Even at his lowest, Dad couldn't stop being charming in female company. 'So, are you eating out tonight?'

'I'll probably go for room service, same as you.' After he briefly ran through his day, we said our goodbyes.

'I love you,' Adam said with more force than usual.

'You too.'

Marginally happier that the call had ended on good terms, my mood dipped when I remembered all the things I hadn't told him. With a heavy sigh, I sat on the edge of the bed and fished in my bag for the padded envelope and tipped the contents onto the duvet, my gaze scanning each item: a pair of *Friends* socks – she'd never been a fan of the show – with a hole in the toe; a worn-down lipstick and tube of black mascara; and a slim, battered book of poetry entitled *Life and Other Absurdities* by a Patricia Russell. I'd never known Rachel read anything other than an occasional true-crime book. I picked it up, foolishly sniffing the pages as if they might contain the essence of my sister, a trace of her perfume. Flipping through, I noticed she'd highlighted the odd letter here and there in yellow: the i in *Imagine life is the shape of a star* and, a few pages later, the f in *fortunes made and lost*, and the t in *aching for the light*, and many more throughout the book. They didn't add up to anything that made sense, as far as I could see. Perhaps the sentences had spoken to Rachel, struck a chord, and so she'd marked them. Had she been looking for meaning in her life? A thought occurred and I turned to the first pages. Had Lucian given her the book? If he had, there was no inscription, only the author's name and a loving dedication to her husband. A Google search revealed that the writer had found brief success with her poetry in the Seventies and died in the late Nineties aged 87. I looked through it again, trying to imagine Rachel's thought process, to picture her with a highlighter pen, but the image fizzled and died. At school, she'd been quick to learn, but easily bored, rarely completing her homework despite our parents' gentle encouragement and occasional bribes.

Then it hit me that someone else could have made the highlights. I put the book down, and stuffed everything back in the envelope. Maybe it was Will's and he'd put the book in there by mistake.

I rose from the bed and located the hairdryer, then blasted my hair before pulling my clothes on over clean underwear and crossing to the window. Through the thick pane of glass, I heard traffic humming in the distance, and the sky was tinged an orangey brown as the streetlights came on. It was never properly dark in the city, unlike in Ulverston. I'd found the solid blackness unnerving until Adam pointed out the scattering of stars that were rarely visible in London.

It was no good. I couldn't stay in my room, and I wouldn't be able to sleep with my mind seething with unanswered questions. I reached for my bag and jacket. I would go to the canal, where Rachel had been seen alive for the last time, and look for the homeless man.

Chapter 21

I was reluctant to get on another train, so decided to go on foot. Unfamiliar with this part of London, I brought up Google Maps on my phone and followed directions to Regent's Canal.

It grew darker as I walked, and my feeling of dislocation strengthened. I considered turning round and coming back tomorrow morning but didn't want to risk the homeless man not being there. *He might not be there now.*

I resisted the compulsion to look over my shoulder. There weren't many people around, but then again, it was a chilly Friday evening in late September – not conducive to wandering by a canal in the dark.

I moved quickly until I reached an activity centre called The Pirate Castle, a large, crenellated building that made me think of a prison. Had Rachel walked past it that night too?

I slowly descended the stone stairs to the towpath, footsteps faltering as I walked beneath the bridge that joined both sides of the castle. Colder down here, the water smelt dank. I drew my jacket more tightly around me, fighting a rush of vertigo. Forcing myself to look at the water, my breath stalled as an image of Rachel, floating face down on the surface, filled my mind. I pictured her fighting for her life, dragged down by her parka and heavy boots.

There had been an unusual weather front that week causing the temperature to plummet. If she'd worn lighter clothing, would she have survived? Unlikely, considering the amount of alcohol she'd drunk. Her reactions would have slowed, according to the coroner's report. She may have blacked out when she hit the water. I hoped so. I hoped she hadn't suffered.

Opposite, water lapped at the dark brick wall, the sound eerie in the silence.

I gripped the top of the railing that ran along the edge of the canal to where the bridge ended, the metal cold beneath my fingers. *Railings.* There to stop people plunging into the water. I imagined Rachel, intoxicated, climbing over, losing her footing. Would there have been a splash? Did she cry out? It had been a Tuesday, past midnight, no one strolling by; just Rachel, and whoever she had come here to meet. If she'd been expecting Lucian and he hadn't turned up, could she have thrown herself into the water deliberately? Her state of mind hadn't been questioned but Will claimed her mood had changed after Lucian's first visit. And her flatmate, Hannah, had told him Rachel was hyped up before going out that night. If Lucian hadn't put in an appearance, it might have literally pushed Rachel over the edge.

Her death suddenly felt crushingly real, and a spasm of grief gripped my chest.

Glancing around, a shiver trailed down my back. Was somebody there? The steps I'd walked down were empty and the path, partly lit by a streetlight from above, deserted. Shaking all over, I clamped my arms around my waist and pressed close to the cold stone wall behind me as my senses adjusted. I could hear faint music now, drifting from pubs and bars further along the canal.

'You lookin' for someone?'

I yelped, clapping a hand to my mouth. The voice was male, rough. I turned around wildly, gaze landing on what looked like a heap of crumpled blankets a few feet away.

'Who are you?' I tried to make my voice strong, but it came out tremulous.

'Who are *you*?' the voice parried.

Neither of us moved. I yanked my phone from my pocket and turned on the torch, aiming the beam in his direction.

'Woah, you tryin' to blind me?' An arm rose from the bundle, covering his face so all I could see was a mass of dreadlocked hair.

'Sorry.' Lowering my phone, I moved closer, then stopped. He could have a knife for protection, be high on drugs.

'You all right?' the voice probed uncertainly.

My body softened with relief. He was equally wary of me. Hoping he was Will's homeless man, I said tentatively, 'My sister died here a few weeks ago.' Tears gathering, I added quickly, 'She drowned. A friend of hers told me there was a witness.'

'Yeah, it was me.' I heard rustling. The figure rose from his makeshift bed and I raised my phone torch, taking in the slight figure. He was younger than I'd expected, no more than 19, dark stubble covering the lower half of his face. Clad in a thick flannel shirt and baggy jeans, he looked primed for a fight, hands clenched by his sides, but his eyes were clear. He didn't seem drunk, or high. 'She was your sister, yeah?'

'Yes. Her name was Rachel.' It seemed important to say it out loud. 'I'm Jess.'

He nodded. 'Sam,' he said, rummaging in his shirt pocket. He pulled out a thin cigarette, rolling it between his fingers, but made no effort to light it. 'Wanna get out from under here?' His voice was low and raspy, giving the impression of someone older, his accent pure East End. 'Bit grim, innit?' He was backing away, to the path at the end of the bridge where the railings ended. *Could Rachel have fallen in there?* It would make more sense – especially if she was pushed.

'Sure,' I said, trying not to dwell on the thought as I followed, taking in his small pile of belongings as I passed: a thin sleeping bag and stained pillow, a Starbucks cup, a fast-food carton, a carrier bag spilling sandwich wrappers, and a paperback novel.

'Not much but it's home.' He spoke neutrally, seeing me looking. 'Don't get hassled so much down here.'

I guiltily stuffed my phone in my pocket, wanting to say I was sorry, to ask why he was homeless and living under a bridge, but I resisted. I must seem like the sort of person who hadn't a clue.

I felt safer on the path, where anybody looking could see us. Not that there was anyone around. A breeze picked up, cutting through my jacket. I thrust my hair back as Sam put his cigarette away and tucked his hands beneath his armpits.

'Bit nippy,' he said.

'I suppose summer's over now.' How ridiculous to be discussing the weather. 'Can you tell me what you saw that night?'

'Not a lot.' He looked at the barely moving water as though considering the question. 'Like I told your mate, I didn't see her go in or anything. I didn't even know what had happened, not then. I was coming down there' – he pointed towards the steps I'd descended moments ago – 'and saw someone going up them. It stuck in my head because of it being late. Whoever it was, they were in a hurry, like they didn't want to be seen, you know?'

Was that true, or the spin he'd put on the sighting after Rachel's body was discovered?

'And you don't know whether it was a man or a woman? You told her friend you bumped into this person.'

'We sort of brushed shoulders, yeah. They kind of muttered, "Watch where you're going." Sounded like a bloke but I got a whiff of women's perfume.' He shook his head. 'Like I said to the police, it was dark, I couldn't tell. They had their head down, like this …' He turned, miming someone running up steps with their shoulders hunched, his dreadlocks swinging forward. 'I didn't take much notice at the time, like, but afterwards it came back to me. I had a feeling, see? Like, something weren't right.' In the orangey glow of the streetlight, his eyes were screwed up, as if seeing the figure again. A chill of apprehension ran through me, as though I'd caught his 'feeling'. 'I'm sorry about what happened to her.' Folding his arms, he scuffed the concrete with the toe of his trainer. 'Would have tried to save her if I'd seen. I'm a good swimmer.'

I had an image of him as a little boy, arms cutting through water.

'She'd been drinking, yeah?'

'Yes,' I heard myself say. 'She had a problem but we … we thought she was getting better.' How odd to be talking to strangers about Rachel when I rarely discussed her with anyone I knew. 'She was supposed to be coming to see me,' I said. 'She wanted to talk.'

'And you reckon someone bumped her off?' Sam moved closer as though drawn in by my words. I caught his smell of unwashed hair and clothes, something decaying on his breath. 'Shoved her in and did a runner?'

'I don't know.' I gave a helpless shrug. 'You're the only witness and I didn't even know about you until I came here today.'

'Police didn't wanna know.' He spoke matter-of-factly. 'I actually don't drink that much, only to take the edge off sometimes, you know?' I nodded, fighting another urge to look around, certain eyes were trained on us. 'I weren't even lashed that night, but …' He raised his shoulders. 'S'pose there weren't no proof. Not like I filmed it or anything.'

I risked a glance over my shoulder. *Did someone shrink into the shadows?* 'The man you spoke to,' I said. 'What was he like?'

'Said his name was Will. Seemed OK.' Another shrug. 'Worried, like. He gave me a tenner.' As Sam's gaze flicked to my bag, disappointment rushed in. I'd gleaned nothing by coming. Sam couldn't tell me anything I hadn't already heard, and he wanted money. Of course he did.

'I ain't gonna mug you.' He rocked back on his heels. 'I'm not a thief.'

Shame heated my face. 'I could get you a room,' I said

impulsively. 'Where I'm staying. You could have a shower and something to eat.' I had no idea how that would work, whether he would be allowed in. 'I'll vouch for you.'

'Nah, you're all right.' He wiped the back of his hand across his nose. 'I'm meeting a mate here soon, but thanks.'

'Isn't there a hostel, a shelter, where you could go?'

'Don't like them places much. Full of druggies.'

'What about family?'

He eyed me warily. 'Long story short, they kicked me out when I dropped out of college. I prefer this.' Maybe reading something into my silence, he added, 'No responsibilities. People are mostly nice or ignore me. I'll go back one day, but not yet.'

'Your mum must be worried.' The thought of Noah running away one day, preferring to be on the streets than at home, turned my blood to ice. 'Does she know you're OK?'

'I can take care of myself.'

Feeling powerless, I took out my purse. I didn't carry much cash and had given Will my only twenty-pound note. 'Thank you for talking to me, Sam.' I found a fiver and a few pound coins. 'Sorry, that's all I've got.'

'Cheers.' Without embarrassment, he took the money and shoved it into the back pocket of his jeans. 'Got to make a living,' he said, in an obvious attempt at levity. 'Sorry I wasn't more help.'

'It's fine, I appreciate—'

'You brought your friend with you?'

'Sorry?'

His gaze had travelled beyond my shoulder. 'There was someone there a minute ago.' He craned his neck. 'I thought they might be waiting for you.'

Heart in my throat, I wheeled around, scanning the path beneath the bridge once more. 'No,' I said shakily. 'I came on my own.'

Chapter 22

After reassuring Sam that he didn't need to walk me back to the hotel, I left him standing at the top of the steps as I hurried away, sticking close to the edge of the road to make myself visible. There had been no sign of anyone lurking as we walked back under the bridge. Even if Sam had seen someone, it could have been a dog-walker, or someone taking a stroll who saw us talking and retraced their steps.

Despite my bravado, I was gripped by foreboding, my senses lurching. I had no idea where Lucian lived these days, but he could be still in London. Unless somebody else had followed me to the bridge.

Breathing hard, I took out my phone. 'Where are you?' I said when Will answered.

'Jess? I'm on the boat.'

There was a ring of truth in his voice, and my shoulders dropped. Of course he hadn't followed me.

'Are you OK?' His voice had sharpened into alarm.

'I'm fine.' I slowed my pace. There was a scattering of people about, the occasional car zipping past. It was only around 9 p.m., not the middle of the night. 'I went to the canal.'

'*What?*'

'I wanted to see if he was there. The witness you mentioned.'

'That was risky.' Will's voice tightened. 'If you'd said, I would have come with you.'

'It was spur of the moment.'

'Was he there?'

'Yes.' I looked back, checking no one was behind me. 'He's called Sam.'

'I know,' Will said. 'He seems like a decent guy.'

'But you don't think I should have spoken to him?'

'Not on your own.' Concern bled into his words. 'Especially after what happened to your sister.'

'I didn't stop to think,' I admitted, eyes darting about as I waited to cross the road. 'I wanted to see for myself where she ... where it happened.'

'I had a feeling you might.' In the pause that followed, I continued walking towards the hotel, shivering as the wind followed me down the street, past buildings with blackened windows. It was like being in a foreign country. 'What was it like, being there?'

'It brought home that she's gone.' My stomach turned over at the memory of the oily dark water, and an image of Rachel's body slowly sinking down. 'But Sam couldn't tell me anything new. I'm none the wiser.'

'Do you believe she was killed?'

'I don't know, Will.'

'What now?'

'I'd like to see the gallery, and the flat where she lived.' I hadn't realized I was going to say it until the words left my lips. 'Can you take me there in the morning?'

'Sure.' If Will was surprised, he hid it well. 'What time are you leaving?'

'Not until four o'clock.' I'd bought an open return, had planned to leave first thing, but knew I couldn't go back with so much unresolved.

'Come to the boat and have breakfast,' Will said. 'It's moored at the Cumberland Basin near Camden Lock. The *Kingfisher*. I'll see you at nine.'

I woke the next morning from a muddled dream about water and a faceless man to see sunlight streaming through the curtains. For a second, I expected Noah to run in demanding breakfast, to hear Adam in the shower. Then I remembered. I was alone, in London.

As yesterday's events rushed back, I fumbled for my phone, which was charging on the shelf by the bed, and knocked a plate to the floor. I'd ordered a chicken sandwich from room service the night before, eating it quickly with a glass of water before shedding my clothes and collapsing into bed, checking I hadn't missed an urgent call from Denny.

I squinted at my phone screen, shocked to see it was already gone eight. I rarely slept for an uninterrupted stretch, used to listening for sounds from Noah's room. Sitting up, I fired off a text to Jennifer, who swiftly replied that she and Noah were having breakfast. *No problems last night. Weather looks promising* ☺

Enjoy your fishing trip! X I should be getting ready to go with them instead of skulking in an anonymous hotel room two hundred miles away.

We will! See you later X

I considered checking in with Dad but worried he might not buy my impromptu shopping-trip story – something I'd shown no interest in doing before. As I was dressing, choosing a clean pair of jeans and long-sleeved top from the few items I'd brought, my phone pinged with a message from Adam.

Hope you had a good night's sleep xx

Nearly 10 hours, would you believe? I hadn't expected to sleep at all.

Wow, that's great! You must have needed it. Are you heading home now?

Soon. My stomach twisted with guilt. *Have a good day xx*

Adam could be hard to read when he was thinking about something, whereas I tended to wear my emotions on my face, and I was glad he couldn't see me. Half-expecting him to call, I jumped when my phone pinged again.

Have a good journey. Love you xx

Expelling a sigh of relief, I typed back, *Love you too xx*

I would come clean about everything when he got home. Regardless of his reaction, I didn't want secrets between us, and he had a right to know about Lucian.

After tying back my hair, I pulled on my trainers and packed my bag. Once I'd checked out of the hotel, I headed quickly towards Regent's Park and the Cumberland Basin, a stretch of canal close to London Zoo. I'd been there once, years ago, for a friend's birthday dinner at the floating Chinese restaurant housed on one of the boats.

The area was busy, with tourists drawn out by the sun sparkling across the water, reflecting trees that were starting to lose their leaves. It was a stark contrast to the dark and rippling canal I'd stood by the night before. I wondered where Sam was this morning. Begging in a doorway maybe, a forgettable face among hundreds. I kept noticing homeless people: an old man on a bench, covered in newspapers; a couple on the pavement with a well-fed dog on a blanket, its imploring eyes doing a better job of attracting attention than its owners.

The towpath was busy with cyclists, runners, and dog-walkers. I spied Will standing on the boatside, hand shielding his eyes as he looked around. I quickly crossed the pedestrian bridge and ran down the steps.

Coming up behind him, I tapped his shoulder. 'Hi.'

He spun round. As a smile lit up his face, my heart gave the same odd thud it had the day before.

'You look better than you did yesterday.' Will's bright blue eyes scanned my face. 'Less tired, I mean,' he added quickly. He had on the same clothes, shirt buttons fastened this time, sleeves rolled up over tanned forearms. 'Sleep well?'

'Fine.' Struck by the intimacy of his comment, I looked away. 'Thanks for the invite.'

'I'm cooking a fry-up.' He stepped aside, gesturing to the back of the boat. 'Unless you'd rather go straight to the gallery?'

'No, that sounds great.' I was suddenly unsure why I'd thought going to the gallery was a good idea, what purpose it would serve. 'Smells good.' I sniffed the air, detecting frying bacon. 'It's ages since I've had a cooked breakfast.'

'It's ages since I cooked for someone.'

Turning, so he couldn't see the flush spreading over my face, I hoisted my bag over my shoulder, stepped over the mooring rope, and pulled myself on-board, a shudder passing through me as I glimpsed the water in the gap between the path and the boat.

'Maybe it wasn't the best idea to ask you here.' It was as if Will had read my mind. 'I suppose I'm used to being on the water, but after … Well, I'm sorry. It was insensitive.'

'Don't be silly.' On deck, I pasted a smile on my face and looked around. 'It's nice,' I said, taking in the smooth wooden surfaces, fresh forest-green and red paintwork, and gleaming porthole windows. It had a cared-for air, tubs of greenery clustered around – unlike the boat behind, which looked in need of a makeover. 'Have you been here long?'

'Since the divorce.' He jumped on deck in an easy movement. 'I've got a permanent mooring, so I don't have to keep moving every two weeks like most boat owners. They don't come up very often. I got lucky.'

Sensing his attempt to put me at ease, I played along. 'So, what's it like, living on a canal?'

'Not much space, cold in winter, the amenities aren't great – I have to empty the toilet – plus the mooring fees are steep, but I've learned skills I didn't know I had, there's running water, Wi-Fi, and a nice little community.'

'You wouldn't go back to living on dry land?'

'In a heartbeat,' he said with a grin. 'It's fine while I'm living alone, but I'd eventually like to settle up in Scotland, preferably with a roof and central heating and a boat for holidays and weekends.'

'Sounds ideal.' A memory crowded in: a holiday on the Norfolk Broads when I was 8 and Rachel a baby, a change from our usual trip to Windermere; a week of golden sunshine on a narrow boat, suppers on deck, being lulled to sleep by the gently rocking boat. Dad, in a peaked hat, insisted on talking like Captain Birds Eye as he steered us along, while Mum sunned herself and played with Rachel, helping push the boat through locks as we travelled downriver. A normal, happy family.

'You OK?' Will was looking at me curiously.

'Fine.' I tried to resurrect my smile, adjusting my holdall with the envelope containing Rachel's belongings at the bottom. 'Just hungry.'

Will stepped past, leading me into a galley kitchen.

'In that case, let's eat.'

Chapter 23

'Can I help with anything?'

'The bacon's keeping warm under the grill while I cook the eggs.' In the reduced space, Will seemed bigger. I was aware of my breathing, his too. 'Make yourself at home.'

As he reached past me for a box of eggs, I slid onto a bench seat behind a small dining table and tucked my holdall underneath. It struck me that Rachel had sat in this seat at some point. I didn't have a sense of her presence here, no ghostly aura or lingering scent. I knew so little about her. I was tracking a ghost, Noah the only solid evidence of her adult existence.

Will turned, catching my gaze. 'It must feel weird, knowing Rachel stayed here.'

'A bit.' I took in the long, low ceiling and narrow spaces. The interior was clean and uncluttered, but despite the white-painted wood and bright furnishings, the jar of wildflowers on the table, it felt claustrophobic. 'To be honest, it's hard to imagine her anywhere,' I said. 'Once she left home, we didn't have any shared experiences, and growing up, the age difference meant she was more like a little cousin than a sister.' I rubbed my forehead, as if I could push the memories back. 'When she was older, that was when it went really wrong. She was difficult to love.' Shame burnt through me at the admission. Loving my sister should have been as instinctive as breathing.

'I barely knew her, but I could see that she could be ... spiky,' Will said. I resisted the urge to reply that she must have been reining herself in if 'spiky' was the worst she had been. Perhaps she really had changed, different when she was sober. 'It's maybe an unfair comparison, but my grandfather on my mother's side was difficult. Distant with me, but nasty to Mum. Had been since she was a child. He seemed to hate the whole world, and I had that sense with your sister sometimes.' Will had his back to me as he found plates and dished up the food. 'He didn't have any redeeming qualities. I was scared of him the couple of times we visited before Mum cut him off.' He flicked me a look over his shoulder. 'Not that I'm saying Rachel was irredeemable.' He got out knives and forks and put the plates on the table. 'My dad helped with Mum's conflicted feelings about her father. He's a therapist.' He gave a small smile as he sat opposite, closer than we'd been in the café the day before. 'I'm sure that's why she married him, but they've been together for nearly forty years now.'

The food smelt delicious, and my appetite returned. 'How do you define irredeemable?' I said after a couple of mouthfuls.

Will deliberated, a crease between his eyebrows. 'My father described it as someone who no longer cares about the effect their actions have on others, someone who even enjoys it. That certainly applied to my grandfather.' He waved his fork. 'He loved to control people, not because of any insecurities that my dad could see. He simply liked it.'

'He sounds awful.'

Will nodded. 'We were better off without him in our lives. Luckily, Mum and her brothers seemed to come through OK. They did well, married, have nice families.'

'Do you have siblings?'

'Two brothers, like she has.' He smiled affectionately. 'Oliver's a lawyer here in London, married with two kids. Dan's younger than me and lives in Manchester, still trying to make it as a musician.'

'You're the middle child.'

'Often overlooked and undervalued.' He made a rueful face. 'Fortunately, having a therapist father meant there was none of that in our family. We were equally valued.'

'Sounds ideal.' I was sometimes wistful about other families, the ones who were uncomplicated, had easy loving relationships, but knew in some cases – in Rachel's case – it wasn't enough. In contrast, it was obvious Will's background had given him a strong foundation, an ease that Adam sometimes lacked. Occasionally, his drive to create a happy family, to not be like his own absent father, meant he couldn't be present in the moment, always looking ahead to how things could be better.

'I don't like to think of Rachel being irredeemable.' I pushed my eggs around my plate. 'I refuse to believe she didn't have any good qualities.'

'She gave you her child,' Will said.

I huffed out a laugh. 'Because it was the easiest option.'

'She could have had a termination.'

'I think by the time she found out she was pregnant, it was too late.'

Will finished his breakfast and stood, holding his hand out for my plate.

'Thanks. It was delicious,' I said. 'Are you into poetry?'

'Sorry?' He turned from the stainless-steel sink and switched off the tap.

'There was a volume of poems with Rachel's things, but she never read poetry. At least, I can't imagine her reading it.'

'It wasn't mine,' he said, squirting washing-up liquid. 'I don't know where she got it, but the last time she stayed here, I caught her sitting where you are, hunched over the book. I think she was making notes.'

'Did you ask her about it?' Odd to think this man had spoken to Rachel more than her own family had in the past year. 'What did she say?'

Will shrugged, rinsing the plates. 'I told you she wasn't good at answering questions. I didn't bother asking, to be honest. I'd only come on board to get my tools.'

'You didn't stay here together?' My gaze fell on a cabin door that I presumed led to a bedroom.

'I did once, but I slept in here.' He pointed a wet finger to the surprisingly plush-looking L-shaped sofa scattered with cushions. 'It pulls out into a bed. I wanted to keep an eye on her in case … you know.' His gaze flicked to me and away. 'You read about people choking in their sleep if they've drunk too much.'

'That was good of you.'

'Like I said, it was only once. The last time, I offered her the boat for the night because she wanted to get out of the flat. I stayed at my parents.'

'You trusted her here on her own?'

'Strangely, I did.' He dried his hands on a stripy tea towel. Behind him, people were passing on the towpath, their legs visible, reminding me of the basement flat Sasha had shared with Jo and where I'd been a regular visitor. 'She wanted some space and was thinking of booking a cheap hotel room, but her salary didn't stretch far so I offered her the boat. There was no sign anyone else had been here when I got back,' he said. 'Only her scribbling in that book.'

'She highlighted bits.' I delved into in my bag and pulled the book from the padded envelope. 'Look.'

As I opened it, Will bent beside me, hands on the table, so close I could have leaned my head on his shoulder. 'See.' Shifting slightly, I flipped through the pages, pausing so he could see the occasional letter brightened in yellow. 'What do you think it means?'

'Probably nothing.' Will angled a sideways look at me, a line cutting between his brows. 'What do *you* think?'

'I don't know any better than you.' Angry without knowing why, I snapped the book shut. 'I haven't a clue what went on in Rachel's mind.'

'Me neither,' Will said quietly, moving away. He lifted a mug off the side. 'Coffee?'

Frustrated, I shook my head. 'I'd rather get going if you don't mind.'

'Of course.'

As he put the mug on its shelf, I stooped to push the poetry book back. As I lifted the bag, something dislodged from under the table and slid to the floor. A photograph. Reaching down, I grasped hold of it and brought it to my lap. When I turned it over, my breath caught in my throat. It was Noah. Not as a newborn but on his third birthday, sitting at the table in our dining room, eyes wide as he gazed at the flickering candles on his dinosaur birthday cake. It was the photo that had disappeared from our mantelpiece, after I thought someone had been in our house – the one Adam confessed he couldn't remember.

Not being funny, Jess, but there are so many photos. Are you sure?

Jennifer had an identical one and so did Dad. I'd convinced myself I must have got mixed up, but I hadn't. It was here … on Will's boat.

'What's wrong?'

I started at the sound of his voice. 'This photo …' I showed him. 'It's mine.'

Shock raced over his face. 'Where was it?'

'Under the table.'

He stared at it, puzzled. 'It's your son?'

'Yes, on his birthday.' My stomach felt as if I'd hit turbulence. 'How did Rachel have it?' I was thinking aloud, mind racing. 'All this time … I knew it had gone. When I got home from work, I could tell that something was different but couldn't put my finger on it. There hadn't been a break-in, nothing valuable was missing, but I was sure things had been moved in our bedroom.

Nothing obvious, but a drawer was slightly open, and I kept looking around the living room, wondering what was missing. I didn't realize for a few days that it was the photo, but even that seemed insignificant, not something the police would be interested in. I thought I was wrong.'

Will listened, an intent look on his face. 'Did Rachel know your address after you moved?'

I went to shake my head, then paused. 'Not as far as I knew, but she could have found out if she'd wanted to. I assumed she didn't want to know.' I looked at him. 'But why take the photo?'

Even before he opened his mouth to reply, I knew what he was going to say. 'To prove something to this Lucian guy?'

I stood up, feeling sick. 'Maybe he wanted proof she'd had his child.' That must have been it, only something had gone terribly wrong. What had Lucian done? *What would he do next?*

'Jess?' Will's voice seemed to reach me from a long way off. 'Jess, you've gone white as a sheet.' His hands were on my shoulders, pressing me gently down. 'Breathe slowly.' His voice was gentle but firm. 'Deep breaths. In … and out. That's it. Look at me. And again. You're fine, Jess. It's OK.'

But it wasn't. As I pulled air into my lungs and puffed it out, keeping my eyes locked on Will's, all I could think of were Noah's words the night of the power cut.

Monsters only come out at night.

Chapter 24

Outside, life carried on as normal, a breeze cooling my overheated face. The ting of a bicycle bell made me jump as a cyclist shot by.

Will cupped my elbow. 'Sure you want to do this?'

I nodded as we continued to the nearest tube station, reassuring myself that – for now at least – Noah was safe with Jennifer and my dad, and maybe Denny would join them for a spot of fishing. 'I'm not sure whether it'll help but if I can talk to Hannah, she might remember something.'

Will had contacted Rachel's flatmate after my call the night before to tell her I was dropping by. 'I wanted to make sure she would be there,' he said, after I'd calmed down enough to listen. 'I know the police spoke to her and she couldn't tell them anything we didn't already know, but she's happy for you to look around.'

We arrived at the gallery on Conway Street half an hour later; a tall, red-brick building with ornamental shrubs outside and a wide glass window displaying an array of twisted sculptures on plinths. I didn't know much about art but there was something arresting about the shapes. 'Is that your mother?' I pointed to the name *Antonia Hanson* in flowing gold script above the window.

Will slowed and nodded. 'She taught art when she was younger, was good at spotting talent. She bought this place with money her parents left her, a sort of two-fingers up to my grandfather. She's done a lot of good for local artists over the years.'

'Is she here today?'

'No, she and my father retired a couple of years ago. They live in Surrey and travel a lot. She employs someone to run the gallery as she can't bear to sell up. She still checks in occasionally. We joke about it being her fourth child.' He paused. 'There's Hannah.'

A young woman had appeared from round the side of the building, wearing a loose hooded top over workout leggings. Happy for me to visit was an overstatement, judging by her expression, though her sullen face lit up when Will spoke.

'Hi, Hannah. This is Jess.'

She flicked a strand of pale-gold hair over her shoulder. 'I hope it won't take long. I've got friends coming round.' Her accent was cultured, her gaze patronizing as it glided over me, dipping to my trainers and back to my face, flushed from the crowded tube ride and walk.

'Any news on Annabel?' Will asked her, gesturing for us to move inside.

'As long as her parents cough up the deposit, she can move in at the end of the month.'

Will gave me an apologetic glance. 'We need a new tenant to cover costs.'

'Of course.' I guessed he'd let Rachel rent the room for less than it was worth. Conway Street was obviously upmarket. Unless Hannah had a highly paid job, I guessed her parents were subsidizing her too.

'Hannah's an intern at an auction house,' Will said, as she disappeared back round the side of the gallery and through a black-painted door. 'Her father pays her rent,' he added, lowering his voice. 'It's her idea of independence.'

'She must have hated sharing with Rachel.'

He held the door open, and I ducked under his arm. 'She

wasn't keen on the previous tenant because she was untidy. At least Rachel kept to herself.'

Following Hannah's toned legs up a well-lit staircase, I had the feeling again of following in Rachel's footsteps. How many times had she run up and down these stairs? What was she thinking the night she ran out to meet Lucian? I imagined her briefly; hair flying, smile bright, thinking she was heading to her future. *No.* That wasn't right. She'd been drinking before she went out. Had she expected a confrontation? Suspected the meeting wouldn't go well? Why didn't she have the photo of Noah with her?

Confusion crowded my brain as we entered a bright room, dominated by a long, grey sofa and glass-topped coffee table. A huge mirror on the opposite wall reflected my dishevelled appearance – hair trailing out of its band, a sheen of perspiration on my forehead, years-old jacket faded around the armpits. It was as if a layer had peeled back to reveal a different version of me; one I barely recognized. 'It's nice,' I said foolishly, taking mental snapshots of polished floorboards, sash windows, and neatly organized bookshelves. It was so far removed from typical student accommodation, I almost laughed.

'My mother had it decorated when my brother moved out,' Will said behind me, as though tracking my thoughts. 'He shared it with a couple of friends from uni. It was a tip when they left.'

In the middle of the room, Hannah turned to face me. She'd kicked off her Converse and her toenails gleamed crimson like drops of blood. 'So, what do you want to know?' She didn't bother with niceties or offer refreshments. 'I already spoke to the police.'

'I know,' I said quickly, reminding myself that she was young – 20 at most – and hearing about Rachel's death must have been a shock. 'I'm sorry to turn up like this, but I hadn't seen my sister for a very long time.' I swallowed a knot of emotion. 'I wanted to see where she lived.'

'Well, this is it.' Hannah spread her hands, but her gaze had softened. 'I don't get on with my sister,' she said. 'She's a total bitch, so I get it.' I doubted she did but appreciated her attempt at empathy. 'To be honest, I wasn't keen on sharing with Rachel at first, but she said it wouldn't be for long and she mostly stayed in her room when she was here. Our paths didn't cross much.' She glanced at Will. 'I'm glad she's gone, but don't get me wrong, what happened was awful and I'm sorry.'

'Thanks.' I tried to place Rachel in this room, on the sofa, watching TV, eating dinner, but the image was like a blurred photo I couldn't bring into focus. 'She said she wouldn't be staying long?'

Hannah flipped her hair again before nodding. 'She didn't say why, but I had a feeling it was to do with that guy she was obviously in love with.'

My heart lurched. 'Lucian?'

'Was that his name?' Hannah's microbladed brows rose. 'She never said. She was sort of happy for a while, like crazy happy, then … she changed.'

'This was before that night?'

Hannah nodded. 'Look, we didn't do girly chats, but she was drinking in her room, not going to work. I panicked a bit one morning because I couldn't hear any sounds from her room. I called Will.' She looked at him for confirmation, nose wrinkled. 'She was a mess,' she said. Will had moved to sit on the arm of the sofa and Hannah dropped beside him, hands tucked between her knees. She looked younger, and I felt bad that Rachel's behaviour had scared her. 'She met him again, whoever he was, before that night.'

'How do you know?'

'I saw him.'

I exchanged a glance with Will. 'What did he look like?'

'You didn't mention it,' he said at the same time.

'I told the police, silly.' She nudged his knee with her elbow. 'I didn't actually see his face, it was from the window. Rachel had been waiting for him and she ran outside. It was raining

128

and she didn't have a coat on. It was like she wanted to get him away from here. She was practically pulling him down the street and it looked like they were arguing.'

My heart revved up. 'You don't remember anything about him at all?'

'It was kind of hard to tell.' She looked into the distance, thinking. 'He was wearing a dark coat with the hood up. Because of the weather.' She mimicked rainfall with her fingers, fluttering them over her head. 'She was worse after seeing him. I mean, she wasn't chatty before but afterwards … she took a bottle of vodka into her room and didn't come out for ages.'

'That fits with when I noticed a change in her.' Will's brow was furrowed. 'She didn't turn up for work much after that—'

'Which is a joke when it was only downstairs,' Hannah chipped in. 'Even with a hangover, I manage to get the train to Notting Hill.' Her big, round eyes swivelled to mine. 'I work at Elmwood's Auction House. I'm going to be their social media manager when my internship's over.'

Good for you, I didn't say. *Amazing how the right connections can get you places.* I immediately regretted the thought. She could be a hard worker, keen to make a mark on the world, for all I knew. One thing was clear: she and Rachel were poles apart.

Hannah tilted her head as though remembering something. 'Before she passed out one night, she came out and looked at me for ages – it was a bit spooky, actually, because her eyes weren't really focused on me – and she said, "Don't bother with relationships. If I could go back in time" … something like that, she was slurring like mad … "I wouldn't have gone to that party."' Hannah paused. 'It was like she was thinking out loud, but then she said, "Scratch that, he was worth it."' Hannah shuddered as though recounting a ghostly encounter. 'Then she ran into the bathroom and threw up everywhere.'

'I'm sorry,' I said involuntarily.

Hannah gave me a pitying look. 'It wasn't your fault.'

'No, it wasn't,' Will agreed, pushing to his feet. 'Is it OK if Jess has a look at Rachel's room?'

'Sure,' Hannah said, rising. 'There's nothing in there though. The police wanted to have a look at her phone or laptop, see who she'd been messaging, but she didn't have a laptop and they couldn't find her phone.' A careless shrug. 'I didn't hear her go out that night.'

'So, you had no idea who she was meeting?'

'I assumed it was that guy again. She was all happy, even though she was drunk.' Hannah's face darkened. 'I went back to my parents' for a few days after I heard the news. It creeped me out.'

About to say sorry again, I closed my mouth. I wasn't responsible for my sister's actions, or her death. *But someone was.* I was growing more certain of it by the minute.

In her room, I searched again for signs of her presence, something of her imprinted between the walls, but it was as if Rachel had never set foot inside. The room was small and basic; bare floorboards, plain white walls, a double brass bed, a white-wood wardrobe with the doors standing open to reveal its empty insides – not even a coat hanger. No fairy lights draped over mirrors and around the curtain pole, like my room in Barnes had been, right up until I left. Even there, Rachel hadn't bothered about décor, uninterested in paint colours and bed linen once she turned 13, more interested in staying at her friend Daisy's house because – we realized later – her parents were often out, and they had unlimited access to their drinks cupboard.

'Nothing to see,' Hannah said in a sing-song voice as my gaze drifted round. I walked to the bed and opened the drawer in the cabinet beside it. Nothing. There was a dark ring on the surface, left by a bottle or glass – maybe the cat-shaped mug that had been among her belongings.

A shaft of dusty sunlight settled on the mattress, and I knelt to look beneath the bed, checking nothing was lying against the skirting board. Finally, when it was obvious I was wasting everyone's time, I dusted my hands together. 'OK, well thanks for letting me look around', I said, hearing the tremor in my voice.

Hannah's face had lost some of its colour and her eyebrows had drawn together. 'Do you think someone might have hurt her?'

Catching Will's warning look, I said quickly, 'No, nothing like that. I'm hoping to find the person she met that night and talk to him, that's all.'

She nodded, brightening. 'I sneaked in here once when Rachel was out.' A look of bafflement crossed her face. 'She didn't really have any stuff. Not like most people.'

'My sister wasn't like most people.' I meant it to sound jokey, but Hannah was looking at Will and didn't seem to hear.

'You didn't find anything either, did you?' she said, her eyes becoming alert. 'When you came to look at Rachel's room.'

Chapter 25

'What was she talking about?'

Will and I were on the pavement after Hannah had ushered us out of the apartment. Rain clouds had swallowed the sun and the street was empty. At the end, the BT Tower soared into the sky like a metal finger. 'Will?'

He started walking and I hurried to catch up. 'I did look around Rachel's room,' he admitted, smoothing his hair as the breeze pushed it around. 'When the police said they couldn't find her phone and there were no leads, I thought maybe it had been missed.'

'Why didn't you mention it before?'

He wheeled around to face me. 'I suppose I was embarrassed. I knew it was snooping.' His eyes fixed on mine. 'Her phone wasn't there so it didn't matter in the end.'

'If it had been, surely the police would have found it?'

Will stuffed his hands in his jacket pockets, shoulders hunched against the strengthening wind. 'To be honest, I wasn't sure how bothered they were about finding this person Rachel had gone to meet. Considering no one knew his name.' He gave a wry twist of his mouth. 'Like I said, with no evidence, proof, or reliable witnesses, it was cut and dried in their eyes. A tragic accident.'

Something about the way Hannah had mentioned his being in Rachel's room niggled at me. Was she implying there was more to their relationship? But Will's eyes were clear and unblinking – no sign of deception.

'I can't imagine Rachel working in there.' I nodded to the gallery behind Will, desperate to fill the silence stretching between us.

'Would you like to look inside?'

I glanced through the window to where a woman – the manager, I guessed – was talking to a well-dressed couple admiring a curvy bronze sculpture. 'Thanks, but no.' I couldn't face meeting anyone else new. 'Did Rachel know much about art?'

Will's started walking again. 'She wasn't that interested. She stuck to cleaning, helped with packing and paperwork sometimes.'

'She was bright,' I said, matching my stride to his. 'But she couldn't be bothered most of the time.'

'That was the impression I got.' We veered round a bearded man in the middle of the pavement, staring at his phone. 'She once told me she used to play the violin.'

'She was good.' I'd hear her practise sometimes, the melancholy notes tugging at my chest. 'Dad was a music professor so it was a given that we would play a musical instrument. I tried the piano but was useless, though I can sing a bit. I think, deep down, Rachel enjoyed playing but Lucian probably didn't approve.'

'He sounds like a piece of work.'

'I'm going to find him,' I said, as we approached the Underground. I hadn't intended to tell Will but wanted to make up for quizzing him about Rachel's phone. 'I want to find out why they were in contact.' I fingered the photo of Noah I'd slipped into my pocket along with the anonymous letter. The photo was mine, after all. 'Forewarned is forearmed,' I added, catching Will's look of concern.

'It's odd that he hasn't contacted you again.'

'If he was the one who sent the letter.'

'No demand for money.'

133

'The thing is, Lucian doesn't need money,' I said. 'His family is loaded.'

'Maybe he's biding his time, waiting to strike when you're least expecting it.'

'That's what I'm worried about.' I tried to think. 'Maybe the letter was a one-off, a warning, while he's consulting lawyers. Like I said, his family is wealthy. They probably have contacts.' I checked the time. 'Look, I have to go. There's somewhere I want to see before I catch my train.'

'Do you want company?'

'I'll be fine.' I belted my arms around my waist, walling myself off.

'Anywhere nice?'

'I thought I'd take a look at the house where I grew up.'

'Where's that?'

'Barnes,' I said. 'I can get the tube from there back to Euston.' I shivered as cold air snaked up my sleeves. 'Thanks for everything, Will.'

He zipped up his jacket. 'Keep in touch, won't you?' I got the impression he was prolonging our goodbye. 'I'd like to know how things turn out.'

'Of course.'

'And take care.'

'I will.' I thought of the figure Sam thought he'd seen under the bridge the night before and suppressed a pulse of fear. 'You don't need to worry about me.'

Being back on Merthyr Terrace was both familiar and strange. In the past it had simply been home; a pretty Victorian terrace in a conservation area, a railway line beyond the fence at the back of the garden.

Walking down the leafy street I realized how lucky I'd been to grow up here. Rachel had dismissed the area as 'not proper London' and 'bourgeois' as though being raised in a slum would have been more authentic. Ironic, considering she'd been happy to take our parents' money when it suited her, like Lucian who – despite his apparent rejection of his family's wealth back then – had no trouble using it to get what he wanted.

I stopped outside number nineteen, which still had the overgrown rhododendron bush spilling over the railings and stared at the front door I'd stepped through so many times. It had been repainted sage green, the blinds at the windows replaced with slatted shutters. A brass Buddha looked out of the downstairs window where I used to stand, hoping to catch Mack Johnson coming out of the house opposite so I could walk to school with him. The Johnsons had long since moved away as several of our neighbours had. Only Caroline remained, at number twenty-one. As if on cue, the door opened and she stepped out, the wind lifting her hair.

'I thought it was you.' Hugging an oversized black cardigan around her ample frame, she came down the steps to the gate. 'How are you, Jess?'

Despite a stiffening in my spine, the sight of her brought a prickle of tears to my eyes. Our families had been good friends once, enjoying barbecues in each other's gardens. I'd bounced on their trampoline with Caroline's twin daughters, now married with families of their own.

'I wanted to see the house. I was in London, shopping.' *Liar*.

'On your own?' Her eyes scanned the parked cars, as if expecting to see Adam in one of them. *Or my father.*

'On my own.' A familiar beat of anger fluttered in my chest, dampening the urge to cry. 'I didn't think you'd be here,' I said. Saturdays used to be Caroline's 'pamper' days, a reward for the hours she worked at a bank. She and Mum went to Champneys once, but Mum had found it stressful.

'I still miss her you know.' Caroline's voice was so faint it faded into the air. She turned to look at the house, fingers working at a silver chain around her neck. 'The Harpers are nice but they're hardly ever there.'

'I miss Mum too.' Memories slid by; the happy times I held close, overlaying the later memories when Rachel's antics had etched premature lines on her face, and her illness took over. 'Be honest.' I turned to Caroline, old feelings swirling to the surface. 'Did you always fancy my dad?'

'Oh, Jess.' Her eyes were wide and sad. 'Of course not.'

'I want the truth.'

Her gaze was pitying. 'You won't believe me.'

'I saw you all over him that day in our kitchen, remember?' My blood boiled, as though I was there again. 'Mum hadn't been dead five minutes and there you were, trying to get your feet under the table.'

Her face crumpled. 'I'm sorry you had to see that, Jess, but it wasn't how it looked.'

'How was it then?' I hadn't spoken to either of them about it afterwards. Caroline had kept her distance, too embarrassed I guessed, to look me in the eye. 'I know what I saw.'

'You saw what you wanted to see, as you always did where your dad was concerned.'

I tensed. 'What's that supposed to mean?'

She was silent for so long, I thought she wasn't going to answer. Someone appeared in her front doorway: James, his steel-grey curls cropped close to his head, a leather bomber jacket years too young for him. Caroline gave a little shake of her head and he ducked back inside. 'I came round to yours that day to see if there was anything I could do to help.' Her fingers moved to the loose skin at her throat. 'We were talking about Helen, and I got upset, started crying. Your dad … He hugged me. He was upset too. But then he tried to kiss me. I was horrified, Jess. I couldn't move for a moment, then I pulled away. He pulled me back, tried to kiss me again. He undid my top and then you came in.' Her gaze held mine, a clipped precision to her voice. 'I would have left anyway, even if you hadn't arrived. He couldn't resist trying, that was the thing with Jon. He never could, even though he loved your mum.'

My heart was banging. The student who came to the house, the mumbled voices in the hall, the girl crying outside. *A silly crush*, Mum called it. *Happens a lot to someone in your father's position.*

'Your mum knew what he was like.' I wondered whether Caroline could read my thoughts. 'She loved him, and he loved her, but he always had what we used to call a wandering eye. He couldn't resist flattery, wanted to charm everyone.'

'You must have flattered him then.' I knew how it sounded, blaming a woman for a man's behaviour, as if he was powerless to control himself, but this was my father. The way Caroline described him … It was true he was charming, but to everyone, not only women.

'Even if I *had* liked him that way, which I didn't, I would never have cheated on James and especially not with the husband of a close friend, who was ill.' For the first time, anger touched Caroline's eyes. 'You must have had a very low opinion of me, Jess.' Trapped words filled my chest. 'I do like your dad, in spite of everything. We talk sometimes.'

A thud of shock. 'What?'

Caroline's face relaxed. 'Why do you think I was at the service?'

'I thought you'd read or heard about Rachel in the news.'

'Your father called me. He wanted to tell someone who knew him well, who understood how things had been with your sister.'

I tried to take it in. Dad hadn't mentioned it. He'd barely acknowledged Caroline that day. 'I didn't know.'

'We can't know everything about our parents, Jess.'

But I'd thought I had – more than most people did. I hadn't properly left home until I married Adam, I spoke to my father every day, had been close enough to Mum to be able to talk to her about anything – at least anything I thought would make her happy.

The ground felt unsteady, as though it might crumble beneath me.

'Look, Jess, I didn't say anything at the time because you had been through enough, and at the funeral … Well, it was hardly the time or the place, but I won't stand here and lie to protect your feelings at my own expense.'

'No, of course not, I'm … I'm sorry,' I stuttered. I was. Sorry she'd told me; sorry the image I'd carried in my head was all wrong, that I had to cast my father in a different light. Sorry he'd put a friend in that position. Everything seemed wrong, upside down.

'Don't read too much into it, Jess.' Caroline's voice grew urgent. 'Your dad, he's still the same person who loves you more than anything. He went through a lot back then and who can blame him if he sometimes felt he—'

'I have to go.' I wanted to hold Noah, feel his arms around my neck. 'I've a train to catch.'

'Jess, wait …'

It wasn't until I was on the train and halfway back to Lancaster, my tangled brain trying to unpick the day's conversations, that I recalled seeing a man on the corner of the street, turning his head as I passed, drawing up his hood as though he didn't want to be seen.

Chapter 26

'And Grandpa said the fish had to go back in the water so I drew a picture so you could see it, Mummy.' Noah launched himself over the side of his bed and grabbed his sketchpad off the floor. 'I don't think the eye is very good though.'

'It's perfect.' I sat beside him to admire the picture. He had a skill for drawing and the proportions and colours were realistic. 'Was it a very big fish?'

He tilted his head. 'Not very, but Grandpa said I could say it was *this* big.' He held his arms wide to demonstrate.

I laughed. 'All fishermen say that.'

I was glad Dad hadn't been here when I got back, Caroline's words still horribly fresh in my mind. What had happened with her was probably due to grief, I'd decided on the train home. Losing Mum before her time had almost broken Dad, and I didn't want this new knowledge to taint our relationship. Whatever the truth, my parents had stayed together, been happy, his eyes rarely leaving her when they were in the same room. If they ever argued, they'd kept it quiet – to protect me and Rachel, no doubt, as Adam and I would for Noah.

Jennifer hadn't commented on the fishing trip, other than to say they'd had a nice time, and I'd found myself wondering what she really thought of my father. Did she detect the same traits that Caroline had mentioned?

Tired of my spinning thoughts, I got to my feet. I'd been hiding with Noah since Jennifer left, helping him get ready for bed, trying to forget about everything else. 'Time for sleep, Buttercup.'

'Buttercup is for girls,' he protested. 'I want you to call me Ninja Turtle.'

I smiled, heart swelling with love. 'Where did that come from?' 'I like it.'

As he drifted to sleep, thumb hovering near his mouth, I crossed over to the window and scanned the garden for the figure I'd passed on the corner of Merthyr Terrace. I couldn't let go of the feeling he'd been following me, though I hadn't spotted him again. It was hard to see through the cloak of falling darkness and I closed the curtains with a shudder.

Adam had arrived home not long after me, relief wiping the tiredness from his features as he swept Noah into his arms and demanded to know where his cake was. Luckily, Jennifer had been busy, providing not only the promised sponge cake, but a cherry pie and a plate of shortbread, gritty with sugar.

That was nearly an hour ago and I couldn't avoid Adam any longer. Despite my resolve to be honest, I still hadn't decided how much to tell him.

When I went downstairs, he was at the island in the kitchen, spooning pie into his mouth, a scattering of crumbs on his shirt front. Adam comfort-ate when he was tired or stressed and from the look on his face, he was both.

'You might catch him awake if you want to say goodnight.'

'I'll go up in a minute.' He took off his glasses and laid them next to his plate. Head bent, he massaged the grooves on either side of his nose. 'Good trip?'

'Like I said earlier, it was fine.'

He raised his eyes. 'You picked up her stuff then?' He rarely said Rachel's name.

'There wasn't much.'

'And you didn't go out last night?'

My heart thumped. 'Why do you ask?'

'What were you doing?'

My chest tightened at his tone. 'Did you have me followed?'

'What?' His head drew back. 'Of course I didn't have you followed. What are you talking about?'

I looked away, the hooded figure I'd been carrying in my head melting away. 'Nothing.'

'You pocket-dialled me about an hour after we'd chatted,' he said. 'It sounded as though you were outdoors. I heard traffic.'

'And you didn't think to call me back and ask?' My cheeks throbbed with colour. 'I went for a walk, OK?'

'With him?'

'Who?'

'The man you picked up her stuff from.'

'His name's Will Taylor.'

'You obviously had quite a chat.'

'I couldn't demand he hand over her stuff and not say anything. I went for a walk because I couldn't settle. I kept going over and over everything.'

He glanced at his hands, teeth grinding his bottom lip. 'So, where is it?' he said at last. 'Her stuff.'

'Like I said, there was hardly anything.' I opened my overnight bag, still on the floor where I'd dropped it before Noah hurled himself at me. 'A pair of old socks, a poetry book, some earrings.' I retrieved the envelope and shook out the contents. They looked so sparse on the wooden surface, exposed to Adam's critical gaze. His eyes briefly touched each item and slid away, as if he couldn't bear to have any reminder of Rachel in our home. 'Hardly worth going all that way for.' He grabbed his plate and took it to the dishwasher. His face in the window was ghostly pale, and when he turned, his expression was guarded. 'Nothing else?'

'Actually, yes.' I knew I had to tell him, if only to bridge the awful space that seemed to have opened up, the two of us on opposing sides in a game I didn't understand. 'Will told me someone came looking for Rachel not long before she died.'

A range of emotions crossed Adam's face. 'Did he say who it was?'

'I'm certain it was Lucian.'

His eyebrows were dark arches. 'Her old boyfriend?'

It sounded so innocent, but Rachel's relationship with Lucian had been anything but. 'Apparently he knew about Noah. He said he wanted to talk about their son.'

Adam dragged his hands down his face, eyes darting about as the implications sank in.

'According to Will, he didn't speak to Rachel right then,' I hurried on. 'From what I can gather they met up and it didn't work out, and I think she went to meet him the night she died, and he had something to do with her death.' *He killed her.* Why was it so hard to say? Because murder didn't happen to families like ours. Murder was for books and films, not real life. 'There was a witness,' I went on when Adam didn't speak. 'A homeless man called Sam. He came forward and spoke to the police because he saw someone leaving the bridge that night, around the time Rachel died.' Now I'd started, the words flowed out. 'But he couldn't give a description, and no one knew about Lucian because he didn't give his name, and Rachel's phone wasn't found so there was no trace of any contact between them—'

'Whoa!' Adam backed up against the sink. 'Hang on a minute.' He pressed a hand to his forehead. 'Her old boyfriend turned up out of the blue and you think he killed her because a homeless person saw someone near the bridge that night?'

'Yes, I do. Hannah, the girl Rachel shared the flat with, said he'd been there, this man who sounds like Lucian, and it looked like they were arguing outside as if he was angry—'

'Let me think a minute, Jess.' Adam shook his head, as if trying to rearrange the information I'd unloaded into something that made sense. 'You're saying this Lucian must be ...' His gaze flicked upwards. 'That he's Noah's ...'

I knew he had trouble saying it, even thinking about Noah not being his biological child. 'Yes,' I said. When he stayed silent, eyes still on the ceiling, I moved over and took his hand. It was cold to the touch, his fingers unyielding. 'I know it's hard to hear, Adam. It was easier to think of him as a faceless one-night stand we would never have to deal with, but I found something.' For some reason, I baulked at telling him I'd visited Will on his boat yesterday morning. 'At Rachel's flat.'

'Why did you need to go there?' His voice sounded thin, as if his strength had been sapped, and a wave of guilt pushed through me. 'I'm sorry, Adam. I wanted to talk to Hannah after what Will told me about Lucian.' I moved to my jacket, draped over my bag by the door. 'Remember, ages ago, I thought someone had been in the house while you were away because a photo was missing?' He half-squinted at the photo as I held it up. 'This is it, Adam. The photo. I wasn't imagining it. I think Rachel came here and took it.'

He seemed lost for words as he took the picture and stared at it. 'It could be a copy,' he said at last. 'Maybe your dad sent it to her.'

'What?' Now it was my turn to look stunned. 'Dad didn't even know where Rachel was. None of us did. And she made it clear she didn't want anything more to do with Noah.'

But his words had sowed a seed of doubt. Could Dad have sent her the picture? But surely he would have asked and not done it behind my back. *Like he hadn't kissed Caroline.* 'But, even if he did, why take this one instead of sending her a copy? He could have emailed it to her.' Except, he wouldn't do it, I was certain. He'd been so angry with Rachel, getting pregnant when she clearly wasn't ready. He said at the time how much better the baby would be with us, that Rachel making a clean break was the best thing she could do. He'd urged us to make it all legal in case she changed her mind one day. *You're his mother,*

Jess. You're not childminding Noah for her. He would have been furious if he'd discovered she was showing an interest now, not sending her photos of Noah. 'Should I talk to Dad about it?' My stomach swayed. I didn't want him to know I was looking into Rachel's death. Bringing someone to justice wouldn't interest him. It wouldn't bring her back.

'I don't think you should say anything.' Adam's words brought a rush of gratitude that we were on the same side, at least in this. 'I can't imagine him sending the photo if it makes you feel any better.'

'So, who did, if Rachel didn't steal it?'

'Maybe she did. But why?'

'To show Lucian. As proof, though Noah looks nothing like him.'

Adam was pale, shaking his head. 'The whole thing is weird, Jess, I get that. But whoever sent that letter hasn't been in touch again, so can we leave it for now?'

I took a step back. 'Aren't you worried that Lucian might try to get custody if he's Noah's father?'

'Stop calling him that.' Adam's arms dropped to his sides. 'If he was going to do that, why wait?'

Lawyering up. I didn't say it. Adam was clearly desperate for it to go away, to resume our comfortable lives – to keep burying his head in the sand. 'I don't know,' I mumbled.

'Look, he wouldn't have a leg to stand on.' A tight smile lifted the corners of his mouth. 'And anyway, I know a good lawyer, remember?'

I thought of Simon, sidelined by Adam since that long-ago bachelor weekend, but kept quiet. Adam must know that Lucian had rights, no matter what it said on Noah's birth certificate – that a DNA test could blow everything out of the water.

He gave my shoulder a weary squeeze. 'We're home now. Noah's safe in bed. Denny hasn't seen anything suspicious. Maybe whoever sent that letter got cold feet and we won't hear from them again.'

'But Rachel—'

'Please, Jess. Leave it.'

His keenness for things to be normal made my worries feel side-lined. The thought that Lucian might have killed Rachel, that he could turn up on our doorstep demanding access – or money, or both – brought a lash of anger I couldn't force down. I wouldn't let that happen. I had to talk to him.

Chapter 27

As I walked from the little car park at the top of the high street to work the following morning, I heard my name being called. Dad was coming out of the bakery wearing polished brogues and jeans, and a dapper waistcoat over his white shirt. He looked smarter than I'd seen him in a while, his hair brushed back and his newly grown beard neatly trimmed.

'What are you doing here?' I wasn't prepared for the sight of him. After pleading exhaustion the night before, I'd gone straight to bed when Adam came down from kissing Noah goodnight, leaving him to unwind in front of the television. I'd feigned sleep when he came up but lay awake half the night. We'd been careful with each other over breakfast, letting Noah fill the gaps, but after I'd dropped Noah at school, my mind snapped straight back to Lucian. Checking in with Dad hadn't been uppermost in my thoughts.

'I fancied some croissants for breakfast.' He waggled the paper bag in his hand.

'With Ruth?'

'Just me.' His mouth pressed into a smile. 'I'm trying to persuade Annie to open a bakery in Rosside, so I don't have to drive out here.'

'What did she say?' I pictured him in action; the silver-tongued charmer unable to resist a pretty female. Annie was at least thirty years younger, dark-haired, slim, and attractive.

'She says the village is too small. It wouldn't sustain a business.' His gaze was wary, his smile strained. I reminded myself he was widower, a pensioner, a grieving father – my beloved dad – and my animosity died. 'How was your fishing trip?'

'I expect you've heard all about it from Noah.' A light came on in his eyes as it always did at the mention of his grandson. 'It was a surprise to see your mother-in-law.'

'I decided to take a last-minute shopping trip while Adam was away.' I dipped my head and pushed my car key in my bag so he couldn't read my expression. 'I wanted to look for a gift for his fortieth.'

'So Jennifer said.' He paused. 'Did you find anything?'

Something about his tone made me look up. I'd never had cause to lie to him before. The bond we'd forged through caring for Mum and despairing over Rachel had negated the need for subterfuge, but I had the impression he didn't believe me. 'No.' My face glowed with heat, despite the chill in the air. 'He's tricky to buy for.'

'Did you see anyone else while you were there?'

My smile froze. 'Such as?'

'Old friends?'

I swallowed. 'I caught up with Sasha. We had a drink at the Three Crowns.' He seemed to be waiting for more and I pulled words up from my depths. 'I went to look at the old house.'

A grizzled eyebrow rose. 'Why?'

'Because … I grew up there, Dad. It's where Mum lived.' As if he needed reminding. 'I have a lot of memories wrapped up in that house.'

'Not all of them good.' His face relaxed. 'Are the Harpers still there?'

'According to Caroline.' *Shit.* Dad's grip tightened on the paper bag. 'She came out to say hello.'

His jaw clenched. 'How is she?'

'Good.' I should ask him to verify what she had told me but wasn't sure how I would feel if he lied. He hadn't explained what had happed the day I walked in on them, only said he was sorry. My imagination had done the rest, casting Caroline as the cheater, the bad friend, taking advantage of a grieving widower; a woman desperate to step into my mother's shoes. *Why had I done that?* I'd been a fully grown adult, but maybe it was a protective mechanism because the alternative – that Dad had tried it on with Mum's best friend – was too hard to bear. But I knew it was simpler than that. It hadn't occurred to me that he might be the guilty party. 'We didn't talk for long,' I said. 'I had a train to catch, and she and James were going out.'

'Ah, good old James.' Dad spoke with genuine fondness. They'd got along well, which made it even harder to accept what he'd done, grief-stricken or not. 'I keep meaning to invite them up for the weekend,' he said, watching my face as though looking for signs of dishonesty.

'You didn't tell me you still spoke to Caroline sometimes.'

'We were good friends, Jess.' His face was inscrutable. 'That didn't stop after your mother died.'

It was a rebuff, despite his gentle tone. 'I understand that. I don't know why you wouldn't mention it.'

'She told you, then?' *Was there a hint of mockery?* Directed at me, or Caroline? No. He was merely being curious. It was good to see him peering out from under his cloud of grief, even if the conversation was uncomfortable. 'How did that come about?'

'She said she was at the service because you called and told her about Rachel.' I glanced at my watch. 'I'm sorry, but I have to get to work.'

He seemed about to say something, but changed his mind and raised the bakery bag instead. 'And I'm ready for my breakfast.' His gaze slipped past me. 'Looks like that colleague of yours is trying to transport you inside with the power of her mind.'

Turning, I caught sight of Kristin watching from the agency window across the street. Her face was stern, unsmiling. Seeing I'd spotted her, she shrank back without acknowledgement.

'She's a funny one.' Dad's words caught my attention. It wasn't the first time he'd described Kristin in an unflattering way. He'd come to the office one day to take me out for lunch, and Kristin had dropped a sheaf of papers on the floor in front of him. When he tried to help her pick them up she'd snapped that she could manage, sounding on the verge of tears.

'Sure you've done the right thing, taking her on?' Dad asked me later. 'She seems a bit all over the place.'

'Give her a break. She's new and keen to make a good impression. She probably feels bad, thinking she showed herself up in front of you.'

'Pretty girl though.'

Now, I had a crushing thought. Had Dad flirted with Kristin – or worse – while I was out of the office? She might not have dared to tell me, worried for her job. 'I really should go,' I said quickly. 'It was good to see you, Dad.'

'You too.' He leaned forward and kissed my cheek, his old-fashioned scent enveloping me like a hug. 'Have a good day, sweetheart.'

'How is your dad?' Kristin's bright smile banished an impulse to ask her whether he'd ever done anything to upset her. Why bring up something that most likely never happened and risk offending her? Not only that, it could damage our friendship and working relationship. Anyway, Kristin wasn't the type to stay quiet. She had a zero-tolerance attitude to what she called 'bad behaviour' regardless of who the perpetrator was.

'OK, I think. Better than the last time I saw him.'

'How come he was in Ulverston?'

'He likes the bakery here.'

Her smile seemed to stretch on for too long before she said, 'And how was London?'

'It made me realize I prefer living here.' I discarded my jacket and sat down, glad to be back on familiar territory. 'I didn't even find a gift for Will.'

'Will?' Kristin paused on her way to the kitchen, flashing me a look of confusion over her shoulder.

'Sorry?'

'You said Will.'

My heart jumped. 'Did I?'

She nodded, turning in the doorway, and folding her arms. She looked chic in a long-sleeved, brown-and-cream spotted dress, hair back in a half-ponytail. 'I've never heard you mention that name before.'

I closed my eyes briefly and massaged the back of my neck. 'Rachel used to work for him ... well, at the art gallery his mother owns. I went to see him and picked up some of her things.'

'Right.' Her tone was curt. 'You could have said.'

I shook my head. 'I'm sorry I wasn't honest with you, Kristin. I ... It sounded ...' I made a frustrated noise. 'I didn't even tell Adam why I was going.'

Stirred out of whatever feelings my confession had elicited, she wheeled her chair over to my desk and sat down. 'Why not?'

I took a breath. 'The other night, he told me he's glad that Rachel is out of our lives for good, because it means we don't have to worry she might want Noah back.' Saying it roused the mixed emotions Adam's words had evoked. 'He thought I shouldn't bother picking up her things and told me to let her go.'

'Right.' Rather than the disapproval I'd expected at Adam's callous sentiment – knowing how highly she thought of him – Kristin looked thoughtful. 'He might have a point.' She smoothed the skirt of her dress. 'I mean, he could have worded it better, but from what you've told me, Rachel could be a loose cannon. Worrying about whether she might turn up one day, might say something to Noah ... that must have been hard to live with.'

'It was, if I thought about it,' I said. 'But I didn't want her dead.'

'No, of course not.' Kristin looked stricken. 'You're far too nice for that.' It wasn't quite what I'd expected her to say. 'So … this Will guy,' she went on cautiously. 'What was he like?' Again, not what I'd expected. All the same, I found myself saying, 'He was nice, I guess. Concerned, you know?'

'Concerned?' A frown settled on her brow. 'What about?'

But I couldn't face going over it again. 'Concerned that all her things were returned, which now they are.'

She nodded slowly but, as with Dad, I sensed she knew I was hiding something. It was as if the truth was written above my head, visible to everyone who knew me. Feeling the need to reveal something, while wishing the phone would ring and distract her, I said, 'I talked to our old neighbour, Caroline. She told me my father is still in touch and that he made a pass at her not long after my mother died.'

Kristin seemed to have stopped breathing. Her lips slightly parted as though about to speak and, with a jolt, I wondered whether my off-kilter assumption had been right, and something had happened between her and Dad. Then she was standing, pushing her chair back to her desk in a flurry of movement.

'I expect he didn't know what he was doing,' she said in her usual tone of voice. 'Grief can cause people to behave out of character at times.'

But was it out of character? 'That's what I thought.' I studied Kristin as she sat down and picked up the phone but when she faced me, her eyes were filled with compassion. 'As if you haven't been through enough,' she said. 'What was the point of her telling you that?'

Inexplicably, tears swam to my eyes. 'Look, it's been a strange couple of days.' I blinked a few times. 'I'm sure things will settle down.'

'I hope so, Jess.'

I forced a deep breath and lifted my tone. 'I'm assuming Vanessa Blake hasn't been in touch?'

'Oh, I got your message and meant to reply but it was late, then it went out of my mind.' Kristin pulled a face at her own forgetfulness. 'She did swing by, but when I said you were away she left.'

'Shame we don't have her number.'

'I know, right?'

Part of me hoped Vanessa had decided Ulverston wasn't right for her daughter, even if it meant losing a buyer for Tarn Cottage. Something about her presence in the area made me apprehensive.

Kristin's cheeks were pinker than usual. Replaying the way I'd said *Will* instead of *Adam* made my muscles clench. What must she think? Especially after not telling her why I was going to London. 'Anyway, shall I bring you up to speed?'

'Sure.' I listened as she ran through the day's itinerary and showed me our updated webpage, which included the pictures I'd taken the previous week. 'We've two viewings booked already,' she said. 'I can do the one this morning, if you like?'

I had a sinking feeling she was keen to get out of the office to avoid hearing any more details about my private life and nodded. 'That would be great, thank you.'

She brought coffees through as usual and kept up a bright stream of chatter while she worked, telling me her brother in Switzerland was laid up with a broken ankle so wouldn't be home for a planned visit. 'I swear he did it deliberately to get out of it. Maybe I should fly out and visit him instead.'

'You should go sometime,' I told her. 'You're owed holiday. Could you get a neighbour or friend to keep an eye on your mum?'

'Maybe.' She fiddled with her hair, pulling out the slide and readjusting it, jumping when the phone rang. 'No peace for the wicked.' She didn't meet my eyes as she snatched up the handset and reeled off the agency name.

I answered some emails and refilled my coffee mug, a jitteriness to my movements that had nothing to do with caffeine.

Once Kristin had left for her viewing appointment – at least ten minutes too early – I waited a few moments, in case she'd forgotten something and came back, then brought up the search engine on my computer and typed in *Lucian West*.

Chapter 28

The link at the top of the page was to a yoga and mindfulness retreat. Breath held, I opened the webpage and read the details.

Serenity Retreat – Brittany, France
Escape to an idyllic location in what was once a Zen monastery to comfort your soul and renew your spirit. Experience the calm and peaceful surroundings and wake up to panoramic views across the valley. Stay in the beautiful main house or pre-erected tents in the grounds and join our guided mindful meditation program led by Serenity founders Lucian West and Astrid Olsson. As well as a new yoga hall, which opened this year, Serenity has introduced silent, mindful walks through the stunning grounds and countryside. Various wellbeing courses, such as self-compassion, are available on request. Book a stay at Serenity and leave your worries behind.

For a moment, I doubted whether it was the same Lucian West. Serenity? Guided meditation? Zen monastery? He must have undergone a dramatic personality change. Will had said he was struck by how 'calm' the man who came to see Rachel was. This must be why.

I clicked *About Us* and there he was: the same 'surfer' hair brushed off a lightly tanned forehead and those eyes … a rush of déjà vu overwhelmed me. They were the palest blue, pulling me in as if he was standing in front of me – as though he knew everything about me. No drink or drug-haze clouding his vision this time. His gaze was clear and lucid, crinkled at the edges in a friendly smile. Will had been right – something about him exuded … well, *serenity* was the only word that came to mind. In a cream linen shirt and light trousers, he stood, looking relaxed, against a backdrop of cobalt sky and greenery, the stone monastery in the background. Underneath, in bold italics, were the words, *I changed my life … let me help you change yours.*

It sounded slightly cultish, but I was probably being uncharitable, stunned by how different he looked to the image I'd carried in my head all these years. Impossible to imagine him sending an anonymous letter with intent to blackmail or shoving his ex-girlfriend in the canal.

His partner, Astrid, was Swedish and a qualified yoga instructor, luminously beautiful with flowing white-blonde hair and sea-green eyes, pictured posing in a sunlit hall in one photo, the sun haloed around her slender body, and standing in the grounds with Lucian in another.

A third image showed Lucian, eyes closed, in a mediation posture opposite a guest – his or her back to the camera for discretion – while the rest of the photos were views of the sumptuous scenery, alongside a 'menu' of wellbeing classes, prices, and healthy food on offer.

My eyes darted over Lucian's biography, looking for a mention of his family, his 'origin story', but there was nothing in-depth, only a paragraph about an epiphany that led him to clean up his life and brought him in contact with Astrid and the monastery.

Hers was a similarly brief run-through of a 'blessed' upbringing in Sweden, detailing the extensive yoga training that brought 'clarity, gratitude, and strength' into her life.

I sat for a moment, flicking around the pages, letting it all sink in; this new version of my sister's one true love, and possibly Noah's biological father.

Astrid was the opposite to Rachel in every way, all light to Rachel's darkness. If she and Lucian were a couple, his taste in women had changed dramatically too. Could Rachel have really believed she had a chance with him, even using Noah as a bargaining tool? And how had meeting him under the bridge that night led to her death? It seemed so unlikely, looking at the crisp, sunny images on-screen, the emphasis on *life* and *personal healing*, that Lucian could have committed murder. Even before his 'epiphany' I doubted he was dangerous or had meant Rachel any harm, however much I'd hated him.

The father's out of the picture. He doesn't know and it's best it stays that way. He's no good.

Rachel would never describe Lucian as *no good*. At least, that's what I'd thought at the time. Maybe she knew things about him I didn't.

I'd thought about putting Denny on the case, but I wanted to talk to Lucian myself, even if the thought of it made my stomach curl. But I could hardly swan off to Brittany, even if I wanted to. I would have to settle for emailing him through the website, or calling the number listed. Only ... it was the sort of conversation that needed eye contact. It would be easier to work out whether he was lying and to find out his next move, his plan – because there had to be one. He couldn't have come all the way to London to talk to Rachel about Noah and then slip back into his perfect life. *Unless he has something to hide.* But there would be proof of his visit to England. Astrid may have known where he was going and why. If they were close, she might lie to the police to give him an alibi.

I wasn't cut out for this third-rate detective work. Head throbbing with questions, palms prickling with sweat, my fingers hovered over the keyboard. About to click on the email address, my attention snagged on the instruction beneath. *Why not arrange a video call for a one-to-one chat and a virtual tour of the venue before you book your stay?*

Not giving myself time to reconsider, I clicked on the email and sent a contact link, requesting a call at eight o'clock the following morning. It was Adam's turn to drop Noah at school and better that I make the call at work where I wouldn't be overheard. Lucian would assume I was a potential guest as my surname was different to Rachel's.

The phone on Kristin's desk was ringing. She – or Moira, if she was in – normally answered, or the call diverted to me. I was tempted to ignore it when it switched, but I was supposed to be working and it could be Vanessa Blake.

Sucking in a breath, I picked up the receiver. 'Hello, Cumbrian Cottages, Jess speaking. How may I help?' My eyes still on my computer screen, I didn't take in at first what the caller was saying. 'Sorry, could you repeat that, please?'

'I was hoping to speak to Kris, only she's not answering her mobile.' A female voice, older, laced with impatience. 'I've locked myself out and our next-door neighbour's not in. He has my spare key. I can't get in without it.'

'Right.' My brain struggled to catch up. 'Kristin's showing someone round a property at the moment. That's why she isn't answering her phone. She'll be back soon.'

'I want the number of the locksmith we used before. I haven't got it on me. It's in the house and I can't remember their name.'

A frown built. 'Are you her mum?'

'That's right,' the woman said. 'Can you get hold of her for me?'

'You said you can't get into your house?'

A gusty sigh came down the line. 'Look, I'm sorry to bother you but my back's playing up and I had to walk home because I missed the bus and I've got two bags of shopping. I don't want to have to wait for Kris to finish work to get back to me.'

The door opened and a tall, well-dressed man came in. I held

157

up a finger to let him know I would be with him in a moment, trying to wrap my mind around what Kristin's mum was saying. If she was agoraphobic, why was she out shopping? 'Is your neighbour likely to be home soon?' I injected a smile into my voice. 'Hopefully, he hasn't gone far.'

'I don't know,' she said. 'He doesn't normally go out. His daughter must have taken him to one of his doctor's appointments. They could be gone ages.'

My head was spinning. I'd never been to Kristin's home but was sure she'd mentioned her next door neighbour was an elderly widow with four cats. 'OK, well, I'll tell Kristin you called as soon as she gets back to the office.'

'I know I'm not supposed to ring her at work.'

The hairs on the back of my neck rose. I spun round in my chair, expecting to see someone looking in through the window, but the street was empty. 'Don't worry, it's fine.' I kneaded my temple. 'It's good to talk to you, actually.'

'Are you the boss?' Her tone was warmer now. 'Kris speaks very highly of you.'

'She speaks highly of you too.' I was still trying to get to grips with the strangeness of the conversation. Kristin had told me her mum was a private person, shy and unsociable, but the woman's tone gave a very different impression. 'Kristin's a great employee. And friend,' I added quickly, frowning when I heard the wail of police sirens in the background. 'She's excellent at her job.'

'She's a good girl,' her mum said, clearly mollified. 'The best.'

Aware of the waiting customer looking at his watch, I smiled an apology. 'I'll tell her to call you the second she gets back if you're OK to hang on a bit longer.'

'I suppose I can make it to the café round the corner and have a cup of tea while I wait.'

'Great. Bye, Mrs Wells.'

I rang off and attended to the man, who wanted to know whether we had anything like Dove Cottage, one of William

Wordsworth's former homes, for sale. 'My wife's a big fan. She's a writer and would love to live somewhere inspirational.'

Momentarily distracted, I said, 'We don't, but there's a house almost identical to Hill Top about to come on the market, where Arthur Ransome lived, and several writers since.'

'Arthur …?'

'*Swallows and Amazons.*'

He nodded, looking embarrassed, and after I'd given him the details and taken his name and number, he left as Kristin returned.

'That looked promising.' Smiling, she swung her bag onto her desk and slid her camel coat off. 'Viewing went well. They want to put in an offer.'

'That's good,' I said. 'Your mum called.'

Her hand froze on the way to smoothing her wind-tossed hair. 'My mum?'

'She's locked out of the house and can't get in.'

'Right.' A tide of crimson spread across her cheeks. 'I'd better call her.'

Seeing her discomfort brought a mix of curiosity and pity. It was obvious she'd lied to me about her mother, but I had no idea why. Kristin was normally so straightforward, no-nonsense. 'You should go home,' I said. 'She was going to wait in the café round the corner but her back is playing up. She doesn't know the number of the locksmith you used before.'

'The neighbour has a spare.' She wasn't looking at me. 'She must have forgotten.'

'He's not in, apparently.'

'Oh.' She pressed a hand to her mouth then let it drop. 'Jess, I'm so sorry.' The words came in a rush, her face a mask of distress. 'I should never have told you my mum was scared of going out.'

'It's fine,' I said, though I couldn't deny it hurt that she'd lied. She knew that Rachel was Noah's birth mother – something I hadn't told anyone else – yet hadn't felt able to be honest with me. Then again, hadn't I lied about my trip to London? And I still hadn't told her about the anonymous letter. 'You obviously had your reasons.'

She pulled her coat back on, a shimmer of tears in her eyes. 'Look, I said it because …' She paused, picking up her bag, clearly struggling with some internal dilemma.

'Honestly, Kristin, it's OK.' I hated seeing her like this, her face pulled down with shame, so unlike herself. 'You don't have to apologize.'

'I do,' she insisted. 'I was embarrassed about still living at home with my mum, so I made up something that made it seem more like I had no choice, which sounds terrible—'

'It's fine, don't worry.' I got up and went to her. 'I didn't leave home until I married Adam.' I tried to lighten the mood, make her feel better. 'There's no shame in living at home if it's what you want, and your mum doesn't mind.'

Her eyes met mine and flicked away. She was nervously running the strap of her bag through her fingers, and I braced myself for whatever she was going to say next. 'I'm sorry,' she repeated, looking miserable.

My shoulders relaxed. 'You probably want to make up for your brother living so far away,' I said. 'To be honest, I felt the same way. Like I had to make up for Rachel. Be more present for my parents because she wasn't around.' Tears pressed behind my eyes. I wanted to unburden myself, talk openly to someone – but it wouldn't be fair to unload on Kristin now. Maybe not ever. 'Really, I do understand.'

'Oh, Jess.' She cupped her hand over her eyes, and I saw she was fighting tears. 'You deserve so much better.'

Taking her by the shoulders, I pulled her to me. 'You're making too much of it.' I stroked her hair, like I did with Noah when he was upset. 'Put it out of your mind and go home and let your mum in.'

'It's fine. I can call her, give her the locksmith's number.'

'That's silly when you have a key.'

'What about work?' She eased away, looking everywhere but at me. 'It's nearly time for your lunch break.'

'I'll call Moira in. She keeps asking for extra hours.' I touched Kristin's arm and tried not to mind when she took a step back. 'Take the rest of the day off.'

'Thanks,' she mumbled. 'I'm so sorry.' She spun away and out through the door, narrowly avoiding a couple coming in.

Watching her almost run down the street, I told myself things would be back to normal tomorrow, once she'd got over the mortification of having her secret revealed, but couldn't brush off the feeling that there was something else. Something Kristin didn't want me to know.

When the postman stepped in, I took the mail on autopilot, agreeing with him that the weather was cold for September. When he'd gone, I glanced down, and my stomach tipped. Another envelope, addressed to me, with a sheet of paper inside.

Have you told him yet?

Chapter 29

'How was school, Ninja Turtle?'

Noah looked up from where he was drawing at the kitchen table. 'Can you tell Daddy I don't want peas for my dinner?'

'Peas are good for you.' Adam turned from the fridge, holding a tray of fish fingers. 'I've put some jacket potatoes in too,' he said to me. His glasses were steamy, his face flushed from the heat of the oven. We took it in turns to cook, depending on my hours at work. 'The fish fingers are home-made. I picked up some hake from the fishmongers after my run this morning.'

'Sounds lovely.' I removed my jacket and went to sit beside Noah, glad of the apparent ceasefire between Adam and me. I'd made the decision on the way home not to tell him about the second letter but had messaged Denny.

I'll be around as long as you need, don't worry. I checked out Rachel's ex. He's lived in France for a while. Came over in September, met with friends, went home. D

I should have known that Denny would have looked into him, but he clearly didn't know that Lucian had tracked down Rachel.

Thanks, Denny. I pressed a kiss on Noah's hair, closing my eyes as I breathed him in, trying to force Lucian from my mind. It was impossible to imagine that Noah was his child. Every time

162

the thought sprang up, I wanted to be sick. He didn't look like him, but I supposed that didn't mean much – Rachel had strongly resembled Mum, while I looked more like Dad – but Noah *felt* like our child; mine and Adam's.

'Everything OK?' I realized Adam had said something while my face was pressed into Noah's hair as he carried on drawing.

'Sorry, what did you say?'

'I asked if you'd had a good day.'

'Fine, thank you.' I picked up a crayon and coloured in the perfectly round sun that Noah had drawn in the corner of his picture. 'Kristin had to leave early, but Moira came in.'

'No, Mummy,' Noah protested. 'Sunshine is yellow, not orange.'

'Oops.' I pulled a silly face that made him giggle.

'You're funny, Mummy.'

'Yes, I am.' I mussed his hair. 'Now, go and wash your hands. Dinner's almost ready.'

Once Noah was in the downstairs toilet, running the taps, Adam gave me a quizzical look. 'What was up with Kristin?'

'A problem at home.' I didn't want to tell him she'd made up the story about her mum having agoraphobia. It wasn't that I thought he would disapprove, but I didn't want to risk him thinking less of her. Since becoming more of a friend, Kristin had been to the house a few times and got on well with Adam. 'Nothing serious,' I added.

'Her mum, I suppose.'

As Adam returned his attention to the food, I made a noncommittal noise. 'How was your day?'

'Productive. I've been speaking to the team in Berlin, going over the new system. They seem happy with it so far.'

'That's good.' I suddenly couldn't stop thinking about the look on Kristin's face as she apologized to me for lying, the way her eyes had brimmed with tears. I was wondering whether I should call to see how she was when Adam caught me round the waist, taking me by surprise. I quickly broke away from his kiss, leaning back in his arms to study his face. 'What was that for?'

'Am I not allowed to kiss my beautiful wife?'

'Jasmine wanted me to kiss her at playtime, but I said no because I'm only 5,' Noah said, running in and squeezing between us.

'You've plenty of time for kissing girls when you're older.' Adam smiled into my eyes, and although I smiled back, I pulled away and adjusted the heat under the pan of peas. How could he be so cheerful after our conversation yesterday? Shouldn't he be more concerned? Maybe he was putting on a happy front for Noah, but it was as if something had shifted – that he'd come to some agreement with himself that I was unaware of.

'You didn't tell me how school was,' I said to Noah once we were seated, our dinner in front of us. It was usually my favourite time of the day when we shared our news. Sometimes Dad would join us, whisking Noah away after we'd eaten to play games in the living room – he'd started teaching him to play chess and was getting him interested in music – but today I was going through the motions. 'Did you show Miss Everly your fish picture?' Miss Everly was the support teacher, and Noah's favourite.

He nodded, chewing his food in an exaggerated fashion until his mouth was empty before saying, 'I talked to that lady at lunchtime.'

'What lady?' I took a sip of water to wash down the paste-like mix of fish and potato in my mouth.

'It was that lady you saw, Mummy.' Noah was carefully pushing his peas to the side of his plate. 'She asked me where I lived when I was a tiny baby.'

Adam glanced from me to Noah. 'Which lady?'

'What is her name, Mummy?' Noah frowned, the way he did when he was trying to recall something important.

'Vanessa.' My voice was a croak. I coughed. 'She's looking for somewhere to live around here for her daughter.'

164

'Why was she at the school?' Adam was studying me as though he'd never encountered my current expression before.

'She's hoping her grandchildren will go there.' I dredged up a smile. 'I suggested she meet with the head teacher.'

'Why was she talking to Noah?'

'Because she remembered him, I suppose.'

'Bit of an odd question.'

'What did you say?' I turned to Noah, hoping he couldn't sense my rising anxiety. 'About where you lived before.'

'I said in a house with you and Daddy that was in London, but I don't remember because I was only a little baby and then we came here.'

'That's right,' I said with forced brightness, noting Adam's jaw had tightened. 'Did she say anything else?'

'She has a house in London, and it is very big, and she was looking at me funny.'

'Funny?' The spark of alarm in Adam's eyes reflected mine. 'How do you mean?'

'Like this.' He stared at us, making his eyes big and round. 'For ages and then she stroked my head.'

'What?' Adam frowned at me. 'That doesn't sound right.'

'Is Daddy cross?' Noah's voice had shrunk. 'She was nice.'

'Of course she was.' I tried to hold my voice steady as panic poured though my veins. 'But it's best to not chat to grown-ups you don't know, sweetheart.'

'But you know her, Mummy.'

What was I supposed to say to that? I could tell Adam was dying to speak and shot him a warning look. 'I don't know her very well,' I said. 'She's going back to London soon.' I widened my smile. 'Now, see how many peas you can eat before I count to twenty.'

'What was that all about?' Adam dropped beside me on the sofa after reading Noah a final bedtime story. 'Who is this Vanessa?'

I guiltily switched off my phone. I'd checked Skype to see that my scheduled call with Lucian had been accepted and hoped Adam couldn't read anything in my face.

'Like I said, she's staying in the area, looking for somewhere for her daughter and grandchildren to live. I advised her to make an appointment to see the head teacher at the school when I ran into her last week.'

'Don't you think it was odd, the way she spoke to Noah?'

I sank back against the cushions, overwhelmed by a wave of exhaustion. 'Yes,' I admitted, unwilling to voice the sense of disquiet Vanessa gave me. 'Perhaps she's missing her family,' I said. 'She recognized Noah from the other day and stopped to talk to him.'

'You'd think she would know better,' he grumbled, running a hand over the back of his head. 'I hope someone was keeping an eye on things.'

'I'm sure they were.' I thought of Denny. Why hadn't he mentioned the encounter? 'Security there is good.'

Adam took off his glasses, stretched, and yawned. He picked up the television remote and put it down again, twisting his body towards me. 'Are you OK?' His brow crinkled. 'You look tired.'

I suppressed a wave of irritation at having to explain. 'It's been a strange few days,' I reminded him. My phone vibrated with a text, and I ignored it. 'I'll be fine after a decent night's sleep.'

Adam rested a hand on my knee, his dark eyes searching my face. 'Things *will* get back to normal.' He said it with a note of defiance, as if nothing less would do. I used to admire his ability to compartmentalize, close off anything messy and complicated, but now it created a distance. 'All that matters is you, me, and Noah.'

'Of course we matter, Adam. But there are things I can't ignore.'

His hand slid away. 'I suppose you mean him.'

'Yes, I mean Lucian.' I lowered my voice. 'I have to know what he's up to.'

'Talk to him then.'

I started, unable to hide my surprise. 'Really?'

166

'If he wants to be found, it shouldn't be too hard.' Adam picked up his glasses and polished the lenses on the hem of his shirt. 'Get it out of the way.'

'And if it turns out he's …' I still couldn't bring myself to say *Noah's father*.

Adam held up his glasses, checking they were clean before slipping them back on. 'Then we'll deal with it.' His neck had flushed red, an indication he wasn't as calm as he sounded.

'And you'll be OK with whatever that brings?' I couldn't quite believe it. 'Because I'm not sure I will be.'

'Not OK, no, but I'll handle it.' I studied his face. 'You wouldn't try to, I don't know … bump him off or something? Hire a hitman to remove him from the picture?'

'I know it's hard to believe, but whatever rights he may turn out to have in law, *we're* Noah's parents. That's got to count for something if it goes to court, regardless of how much money he and his family might throw at the situation.'

'It'll involve a DNA test.'

'We can make a game of it for Noah, so he won't be—'

'I can't let that happen,' I cut in. 'If Lucian pursues it, I'll tell the police he murdered Rachel. It won't get to court.'

Disbelief filled Adam's eyes. 'You would do that?'

'He won't want to risk being accused,' I said. 'He's got a nice lifestyle in France, a business, a reputation. He doesn't even know Noah. I can't imagine how a child would fit with his environment.'

'Wait … you've found him?' Adam's voice tightened. 'Why are you doing things behind my back, Jess?'

I let out a sigh. 'After our last conversation, I felt like you didn't want me to pursue it.'

'Yet, you did anyway.' His face was stiff like a mannequin's. 'I might not like it, but I still prefer you to be open with me.' Annoyance flared in his eyes. 'I can't believe she's still got you running rings, even now.' That bitter tone again, the one I'd heard when he called me from Berlin.

'You're sorry for suggesting I be honest with you, yet you say something like that?' Anger ignited. 'I'm sure Rachel didn't die on purpose to mess up your life.'

'Isn't that all she was ever good for? Messing up lives.'

True or not, his words cut deep. 'If it weren't for her, we wouldn't have a child,' I said tightly.

Instantly, he crumbled. 'You're right. I'm sorry, Jess.' I shrank away as he reached for me, not ready to make up. 'My head's all over the place. I don't like it.'

'I don't like it either,' I said. 'I want things how they were but, right now, they aren't.' I paused for breath. 'I've booked a call with Lucian tomorrow morning at eight.'

'Right.' There was a glint of tears in Adam's eyes. 'I guess that's that then.'

'You were the one who told me to talk to him.'

'I didn't know you'd already arranged it.'

I grabbed my phone and got to my feet. 'I'm going for a bath.'

He nodded without looking up, seeming somehow adrift in the middle of our supersize sofa. Seconds later, I heard the TV come on.

After checking Noah was sleeping, the top of his head just visible above his duvet, I sank into a bubble bath, letting the hot water ease some of the tension from my muscles. I submerged myself, then remembering the text that came in earlier, I leaned over and reached for my phone on the floor by the tub.

My heart leapt when I saw Will's number. I grabbed a towel and dried my hands before opening the message.

Wondering how you are. It was nice to meet you, by the way. I don't think I mentioned that. Any news? I had a thought today about the random letters Rachel highlighted. Could it be a coded message? Will.

Chapter 30

I arrived at the agency well before eight the next morning, checking the main door was locked in case someone saw me and thought the shop was open. After making coffee, I settled at my desk and booted up my computer, trying to ignore the coating of nerves in my stomach that had made eating breakfast impossible.

'Are you sure you don't want me there when you talk to him?' Adam's question had been an afterthought, thrown at me while packing Noah's lunchbox. I said no, worried Lucian might disappear when he realized who I was. 'Promise you'll call me when you're done.'

We hadn't had a good night, each pretending to be asleep on our separate sides of the bed. I knew Adam's sleep pattern by heart; the little jolt as he fell into a dream, the catch in his breath that wasn't quite snoring, and knew he was faking. I suspected he guessed I was too and had tried not to cry, desperately missing the nights we'd lain awake, talking, or making love, drifting to sleep wrapped around each other. When Noah came, we would try to stay awake to keep each other company during his night feeds, taking turns to walk him up and down when he wouldn't settle. *A team.* That's how I would have described us.

It hadn't helped that after my bath, propelled by Will's text,

I'd gone in search of the poetry book, only for Adam to tell me I was being ridiculous.

'A coded message?' Still on the sofa where I'd left him, he'd given me an incredulous look. 'I can't believe you're taking the word of someone you don't even know.'

'I'm not *taking his word* for anything. It was just an idea and I thought I'd have a look.'

He got up. 'A message about what?'

'I don't know, Adam.' I backed away, not liking his expression. 'It's probably nothing.'

He trailed me to the bookshelf, where I'd left the envelope with the book inside, but knowing he was watching with barely suppressed irritation had been too much. 'Fine.' I put the envelope back. 'It was a stupid idea.'

'Why is he texting you anyway?' He watched me, waiting for my defence. Adam had never been the jealous type, but I'd never given him reason to be.

'He's not *texting* me. He wanted to let me know about this theory he had.'

'Sounds like an excuse.' A muscle in his jaw twitched. 'You didn't mention anything odd about the book to me.'

I'd felt a slipping sensation inside, a feeling that I was losing something precious as Adam looked at me with suspicion, tension winding between us.

'Forget I mentioned it.'

He'd made an effort to relax his face. 'I will if you will.'

I'd slipped the book into my bag before leaving the house earlier and pulled it out now, more to stop myself checking the time than because I seriously thought Rachel had left a secret message.

I'll look into it, I'd texted Will back. *I'm OK, thanks for asking. It was good to meet you too.* The last bit had sounded overfamiliar, so I deleted it and wrote, *I'll be in touch* instead.

I glanced at my computer once more, imagining Lucian

preparing to take my call. It was a relief to know he was far away, not lurking in the UK. I thought again of the figure under the bridge, the man I'd brushed past on Merthyr Terrace and shuddered. It couldn't have been Lucian. Unless … unless he'd flown back to France on Saturday evening and that's why I hadn't spotted him since. *Had he sent the anonymous letters?*

It was cool in the office, the weak sunshine that had pushed through the clouds on my drive over not warm enough to penetrate the building. I pulled on the cardigan draped over the back of my chair and sipped my coffee as I flipped through the book of poetry. A handwritten message caught my eyes on the inside of the back cover. *To Will, thanks for everything. R*

Rachel. Her writing was different from the looping scrawl from childhood. I stared at the words for a moment, wondering why Will had said the book wasn't his. Was the message inside for him, something secret?

Frowning, I looked through the pages again, at the letters she'd dabbed with a highlighter pen. What was going through her mind? If she'd been drinking, it might not mean anything, or be total gibberish, but the more I looked, the more certain I was that Will was onto something.

Taking a pen and a sheet of paper from the desk drawer, I wrote the letters down in the order they appeared. Thirty-one in all, several of the letters repeated; no pattern that I could detect.

When I'd finished, I glanced at the time. Eight o'clock. Nerves springing back, I clicked the call link and barely had time to take a breath when his face filled the screen.

'Good morning, Jess. It's so good to meet you. Is it OK to call you Jess?' The drunken drawl had gone, replaced by a plummy tone that spoke of good-breeding and his expensive schooling – amazing, considering he'd encouraged my sister to reject a formal education in favour of hanging out with him.

'Good morning, Lucian.' My heart was beating too fast, and my voice shook a little, despite my resolve to be brisk and to the point. I hadn't factored in the effect of him in 'real life'; a solid person, older of course, but magnetically attractive, his streaky-blond hair thick and wavy, his mesmerizing eyes clear and bright, something about them prompting a snatch of memory I couldn't hold onto. His collarless white shirt offset a deep tan and his teeth, when he smiled, were the right shade of white. He was sitting outside, sunlight warming the pale-stone building behind him, a hint of blue sky to the side. As I took it all in, trying to decide whether someone could commit a crime and look so at peace with the world, I wondered how I looked to him in my sensible cardigan, nothing behind me but a plain wall, my face cast into shadow as I'd left the overhead lights off. He gave no sign of recognition, but we'd only met twice, years ago, and both times he'd been drunk.

'Jess, do you mind if I ask how you came across Serenity?'

I shifted so the light from the window fell on my face and leaned closer to the screen. 'I was looking for you.'

'For me, specifically?' He was still smiling, but a tiny frown appeared. 'Did someone recommend us?'

'I wanted to talk to you about Rachel Beresford.'

The smile slid from his face as though slapped away. He looked around, as if checking there was no one within earshot, and pushed a hand through his hair. The tattooed spider's web was still there, faded but visible. 'Who are you?'

'I'm her sister,' I said. 'Jess.'

His face loomed closer, pupils dilating. Was he searching for a resemblance? I had to stop myself reeling back and turning away. Instead, I tilted my chin and forced my eyes wide open. 'You won't remember me. You weren't sober when I had the displeasure of meeting you.'

'The teeth.' He sank back, face resuming its previous calm. 'You have the same little gap between your two front teeth.'

'Why did you come over to see her, Lucian?'

'She told you?' His forehead creased. 'You know, she never

172

had a good word to say about her family. Looking back, I think that's a shame.'

Surprised he hadn't denied their meeting, I pushed out a humourless laugh. 'Like you didn't encourage her to hate us.'

He surveyed me for a moment, as if recalibrating: this was hardly the call he'd been expecting, but he was going to deal with it. 'At the time, I hated my family too.' His eye contact was intense. 'Their money, the millionaire lifestyle. It was all about material things with my parents, about achieving wealth and status, a good reputation, proving your worth. I came to understand that it wasn't their fault. They'd been conditioned by their own upbringing, their families, their families before them, and so on.' He shook his head, as if throwing off bad memories. 'They didn't approve of my choices then, which I can understand looking back – though it was no more of a rebellion than most of my friends were staging at the time. They still don't approve, despite all this.' He looked off to the side, a ripple of sadness on his face.

'So, why did you come over to see Rachel?' I didn't care if he was estranged from his family. 'I was told it was about …' I swallowed, determined not to utter Noah's name. 'About your son.'

He leaned forward again, fingers steepled beneath his chin, his expression earnest. 'When Rachel told me that she was pregnant six years ago, I admit I reacted badly, Jess.' I wished he wouldn't use my name. 'I wasn't ready to be a father. I'm afraid I suggested she get rid of it. Told her that she wouldn't be a good mother.' He briefly shut his eyes, as if reliving his reaction. It was a momentary reprieve, then his gaze was blazing through the screen once more. 'I'm ashamed of that, Jess. At the time, I felt she was using it to get a commitment from me that I wasn't ready for.'

'She loved you.'

'I know and it wasn't healthy. I see that now. I saw it then, actually. It was why I ended our relationship. She was too dependent.'

'But you didn't end it permanently.'

'I had strong feelings for her too. I couldn't just switch them off.'

173

'But then you did.'

'I moved on.' His gaze flicked away and back again. 'Your sister couldn't. I thought it was kinder to break contact.'

Well, she's not moving anywhere now. 'And you came to see her because?' I wished he would get to the point. I wanted to hear him recount it, to give me a clue about what had happened, about his intentions now.

'Meeting Astrid was a turning point for me.' His voice softened. 'She never wanted children – long story – but it got me thinking about the child, about whether Rachel went ahead with the pregnancy. When I told Astrid about it, after we had saved enough money to open this place, because I wanted us to be completely honest with each other, she urged me to find out. She said if there was a child, I should be present in his life.' The choke of emotion in his voice caught me by surprise. 'I realized she was right. It was time to accept some responsibility, do the right thing.' *Noah. He was talking about Noah.* 'I put out feelers and learned Rachel was living in London and got in touch—'

'Wait,' I interrupted. 'You found Rachel, not the other way round?'

'That's right.' His forehead crinkled. 'She wasn't that hard to find.'

I was taken aback. I'd assumed that Rachel sought *him* out. I had no doubt she would have tracked his whereabouts over the years, looking for a way back in, deciding Noah was the answer. But if Lucian was telling the truth, could she really have been sorting her life out instead, had wanted to meet me to talk about a reconciliation? Maybe she'd had an epiphany, as Lucian had. It would have been confusing, and I had no idea how I felt about the possibility, but didn't it make more sense than clandestine meetings under a bridge and murder? And yet ... somehow, Rachel had ended up drunk, in the canal, after meeting someone that night.

'So, you arranged to see her, and ...?' My phone pinged. Kristin, saying she was running late.

'I flew over, we had coffee—'

'At her flat?' Hannah had seen Rachel with a man in the rain, witnessed their argument in the street.

'No, at a café near the gallery where she works.'

Was he lying? Something didn't sound right about the way he said it. 'What happened?'

He hesitated. 'To be honest, Jess, she was a bit manic. She wanted to kiss me and got angry when I explained I was with Astrid now. She said she'd got the impression I wanted us to be a family; me, her, and our son.' His words made my throat burn. 'Then, when I asked if I could meet him, she became evasive and said he was being looked after by someone else while she got back on her feet.'

'Someone else?' My heart drummed against my ribs.

'Friends, she said, but … I know this sounds harsh, but Rachel was never interested in making friends in the past and she wouldn't tell me their names. To be honest, I thought she was lying, even when she showed me a photo of a little boy blowing out candles on a birthday cake.' Every inch of my skin froze. 'It could have been any child. She wouldn't even tell me his name, so I suggested doing a test to be sure.' Was *that* why Rachel had contacted me? Some crazy plan to get hold of Noah's DNA. 'She lost it after that,' Lucian continued. 'She couldn't believe I was doubting her, knowing I was the only man she would ever want a child with, that sort of thing.' I pictured it, a scene in a café, staff and customers looking on in horrified fascination, and wished I understood what had driven Rachel – why she had always made everything so difficult. 'When I insisted, she told me to go to hell, that she wished I hadn't got in touch, she'd been doing fine without me and now I'd spoiled everything.'

My head was starting to ache. 'What did you do?'

'I asked her to tell me honestly whether the boy was mine. She said I would never know and that I didn't deserve to be a father and shouldn't contact her again. I wished I hadn't if I'm honest.'

'So, you left?'

He nodded, expression sombre. 'The whole thing was a mistake. I'm not sure what game she was playing, whether she even had the baby, but if she did, I don't believe I was the father.' Regret played over his face. 'She hadn't expected me to insist on proof. When I did, her plan fell apart and she stormed out.' He looked at me squarely. 'Do you know if she went through with it? The pregnancy?'

She hadn't told him the whole truth. Unless Lucian was putting on an Oscar-worthy performance, he had no idea that Rachel had given her baby to me – which meant he couldn't have sent the letters. Not stopping to consider the ethics, I said quickly, 'No. We lost contact a long time ago. I had no idea she was pregnant.'

'I guessed that was the case.' He gave a slight shake of his head. 'I should have known, really.'

'But you thought there *could* have been a child?'

'We … reconnected around that time, in Ibiza. She was working in a club there and I was visiting with friends. It was a mistake. I told her it was a one-off, but when she got in touch through my family – my parents were furious – and told me she was pregnant, it was feasible, though we'd always been careful in the past. Neither of us ever planned on being parents. Like I said, I'm not proud of myself, but I made it clear back then that I wasn't interested and thought that was the end of it.'

He sounded so reasonable. Not angry. Not like someone who might have lost his temper with her and pushed her in the canal.

My mind shifting gears, I said, 'Did you meet with her again, at night?'

'Only once, early afternoon.' Taking my question in his stride, he added, 'I saw some old friends after Rachel, stayed overnight, and returned to France the following day.'

'And you definitely didn't meet her again?'

He shook his head, a frown gathering. 'That was the last time I saw her.' He refocused on my face, which felt too hot though my fingers were icy cold. 'We didn't part on good terms, but I hope she's doing OK, Jess. I suggested she join AA. Their programme worked for me.'

My breathing grew shallow as I realized what had been obvious from the start. He kept talking about Rachel in the present tense. 'You don't know, do you?'

His posture changed, as though he sensed what was coming. 'Know what?'

'Rachel is dead.'

Chapter 31

The momentary shock that stripped Lucian's face of expression was the final proof I needed. He'd had no involvement in Rachel's death, or with Noah.

'I assumed you knew.' *Because I thought you'd killed her.* 'She drowned in Regent's Canal.'

He lowered his hands, disbelief giving way to sadness. 'I'm so sorry. I had no idea.' But he wasn't surprised, I noted. Like the rest of us, he had suspected that Rachel's life would end tragically. 'I don't—'

'Hi, there!' A woman dipped into shot, snaking an arm around Lucian's neck, her long hair falling across his shoulder. 'I'm Astrid.' Her lips parted in a gleaming smile. 'I hope Lucian is giving you a good impression of our wonderful facilities!' Her Swedish accent was strong. 'Has he given you the tour yet?'

Lucian caught her hand and kissed her fingers, turning to whisper close to her ear. Her expression morphed into sympathy as she switched her gaze back to me, eyes so green I thought they had to be coloured lenses. 'I am so sorry for your loss,' she murmured, giving Lucian's shoulders a squeeze before moving out of frame.

Watching her go, he pushed his hands through his hair and

I saw fine lines around his eyes, caught in a pattern of sunlight, that made him look older than he'd first appeared.

'Is that why you wanted to talk to me?' He leaned close to the screen, his face composed once more. 'Am I a person of interest to the police?'

'Oh ... er, I don't think so.' I tried to maintain control of my voice. 'Nobody knew about you, or who she was meeting the night she died. It was a friend from the gallery who told me someone came looking for her. From his description, I guessed it was you.'

'I must have made a lasting impression.' His tone told me he knew it wasn't a good one. 'So, you thought I was the last person to see her alive?'

I assumed you were living in England, that you arranged to see her again, the meeting didn't go well, and you killed her. 'She died a couple of weeks after your meeting, so if you went straight back to France after that, then ... no.'

'But you think it wasn't an accident?' Before I could summon a reply, he went on, 'You know, before our meeting went sideways Rachel was chatty, talking fast as if trying to impress me, bringing me up to date with her life, and she said something odd.'

'Odd?'

'That she was being followed.' The remaining heat drained from my face. 'I asked what she meant, and she said it was fine, that she wasn't worried because she was onto them. Said she knew who it was, and it was all good.'

My heart galloped as I thought of the figure I'd seen near my old house. 'Did she know who it was?'

'To be frank, I was struggling to keep up.' A flash of bemusement crossed his face. 'I wanted to talk about the child, but she was clearly trying to put it off because ... well, you know why. That's when alarm bells starting ringing for me. I knew things weren't what they seemed.' His tone was suddenly more assertive. 'It happened in early September, right?'

I nodded, trying to organise the jumble of thoughts crashing around my head. 'The third.'

His brow relaxed. 'I was running a series of workshops that week: sunset yoga, evening mediations, forest bathing. Plenty of people can confirm I was here. I'm happy to talk to the police.'

'The investigation is closed.' A trickle of something was working its way in – the realization that Lucian wasn't Noah's father, that we wouldn't have a court case on our hands, no custody battle, was bringing a tentative relief, loosening the knots in my stomach. I still had questions – *was Rachel really being followed? Was I? Who had sent the letters?* – but a couple of big ones had been answered. 'Thank you for talking to me,' I said, formally. 'I appreciate it.'

'I'm glad you called.' His words were heartfelt, and I wondered for a second whether, like Adam, he saw Rachel's death as a line in the sand – one less piece of his past to haunt him in the future – but then he said, 'I really am sorry for everything you and your family suffered, and for my part in it.' His eyes flooded with emotion. 'I tried to persuade her to get in touch with her parents. As much as she rebelled against them, Rachel never had a bad word to say about you – even when you came looking for her, and tried to get her to go home, to sit her exams. She said she felt sorry for you but wouldn't say why.'

For some reason, this upset me. 'I wasn't the one she should have felt sorry for,' I snapped. 'She made my parents' life hell. If you hadn't invited her to your eighteenth birthday, everything might have been different.'

He fell silent and still, eyebrows raised. After a moment, he said, 'I didn't invite her, Jess. She gate-crashed the party with her friends and lied about her age.' He spoke with quiet authority. 'Maybe if I'd known she was underage, I would have sent her home, but what happened, happened. I think if it hadn't been me it would have been someone else, but I'm still sorry for the way I behaved and I'm sorry that she's gone.'

All I could manage was a stiff nod.

'I take it you won't be booking a stay at the Serenity Retreat?'

It was an effort to end on a lighter note, but despite his transformation, I couldn't quite forget that I was talking to Lucian West; the man my sister had chosen to the exclusion of everyone else. Maybe it wasn't his fault, and perhaps he wouldn't have encouraged her if she hadn't lied about her age, but the truth was, Lucian was the reason Rachel had slipped from our lives and beyond our reach. He might not have been there when she died, but there was no doubt in my mind that she wouldn't have been under the bridge that night if they'd never met.

'Bye, Lucian.' I ended the call before he could respond and fell back in my chair, freed from his gaze at last. Staring at the blank screen, I tried to work out how I was feeling but there was too much to unravel. I reached for my mug of half-drunk coffee, but it had gone cold. I took out my phone to call Adam, surprised to see it wasn't yet nine o'clock. I glanced through the window for a sighting of Kristin. Rain bounced off the road and the window-box plants drooped miserably under the onslaught. I hoped Adam had remembered Noah's coat.

'Hello?' He sounded distracted, no doubt absorbed by work.

'He isn't Noah's father.' I threw the words out like a lifeline, hoping they would rope us back together. 'He says Rachel lied to him. All she wanted was for them to get back together.'

I wished I could see the relief flooding his face. In the brief silence, I imagined him removing his glasses, gripping the bridge of his nose and inhaling deeply.

'She told him that Noah *wasn't* his child?' He sounded puzzled.

'No, she tried to convince him he was. She showed him that photo she stole, but he wanted a DNA test and she refused. He said she got angry, defensive, told him he didn't deserve to be a father and to never contact her again.'

'Wow.' I could almost hear the cogs turning but couldn't work out what he was thinking. I'd expected him to be happy, but he probably needed time to take it in. 'So, that's it?' he said at last. 'He's not going to pursue it?'

'No.'

'Because he could take a test if he wanted to be certain.'

'He is certain. He said having known Rachel for so long, he could tell when she was lying. Oh, and *he* contacted *her*, not the other way round.'

'What?'

I explained quickly, standing up on rubbery legs to switch on the lights and unlock the door, rotating my head to release the tension in my neck. There was movement out the back, the sound of a door opening and closing. *Kristin.* 'He didn't even know she was dead,' I finished, keeping my voice low. 'Let's just say, you won't need to contact Simon.'

'Sorry?'

I let out a sigh. 'You said you knew a lawyer if we needed one?'

'Oh.' He gave a short laugh. 'Thank God for that.'

'I think we can relax on that score.' *Relax.* It sounded impossible, but I wanted to end the conversation on a brighter note.

'And you're happy to let it go now?'

'There's still the anonymous letter.' *Letters.*

'For fuck's sake.'

I drew my head back. Adam never swore.

'Sorry, sorry, it's just … I want it to be over, Jess.'

'Maybe it was from Rachel.' I wasn't sure why I said it. An urge to reassure him.

'How would that work?' I heard the hope in his voice – that the letters might be easily explained, and not from Noah's *actual* biological father.

'Maybe she'd written them to send and … I don't know, gave them to someone to post in the event of her death.' It sounded ridiculous – the least likely explanation. 'Either way, whoever it is will come out of the woodwork at some point.'

'That's what I'm worried about.'

I almost told him what Lucian had said, about Rachel believing she was being followed, but Kristin was in the kitchen. She poked her head round the door and made a drinking motion. I gave her a thumbs-up, scouring her face for signs of awkwardness from the day before, but she'd already turned away.

'I have to go,' I said. 'I wanted to let you know.'

'Thanks.'

I waited a beat.

'I love you, Jess.'

'How long have you been in?' Kristin sat down and swivelled to face me. 'Looks like you've already been at the coffee.'

'I wanted to catch up on some paperwork.' I opened the company webpage as though I'd been working on it but seeing her smile drop knew I had somehow given myself away. She had dark crescents beneath her eyes as if she hadn't slept well, perhaps dwelling on her own lie. 'Actually, I had to make a call I didn't want Adam overhearing.'

Her face relaxed. 'Are you going ahead with a trip for his fortieth?'

'There's a retreat in Brittany I was looking at.' Lying by omission felt as bad. 'I'm not sure it's his thing, but a week away might do him good.'

Seeming to take my words at face value, she smiled. 'I don't think he'd like being away from Noah for that long.'

'Neither would I.'

The atmosphere eased a little. She obviously wasn't planning to revisit yesterday's conversation and I wasn't going to probe.

While she took a call, slipping into work mode, I quickly texted Will.

Spoke to Lucian. He was in France the night Rachel died, has convincing alibi. He's not Noah's father. J

He replied straight away. *That's good, about him not being related to your son.* I liked how he avoided the word 'father'. *Are*

183

you satisfied with that? She still went out to meet someone that night. Will.

I typed, *Could have been a stranger,* trying to think it through. *Maybe she matched with someone on Tinder and things turned bad.*

Possible. Doesn't make it right though.

No. And impossible to prove. It's a shame her phone wasn't found.

Probably at the bottom of the canal.

Would police have checked?

The bottom of the canal? Doubt it.

Maybe she told whoever she met about me having Noah, that it's some big secret, and they're the one sending me letters.

You've had another??

Yep. Said, 'have you told him yet?'

Jess, I'm sorry. You must be so worried.

Trying not to be, but yes. Want it to be over.

'Excuse me.'

I started, almost dropping my phone. A pair of white-haired women had materialized while I was texting, leaving the door ajar so a breeze was blowing in. 'I'm so sorry,' I said, flustered, realizing Kristin was on the phone. 'How can I help?'

With a gargantuan effort, I pushed everything else to the back of my mind and focused on work for the next few hours. It was no longer raining, and the town filled up, several people dropping in to see what was on the market. Occasionally, I was aware of Kristin casting me troubled glances, and saw how swiftly her face dropped when she thought I wasn't looking. In her black shift dress and loafers, she looked like a student, her cheeks paler than normal. I wondered whether I should say something about yesterday, but decided to let her bring it up if she wanted to.

At one o'clock, Moira came in and Kristin got up to leave.

'Would you mind getting me a sandwich if you're going to the bakery?' I asked her, reaching for my bag. My stomach growled with hunger. 'Something with chicken if they have it.'

'I've got the afternoon off to go to the dentist.' Kristin focused on tying the belt of her coat. 'A root canal filling.'

She'd mentioned a recurring toothache a while ago. I should have remembered her appointment. 'Of course,' I said. 'I'm sorry. I haven't been concentrating.'

'Don't be silly, you've had a lot on your mind.' Her gaze darted to the rear of the building, where Moira was hanging up her coat. 'Sorry,' Kristin whispered. 'I don't think she heard.'

'Don't worry about it.' Moira knew I'd had a death in the family but hadn't pressed for details. With her preference for work-only chat, the only personal comments she made were about the habits of her rescue dog, Charlie. 'Good luck with your appointment.'

'Thank you.' There was a moment of tension when our eyes locked, and she seemed on the verge of saying more, but Moira came through and Kristin left before I could say goodbye.

'You go and get a sandwich.' Moira followed Kristin's departure with a worried gaze. 'I can hold the fort until you get back.'

'Actually, I'm not that hungry,' I said with a grateful smile. 'Shall I make us some tea?'

There was a lull around 2.30, no viewings until the following day. While Moira was occupied, I found the sheet of paper with the letters I'd written down and copied them into a text to Will, adding *Hope you're good at anagrams, because …* I froze. I'd always enjoyed doing the word search puzzles my grandmother had been fond of, and a word had formed from the jumble of letters. I checked I wasn't mistaken.

It was *FATHER*. My breath stalled. It could be a reference to Noah's father. Or a reference to Dad. After checking Moira was busy, eyes skimming across her computer screen, I deleted my half-written text and after the row of letters typed, *I can see the word 'father', can you? Maybe you're onto something. Hope you're good at anagrams. J*

Chapter 32

Rachel

Before

From: RBeresford@gmail.com
To: JessSanderson11@gmail.com
Subject: Getting things off my chest

So yeah, I'm being followed. Obviously, I recognize him. The moustache did it, like an ageing Magnum PI. I watched a couple of episodes of that recently. It was so dated, but cool. I remember Mum saying it was her favourite programme growing up. That's what happens when you're trying to be sober, you start watching a lot of rubbish telly. It keeps me from having to talk to my flatmate, Hannah. We're not mates. We have zero in common, but at least she's not throwing parties every night. Not sure I'd be able to resist. I almost understand Lucian getting all yogic and mindful (yes, I stalk him secretly on Facebook, so sue me). I bought a book about it, tried it out, but fell asleep. Seems to be my default with anything 'improving'. Although, I suppose falling asleep could be classed as mindful. Maybe I want to impress him when we meet again. It's what keeps me going, the thought of us being together again. You have your boy, I have him. Always him. A curse and a blessing. Granny Beck used to say that about me because I was 'pretty'. A curse and a blessing. Silly old moo, Dad's mum. And no relation to me, it turns out. Maybe that's why we never got on. She used to look at me as though I had horns but loved you. Everyone loved you.

I don't blame them.

Chapter 33

After diverting the phones to my mobile so Moira wasn't over-whelmed with calls while I was out, I left to collect Noah from school. Adam would have done it, but it was my turn and I guessed he was keen to burrow into work now things had been resolved with Lucian.

Noah loved coming to the office, especially if Moira was there. Her demeanour softened around him, and she kept snacks in her bag just in case. Last time, she'd set him the task of drawing a picture of Charlie from a photo on her phone and was so impressed with his efforts she had it framed.

My phone rang as I walked from the car to school and half-expecting it to be Will, I was surprised to see Adam's name.

'What did you do with that poetry book?'

Thrown, I stumbled off the kerb as I passed a clutch of mums hogging the pavement. 'What did you say?'

'The poetry book has gone.'

My heart sank. 'What did you want it for?'

'It was playing on my mind, what you said about a coded message.' He sounded sheepish. 'I thought I'd have a look.'

'Oh.' A flare of relief quickly died. 'I brought it to work with me.'

'Why?'

'Same reason as you,' I said. 'I was curious.'

'Not busy today then?'

At the edge in his tone, my hackles rose. 'I could say the same to you.'

A pause was followed by a sigh. 'Touché,' he said. 'Sorry.'

'It's fine.' I wasn't in the mood for a disagreement. 'I couldn't make sense of it anyway.' Confessing I'd spotted the word *father* would only ignite more worry, possibly anger. 'You're welcome to have a go if you want to.'

'No, it's OK. It was stupid of me, especially after telling you off.' He was repentant now. 'Like I said before, I don't like the way all this is affecting us.'

'Me neither.' There was the usual huddle at the school gates. The end-of-day bell had already rung, and children were flowing out. Jasmine's mum beckoned me over with a friendly smile. 'I'd better go. We can talk later.'

'I'll crack on with dinner,' he said. 'Chicken curry and rice.'

'Sounds great!' My voice was overly cheery. '*Arrivederci.*' It was a joke from our long-ago Greek holiday, when neither of us could remember the local word for *goodbye* and had settled for the Italian version.

His chuckle sounded strained. '*Arrivederci.*'

Jasmine's mum – I did a mental roll call of the class contacts list and came up with Meredith – launched right in. 'Can Noah come round for a playdate with Jasmine after school tomorrow?'

I looked down at her eager face. 'He would love that,' I said, pushing my phone in my pocket, though in truth, I didn't want him out of my sight unless he was at school. 'It's lovely to see them getting on so well.'

'They're so sweet together.' Meredith wrinkled her nose, which was freckled like her daughter's. 'He's her first "boyfriend"' – she made air quotes – 'and I'm *so* pleased. At this age they don't discriminate, do they?'

'No, they don't.'

189

'You work in the estate agents, don't you?'

I returned her smile with an effort, half-wondering why Adam had changed his mind about the poetry book. Was not knowing Noah's full parentage starting to eat away at him? 'Cumbrian Cottages,' I said. *Estate agent* had negative connotations for a lot of people. I usually felt compelled to change people's minds if they made a face, but she was smiling.

'I would *love* to be able to afford one of those places. I look in the window sometimes and dream,' she said. 'We're due an inheritance now that my father-in-law has passed and Jack, that's my husband, has got his eye on that place in Broughton Beck.'

'Tarn Cottage?'

'That's the one.'

'It's over the market price, I'm afraid.'

'Jack reckons it's worth it.'

I thought of saying that someone was interested already, but the more I thought about it, the less certain I was that Vanessa Blake's daughter and family would ever live there. 'I can show you round sometime if you like.'

Meredith's eyes gleamed. 'I would *love* that.' Conversations were breaking up, the playground emptying. 'I'm surprised to see you, actually.'

'It's my turn to pick up Noah.' The mums were used to seeing Adam, one of the only dads who turned up on a regular basis. 'What time should we collect Noah from yours tomorrow?' I glanced at the doors. *Where was he?*

'No, I mean, Noah's already gone.' Meredith was frowning. 'I saw him go past with a woman. He was one of the first out.'

'*What?*'

Alarm ran over Meredith's face. 'Didn't you know?'

Had Jennifer picked him up? I racked my brain but knew we had no such arrangement. She lived too far away, only came to the school if she was staying with us. 'Did you see what she looked like?'

'I'm afraid I didn't take much notice.' Meredith's eyes were wide. 'He was holding her hand and chatting. It made me smile because he's always so polite.'

I was looking around me, about to run into the school, when my phone vibrated. I fumbled it from my pocket with clumsy fingers.

Relief smoothed Meredith's face. 'That's probably her, wondering where you are.' She gave a sympathetic smile before stepping towards the gates, holding her hand out to Jasmine. 'See you tomorrow.'

The text was from a number I didn't recognize.

If you want to find Noah, don't tell anyone, and don't call the police. He's safe. I want to talk.

Fingers of fear crept up my neck. Heart thudding, I started to reply but my hands were shaking so badly I had to start again. *Who are you? Where is my son?*

Go back to your car. Behave naturally.

Naturally? I frantically looked around, wanting to storm inside and demand to know who had walked out with my child. Only someone approved by Adam and me was allowed. *Don't tell anyone.* The world shrank as I tried to think, to look less panicked. I should call Adam. *No.* I didn't know what this person was capable of. *Dad?* My fingers hovered, but what if the woman could see me? She might be watching. *Where the hell was Denny?*

I raced from the playground and back to the car, fighting a tight knot of panic in my ribcage. Throwing myself into the driver's seat, I jabbed out another message. *Where is he?* My palms were slippery and the phone shot into the footwell. I retrieved it, bashing my head on the steering wheel, and read the reply.

Tarn Cottage.

My brain froze. Seeing the words so soon after talking to Meredith didn't make sense. I stared stupidly, then reality rushed in. I typed, *On my way. Alone. Please don't hurt him.*

Gunning the engine, I almost hit a black SUV as I pulled away

191

and headed towards Broughton Beck. A sob pushed out of my throat. 'Please, please, please, let him be safe.' The words ended in a storm of tears. My job was to take care of Noah. He had walked out of school with a stranger. Except ... *no*. I brushed the back of my hand over my eyes. The school wouldn't let Noah leave with someone they didn't recognize. With a jolt, I thought of Kristin, slipping out at lunchtime, claiming a dental appointment I was certain she hadn't mentioned before; the way her gaze had shifted, a final furtive glance before she left. She wasn't herself at the moment. She had lied about her mother. *What else had she lied about?* And the letters ... Could she have sent them? But why? And Kristin cared for me, I was sure of it; she cared about Adam and Noah, knew how deeply I loved my son. *And she was the only person – apart from Will – who knew I wasn't his biological mother*. And she knew Tarn Cottage. Kristin had access to the keys.

I swerved round a bend, veering into the middle of the road, and eased my foot off the accelerator. If I were to die in an accident, no one would know where to find Noah.

Remembering my phone was synced with the car, I hit the call button, but Dad's mobile went straight to voicemail and the landline was engaged. '*Shit!*' I slammed my fist on the steering wheel, fear chasing away a momentary burst of hope.

Outside the car, white clouds trailed across blue sky, sun glittering off rain-soaked leaves. It had been sunny like this the day we got Noah; cold but bright. A good omen, I'd thought at the time. I had gently lifted him out of his Moses basket and held him for the first time, marvelling at how easily he'd slotted into my arms – at the rhythmic flutter of his breath, and the soft, downy fuzz of light hair that gradually darkened. According to Rachel's note, he was seven pounds and six ounces, and I'd studied every centimetre, from his tiny, wrinkled feet, to his chubby hands and perfect, cupid's bow mouth. When his eyes sought mine, my heart had overflowed. In that split-second, I had a flash of recognition, a sense that I had always known him, had been waiting for him. *You're my son,* I'd whispered, rocking gently, reluctant to relinquish him to Adam, waiting impatiently for his turn. *Oh, God.* If Adam knew about this. He would call the police, and I couldn't risk it.

Infused with fresh panic, I bounced the car over the tiny bridge in Broughton Beck, through the village and out the other side, almost missing the turn to the cottage. I slammed my foot on the brakes, forcing the car to round the corner at the last second. *Hang on, Noah. I'm nearly there.*

My teeth chattered as adrenaline flooded my body, but my forehead was damp with sweat. I drove as fast as I dared down the winding road to the cottage hidden at the end, and even before I saw the car, parked by the gate, I knew who had taken Noah – realized I'd known from the start. I just didn't understand why.

Chapter 34

She was round the back, sitting at the patio table, a dreamy smile on her face as she watched Noah pushing himself on the swing.

When he saw me, he leapt down and ran across the grass. 'Mummy, you're here!'

'Of course I'm here, sweetheart.' Kneeling, I wrapped him in my arms, pressing my lips together to stop myself crying, trying to calm my breath.

'I thought you wasn't coming.'

Holding him at arm's length, I searched his face and smoothed his hair. 'I was a bit late. I'm sorry, Buttercup.'

'Muuu-um.' He did his usual pretend scowl.

'Sorry.' I pushed a wobbly smile to my lips. 'Ninja Turtle.'

'You look funny, Mummy.' He tipped his head, eyes scrunched. 'Your face is red.'

'That's because I was running, so I could get here.' I tugged down his school jumper, resisting the urge to pull him to me again. 'Where's your rucksack?'

'In there.' He pointed to the house. 'Lady got me an orange juice.'

How the hell did she get in? 'That's nice.'

'She's going to live here, and she wanted me to go on the swing

194

to see if it worked while we waited for you, and she might have a dog. Can we get a dog, Mummy?'

'We'll have to think about that.' My mouth was dry, my breath too fast. 'Have another go on the swing while I talk to … the lady.'

'Will you watch me?'

I nodded, blinking back tears at the sight of his earnest expression. 'Be careful.'

When he'd returned to the swing and hoisted himself up, I dragged my gaze to Vanessa. She was watching me through narrowed eyes.

I moved closer, out of Noah's earshot. 'How dare you bring him here under false pretences!' I wanted to grab her, throw her to the ground, throttle her with my bare hands, but sat down at the other side of the table where I could see Noah. 'I don't know what kind of sick game you're playing, but you won't get away with it.'

'Look at him, having fun.' Her voice was sing-song, and although her expression was filled with affection, it was oddly removed – as though she wasn't seeing Noah but someone else.

'How did you get in here?'

'Oh.' Seeming surprised by the question, she glanced over her shoulder at the half-open sliding door. 'I didn't close it properly the last time.'

I should have checked. 'You planned this.' My mind reeled with realization. 'The whole thing was a set-up.'

'It was good of you to give me your number.' She gave a tinkling laugh. 'You're very trusting. Like your son.' Her eyes returned to Noah. 'Only … he's not your son, is he, Jessica?'

My stomach turned. 'Of course he is.'

'Come on now. Don't pretend you don't know what I'm talking about.' Her tone was chastising, as though I was a naughty child. With her hands folded in her lap, hair drawn back in a silver clasp, and a floaty scarf trailing over her top and wide-legged trousers, she looked utterly respectable.

195

'You sent me those letters.'

'Well?' She turned to look at me, raising her eyebrows. 'Have you told him the truth? He deserves to know.'

'It's none of your business.'

'I have rights.'

'Rights?' My eyes flicked from Vanessa to Noah, who was swinging higher. I wanted to grab him and run, but felt pinned to the chair. 'I don't understand.'

'I want to spend time with my grandson.'

The world tilted. 'Grandson?'

She turned to look at me fully, ice-blue eyes like lasers. I had the feeling of vertigo I'd experienced the first time we met, the sense that I knew her, and suddenly understood.

'You're Lucian's mother.'

She inclined her head. 'Not that you'd know it. He hasn't spoken to me in years.'

Numb with shock, I stammered, 'I ... I don't know what you're saying.'

'Mummy, can I get down now?'

'Come and drink your juice,' Vanessa called in a syrupy tone. 'Then you can sit with us.'

Anger took flight in my chest. 'I don't want Noah hearing any of this.'

When he reached the table he paused, looking from my face to Vanessa's as though seeking reassurance.

'Go and wash your hands, sweetheart,' I said calmly. A daily request he was used to hearing. 'Do you know where the downstairs toilet is?'

He nodded. 'I had a wee when we got here.'

When Vanessa smiled indulgently, I wanted to scream at her to stop looking at Noah, stop talking to him as though she had a right to. I waited until he'd gone inside, trailing damp footprints across the wooden floor, before saying, 'You took him out of school.'

She crossed her legs and wrapped her hands around her knee.

'Too easy.' Her voice held a hint of disapproval. 'I had my meeting with the lovely head teacher, made sure it was close to home time. On the way out, I explained to Noah's teacher that his mother was taking an important work call and had asked if I would walk him to her car.' She shook her head. 'She didn't bat an eyelid.'

And Denny hadn't taken notice. It was easy to see why. Vanessa was well-spoken, polite, clearly had money. How could she be a liar, a kidnapper? A choking fury filled my throat. I should report the teacher.

'I could have taken him from your house and disappeared the other night,' she said. 'But you're rather good at locking up.'

'Oh my God … *you* were the monster.'

Her laugh held no humour. 'I wouldn't go that far,' she said. 'I'm no monster.'

'Noah saw you in the garden.'

'Ah, yes. I think my torchlight woke him up. He clearly needs a lesson in stranger danger,' Vanessa continued. 'But then, I'm not a stranger.'

'You're not his grandmother.' I shot to my feet. 'I spoke to your son this morning, as it happens. He met with Rachel before she died, was under the same illusion you are – or he was, until they spoke. She lied about Noah to get Lucian to meet her. She wanted him back.'

For a second, Vanessa's composure slipped. 'That's rubbish.' She bent to take something from the leather bag at her feet. 'He looks exactly like Lucian at that age.' She held out a photo, but I refused to look. She was deluded, trying to relive the past, make up for being an awful parent.

'How did you know about Noah?'

'I knew there was a child, that your sister' – she spat the word – 'tried to trap my son by getting pregnant, or that's what he told us. She called us you see, to ask for his number, took great delight in telling me I was going to be a granny' – she ground the word out. 'I was so angry because I thought they were over for good. I

197

didn't know Lucian's number at that time, so she must have got it from one of his friends, but he called to ask me what she'd said. We only spoke briefly. He confirmed she was pregnant, but said he wasn't interested in becoming a father. I thought it was for the best, back then.' Her eyes flickered down. 'I wasn't ready to be a grandmother ... not under those circumstances. But since losing Lucian' – she made it sound as though he'd died – 'I've thought about the baby more and more often. I wanted to make amends, do the right thing. And I thought the child might bring Lucian back.' Someone else using Noah to get what they wanted when it was convenient. Vanessa and Rachel had more in common than she realized. 'It could be the making of him, but Noah needs to know the truth about who his father really is.'

'Shame it's not Lucian.'

'You're forgetting, I spoke to your sister at the time. There's no doubt in my mind she was telling the truth, no matter what she might have told you since.'

'She was lying.'

Vanessa's face pinched with anger. 'Believe me, I would rather it had been anyone but her,' she said coldly. 'She was like a virus, poisoning my son.'

'Hang on.' I was shocked by her venom, even as a treacherous voice whispered, *You felt the same about Lucian.* 'It's not like he was blameless and didn't have a mind of his own.'

'She was a drunk.'

'So was he, and don't talk about Rachel as though she was scum from some awful, deprived background. We did everything we could to bring her back to us, to help her. What did *you* do? You and your husband were never around, too busy with your important lives, too busy making money.' I drew a breath and sat down again. 'You weren't interested in Lucian because he wasn't like you. You left him to his own devices, didn't care what he was up to. You disowned him. Rachel had a loving home to come back to.'

'Yet she chose not to.'

I couldn't argue with that. I watched Noah in the kitchen area, reaching for a glass of liquid on the counter. 'Rachel died,' I said. 'Obviously, you know that.'

'There was a piece on the local news.' Vanessa's anger died as quickly as it had flared. 'When I heard that name ...' She gave a dramatic shudder and I realized it wasn't possible for us to ever see the past from the same side. For her, Rachel was the reason her son no longer spoke to her; for us, Lucian had been the one to take Rachel away.

'I decided to take things further,' Vanessa said. 'I found out where the funeral was being held and thought I might speak to one of you, see if you had any information about the child.'

My mind swam with confusion. 'You came to the service?'

She shook her head, a coil of hair springing loose. 'I watched you turn up with your little family. As soon as I saw the boy, I knew.' She clicked her fingers, miming something falling into place. 'Her sensible big sister took on the baby.'

Noah was walking towards the doors now, taking tiny steps, the glass of juice clasped between both hands. My heart squeezed with love. I would rather die than let Vanessa anywhere near him.

'I know what you believe, but you're wrong. He is *not* your grandson.' My voice cracked. 'Please, leave us alone.'

'I want access.' She tilted her chin. 'I want him to come and stay with me. I have a lot to offer. I could pay for private—'

'He is *not* your grandchild,' I repeated, stronger this time. 'Noah isn't related to you. Speak to Lucian. He'll tell you.'

She was shaking her head again. 'He won't talk to me. And I don't need his permission. He might have forfeited his rights, but I know mine.'

'I'll call him.' I scrabbled my phone out, brought up the webpage I'd found only two days ago. 'Wait there, Noah,' I said as he reached the door. He froze, poised with the glass like a statue. I found the Serenity number and pressed call. 'Lucian

West, please,' I said to the woman who answered, cutting her introduction short. 'It's urgent.'

I tried to smile at Noah, as though we were playing a game.

'Mummy, can I put my drink down?'

I nodded and he placed it carefully on the floor.

'Hello?' Lucian sounded cautious.

'It's Jess Sanderson. I have your mother here. She took my son from his school today. She believes he's her grandchild and is demanding access.'

'What?' Shock resonated down the line. 'Jess, I—'

'Can you talk to her?' I handed my phone to Vanessa, who took it and, without moving her eyes from mine, cut the call, and handed it back.

'He won't be truthful,' she said sadly. 'He never wanted to be a father. He made that abundantly clear. He's lost to me, but I have my grandson now.' My phone started ringing, but Vanessa had turned to look through the glass at Noah. 'I won't leave without him.'

'No!' As she moved forward, I pushed myself between her and the door, arms spreadeagled. 'Stay away from him.'

'Mummy?' Noah's voice was querulous.

'It's OK, sweetheart, we're playing hide and seek.' A surge of hatred rose. How dare she invade his innocent world and bring him here, telling him lies?

'I'm going to find a hidey-place,' he said cautiously.

'Good idea!' I infused my voice with enthusiasm, shifting to the side so Vanessa couldn't get past me. 'I'll count to twenty.' My phone stopped ringing and started again. 'Lucian will call the police,' I said to Vanessa.

'They'll understand once I've had time to explain.'

'You can't have him because you want a second chance at being a mother.'

Her arm shot out and she struck me across the face. 'You little bitch.'

200

I gasped, hand flying to my cheek. 'Get away from me.' I ground the words through gritted teeth, tears spilling down my burning face. 'Noah is not your grandson.'

Her hand reached past me for the door. 'We'll let the courts prove that.'

'You won't have to.' A familiar voice cut through the air. 'Get away from my daughter or I'll call the police right now.'

My heart slammed against my chest. 'Dad!' He'd come around the side of the house and was standing on the patio, waving a sheet of paper. 'This is all the proof you need,' he said. 'Your son isn't Noah's father.'

'Grandpa!' Hearing Dad's voice, Noah charged out from wherever he'd been hiding and wriggled through the gap in the door. 'I was playing hide and seek!'

'Noah, wait!' I called, wiping tears from my face, but Dad had dipped to his knee to catch him, his forearm gripped around Noah's back.

Vanessa's hands clenched at her sides. 'I remember you coming to our home,' she said slowly to Dad. 'You ordered us to keep my son away from your daughter.' Her face sagged. She looked years older. 'It would have been like trying to stop the weather.'

'You didn't even try, didn't care.' Dad's tone was measured, but his eyes were glacial. 'You threatened to have *me* arrested that time, as I recall.'

He came home that day with a defeated slope to his shoulders, barely able to look Mum in the eye. *I tried.*

I crossed the patio and rested my hand on Noah's hair, relishing the silky texture beneath my fingers. He turned, throwing himself at my legs. 'I don't like it here.' I lifted him up and held him tight, felt the rapid beat of his heart, his hot breath on my neck. 'I want to go home, Mummy.'

Blinking back fresh tears, I said, 'We're going very soon, I promise.'

Vanessa strode over and plucked the piece of paper from Dad's

201

outstretched fingers. Dismay filled her face as she scanned the document. 'DNA test results.'

My arms stiffened around Noah. I looked at Dad, but his attention was focused on Vanessa.

'How did you get this?' She tossed the paper to the ground, where a gust of wind caught it and blew it along the path.

'I had ways.'

'Illegal, no doubt.' Vanessa's voice lacked emotion. 'You're the type, aren't you, Mr Beresford?'

'And what you've done is legal?' Dad pulled himself to his full height, towering over Vanessa. 'Go home, Mrs West.'

'I'm divorced.' Her eyes looked glassy. 'I prefer the surname I was born with.'

'Handy, when you're pretending to be someone you're not,' I couldn't help saying, but her gaze drifted past me as if I hadn't spoken. Perhaps she was wondering how to explain all of this to Lucian. My phone was ringing once more. Keeping hold of Noah, I grabbed it off the table where I'd dropped it. 'It's OK,' I said, before Lucian could speak. 'She's going home now.' I hung up before he could reply. It was for them to sort out now.

'And don't come back,' Dad said.

'Why is Grandpa being mean to the lady?' Noah lifted his head, his eyes shiny with tears.

'Oh, sweetheart.' I kissed his cheek. 'Grandpa's cross because the lady shouldn't have picked you up from school. But it's OK. She's going back to her own house today and we won't see her again.'

I threw her a pointed look and she backed away, sinking her knees as her fingers scrambled for her bag. Straightening, she smoothed her scarf with a trembling hand. 'I would be grateful if this didn't go any further.'

'That's up to you,' Dad said grimly. Turning, he gave Noah a reassuring smile. 'Say bye-bye to the lady.'

'Bye.' Noah gave her a little wave that broke my heart. 'Thank you for the juice,' he added politely.

Vanessa barely glanced up, as if wanting nothing to do with him now that she knew he wasn't related to her. Or maybe she'd come to her senses and realized how close she was to being arrested.

We watched in silence as she picked her coat off the chair and looped it through the handles of her bag. She patted her hair and squared her shoulders before walking back the way she'd come, leaving, once more, without looking back.

Chapter 35

'Is this genuine?' Back at Dad's, I waved the document I'd retrieved from the garden at Tarn Cottage. I had so many questions, I barely knew where to start. 'I don't understand how you got it.'

'Let me make some tea and I'll explain.'

When he'd gone through to the kitchen, I sat on the sofa then got up, needing to pace around to work off the stress. Noah had shot upstairs after Tiger, seeming none the worse for his ordeal, easily distracted by the cat and a promise of chocolate cake.

After Vanessa had left, I'd checked the house while Dad gave Noah a push on the swing in an effort to restore normality, before securing the door and returning to the car. Dad's Aston Martin had been parked haphazardly, the driver's door still open, and Noah had insisted he wanted to go in Grandpa's car. There had been no opportunity to talk. I'd followed them back to Rosside, mind buzzing, calling Moira on the way to tell her something had cropped up and I wouldn't be coming back to the office. To her credit, she took it in her stride, explaining that Kristin had returned after her appointment, which turned out to be a small filling, and everything was fine. I went hot with guilt at how easily I'd suspected Kristin of taking Noah. I debated calling Adam but couldn't face the barrage of questions and accusations he was bound to unleash, especially as I hadn't got everything straight in my mind. The main thing was that Noah was safe, Vanessa no longer a threat, and no one would ever walk out of school with Noah again once I'd spoken to the head teacher.

I looked again at the document in my hand, crinkled around the edges from being blown around the garden at Tarn Cottage. My eyes strayed to the box at the bottom of the page.

Lucian West is excluded as the biological father of Noah Sanderson. This conclusion is based on the non-matching alleles observed at the STR loci listed above with a DI equal to 0. The probability of paternity is 0%.

There were columns of numbers and letters above, none of which made sense, but the result was irrefutable. Tears of relief sprang to my eyes. It was so good to know for certain.

I heard Dad run upstairs and say, 'Cake for Sir Noah,' in a theatrical voice and knew he was playing for time.

'What would you make of this, Mum?' I looked at the photograph on top of the piano, where she smiled out at me from our living room in Barnes. 'I wish I could talk you properly.'

Finally, Dad came through with two mugs of tea and placed them on the windowsill. Digging his hands in his trouser pockets he peered out at the garden. 'I'm definitely going to make a start out there tomorrow.'

'Dad.' He glanced at me sideways, a hunted look on his face. 'The paternity test. How did you get it?'

'Do you really need to know?'

'You must have broken the law if Lucian doesn't know about it.'

'How do you know he doesn't?'

'Did you break the law?' I persisted.

He turned so I couldn't read his face and was quiet for so long, I thought he wasn't going to answer. 'Only by proxy.'

'What does that mean?'

He paused, as if weighing up what to say next, and briefly met my eyes. 'Denny.'

Of course it was Denny. Hadn't I turned to him myself?

'Right.' I couldn't work out how I felt.

'Don't look at me like that,' Dad said. 'When Rachel gave Noah to you, I wanted to know for sure that waster wasn't the father, that he wasn't going to cause trouble.'

'So you got an illegal paternity test.'

'There are ways if you know what you're doing,' he said.

I didn't want details but had to know one thing. 'Noah. How did you—?'

'A cheek swab.' His words came quickly, a hand waving them away. 'He was only a few months old. You were taking a nap, I was babysitting. Adam was at work. It was fast, didn't hurt, and he won't remember it.'

I was speechless. This had happened without me knowing, never guessing for one second my father – always on hand to babysit his precious grandson – was capable of such deception. *You saw what you wanted to see, like you always did where your dad was concerned.* Caroline's words rang loud in my ears.

'I'm sorry, Jess. I thought it was for the best.' He looked contrite. 'Insurance, if you like, in case that waste of space somehow found out and came asking questions.' He ran a hand across his face. 'I wanted to protect my family.'

Hating to see him vulnerable, I tried to reframe his words. He'd broken the law, yes, but he'd done it for me, for Noah. 'You should have told me. I wondered about Lucian too and all this time, you had this.' I thrust the printout at him.

'You never asked.' He took a step back, knocking his mug with his elbow. 'If you had, I would have told you.'

Really? 'I spoke to Lucian this morning.' I might as well tell him. 'I got it into my head he had something to do with Rachel's death,' I said. 'He came to see her.' Dad didn't react. 'I worked out that it was Lucian and tracked him down.'

'Sounds like you've been going behind my back too.'

'I didn't want to worry you.' When he gave me a pointed look, I said, 'OK, I get it.'

'What did he have to say for himself?'

'Rachel had him believing he was Noah's father. She even stole a photo from our house. She was there, Dad.' His face jolted with shock. 'And all because she wanted Lucian back.' My voice had risen, and I lowered it, mindful of Noah upstairs. 'If I'd known about this' – I crumpled the sheet of paper in my fist – 'it would have saved a lot of heartache. I wouldn't have got in touch with him and stirred things up.' When Dad didn't speak, continuing to stare out of the window, my anger grew. 'Adam and I have fallen out about all this. Things are weird between us and all because …' I trailed off. 'You knew, didn't you?'

His head whipped round. 'Knew?'

'That I went to London and spoke to Will Taylor,' I said. 'You had Denny follow me, didn't you?'

Turning, he gripped my shoulders, a fierce look in his eyes. 'I was worried about you, Jess. When you asked me last week if I thought your sister's death was really an accident … you had this look on your face. I had a feeling you weren't going to let it lie. I dropped into your office last Friday morning. I'd been to the bakery and that girl you work with told me you were in London. She seemed … furtive, as though she didn't want me to know.'

'So, you asked Denny to keep an eye on me and report back. Is that it?' I wrenched out of his grasp, remembering the feeling I'd had that he didn't believe me when I told him about my trip. 'You could have said. I thought whoever pushed Rachel into the canal was after me—'

'*Pushed* her?' He paled. 'Is that what you think happened?'

'I don't know.' I pulled my hands through my hair. 'Maybe.'

'This Will Taylor. What's he got to do with anything?'

'He's a concerned friend, that's all.'

'And he put these doubts in your mind?'

I nodded, not liking Dad's darkening expression. 'He wanted

to talk it through, but he knows now that Lucian had nothing to do with Rachel's death. He wasn't even in the country that night.'

'But you still think she was killed?'

I didn't like the way he was breathing, how his hand had covered his chest. Dad wasn't fragile, but he wasn't a young man either. He'd suffered unimaginable losses, been brought to his knees by grief. If I told him about the letters in the poetry book among Rachel's things, how even as we spoke Will was trying to decipher them, convinced something didn't add up ... it might kill him. 'There's no evidence,' I said, banishing the image of Sam that flew into my mind. 'It must have been an accident.'

He nodded slowly, his colour returning. 'Don't be angry with me, Jess. I—'

'Wait.' I was struck by something. 'Was Denny following Rachel?' My thoughts lost themselves once more in a labyrinth of questions. 'Did Denny ... Did he see what happened that night, Dad?'

'Did Uncle Denny get your sister drunk and push her in Regent's Canal?' Dad looked at me with horror etched on his face. 'You think he's capable of something like that, Jess?'

'No, of course not.' His expression brought me to my senses. But I thought how readily Denny had agreed to help me and keep it from Dad. How, at Dad's bidding, he'd bolted to London to follow me when he was supposed to be watching Noah. 'Of course he wouldn't, I'm sorry. But he was following her, wasn't he?'

Dad sank heavily into the armchair. 'I can see you think less of me, but—'

'I don't.' I dropped to my knees in front of him and took his hands in mine. They were cold and slightly clammy. 'I'm having a hard time getting my head around it, that's all. I'm trying to understand.'

His eyes were damp, his mouth working, and I wanted to tell him it didn't matter, that I knew he'd had his reasons, but he started talking again. 'I wanted to know why she was back, that's all. I could pretend she was happy in Thailand or India, or wherever, having a great time. I tried to get on with my life, but then she came back to London.'

'How did you know?'

'I had Denny keep an eye on the databases. You know, she was in the system because of that shoplifting business, and the time she ran away from rehab.' I nodded. 'Her name came up at the beginning of the year. She was arrested and fined for drunken behaviour. Denny made it go away – he's still got contacts in the force – then kept an eye out. She kept her head down after that, got a job. I couldn't understand why she was back. I wanted to know …' He broke off, looking at our joined hands as if saying the rest was too hard.

I let go, resting my arms on his knees like I used to when I was a child and he read to me. 'I think I understand.' And suddenly, I did. 'You were hoping she might be on her way back to us.'

He closed his eyes, chin dropping. 'When you told me she'd emailed you out of the blue, that she wanted to meet, to talk—'

'You thought she was hoping for a reconciliation,' I said. 'So did I, Dad.' I couldn't – wouldn't – tell him I'd been scared she was coming for Noah. Dad had wanted his younger daughter back, of course he had, but hadn't quite dared believe it. 'It's OK.' I leaned over and gently kissed his forehead, wanting to wipe the haunted look from his face. 'I mean, I don't condone how you've gone about things, but I get why you did it.' Even so, a slither of unease uncoiled in my stomach. Sam had bumped into a figure hurrying away from the bridge that night. Could Denny have seen Rachel fall, recognized the person she had met with? Perhaps he'd thought it better to keep quiet, knowing how devastated Dad would be if the truth came out that whoever it was had pushed her.

Another thought struck. 'How did you know I was at Tarn Cottage?' When Dad's face sagged, I wished I could stop asking questions and let him off the hook, but I had to know. 'Denny?'

He nodded, wearily. 'You know he's been up this way on a fishing trip?'

I nodded. So Denny hadn't told Dad everything. 'He was on his way over to see me and passed you coming out of Ulverston. He said you were driving recklessly and looked upset.' He must have been near the school. 'He followed you there and overheard that woman telling you Noah was her grandson.' I sat back on my heels, taking it in. 'He called me, said I should get up there quickly. I knew it had to be her, *his* mother.' He couldn't say Lucian's name. 'So I found the document and drove up.'

'It's a good job you did.' For the first time, I allowed myself to wonder what would have happened if he hadn't. 'I really think she was planning to grab Noah and take off with him.'

'She wouldn't have got very far.' Dad slapped his knees and stood up. He looked better, more animated. 'She didn't think it through, did she? Even if she had been his grandmother, a charge of kidnapping would have put paid to access.' His tone was derisive. 'I doubt we'll hear from her again.'

'I hope not,' I said. 'I'll have a word with the school tomorrow. She should never have been allowed to take Noah out.'

And Denny should have spotted something was wrong. Maybe he was losing his touch.

Noah thundered downstairs wearing a ghostly chocolate moustache, trailed by Tiger. 'Finished my cake,' he said, looking hopefully at his grandfather. 'Can we see the fishes?'

'Not now, Ninja.' I picked his rucksack up off the floor and hugged him. 'It's time to go home, young man.' Adam would be cooking dinner. Our conversation from earlier seemed a hundred years ago.

'You don't have to tell him.' Dad clearly hadn't lost the knack of knowing my thoughts, but I didn't like the collusive glint in his eyes. Maybe if I lied – or withheld the truth – he would feel better about his own deceits.

I turned away, helping Noah thread his arms in the sleeves of his coat.

'Ruth's coming round later.' Dad blurted it like a confession, perhaps wanting to say something honest. 'I like her.'

'I'm glad,' I said.

'Grandpa's got a girlfriend,' Noah sang.

We smiled and Dad playfully swiped his hair. 'It's going to be OK,' he said softly, wrapping me in a hug on the doorstep. 'Look after the boy. That's all that matters.'

'I will.' I hugged him back, but as I drove home, glancing at Noah in the rear-view mirror every few seconds, I had the weirdest feeling the worst was yet to come.

Chapter 36

'You weren't keen on the curry, then?'

I placed my bowl in the dishwasher, shoulders tensing. 'I wasn't very hungry.'

'I got a bit carried away with the spices,' Adam said. 'Noah seemed to enjoy it.'

'It's good for him to try new things.'

'I didn't eat a proper curry until I was 28.'

'I know.' I turned to him, realizing he was trying to connect after my hushed confession about Vanessa taking Noah, believing he was her grandson – the fact that she was Lucian's mother, and had sent the anonymous letter. Seeing Adam's face pale, I found myself playing it down, even saying how sorry Vanessa was, and making more of Dad coming to the rescue as if to put him in a good light. Expecting fury – at Vanessa, at me for letting our son be taken, at Dad for not revealing he'd known that Lucian wasn't Noah's father – I was surprised when, after a breathless silence, a sheen of hope filled his eyes.

'I knew there was something off when Noah told us she questioned him in the playground,' he said. 'She's obviously unhinged, but at least she didn't hurt him.'

I couldn't believe he was being so reasonable. 'But if Dad had told us in the first place that—'

'It's over, Jess.' His smile was like a light coming on. 'Oh my God, it's over and we don't have to talk about any of this again.' I smiled hesitantly as he pressed his hands onto my hips. 'Let's get him in from the garden and have dinner.'

And that had been that as far as Adam was concerned, the lid slammed shut on the topic.

Now, I tried to smile as I responded to his comment. 'Yes, I know. You had a terribly deprived palate and it made you wonder what you'd been missing all those years.' I half-wished Noah wasn't tucked up asleep in bed now, leaving us alone.

'Come here.' Adam curled a beckoning finger. 'You look like you need a hug.' I moved into his arms – more so he couldn't keep searching my face as if checking we were on the same page. 'Noah doesn't seem affected at all, does he?'

I waited for him to ask more questions – why hadn't I called him on the way to Tarn Cottage? How had Dad known we were there? Had Lucian called me back? – but he'd clearly been serious about not discussing it again.

'No,' I said truthfully. 'But we'll need to keep a close eye on him.'

I already knew I wasn't going to tell Adam about Denny. It was a step too far, something he wouldn't understand, Dad having his daughters followed. He would see it as a betrayal and it was, in a way, but I knew what was in Dad's heart, what family meant to him. Adam would go to any lengths to protect Noah – we both would – but he might draw the line at 'spying'. Even so, I was uncomfortable with how economical I'd been with the truth. In order to protect Adam, I had isolated myself from him.

'You've had quite a day,' he said, letting me go – as if I'd told him about a difficult client at work. I closed my eyes and heard the suck of the fridge door opening. 'Fancy a beer?'

'Not for me, thanks.' A gnawing desire for sleep was growing, for the sort that would pull me under for at least eight hours. 'I'm going to have a shower.'

Adam nodded, flicking the top off a beer bottle. 'Good idea.' Tipping his head back, he took a long swig then wiped his mouth on the back of his hand. Despite his cheerful tone, he looked tired and scruffy in mismatched socks, hair curling over the collar of his polo shirt. 'I thought I'd take Noah to Mum's on Saturday.' *I*, not *we*. He dangled the bottle at his side. 'We haven't been there for a while.'

'Boys' trip?'

'I can take him to the nature reserve. He loves it there.'

'You don't want my company?'

'Isn't it your Saturday at work?' He nodded to the wall-planner by the fridge, dates blocked in different colours; green for Noah – I'd already added the playdate with Jasmine tomorrow – blue for Adam, orange for me.

'It's Kristin's turn.' He must have looked, had surely known I wasn't working. 'I like the nature reserve too.' I loved seeing Noah there, his excitement at spotting an owl, or a roe deer peering through a shrub.

Adam shrugged, tracing his thumbnail in a figure eight on the worktop. 'OK, come with us.' The trace of irritation was faint but unmistakeable.

'No, it's fine,' I said, understanding he wanted to spend time alone with Noah – 'bonding time' he called it. 'I've lots of stuff to catch up on.'

He picked up his phone, glanced at the screen, and winced. 'Problem with the server,' he said, ploughing a hand through his hair. 'I'd better make a call.'

'OK.' I smiled as he brushed past, but his mind had clearly switched gears and he didn't respond. He was still in his study after I'd showered, his voice a low murmur, the light from his computer screen bright where the door was ajar. I went to check on Noah, adjusting his duvet and gently kissing his forehead before double-checking his window was firmly closed.

On the way back I peered round the study door to see Adam stooped over his desk, head cradled in his hands. Something about his posture stopped me going to him – a sense that whatever it was, he wouldn't welcome being disturbed.

I got ready for bed and climbed under the duvet with a book, but my head ached, and my mind wouldn't settle, circling around and finally landing on Rachel. Wasn't the simplest explanation usually the right one? She had slipped and fallen into the canal.

I checked my phone, but there was nothing from Will. I typed out a text.

I have to accept that Rachel's death was an accident and let it go. I'm sorry. J

When I eventually drifted to sleep, Adam still hadn't come to bed.

'I can't believe she walked out with him.' Horror widened Kristin's eyes. 'Or that the school didn't double-check with you.'

'Apparently, it all happened fast because the bell went and the children were coming out of their classes and suddenly she was there, reaching for Noah's hand, saying I was waiting in the car and Miss Everly didn't think there was a problem.'

I'd joined Kristin in the office kitchen before we opened up and recounted what the head teacher had told Adam and me when we took Noah to school. She called in the support teacher Miss Everly, whose frightened and tearful reaction had reassured us it had been a mistake she would never make again.

'She said that Vanessa seemed so nice and normal, it didn't occur to her that she wasn't a friend of mine.'

Denny had messaged an apology overnight. *I'm sorry I let you down, Jess. D*

At least he'd seen me shoot off in the car and called Dad, but I couldn't forgive him for trailing me to London even if – like Dad – he'd done what he thought was right.

'God, you must have been terrified.' Kristin's eyes were wide, as though picturing the dash to Tarn Cottage.

'I was.' The scene had seemed like a nightmare on waking that morning, fear turning to relief. *Noah was safe.* 'I don't think she would have hurt him, but ... I can't be sure. As soon as she knew he wasn't her grandson, she lost interest.'

'Sounds like she needs a lot of therapy.' Kristin was still in her coat, a jar of coffee in one hand. 'She's obviously not well to have behaved like that in the first place.'

'I'm not ready to feel sorry for her,' I said abruptly. I'd wanted to confide in Kristin, hoping it showed I trusted her, but she didn't have children. She couldn't fully understand.

'I'm sorry.' Kristin winced, as if in tune with my thoughts. 'She was lucky you didn't have her arrested.'

'Hopefully, we won't hear from her again.' I'd half-expected Lucian to make contact, but suspected he was as keen as I was to distant himself from Vanessa and the whole situation. If he knew from his mother that I'd lied about Rachel not having the baby, he either understood why, or didn't want to know. 'It's as well my dad's friend was keeping an eye on things,' I said without thinking.

'An eye on things?' Putting down the jar of coffee, Kristin gave me a startled look.

I tried to laugh it off. 'I know it sounds a bit creepy, but we have this family friend who was in the police force for a long time and does private investigation work. He spotted me driving to the cottage and told Dad.'

'He was following you?'

'Not then ... not exactly. He was keeping an eye out for Noah.'

'Not *then?*' Kristin's skin drained to a sickly pallor. 'You mean he's followed you before?'

I sighed, wishing I hadn't brought it up. 'Dad told him I was in London last Friday and had him look out for me. I thought I was being followed while I was there but—' Kristin clamped a hand to her mouth as though she was going to be sick. 'What is it?'

'Oh, Jess, I'm sorry. I shouldn't have told him you'd gone into London.' She burst into noisy tears. 'I've been feeling bad about it ever since, but he kind of demanded to know where you'd gone.'

I fished in my pocket for a tissue but couldn't find one. 'Kristin, it's fine,' I said. 'I didn't tell you *not* to tell him.' I touched her shaking shoulder. 'I didn't think he'd come in here.'

'I wouldn't have mentioned it if I'd thought you didn't want him to know.'

'But you didn't know that. It's fine, I promise.' I grabbed a paper towel from the basket by the sink and thrust it at her. 'He only told me about it because when he turned up at the cottage yesterday, I asked how he knew I was there, and it all came out. He'd been following Rachel in London too, after she came back to London.'

'God, that's awful.' Kristin dabbed her eyes then blew her nose. I'd never seen her so upset.

'Not really,' I said. 'He was hoping that Rachel was on her way home. He wanted to check she was OK.'

A fresh bout of tears erupted. 'Kristin, please. Don't cry.' When I tried to hug her, she squirmed away. 'It's fine, really. You don't have to be upset on my behalf. It sounds extreme, but that's Dad, his way of trying to protect us.'

'It didn't work for your sister.' Her words were muffled by the paper towel. 'How come it didn't stop her dying?'

I tried to smile, but inside my heart was pounding. 'He wasn't having her followed all the time.' I spoke with a brightness I didn't feel. 'We'll never know for sure what happened, but I think it's most likely Rachel went to meet someone who didn't turn up, got drunk and took a walk along the canal, and … she fell in.' It sounded as though I was trying to reassure myself.

'That man you talked to, he didn't think so.' Kristin's eyes were blurry. 'He didn't think it was an accident.'

'Will?' I swallowed. 'I didn't say that.'

'It's why you went there, isn't it? To talk to him.'

I couldn't look away. 'Yes, but he was wrong.'

'Are you sure?' She sounded scared, like a child.

I nodded with as much conviction as I could muster. 'As sure as I can be.'

She looked at the sodden ball of paper in her hand, chewing her bottom lip. I could sense her balancing something in her mind, trying to decide what to say next.

Wanting to put her out of her misery, I said, 'Look, Kristin, it hasn't been fair of me to bring my personal problems to work, and if you've felt under pressure because of that, I'm sorry.' I risked laying a hand on her arm. She didn't pull away. 'Let's get to work and try to pretend the last week or so hasn't happened.'

After a moment, she nodded, wiping her face. Her eyeliner had smeared, giving her a clownish look that made me feel protective. 'I don't want you to feel bad,' I said. 'Let's try to get back to normal.'

'Fine.' Her tone was flat, indicating that it wasn't fine at all. She was too involved, I reasoned as I gave her arm a final pat before hurrying to unlock the shop, leaving her to compose herself. She was hurt that I hadn't told her the whole story, but she had secrets too that she wasn't willing to divulge.

I switched on my computer and opened my emails, telling myself it was time to pull back, to focus on work and keep my personal life to myself, but when Kristin came through with our coffees and commented on the weather as though we were strangers, I was hit by a wave of loneliness.

I missed her already.

Chapter 37

Ordinary life reasserted itself over the next few days. I tried not to fuss too much over Noah, though I found myself turning up early to collect him from school, guiltily relieved when Adam announced he was too busy to do the pickup.

Problems with the IT system in Berlin continued to crop up, and he was spending a lot of time in his study, only coming out to eat dinner and read Noah a bedtime story.

Dad called round to see Noah but really to check up on me – an unexpected turnaround – but I made sure we weren't alone. I needed space to process our last conversation.

At work, my thoughts were occupied as long as I concentrated but it was difficult being around Kristin who was being unnaturally bright and breezy, taking the lion's share of viewings as a way, I suspected, of avoiding me. Left on my own – or with Moira – I took to checking my phone for a message from Will, debating whether to call him, deciding he must have put the whole thing behind him after my last message.

During a lunch break, I typed his name into Google, and this time found a small mention of him on a blog about people living on canal boats in London, where he detailed the pitfalls he'd mentioned to me, the 'loo topic' being the main one. *But limited space leads to a simpler existence and I like that.* Envy gripped me as I pictured him on deck watching the sun go down.

Whenever my mind snapped to Rachel, I told myself I had done everything I could, and that even if I were to talk to the police the chances of re-investigating her death with no fresh evidence was zero. Even so, unease crept down my spine, the sense there was something just out of sight niggling at my subconscious.

At least I didn't have to worry about anonymous letters any more. I'd torn them up and pushed them into a wastebin on my way to work this morning.

On Saturday, Adam was up early, waking me as he leapt out of bed and pulled the curtains back while I blinked and covered my eyes. He seemed happier. His work issues were resolved, and he didn't have to return to Berlin – something he'd thought was on the cards. 'A perfect day for bird-spotting.'

Catching his high spirits, Noah bounced around in a giggly mood, pleading to be able to use the 'noculars' that used to be Dad's.

'Eat your breakfast,' I instructed Noah, smiling when he crammed his toast into his mouth, chewing fast. 'Come here,' I said, once he was dressed in jeans and a red hoodie and his favourite trainers, enfolding him in a cuddle. 'You have a lovely day.'

'Mummy, it's too tight.' Wriggling away, he grabbed the little camera we'd bought him for Christmas. 'I'll take lots of pictures.'

'Make sure you do,' I said. 'And say hello to Nanna from me.'

'What are you going to do with yourself?' Adam leaned in for a kiss. He'd showered and shaved and was wearing his contact lenses. 'Go back to bed if you like. Have a lie-in.'

'I'm wide awake now.' I recognized the smell of my shower gel on his skin and affection flowed through me. 'I might give the grass a final cut while the sun's out.'

'Be careful. You know the starter motor is tricky.'

After I'd waved them off, shivering in my dressing gown, I

wandered around the house, feeling lost. I wanted to be with Noah and wished I'd insisted on tagging along.

Once dressed, I went into the garden and picked up a couple of waterlogged toys left out since the start of the summer holidays.

Back inside, I made a bowl of porridge, scattering in some blueberries, and ate at the kitchen window, watching a plane cut through the sky.

A desultory bout of vacuuming later, I decided to visit Dad. His car was there when I arrived, and the front door was unlocked. I let myself in.

'Hello?' I stooped to stroke Tiger as he padded over and wound around my ankles. Concerned Dad might be upstairs with Ruth Duncan, I called out more loudly, but there was no response. I headed up and found his bed neatly made, his favourite tweed jacket hanging on the wardrobe door, and a hardback book on his bedside table. Ted Gioia's *The History of Jazz*. Mum bought him it a long time ago, her inscription inside the cover in blocky handwriting. *Happy birthday, Jon. All my love, Helen xx*

I thought again of the student who came to our house, and Caroline's revelation about Dad. *Had Mum known?* If she had, she'd forgiven him. I doubted I could be that generous if Adam cheated on me, but maybe Mum had once thought that about Dad.

I replaced the book and went down into the kitchen, Tiger following. Perhaps Dad was in the garden, though I couldn't see him when I peered through the window.

On the way to the back door, I stopped, catching sight of a cardboard box on the table. My stomach flipped. It was the box containing Rachel's belongings, the flaps open as though Dad had been looking through them.

My heart twisted. Perhaps after the events of the past week or so, he'd needed to feel close to his daughter, to get a sense of her from the meagre selection of items. Tiger miaowed, making me jump, and I filled his bowl with biscuits before moving to the table.

Taking a breath, I peered inside the box before plunging my

hand in and pulling out one of the prints. It looked like an abstract seascape, all blues and greens with acid-yellow stripes. I decided to keep it – a benign link to my sister – imagining her looking at it and taking pleasure from the shapes and colours.

Sifting through the small jumble of clothes, something felt different. My breath quickened as my fingers closed around something hard and shiny. *A phone.* I took it out and stared. It was Rachel's, it had to be. It must have been in a pocket and fallen out while Dad was looking through. Heart racing, I searched for the button to turn it on. It was an old model, badly scratched, and of course it wouldn't come on. The battery was dead.

'What are you doing?'

With a scream, I turned, dropping the phone in my jacket pocket. 'Dad!' I said, clutching my chest. 'You scared the life out of me.'

'So I can see.' Removing his old navy-captain's hat, he ruffled his hair and put it back on. 'I wasn't expecting you.'

'Adam's taken Noah to his mum's. I was at a loose end.'

'So you thought you'd see what your old man was up to?' His hand reached past and closed the flaps on the box.

'Something like that.' Tiger shot through the back door and into the garden, making me jump again. 'I noticed you'd been going through Rachel's things.'

'I decided to burn them.' He patted the box like a pet. 'Can't see the point of keeping it.'

'Why now?'

'It's not Rachel.' His mouth was set in a determined line. 'There's nothing here that makes me feel close to her. If anything, it's a reminder ...' His voice caught. 'Look, take it if you want.'

'No, it's fine,' I said quickly, annoyed that I'd read the situation wrong. I should have known having her stuff in the house would cause more pain than comfort. 'Of course you should do what you want, Dad. Whatever helps.'

'Do you forgive me?' he said unexpectedly, gripping the edge of the table. 'It's been playing on my mind, what we talked about the other day. About Denny—'

'Dad, it's fine.' I couldn't bear to see him upset, tears pooling in his eyes. 'It's all in the past now.'

'I don't deserve you.'

Shocked, I said, 'Don't be silly.'

'I mean it, Jess. You're a good girl.'

'Where's this coming from?' I tried to laugh it off, but it sounded forced. 'We're the only family we have, Dad. We're a team, remember?'

'You know I loved your mother, don't you?'

I grew still. *Was he about to confess something?* 'Nobody loved her more. Everyone could see it.'

He looked down at his hands, roped with veins. 'She deserved better too.'

'She would have argued with that.' I didn't feel ready for this, whatever it was. 'No marriage is perfect, Dad, but she wouldn't have had it any other way.'

He took off his hat and laid it on the table. His face was shadowed with tiredness. 'Your mother could have done better and so could you.'

'Dad!' Rounding the table, I dipped my head, forcing him to meet my gaze. 'I thought you liked Adam.'

He made a dismissive gesture with his fingers. 'You should have played the field a bit, not married the first man who proposed.'

'It wasn't a proposal exactly. We just decided we wanted to get married.'

'Exactly.' A flash of outrage crossed his face. 'Why didn't he propose properly?'

'It's a bit of an old-fashioned concept, Dad, the whole hand-in-marriage thing, and you didn't have an issue with it at the time.' Why were we talking about *my* marriage all of a sudden?

'I wanted you to be happy. That's all I've ever wanted, Jess.' His voice was low and scratchy, as though he had a sore throat.

'I am.' The words sounded unconvincing. 'Well … I was, and I will be again,' I corrected. 'Things have been a bit tricky, but we're getting there. Adam and I are good together.' *At least, we had been.* 'We've been through a lot,' I said. 'It's bound to take time to get back to where we were.'

Dad was nodding, the warmth in his eyes tempered with regret. 'I'm sorry.' He shook his head, replaced his hat once more, tugging the peak down. 'I don't know what's got into me this morning.'

Relieved whatever had held him in its grip was passing, I smiled. 'Too much coffee, knowing you.'

Before he could reply, there was a tap at the door and a cheery voice said, 'Jonny? Are you decent?'

I spun round to meet a startled pair of hazel eyes.

'Hello!' Ruth Duncan smiled as she came inside. 'I didn't realize anyone else was here.' Close up, she was attractive, her low-cut top revealing a freckled cleavage where a pair of reading glasses dangled from a chain. 'You must be Jess.' She held out a slender hand. 'Nice to meet you.'

Her grip was firm, and I could see how she might be good for Dad. Fiftyish, generous smile, and that amazing red hair. 'Good to meet you too.'

'I'm here for my piano lesson.'

I glanced at Dad, who looked torn between wanting us to continue talking and welcoming his guest.

'I can leave.' Ruth half-turned.

'I was just going.' Reaching for my keys, I touched Dad's hand. 'I'm going to take this print if that's OK.' I avoided looking at the cardboard box.

He nodded. 'Thanks for coming today, Jess.'

I tucked the print under my arm and left, wondering what they would talk about once I was gone – whether she knew about Rachel.

As I got in the car, my phone began to ring.

Chapter 38

'Where are you?'

My heart jumped at the sound of Will's voice. 'Leaving my dad's house,' I said, pleased to hear from him. 'Where are *you*?'

'About twenty minutes from Ulverston.'

I almost dropped my phone. 'You're joking.'

'No.'

'What …? *Why*?'

'I need to talk to you.'

I tried to analyse his tone. 'You couldn't text?'

'I would rather be face to face.'

In the pause that followed, sounds sharpened around me: birdsong outside, an engine revving, piano scales drifting from the cottage. Aware of Dad watching, I started the car. 'Hang on.'

I drove off, waiting until the cottage was out of sight before pulling the car onto the kerb. 'I'm on my way home,' I said and gave Will my address. 'I'll see you soon.'

Once there, doubts set in. Why hadn't I demanded he talk to me on the phone? Then again if he was driving all this way it must be serious.

As I hurriedly searched through the kitchen drawers and found a charger for Rachel's phone, the words she'd written in the back of the poetry book floated into my head. *To Will, thanks for everything. R* He'd denied the book was his, but what if it was? And the photo of Noah I'd found on the boat ... I couldn't think how, but what if Will was connected? Was he worried I might still be digging for the truth?

Still in my jacket and trainers I paced up and down, dragging my thumbnail across my lower lip. Should I call him back and insist we meet somewhere public? Or tell someone he was coming and have them drop by? *Who?* Dad was busy with Ruth, Adam was at his mum's, and Kristin was working. Denny would be back in London with his wife.

I stood by the sink in an agony of indecision, but it was already too late. A dark blue car swung into view and pulled up next to mine. As Will got out, glancing around him, I told myself I was being ridiculous. Will was the one who raised doubts about Rachel's death in the first place. I wouldn't have gone poking around otherwise, and why risk me looking into it if he was involved? It didn't make sense. My stomach turned over as another thought struck. What if *he* was Noah's father, and getting me to London had been a trick to find out whether I knew? Maybe that was why he'd given Rachel a job – a guilty conscience linked to a one-night stand that had resulted in a pregnancy she then used to try and win Lucian back. Had he found out everything, decided she wasn't a fit mother and killed her in a bout of anger? The idea rang loud in my mind, drowning out every other thought.

When the doorbell pealed, I went hot with panic.

I needed Adam to be here.

Diving into the hall, I looked at Will's looming shape through the stained-glass panel of the door and called out, 'Won't be a minute!' as I dug my phone from my pocket and brought up Adam's number. *Come home NOW.* My hands shook as I typed, *Don't bring Noah.* My son couldn't be here for whatever was about to happen. I quickly added, *Don't call me.* I didn't want to alert Will.

226

I ducked out of sight of the door, giving Adam a moment to reply. His phone was rarely out of his hand because of work. I prayed he hadn't decided to put it away for the day. Peering round, I saw Will's face come close to the glass as if he was searching for me. Seconds later my phone buzzed. *On my way.*

'Sorry about that,' I said, pulling the door wide to admit Will. The rational part of my mind told me he wasn't here to hurt me, that he only wanted to talk. He had such an open, honest expression it was hard to imagine he was capable of deceit, let alone murder. 'I found Rachel's phone,' I blurted out, inwardly cursing myself.

He stepped past me into the hallway, his expression changing to confusion and surprise. 'Really?'

I nodded, not quite closing the door, mentally calculating that it would take Adam at least half an hour to get here, driving at full pelt.

'Where was it?'

'Among her things at my father's house.' I couldn't seem to switch off an instinct to trust him. 'It must have been in one of her pockets.'

'Will you tell the police?'

Was he suggesting I ought to, or checking my intentions? 'I don't know what's on it yet.'

I looked at him properly, taking in his well-worn jeans, the plain grey sweatshirt under a bomber jacket, the kindness of his blue eyes. 'You cut your hair,' I said.

He ran his hand over the shorter layers. 'Needed a trim.'

'Come in, come in,' I chirruped, like a hostess remembering her manners. 'Can I get you a drink?'

'Tea would be good.' He was eyeing me warily now, no doubt sensing something was wrong. 'I'm sorry to turn up like this. I was in two minds but thought I should be here in person rather than a voice at the end of the phone.'

My heart was thumping so hard, I grew dizzy. 'I know what

you're going to say.' I filled the kettle at the sink, turning the tap on too hard. Water gushed out, splashing my arm. 'I worked it out.'

'You did?' Still cautious. 'Why didn't you say something?'

'I worked it out just before you got here.' I swiped at my arm with a tea towel, hoping he couldn't see my hand was shaking. 'I've asked Adam to come back, so we can discuss it together.'

'He's not here?'

'He took Noah to his mother's. He won't be long.' I realized he couldn't have known that Adam and Noah wouldn't be home.

'That's why you're upset.' Will came closer, stopping by the table. 'I'm sorry, Jess.'

'Why are you sorry?' I threw down the tea towel and rolled up my sleeves. 'Let me make that tea.'

'Jess, I—'

'I don't want to say anything else until Adam gets here.' I found a pair of mugs, dropped tea bags in, face burning under Will's gaze.

'I know it must be difficult,' he said gently. I had no idea what to say. Was it an admission? What did he think I knew? He clearly didn't mind that Adam was on his way. Access … was that it? To Noah. He would be reasonable, I was sure. Even so, tears flooded my eyes. I had to be strong, stay calm and rational. If Will was Noah's father it would break Adam's heart, but Will was a good person, not a murderer, I was almost certain. He was a far better option than Lucian.

I scoured the cupboard for biscuits, playing for time. Could Will's concern over Rachel's death be for the mother of his child? He wanted justice for her – to make sure her death was properly investigated.

'I hope you had a good journey,' I managed, an ache at the base of my skull as I racked my brain for a neutral topic. 'The roads are usually busy at the weekend.'

'No worse than your trip to London, I imagine.'

Was it really only two weeks ago? 'I prefer travelling by train to driving.'

'I rent a friend's garage for my car.' He accepted the change of subject, though when I met his eyes he looked troubled. 'I don't need it day to day, only when I'm visiting my parents in Surrey.'

'Handy to have it though.' God, this was excruciating. 'We need a car each out here, being in the country.'

'I can imagine.' He looked around him, taking in his surroundings. 'Nice house.' His gaze seemed to linger a little too long on a photo stuck to the fridge door, of Adam and Noah wearing life-jackets, in a rowing boat on Lake Windermere. 'It's years since I've been up this way.'

I placed his mug of tea on the table before taking mine and moving to stand in the doorway. 'It's a good place to raise children.'

He turned, keeping me in his eyeline. 'I expect once they're old enough, they long to escape somewhere more exciting.'

'Probably.' I took a sip of scalding tea and discreetly glanced at my watch. *Please hurry, Adam.* 'How's the boat?'

Will nodded, hand closing around his mug. 'I left Sam in charge.'

'Sam?' Forgetting myself, I said, 'How come?'

'I've been back to the bridge a few times to see him. We got chatting. I offered him some work.'

'That's nice of you.'

'I figured he deserves a break.'

I couldn't imagine too many people doing the same thing. 'And you've left him alone on the *Kingfisher*? Aren't you worried he'll trash it, or steal your stuff?'

He raised a hand in casual defence. 'It's a leap of faith, but if that happens, I'll know better next time.' He took a drink of tea. 'I've a feeling he won't do that.'

For a second, I wished we could keep chatting, that there was no hidden agenda. My senses were alert for the sound of Adam's car. 'It's probably good to intervene while he's young enough to want to change.'

'I agree,' Will said. 'The older ones, you can tell it's their life now.'

'Hopefully, it's not too late for Sam.'

Will's expression clenched as though he'd remembered the purpose of his visit. Anxiety flowed back as he drained his mug, then crossed over to the worktop. 'Is that Rachel's phone?' He nodded to where it was charging and I nodded. 'Won't there be a password?'

Stupidly, I hadn't considered it. I joined him and we stared at the screen, elbows touching. Impulsively, I picked up the phone and turned it on, partly to see what Will would do. Rip it from my hands, concerned there might be incriminating evidence on there? Instead, he watched closely as the phone sprang to life, the plain home screen displaying a row of apps.

'No password.' Somehow, I wasn't surprised. Apart from a lack of interest in any kind of technology – Rachel had a phone when she was younger only so Lucian could easily contact her – she wouldn't have cared about anyone seeing her messages. Which meant she had nothing to hide.

Will didn't make a move to take the phone. 'Anything there?'

I stared at the email app – the one she used to message me from. Resisting the urge to open it and search for more emails, I clicked on her contact list, looking for text messages.

'Wait.' Will put his hand over mine then drew it back. 'Didn't you want to wait for your husband to get here?'

Frustration bubbled up. It was taking too long. I looked at Will, standing so close I could smell his skin, his hair, a hint of the tea he'd drunk. I raked his features for signs of Noah. Were his eyes the same shape, his lips?

His gaze held mine. 'What is it?'

I looked away, my heart rate elevated. 'Did you manage to decipher the letters from the book of poems?'

He was silent for a moment, tension spiking the air. 'I spent a couple of nights trying to work it out. I didn't think it was going to be possible.'

My attention whipped back to him. 'But you did it?'

He nodded, a frown etched deep into his brow. 'I didn't realize you'd worked it out too.' His expression softened. 'I'm so sorry, Jess.'

Goose bumps spread across my skin. 'But I didn't.' My breath slowed. 'You mean … those letters really spell out a message?'

'Wait.' His frown deepened. 'You told me you knew.'

'I wasn't talking about that.'

His face changed as he realized we'd been at cross-purposes. 'What *were* you talking about?'

My chest felt tight. 'I thought you were going to tell us you're Noah's father.'

'*What?*'

'I'm sorry, I—' There was the sound of a car engine out front and Will's gaze shot to the window. 'I asked Adam to come home. I thought …'

'Oh, God,' Will muttered, sticking a hand in his pocket. 'I need to show you something.' Watching his hand, waiting for Adam to come in, I dropped my gaze to the phone. A single message was visible: *Meet me at 12.30. You know the address. Bring the stuff. R.*

Will was handing me a slip of paper. 'This is why I came.'

I took the note as the front door slammed open. My eyes skated over the capital letters, rearranged into a message from beyond the grave.

'No.' I shook my head, tears spilling from my eyes. I read it again and fell against Will as the words scrolled across my brain.

JESS THE BABY'S FATHER IS YOUR HUSBAND.

Chapter 39

Rachel

Before

From: RBeresford@gmail.com
To: JessSanderson11@gmail.com
Subject: Getting things off my chest

I didn't set out to sleep with him. Sleep. Why do we say that? I didn't set out to have sex with your husband, Jess. Maybe if Lucian hadn't rejected me after we spent the night together in Ibiza, breaking my heart for probably the thousandth time (WHY did I keep doing that to myself??) I wouldn't have been in that frame of mind.

Your husband came looking for me, by the way. He was with a bachelor party, only he's not a 'bachelor party' kind of guy, though I expect you know that. He knew I was in Ibiza because of my email to you – remember those pathetic emails I used to send? "I'm alive!!" and a snapshot of where I was. Poor Jess, you probably felt you had to share whatever titbits (great word) I threw your way. Anyway, I'd finished my shift at the club, and he was waiting outside. I wasn't that drunk, because it had been so busy (I know, I know, bar work when you're an alcoholic isn't ideal, but I was doing OK before hooking up with Lucian again) but anyway, I admit I was intrigued to see Adam Sanderson in person. He asked if I knew who he was, as if I've spent my life so sozzled, I literally can't remember a thing (actually, there's loads of things I've forgotten) – as if you didn't invite me to your wedding, didn't send photos, tell me all about him as though I cared. Sorry for ignoring the invite by the way, I didn't think you'd want my miserable mug spoiling your pictures.

To be honest, I think he had good intentions by coming to find me. Wanted to bring about some sort of family reunion – reunite the sisters. He even mentioned Dad would be glad to see me (ha!). Naturally, I put paid to that idea, suggested we have a drink instead and he started going on about how you're trying for a baby, but you can't get pregnant. Shame men can't get pregnant and give birth, they'd soon stop banging on about it. Anyhow, long story short, he might have had a tiny bit too much to drink and we ended up down an alley. Not very glamorous, but fitting somehow, because the whole situation was sleazy when you think about it, and I didn't much at the time. He wanted to, Jess. I gave him an out – I think he was unzipping his trousers at the time. I said, Are you sure you want to do this? and he nodded, looking all sweaty, and I realized he was a total shit like most men. He said I was beautiful (God, it would hurt you so much to read this, but it's OK because you never will) and that it was a 'shame' by which I supposed he meant if I wasn't such a hopeless loser I might have a chance with a 'decent' guy like him. Yeah, right. Like I'd look twice. I felt a bit bad actually. I even thought about telling you then – a special email delivery – but he got all weepy and desperate afterwards, going on about how much he loves you, he didn't know what he was thinking, things have been 'tough' between you, blah, blah, blah. I mean, it was obvious he loved you and felt awful, and it clearly wasn't ever going to happen again, so I figured the thought of it hanging over him, wondering whether I would change my mind and tell you, was enough of a punishment. I hope it was, and I hope he was kind to you when he got home. I didn't expect to end up 'with child'. First instinct, no way, not having it. Not part of the plan if I ever had one. Then I thought about Lucian. My thoughts always end up with him. If I could convince him the baby was his – and we had recently 'slept' together after all – maybe this time he would stay around, we could make a proper go of it. Grow up and all that. Should have known better. Mind you, it wasn't his kid – but he didn't know that. Told me to get rid of it, only it was too late by then. I really wish I didn't love the bastard. Anyway, I remembered Adam going on about you not getting pregnant and that you might never be able to have kids, even though you were desperate to be a mum. (Really? I thought you'd have had enough of all that, looking out for me, and helping care for our dear mother, but maybe you got my share of mothering instincts.) I figured the one decent thing I could do was give you a chance to have a baby, even if you didn't actually birth it. Obviously, I couldn't tell you the truth – though with hindsight, I think you would have wanted the baby anyway, and you might even have forgiven Adam, but when I told him (the idiot gave me his number before he got drunk, when he was going on about us having that cosy family reunion – I think he forgot) he was angry and terrified, but excited too, I could tell. It was what he wanted, more than anything I think (to be a father – what's that about? Reckon he has daddy issues of his own), and I half-wondered whether the whole thing had been calculated. The baby would have some of your DNA as its auntie, so could almost be yours. Almost. He was quick to suggest you both raise it but made me promise I would never tell you the truth because you wouldn't forgive him, and he couldn't cope with that. God knows why I agreed. Maybe I wanted the baby to have a proper family instead of a broken one, or maybe I felt sorry for you, and I thought now he'd got what he wanted he wasn't likely to have an affair, but I went along with it. Or maybe it was all the money he gave me. Yeah, sorry about that, but I wasn't earning much, and I really wanted to go back to Thailand, so … I guess I sold my baby.

It wasn't that hard really, 'being with child', even though I had to stop drinking properly, not the occasional session now and then. And I'd been good for a while before that because I had a bug and couldn't eat or drink, and then I carried on feeling ill and being sick and thought I had a parasite or something, and that's why I didn't realize for nearly five months that I was pregnant. D'oh. Being pregnant was awful and weird and I was glad when it was over, but in some ways, I'd never felt better (once the vomiting stopped). Well, I say that now. At the time, I wanted to unzip myself and take it out and the stretch marks aren't pretty, and I have what I call a 'jelly belly'. Attractive.

Giving birth wasn't a breeze either. I came back to London to do that. Did I mention Adam sent me more money to cover costs? Trying to put things on a professional footing, the fool. I didn't say no. I guess he owed me. Anyway, I flew back a few weeks before the due date, stayed with a mate who was sorry for me, thought she was being a good Samaritan, then when the contractions started, took myself to hospital, gave them a made-up name, did a ton of screaming and more throwing up – you're not missing much there, I promise – and as soon as he'd been fed a few times, I took a cab to Dad's and … well, you know the rest. And you don't need to worry. I didn't come over all maternal when they put him in my arms. I mean, I didn't drop him or anything, but there wasn't much cuddling.

Being brutally honest, I was glad to feel like me again, though most people would say that wasn't a good thing. I couldn't wait to have a proper drink to celebrate. I'm not cut out for parenting. Not unless it was with Lucian. I would change my mind for him.

I hope he makes you happy. The baby, that is. Maybe Adam will end up cheating again – perhaps when he wants a brother or sister for the baby – and you'll find out and see for yourself what kind of man he is.

Well, sis, it's been good to get that out there.

Time to delete …

Chapter 40

I was distantly aware of the front door opening, Adam calling my name.

Adam. It was Adam. All along, Adam knew he was Noah's father. Adam slept with my sister.

'Jess?' An edge of anxiety. 'What's going on? Whose car is outside?'

I felt his presence in the kitchen, sensed his confusion as he took in the scene: Will propping me up while I sobbed.

'What the hell?' Fright competed with anger. 'Who are you?' Perhaps he thought Will was a burglar, holding me hostage.

My mind looped around, stuck on facts I didn't want to believe. *Adam is Noah's father. His biological father. Adam and Rachel. He slept with my sister. Adam is Noah's father.*

Sounds emerged, sobs that threatened to choke me. I let go of Will and hurled myself at Adam. 'You bastard!' My arms thrashed, fists connecting with his head, his chest, his cheek. I shoved him and he stumbled back, knocking a chair over. He tried to grab my arms, but I kept lashing out, wanting to hurt him for what he had done, for how he had lied to me for so long. *Five years.* Nearly six. That was how long he had kept the truth from me, how long he had hidden this one big fact, this crucial, life-altering fact: Noah was his son. In every possible way.

'God, you must have been laughing all this time.' My voice was weak, spent. 'Me talking to Lucian, thinking we might have to go to court, knowing all the time that *you* were safe, that *nothing*,' I slapped his chest, 'nothing could touch you. No one was ever going to claim Noah, because Rachel is dead and you … *you* are his father.'

'What are you talking about?' His face was ashen, his voice a wobble.

I snatched up the slip of paper and shoved it under his nose. 'She left a message in that poetry book. You guessed, didn't you?' Spittle flew from my lips. 'You were terrified of what might be in there, that's why you were looking for the book the other day.' My stomach rose. I ran to the sink retching over and over, jerky images playing through my head like an old-fashioned cine-reel; Adam and Rachel, laughing behind my back—

'When?' I spun round, dragging my hand across my mouth. Will was standing frozen by the back door, making no move to leave, perhaps understanding that anything could happen without someone to intervene. 'Don't tell me.' Things snapped into place. Things that – at the time, or taken singly didn't add up to much, things that niggled at the time but were brushed aside – took on a depressing new significance. 'That stag do. Spain.' I pushed my hair off my face. 'She was working in a club in Ibiza,' I said. 'I told you that. You must have looked her up while you were there.' I forced myself to look at him. 'That's why you fell out with Simon, isn't it? He knew what you'd done, or he guessed, and you couldn't face him.' Adam looked as though his blood had been drained. His shoulders sagged and his mouth hung open.

Anger burnt like a fire. 'You know … if you'd had the guts to tell me … I would have been devastated, of course I would, but I could have forgiven you, Adam. Because of Noah. We could have got past it.' I didn't know whether that was true but would never know now. 'You took that choice from me, by lying.'

'I didn't lie …' he started to say, his voice a groan that inflamed me further.

'You didn't tell me the truth.' I shook my head, tears flying from the corners of my eyes. 'It amounts to the same thing, Adam. You weren't honest with me.' Suddenly, honesty was all I wanted. 'Just tell the truth!'

'Jess, please.' He spoke with difficulty, as though my hands were clasped around his throat. 'I thought it would break us if I told you. What I did, it was unforgivable. I considered coming clean, I did, I swear. I came close so many times after that trip, but I couldn't bear to risk losing you, and then …' He swallowed, held out a pleading hand. 'Then there was Noah and it felt like our prayers had been answered.'

'*Your* prayer.' I let out a shaking breath. 'You wanted a child more than you wanted me. At least be truthful about that.'

'No.' His face crumpled, but his eyes were dry. 'I love you, Jess. I have since the moment we met.'

'If it hadn't been Rachel, it would have been someone else.' I was suddenly surer of that than anything. If I hadn't given Adam his longed-for child, he would have left me. 'Why did it have to be her?' My voice rose again. 'My *sister*, Adam. And knowing how difficult things were between us … how could you *do* that?'

'I wasn't thinking,' he almost wailed. 'I didn't go there for that. I actually thought I could talk to her, persuade her to come home and—'

'Let me guess.' I held up my hands to stall him. 'One thing led to another, you had too much to drink and didn't know what you were thinking.' I choked out a laugh. 'Spare me the clichés, Adam.' Maybe when he'd looked at the photo of Rachel in her bikini top at my parents' house, he was wondering whether he'd picked the wrong sister. 'You must have been attracted to her, or it wouldn't have happened.' It was the sort of thing Rachel would

239

do, with her desire to hurt those she cared about, detached from the consequences, but I would never have expected it of Adam. 'Being sober might have stopped you acting on impulse, but it had to have been there in the first place.'

'Oh God, Jess, that's not true. It was just—'

'I don't want to hear what it was.' I belted my arms around my aching stomach, my brain seething. Had giving me Noah been Rachel's way of making it up to me? What had Adam told her? *Oh God* ... the thought of them discussing me. I straightened, took a gulping breath. 'Are you sure he's yours?'

'What?'

'How do you know for sure?' I sensed a change in Will's breathing and wondered if he'd been thinking the same thing. 'Don't lie to me, Adam.'

Bending, he picked up the chair and sat down. He lowered his head, arms dangling between his knees. 'When she told me she was pregnant and said the baby was mine I knew it was true.'

'How?'

'If it had been his – Lucian's – she would have kept it,' he said. 'At the time ...' He stopped, buried his hands in his hair. 'When we ... When he had ...' He swallowed. 'She told me she hadn't slept with anyone but him for nearly a year and I should be honoured.'

Sickness rose again, saliva filling my mouth. 'And you believed her.'

'Why would she lie about that?' His gaze flickered to mine. 'She had nothing to lose.'

'But you couldn't be a hundred per cent sure.'

He cast his eyes to the floor. 'I wanted a test as soon as he was born, to be certain.' He was talking about Noah. Noah, my son, whom I loved with every beat of my heart. If the test had shown that Adam wasn't the father, I would never have met my little boy, never felt that tsunami of love – wouldn't have known he existed. 'I didn't know him then.' Adam's anguished voice broke in, as if my thoughts had been transmitted. 'As soon as I saw him that first day, I knew. Even if he hadn't been mine, at that point I would have fought tooth and nail to keep him. But the test was positive.'

My head spun. My son had been tested, not once, but twice – once to prove paternity, once to disprove it, and I'd only just found out, and only because circumstances had forced the truth. Dad had wanted to know that if Lucian came looking for Noah, he had no rights. Adam – and I knew him well enough to know this much – wouldn't have wanted to raise another man's child.

'I despise you for what you've done.'

'Jess, don't say that.' Adam looked up, chin trembling, tears clinging to his lashes. 'You were better off not knowing. That's why I didn't say anything.' He rose and took a step forward. 'We were happy, had everything we wanted. If it wasn't for him' – he pointed to Will – 'you'd be none the wiser. We would still be happy.'

'And part of me would always wonder about his birth father.'

'You thought it was Lucian at first, and then convinced yourself it was a stranger who knew nothing about Noah,' Adam raged. 'You were happy, Jess. I know you were.' It was like meeting him for the first time. The real Adam, not the watered-down version I'd thought I loved. 'It hasn't been easy for me.' His voice broke as he added, 'I was always on edge, wondering whether she—'

'Her name is Rachel.' I gave a bitter laugh. 'No wonder you could never say it.'

With a pained expression, he continued. 'It was always at the back of my mind that she might change her mind and tell you the truth.'

'Oh my God, that's why you were jumpy whenever our phones rang after she left Noah with us. It's why you always wanted to read her emails.' Pieces were slotting into place, the full, horrible picture emerging. 'You were terrified it might be Rachel calling, of what she might reveal to me in her messages.'

On my right, Will was motionless, his gaze fixed on Adam. I

was suddenly, fiercely, glad he was there – a witness, someone who later would know what had happened, had seen with his own eyes the moment my marriage disintegrated. Why had I doubted him? I trusted Will more than I did my own husband.

'After the first six months, I relaxed a bit.' Adam voice turned cajoling, trying to persuade me to see his point of view. 'She was in Thailand, she wasn't emailing you and then we moved here, started afresh, and I thought it was going to be OK. I truly believed I had done the right thing, saving you from …' He waved a hand between us. 'From this.' I wondered how he had lived with the knowledge inside him all this time, and what it said about me that I hadn't suspected. 'Like I said, we were happy, Jess. You, me, and Noah, our little family, his grandparents close by.' *Grandparents.* Jennifer was Noah's grandmother. His *actual* grandmother. 'You can't tell her.' As if reading my thoughts, Adam held out his hands in an appeal. 'You know my father cheated on her. She expected better of me. *I* expected better of me.' He clapped his palms to his chest. 'It would kill Mum to know the truth.'

'So this is about you saving your own skin.' My voice was sour. 'You can't bear the thought that you might be more like your father than you realized.' Wanting to cut him more deeply, I added, 'They say the apple doesn't fall far from the tree.'

His lips turned white. 'Don't say that.'

'The truth hurts.'

'I'm *not* like him.' He came closer, finger stabbing the air. 'I will be here for my son. Always.' His expression darkened. 'I won't be an absent father like he was. That will *never* happen.'

My eyes were hot with tears. 'You're telling me you have rights. That if we divorce, you'll fight me for custody.'

Instantly, his face changed. 'Christ, Jess, we don't have to split up over this. You're Noah's mother. *You.*' He moved suddenly, grabbed a framed photo from the shelf of cookbooks behind him, the three of us at the nature reserve, holding it out like a peace offering. 'We're a family, Jess.'

But he hadn't denied it. He was prepared to use the fact he was Noah's biological father against me if it came to it. 'No wonder you're happy she's dead.' A seam of hatred strengthened my tone. '"*I'm glad she's gone, Jess.*"' I mimicked his voice from the night he called from Berlin. 'What a relief it must have been to know you could never be found out. You must have been rubbing your hands together, thinking she'd taken your secret to her grave.'

'Jess, that's not what I meant at all.' But we both knew it was. He threw Will a poisonous look. 'Why were you poking your nose into things that are none of your business?'

'In a way, it was my business.' In contrast to Adam's belligerent tone, Will's voice was measured. 'She was a friend. I knew there was more to her death.'

'That's rubbish,' Adam blustered, combing his fingers through his hair. He was shaking. 'She was drunk, the police said so.' He paused, as if something had occurred to him. 'You came all this way to tell Jess about *that*?' His gaze dropped to the piece of paper on the floor, then turned to me. 'You asked him to help you?'

'I don't think you're in any position to criticize.' I was shaking too, with anger. 'I couldn't talk to you about it. I didn't know why, but I do now. You were desperate for me to drop it in case I found out the truth.'

'What does it matter how she died?' His voice was a roar that made me gasp and clamp my hands to my ears. 'She's *dead*.' His eyes were wild, the veins in his neck standing out as he advanced towards me. 'What does it matter how she died?'

'It matters.' I dropped my hands and stood my ground. 'It matters to me.'

'She was poison. Nothing but trouble. Nobody liked her, not even her ex-boyfriend in France.'

'I liked her.' Will stepped between us, a restraining arm held in Adam's direction. 'And it matters if she was murdered.'

'The police said it was an accident.' Confusion slid over Adam's face. 'Didn't they?' He looked from me to Will and back. 'Why didn't they arrest anyone?'

'No evidence,' Will said quietly.

In the swollen silence that followed, I cradled my banging temples between my fists before reaching for Rachel's phone. 'This might change things.' I held up the mobile.

As though hypnotized, Adam stared at the screen. A slow tide of scarlet chased away his pallor. 'Where did you find that?'

'At Dad's, in the box he brought from Rachel's apartment.'

His jaw worked briefly, a pulse twitching. 'And you think …?' He swallowed. 'Are you accusing me of something?'

'Was this message for you?'

He moved closer, eyes scanning back and forth.

Meet me at 12.30. You know the address. Bring the stuff. R.

The sun had disappeared and the temperature in the kitchen dipped. A shiver racked my body. 'What does it mean?'

'It doesn't mean anything.'

I glanced at Will, encouraged by the look of belief in his eyes. *Keep pushing*, he seemed to be saying.

'It must mean something, Adam.' I tried to hold onto a sliver of calm. 'What stuff?'

For Noah's sake, I had to know if his father was capable of murder.

Chapter 41

I waited, holding my breath.

Adam, clearly deciding there was no point pretending, dropped his gaze. His shoulders slumped, and when he looked up there was a new directness in his eyes. 'Honestly, Jess, I don't know why she wanted it.'

'Shall I wait outside?'

I heard Will's softly spoken question and shook my head, unable to wrench my attention away from Adam. 'What stuff?' I repeated.

'She called me one day, completely out of the blue.' His face twisted with remembered shock. 'I didn't even know she still had my number. She said she wanted to meet me in London and told me to bring a picture of Noah and something that belonged to him when he was a baby.'

'*You* gave her that photo? The one you said wasn't missing. The one I told you about last week that she showed to Lucian, and all the time, *you* were the one who gave it to her?' My heart thumped with such intensity I could almost hear it. 'You said you were seeing a client that day.'

'I came back to the house while you were taking Noah to school.' His tone was wretched. 'I took the photo and the bootees Mum knitted.'

'*What?*' It was as if I'd entered a twilight reality. 'I knew someone had been in the house.' I'd stood in the bedroom, wondering what was different; the bottom drawer of the dressing table slightly open – the drawer where I kept a few of Noah's baby clothes.

'This must be yours then.' In slow motion, I turned to see Will unfurl his hand. In his palm was a delicate white bootee laced with blue ribbon. Jennifer had insisted on *blue for a boy, though I know it's stereotyping.* She was proud that she'd mastered the art of knitting, especially for Noah. Those bootees had been precious, worn until Noah grew out of them, then wrapped in tissue and placed in the drawer, alongside other mementoes of his babyhood. 'I had a good look around the boat yesterday and found it tucked down the back of the sofa,' Will said. 'I couldn't find the other one.'

I took the bootee and stroked the soft wool. 'Did she tell you why she wanted them?' I addressed the words to Adam, my throat thick with tears. 'Did you ask?'

'Of course I asked.' He sounded on the verge of tears too, as if the sight of the bootee had unfastened something inside him. 'She said she wanted some keepsakes of Noah's and threatened to tell you the truth if I didn't do as she asked.'

Glancing at Will through tear-blurred eyes, I saw deep sympathy in his. He had concluded his grandfather was irredeemable. I hadn't wanted to think of Rachel that way, but I'd been wrong.

'You must have wondered why she wanted keepsakes after so long.'

'Yes, I wondered.' Adam looked up with an irritated expression, as though I was being obtuse. 'Obviously, she wasn't going to tell me the truth, but I knew she was serious about telling you everything if I didn't comply.' *He had sneaked home while I was out, stolen treasured items, and told me I was imagining it. Who was this man?* 'Things were quiet for a few days,' he went on. He'd been edgy around that time, blaming it on work. 'And then she called again. She was incoherent, drunk. Said something about Lucian, that he hadn't changed. I guessed that's what it had been about, that she'd hatched some half-baked plan using Noah to get him back.' And all this time, Adam held onto that information while I remained clueless. He'd watched me blundering around after Rachel's death, asking questions, and all the time he *knew*. While I was relaying my Skype conversation with Lucian, he'd known, yet looked me in the eye and kept quiet. 'I asked how she could seriously have thought I would let Noah go because it suited her, even if Lucian had somehow believed he was the father.' Adam gave an incredulous laugh, as if reliving the conversation – a conversation I would never in a million years have imagined him having with my sister. 'She said I would probably have done anything to stop you from finding out the truth. She wanted to convince Lucian he was Noah's father as a way of getting him to come back to her. At least, that was the plan until he demanded a paternity test.' Anger bit down at the thought of her playing around with people's lives, prepared to use Noah as a pawn, to lie to Lucian, threatening Adam … not that he deserved a second of my sympathy. 'She changed her tune after that. She was angry, blaming everything and everyone. I think she wanted revenge because she started saying what a shit I was to have lied to you, how she should have told you from the start, that she wanted to make things right because you deserved to know the truth.'

Can I come and see you? We need to talk.

A ball of emotion rose and cut off my breath. I'd been right to be worried. I just hadn't known why. 'And you went to see her.'

He nodded. 'I went to the flat. She'd been drinking, even though it was only lunchtime. She looked awful. We argued.' I thought about Hannah seeing them from the window. *The man had been my husband.* 'She wasn't making much sense and I pleaded with her to leave us alone, told her it could ruin Noah's life if it all came out, that it would make *you* unhappy.' He turned tear-soaked eyes to the window, as if seeing the scene play out on the rain-spattered pane of glass. 'I suppose I was trying to appeal to her better nature, but she didn't have one. She was acting out of spite. She wasn't happy and couldn't bear that we were.' He rubbed his face, turned back to me. 'I offered her money. More money,' he amended. 'I had to pay her quite a lot in the first place to keep quiet.'

'For God's sake, Adam.' I couldn't look at him. My head felt encased in concrete, full to bursting. 'I can't believe this.'

'She kept saying she had to make it right.'

'She said something similar to me.' Will's words reminded me of our conversation. 'She didn't say what.'

'Well, now you know.' Ignoring him, Adam came closer. His breath smelt stale, and something had dried in the corner of his mouth. 'And then she sent you that email, wanting to see you.'

'You must have panicked.'

'Obviously.'

A detached air of calm settled over me. 'So, you went to see her again.' My mind was working it out, fitting together the awful pieces. 'That first trip you took to Berlin, staying overnight. You went to London, arranged to meet Rachel late at night on the towpath. You argued and then …' I paused, felt Will's presence behind me. 'You pushed her in the canal and ran away.'

Adam's staggered backwards as though I'd shoved him. 'You can't believe that's true.' His face was aghast. 'Jess, that's crazy—'

'Like I was crazy to think Noah's photo was missing?'

'That's different.' He looked at me as though I'd grown two heads. 'You honestly think I'm capable of killing someone?'

It was a good bluff, a great performance, but how could I believe anything he said? 'I really don't know.'

'This is your fault, you interfering bastard. Filling her head with stupid ideas.' Out of nowhere, Adam launched himself at Will, wrestling him to the floor. Kneeling over him, he brought up his fist and smashed it into Will's face.

'Adam!' Dropping the bootee, I grabbed his shirt and tried

to pull him away as Will fought to free himself, but Adam was bigger than both of us, fuelled by an anger that made him strong. 'No!' I cried as his hands closed around Will's throat, squeezing hard. 'Get off him!'

Will's face reddened, eyes bugling, his legs kicking uselessly while his fingers clawed at Adam's hands.

I tried once more to yank Adam away, to loosen his grip, pleading and crying for him to let go, but he was lost in rage and didn't hear me. I screamed for help, but of course nobody was there.

I looked around frantically, gaze landing on a Pyrex casserole bowl in the open dishwasher. Scrambling across, I grabbed it, lifted it high, and slammed it against Adam's head, watching in horror as he tipped sideways and crashed to the floor.

Will rolled onto his side, gasping for air, clutching his throat.

'Are you OK?' I knelt beside him, then got up and ran water into a glass at the sink, slopping it everywhere as I took it back, stepping over Adam, who was groaning in pain on the tiles. 'Here.' I handed Will the glass and he managed a few sips, his colour slowly returning to normal. 'Oh God, Will. I'm so sorry.'

'Not your fault,' he managed to croak, shifting to look at Adam, who was shuffling to a sitting position, hand clasped to the back of his head.

'That really hurt,' he said churlishly.

I stood over him, trembling. 'So much for you not being capable of killing anyone,' I said, as Dad walked in.

Chapter 42

Rachel

Before

From: RBeresford@gmail.com
To: JessSanderson11@gmail.com
Subject: Getting things off my chest

OK, so spelling out a message in a book of poetry wasn't my finest hour. In my defence, I was a little bit drunk because of the showdown with Lucian in the café. I was so, so pleased and excited to see him, but he's changed and not for the better. Sanctimonious, I would say. I still love him though. Maybe even more. He's aged well. Makes me sick when I think of him with his new woman, even if it's not her fault. When will he realize I'm The One? And don't say never, Miss Clever Clogs. Some things are meant to be. They need a little help, though I probably didn't go about it the right way. I think I read it wrong, got carried away. Shouldn't have mentioned Noah, why did I do that? I blurted it out when he called me out of the blue, asking about the baby. I'd made myself easy to find by setting up a Facebook account, mostly so I could stalk him – obviously – (did I mention that already?) posting bits about myself at the gallery, making it look like I was doing well (which I was, comparatively – ooh, big word) if he looked. I knew he would look eventually. I didn't expect him to call. I was going to contact him when I was ready.

'He's nearly 6!' I chirped like a big idiot when he asked, nearly fainting with shock and excitement. 'Would you like to meet him?' I went a bit mad after that when he said he was coming over from France. Spiralling, they call it, or is it spinning? I never could keep my head straight around Lucian. That was my downfall really. I started making a stupid plan that obviously couldn't work but made sense at the time. Not thinking properly. Desperate to see him, have him close again. Keep him from going back to France.

Anyway, it did NOT go well. You can't imagine. I thought, yeah, I think it's over for good this time. Until I can work out a better plan.

So, I was on the boat that night feeling deeply sorry for myself (i.e., very, very drunk). Will let me stay there while he was visiting his parents because he's good like that and I couldn't afford a hotel. I wanted to get out of that flat, what with Hannah mooching about with her ridiculous 'Instagram friends'. When she said she was working at an auction house, I almost thought it sounded interesting. I nearly asked her to tell me about it – even though I can tell it scares her a bit when I speak to her – but then she said something about media content, and I lost the will. SOOO – I was a teeny bit (OK a lot) drunk, and I was looking through the book of poems I bought because Lucian told me his grandmother knew the author and he'd had a copy for years and lost it. I was going to give it to him only I didn't get the chance, and I thought it might be fun to send you a message, like they did in the war. Trust Will to have pens and highlighters lying around. He's a keeper, that one. Shame you didn't meet. I bet you could have kids of your own with him!! Hey, you're still young enough! Anyway, I doubt you'll ever see my 'secret reveal' and I shouldn't think Will would be able to work it out if he even looks, but anyway, I did it and I left the book on the boat with a thank you in the back because he's been a mate and I think he's the sort of man who likes a nice poem. I've met his mum a few times. Antonia. She's nice. Classy. He's nice. They're nice, nice, nice. Like you.

Not like me.

I might get the book back actually. And the photo of Noah and his bootees. I'd taken them out and was staring at the bootees thinking they looked too small, even for a baby (did you knit them?) wondering whether you'd noticed they were missing (yeah, that was my big idea to convince Lucian he was Noah's dad!! Can you believe it? Don't answer that) and I must have dropped them because when I came round and went back to the flat, they weren't in my bag. A job for another day. Sleep beckons. Time to delete.

Night, Sis x

Chapter 43

'Who killed who?' Dad's face was pale and tense as he stared at his son-in-law on the floor, before turning to look at Will, who was struggling to his feet. His hair was dishevelled, and there were angry red marks at his throat. Finally, Dad's gaze landed on the Pyrex dish at my feet, cracked across the base. 'What the hell is going on?'

'What are you doing here?' Surely this was a nightmare.

His gaze picked out the mobile phone on the table. 'After Ruth had gone, I looked in the box and realized you'd taken it,' he said. 'I didn't want you to see it.'

'You knew the phone was there?' There was a buzzing feeling in my head.

'Denny found it in her room when he picked up her things.' Dad was clearly reluctant to explain, eyes moving once more to Adam. 'I saw her message—'

'You saw it and didn't say anything?' I wheeled around, not sure how much more I could take. 'You didn't think it might be important?'

'I knew it wouldn't do any good to show you.'

'You knew the message was for Adam though, didn't you?' I advanced towards him. 'You must have got *Denny* on the case.'

Fresh rage spiralled through me. 'You knew Rachel sent Adam a message asking to meet, and you didn't say a word. You didn't even tell the police.'

'How could I?' His voice was edged with steel. 'I wasn't going to risk breaking up your family.'

'But … but Adam killed her.' I looked at Dad incredulously. 'Her death wasn't an accident.'

'There's no proof of that, Jess, but even if—'

'But even if he did, he shouldn't go to prison for the sake of *family*?' I spat. I could hardly believe what I was hearing. 'What about Rachel, Dad? *Rachel* was family, but she clearly doesn't matter.'

'I didn't kill her,' Adam bellowed. 'Christ, Jess! I am *not* a murderer.'

Will was silent, propping himself up in the doorway, rubbing the back of his neck as his eyes flickered between us.

'Do you really think Adam killed her?' Dad looked at me, almost scared now, a sweaty sheen on his forehead. I prayed he wasn't about to have a heart attack. 'The police didn't find any evidence of foul play.'

'"Foul play",' I mocked. 'God, Dad … you and Denny—'

'I can prove I wasn't in the country.' Adam was patting the pockets of his jeans, a feverish red to his cheeks. He tugged out his wallet and flipped it open, manically throwing receipts onto the table. He kept everything he could claim as an expense for his tax returns. 'Here, look.' He picked one up, then flung it down again. 'Hang on, it's here somewhere.' Desperation made him clumsy. 'I know I kept it.'

Dad and I closed in. When he put his hand on my arm, I jerked away, struggling to untangle his woolly mess of secrets; his dismissal of Rachel's murder, even if it had been in favour of saving my marriage. 'Did you know that Adam is Noah's father?'

Adam paused in his frantic search and briefly closed his eyes. It was as if I'd mentioned an unsavoury habit, instead of the earth-shattering news that he'd had sex with my sister.

Dad swung guilty eyes to mine. 'When I saw that message on her phone and worked out it was Adam's number, I thought they'd been having an affair. I put two and two together.'

'That's why you've been off with him lately, isn't it?'

Nodding, he looked away, but I'd caught the flash of dislike in his eyes. *Your mother could have done better and so could you.* Now I knew what he'd been referring to.

'Here.' With a desperate flourish, Adam held up a receipt. After scanning it with narrowed eyes, he passed it to me. Our fingers brushed, and goose bumps crawled over my skin. 'I ate out that night with the client.' He pointed, a nerve pulsing underneath his eye.

I stared at the slip of paper, letters and numbers leaping out. At 8.45, he'd paid for two draught beers and a mixed meat platter at Zweistrom, Berlin.

'No way I could have flown back to London in time to meet Rachel. We didn't leave the restaurant until nearly eleven. There's probably camera footage if you don't believe me.' I looked into his bloodshot eyes. 'For God's sake, Jess. I didn't kill her.' For the first time, his voice rang with conviction. 'I was nowhere near that bridge, and I'd already decided that, whatever happened, whatever she was going to tell you, I would face it and take the consequences.'

'You didn't get someone to push her in the canal for you?' I had to ask, because I didn't want him anywhere near Noah in the future if he had played any part in Rachel's death. I would go to the police myself if I had to.

'Jess, for Christ's sake.' A tear slipped down his face. 'I've behaved terribly, OK? I get it. I'm an awful husband. I shouldn't have lied, but the last thing on my mind was hurting anyone. I can't believe you would think that of me.' He buried his face in his hands and gave way to a series of guttural sobs that made my stomach turn.

'I believe you.' I did but my voice was cold because I couldn't locate the love I'd felt for him less than an hour ago.

'I should go.'

I started at the sound of Will's voice. 'You're not fit to drive,' I said automatically. *Not after my husband nearly strangled you.* 'You could stay here tonight.'

'I'll be OK.' He gave Adam a stony stare, but Adam was still crying, his shoulders jumping.

Dad came back from wherever his mind had been, his face creased with bewilderment as he turned to Will. 'Why is he here?'

'He figured out that Adam was Noah's father.' The thunderbolt shock of it hit me all over again. 'Rachel left a coded message in a book.'

'A book?' Dad screwed up his face. 'What book?'

'It doesn't matter,' I said tiredly. 'I know the truth now.'

'And you know I had nothing to do with her death.' Adam sniffed and wiped his sleeve across his face. 'Can we at least let that go now, please?'

I looked at Will, who gave a reluctant nod and said, 'I guess we'll never know for sure what happened.'

Seeing his pale face, the marks I was sure would become bruises around his neck, the red imprint on his cheek where Adam had punched him, made me want to weep. 'I'm so sorry you got dragged into this.' *And I'm sorry I suspected it was you.* The irony, that I'd begged Adam to come home.

'I dragged myself into it, remember?' A faint smile hovered at the corners of his mouth. 'Call if you want to,' he said as I walked with him into the hall. My whole body felt weak, and my teeth chattered. 'It's going to take time to process all this. You should ask someone to be with you.' He cast his gaze around, pausing on the gallery of photos of Noah on the wall. 'If you want to talk anytime, you know where I am.'

'Thanks, Will,' I said. 'For caring about Rachel.'

256

A spasm of emotion passed over his face. 'I'm sorry you've had to go through all this.'

When he'd gone, I leaned against the front door until I heard him drive away, overcome with dread at the thought of facing Adam and my father.

They were standing where I'd left them, at opposite sides of the table. Adam was standing over it, knuckles pressed into the wood, his face a blotchy mess. Dad was staring through the window where rain was falling on the garden. The branches of the plum tree rocked in the wind, sending leaves flying across the lawn.

'You can go now,' I said.

They turned. Dad's expression was vacant, Adam's twisted with pain.

'What are you going to do?' Adam said.

'I don't know.' My mind was overflowing, and I couldn't think straight. 'Go back to your mum's and act normally for Noah's sake.'

'You don't have to tell me how to behave with my son.' *My son.* Hatred swept over me as the words took on new meaning.

'If you want to stay with me for a while,' Dad began, his voice subdued, but I shook my head.

'I need to be on my own.' I looked back at Adam. 'Stay overnight at your mum's. I want to get my head clear before Noah comes home.' I pressed my fingers to my tear-swollen face. 'He can't see me like this.' He nodded. 'I'll pick him up tomorrow.'

Surprise streaked over his face. 'I'll bring him back.'

'No,' I said. 'You won't.'

Silence fell. When Adam opened his mouth to speak again, I turned to leave the room. 'When I come back downstairs, I want you both gone.'

'Can I at least get some of my things?'

I paused, steamrollered with exhaustion. 'Fine. Be quick.'

Reluctant to follow him into the bedroom, I went into Noah's room instead and dropped on the edge of his bed, staring at the clutter of toys on his rug. I heard drawers opening

257

and closing, the sound of a zip being drawn, then Adam's feet on the stairs.

There was an angry exchange of words between him and Dad below, followed by the front door slamming shut and hitting the wall as it bounced open again. Adam's car revved and he pulled away in a squeal of tyres. Seconds later, Dad followed suit.

I sat in the fading light, my mind a blissful blank until my phone rang, making me jump. I still had my jacket on and fished my phone from the pocket.

'Hello,' I said dully.

'It's Kristin.' A pause. 'Jess, is it OK if I come round after work? I really want to talk to you.' I couldn't speak. 'Jess?'

A sob broke out then another, and suddenly I couldn't stop as I slipped from the bed to my knees.

'What's happened?' Kristin's voice tensed. 'Is it Noah?'

'Not Noah,' I managed, but couldn't catch my breath.

'Stay there,' she ordered. 'I'm on my way.'

Chapter 44

Rachel

Before

From: RBeresford@gmail.com
To: JessSanderson11@gmail.com
Subject: Getting things off my chest

I wouldn't have told you the truth, Jess. At least, I don't think I would. I can be mean when I'm drunk and upset and I was both for a while, after the whole 'Lucian still hasn't realized he loves me' thing, but I think I wanted to wind Adam up more than anything. He's such a sap. Offered me money again to keep quiet. He can't have much left by now. Do you know? Does he have a separate savings account? Anyway, things are looking up, as they say (whoever 'they' are)!!

Lucian has been in touch!! I KNOW!! He wants to meet, to talk things over after our last disastrous get-together. WHOOP!! I thought he was back in France, but he's obviously had a rethink. I knew he would. It was obvious he still has feelings, or he wouldn't have come over in the first place. He's accepted I lied about Noah, understands why I did it, and still wants me. I hope he does. I can't think why else he would want to meet. If I could spend the rest of my life with him, I would die happy. Hopefully not for a long time. Do you wonder sometimes whether we might have inherited Mum's illness? I don't think it's genetic, but you never know.

Oh, and I had a great idea. I'm going to send you an email. A proper one, after I delete this. I'll schedule it to arrive on Noah's birthday, so it'll be like a gift for you too. How about that?! I'm going to do The Right Thing.

OK. Time to delete, then get ready for my 'hot date'. Probably wear my parka and boots. It's FREEZING, what's happened to the weather??

I'm going to need a lot of Dutch courage, in case things don't go my way. I think maybe Lucian prefers me drunk. I know I do.

Bye, Sis xx

Chapter 45

When I'd finished talking, Kristin was quiet for a long time beside me on the sofa, where she'd led me after she let herself in through the open front door and found me in tears on Noah's bedroom floor. She wrapped me in a throw and brought me a cup of tea with two sugars. 'For shock,' she said, before I'd spoken a word, her worried eyes taking in the state of me as she slipped her coat off and turned on the heating. I couldn't stop shaking.

'I can't believe it,' she said now, rubbing at an ink stain on her finger. 'That all this time, Adam … he …' Seeming lost for words, she shook her head. 'I thought he was one of the good ones.'

'Well, he *is* a good dad.' He'd found it so easy, changing nappies, singing lullabies, sitting by the cot until Noah slept, encouraging me to sleep while he took Noah to the park in his buggy. *No wonder it had come naturally.* 'And I guess it's a good thing that Noah's birth certificate isn't a lie.' No wonder Adam had filled it in without a qualm, while I'd fretted about whether we were doing the right thing. Snippets kept coming back – things that made sense with new awareness, like how readily he'd accepted what I thought was another man's baby and how, over time, he would say proudly, *He's just like me* and *Mum said I used to do that when I was his age* and *I think he's going to be left-handed like his dad.* I would think it sweet that he was seeing similarities, when all the time it was real. I had thought it a lucky coincidence that Noah had his dark hair and eyes, not guessing for a second he'd inherited Adam's colouring.

'And you say your dad suspected he was having an affair with Rachel and didn't say a word?' When I nodded, Kristin sat forward, hugging her knees. In the light of the lamp she'd switched on, her face was pensive. 'And he would have kept quiet if Will hadn't worked out that Adam was Noah's dad from the poetry book.'

'I can sort of understand why,' I said, though in truth, I wasn't sure how I felt about all the things Dad knew and hadn't told me. 'He's so protective of Noah and me. He would have been worried about my reaction and probably thought there was no need to tell me as Rachel was dead.' Tears threatened once more. 'He and Noah are all the family I have left.'

Kristin shuffled closer and put her arm around me, her perfume familiar and soothing. 'They're lucky to have you,' she said gently, giving me a squeeze. 'You've got me too.'

I managed a weak smile. 'Thanks for coming over. Did you lock up the shop?'

'Of course.' She pulled back, mock indignant. 'It wasn't busy today.'

I was spent now that the words had tumbled out, but something came back to me. 'You wanted to talk.'

Kristin looked at me with a puzzled pinch of her brow.

'When you called,' I reminded her. 'You asked if you could come over because you wanted to talk.'

'Oh.' Flushing, she flapped a hand. 'It was nothing, really.' She looked across the room, fixing her eyes on the blank television screen. 'The last few days have been a bit awkward at work. I know it's my fault,' she said, haltingly. 'I wanted to apologize again, set things straight between us.' Her hands were laced tightly in her lap. 'I feel even worse than I already did for lying about Mum after what you've found out.' She pressed her lips together, then turned. 'You must feel like there's no one in your life you can trust right now.'

'I trust you.' Putting down the mug of cold tea I'd been clasping, I reached for her hand. 'You're a good friend, Kristin. I understand why you said what you did about your mum, but I want you to know you can tell me anything. I would never judge you, like you don't judge me.'

Her eyes swam with tears. 'Jess, I—' She stopped, shook her head. 'I'm here for you, OK? If you want someone to babysit Noah, even cook dinner for you.'

'Are you offering to move in?'

She gave a teary smile. 'If you want.' She added, 'Seriously, do you think you and Adam will stay together?'

Fresh pain clawed my insides. 'Right now, I can't think of anything I want less but I'll sleep on it and see how I feel in the morning.'

Kristin nodded slowly, searching my face. 'And Rachel?'

I thought for a moment. 'I've accepted whatever happened that night was an awful accident.' I breathed out the heaviness around my heart. 'It sounds silly, but I think that maybe she wanted me to look closer because it was the only way I would ever find out the truth about Adam.'

Kristin considered my words. 'Maybe,' she said. 'And now she can rest in peace.'

'While the rest of us suffer.' I surprised myself by smiling. 'That was Rachel all over. Leaving a trail of chaos wherever she went.'

Kristin returned my smile, but her eyes were sad. 'Now *you* need to rest,' she said. 'You look wiped out.'

I was desperate to lie down, for the day to be over, but first, I wanted to talk to Noah.

'Are you sure I can't make you something to eat?'

'I wouldn't be able to, but thanks.' I stood up, feeling wobbly. 'I'm going to have an early night.'

At the door, Kristin held me tightly. I relaxed for a moment in her embrace, grateful to have been able to talk through what had happened, knowing I had someone on my side. *Someone else.* Will had texted while Kristin was in the kitchen making tea. *When you're ready to talk, I'll be here. Look after yourself, Jess xx*

Right now, the only person in the world I wanted to talk to was my son.

Despite everything, I slept, unable to stop my eyes from closing once I'd crawled into bed fully-clothed and woke with my mind clearer than it had been in weeks. I was starving and ate breakfast at the kitchen table where Noah's baby bootee lay beside Rachel's phone.

The receipt from Berlin, the slip of paper with Will's decoded message on it, and the broken Pyrex bowl were gone, cleared away by Kristin.

After I'd eaten and drunk a cup of coffee, I threw the phone away and replaced the single bootee in the chest of drawers before pulling a couple of suitcases out of the wardrobe.

When I called Dad, he answered on the first ring. I guessed he'd been up all night, worrying whether I would ever speak to him again. 'I'm fine,' I told him. 'We're going to be OK, Dad.'

'I love you, Jess.' His relief was palpable. 'Come round for dinner later.'

I messaged Will: *I hope you got back safely X* and he replied with a thumbs-up and a photo of a sleeping Sam, mummified in a sleeping bag on the cabin-bed on the boat. *Clearly not a party animal! X*

I smiled, something inside me beginning to loosen as I stood by the bedroom window for a moment, looking out at the flat white sky. I felt as though a layer had been stripped away and someone new was emerging. Someone stronger.

On the way to Jennifer's I switched on the radio and listened to cheesy pop music – the kind Mum used to love. 'I miss you,' I whispered, a swell of emotion in my chest. 'I hope you and Rachel are together wherever you are.'

Chapter 46

When I arrived at Jennifer's semi-detached house, on the quiet street where she had lived for forty years, she came to the door with a look of slight surprise.

'Jess,' she greeted me, her face pouchy from crying. 'It doesn't have to be like this.'

I'd spoken to Adam the night before, after I chatted to Noah.

'I told Mum I've been having an affair,' he'd said, sounding broken. 'I had to say something because she kept going on at me to tell her what was wrong.' He sniffed. 'She's gutted.'

But not as gutted as she would be if he'd told her the truth.

'I'm afraid it does have to be like this,' I said to Jennifer. 'I can't forgive him.'

She clasped a hand to her mouth, eyes filling with tears.

'It won't affect anything between us.' I put down the suitcases I'd lifted out of the boot and hugged her. 'You know how much I care about you.'

She clung to me, stifling a sob. 'Noah ...'

'Noah will be fine.' I stepped back. 'He still has his grandma.' *His real grandma.* 'Nothing will change, I promise.'

She pulled a tissue from her sleeve and wiped her eyes. 'Maybe after their holiday, you'll see things differently.'

'Holiday?' I glanced into the hallway behind her. 'I'm here to pick up Noah.'

Jennifer's brow crumpled. 'Adam said he spoke to you last night and you agreed he could take Noah away for a few days.' She sniffed, dabbing her nose. 'It was so kind of you, Jess. It will do them good to spend some time together.'

'I would never have agreed to that.' My heart turned over. 'Especially not now.'

'What?' Her eyes widened. 'You didn't—?'

'Of course I didn't agree to them going on holiday.' Fear clutched my throat. 'Noah has school tomorrow, for one thing.' I pushed past her, into the house, nerves alive with panic. 'Adam!'

'They're not here.' Behind me, Jennifer radiated alarm. 'They left about half an hour ago. I was surprised to see you, and thought you were bringing suitcases for the trip even though they'd already ...' Her voice petered out. 'Oh, Jess.'

'Where have they gone?' My heart was beating wildly, eyes raking around as if Noah might magically appear.

'Windermere.'

I let out a shaky breath. *Not far.*

'Noah wanted to go on a rowing boat, then they're heading to the airport.'

The ground seemed to fall away. 'Airport?'

'Spain, Adam said.' Jennifer's hands were pressed to her cheeks. Seeing her so anxious made everything worse. 'He had their passports, and some clothes in a rucksack.'

I thought of Adam in our bedroom the day before, rummaging through the drawers. He must have been planning this even then – to take Noah away. 'Call him,' I instructed, but Jennifer already had her phone in her hand.

'He's not answering.'

Terror clutched my insides. 'I have to find them.'

'Jess, I'm so sorry.' Jennifer was crying again, frightened little sobs. 'If I'd known you hadn't agreed to it …' She broke off. 'You know he wouldn't harm a hair on Noah's head.'

'No, but he might not bring him back.'

'Oh my God.' She covered her eyes. 'He's not himself, Jess. He doesn't know what he's doing.'

'Keep trying his phone.'

I hurtled out of the house to the car and made the twenty-minute drive to Windermere in record time, my mind empty of everything but the need to bring my son home.

The car park was half-empty, the overcast morning off-putting to visitors.

Not bothering to pay for parking, I ran to the ticket office I'd been to so many times in the past, barking out my request for rowing-boat hire to the woman behind the glass.

'You OK?' She looked startled.

I forced a smile as I dug my debit card out of my bag. 'I'm running late. I promised my husband and son I would join them.'

'Ah.' A smile replaced her frown. 'Rain forecast for later. You've come at the right time.'

I paused on the other side of the ticket office, breath heaving in and out of my lungs as I scanned the red-and-white-painted boats scattered like toys across the lake. It wasn't hard to spot the one I was looking for. About a quarter of a mile out, it was the only boat not moving, two dark-haired figures in orange life-jackets motionless in the middle. Adam was bent forward talking to Noah, who was peering over the side.

My stomach lurched. My boy was a strong swimmer, Adam too, but what if he … *no*. I snatched my mind away from the horror stories I'd read, about the frightening lengths some parents went to if denied access to their children. *He wouldn't harm a hair on Noah's head*. I had to believe that Jennifer was right.

I sprinted to the jetty farther down, where the traditional wooden boats were lined up. Fumbling on my life jacket, I interrupted the attendant's instructions.

'I've done it before.'

'Forty-five minutes,' he said, glancing at his watch.

Grasping the oars, I managed to turn the boat around, muscle memory coming back from those long-ago family holidays when Dad insisted we all take a turn. I steered the boat in a straight line to Adam and Noah, blowing my fringe from my eyes, trying not to think of Rachel's waterlogged body in the canal.

I'm going to get him, I'm going to get him, I chanted to her in my head. My upper arms burnt with exertion, my face growing hot with the effort. I imagined Mum with me, urging me on, hearing her voice in my mind. *Go, Jess! You can do it!* and a feeling of calm descended as I turned with a heave of the oar, the front of the boat nudging the stern of Adam's.

His head jerked round, hands shooting out to grip the sides. 'Jess!' His utter astonishment lit a flame of anger. Had he really thought I wouldn't care where he was, that I would let him leave the country with Noah? 'What—?'

'Mummy!' Raising his head from the opposite side, Noah stood up, the boat rocking as he swapped sides. 'I asked Daddy if you would come, but he said no.'

'Well, I'm here.' My voice had a tremor flecked through it. Reaching over, I grabbed the side of their boat as I began to drift. 'Get in,' I said, stretching my other hand out to Noah. 'We have to go now.'

'But, Mum, we were looking for fishes.' Noah plopped onto the seat and folded his arms with a mutinous frown. 'Daddy said we might see some trout.'

I risked a look at Adam, glimpsing the rucksack between his feet.

'Mum told you where we were,' he said tightly.

'Did you think she wouldn't? You knew I was coming to pick him up.'

His eyes were fixed on the bottom of the boat.

'Don't do this, Adam.'

'I was going to bring him home.' I'd been expecting a fight, but his voice was soft and when he lifted his eyes they were filled with shame. 'Noah didn't want to go on an aeroplane without you, and …' He lowered his voice further as Noah lost interest and dipped his head over the side of the boat once more. 'I don't want to be a weekend dad, to not be there every night.'

'You should have thought about that sooner.' My voice was choked. 'You think behaving like this is going to win my trust?' I was trembling all over, my words pushed through gritted teeth.

'Don't deny me custody, Jess.'

'I never said I would.' I looked at the rucksack. 'Give me his passport.'

Adam hesitated, then unzipped one of the pockets and took it out, not looking at me as he handed it over.

I grabbed it, checking it was Noah's before pushing it into my pocket. We'd intended to go abroad as a family for the first time the following spring. That would never happen now. 'Come on, Noah.'

This time he let me hoist him into the boat, which rocked precariously as he dropped into my lap. Drawing him close, I kissed his cold cheek and briefly closed my eyes, sending up a prayer of thanks. 'I thought we could invite Jasmine round to play tomorrow.'

'Yay!' Brightness flooded his face once more. 'Is Daddy coming?'

'No,' I said with forced lightness. 'Daddy's going to live with Nanna for a while, and then he's going to buy his own house and you'll be able to stay with him sometimes.'

I hoped Adam would get the message. I wasn't going to deny him access, however much I wanted to at that moment. When I met his guilty gaze, he gave a single nod.

Noah thought for a moment, the aeroplane trip apparently forgotten. I held him, our hearts beating in tandem. 'Cool,' he said finally, in the casual, accepting way of children – in a way I knew would break Adam's heart – though I was sure when it sank in that his dad wasn't there every night to read him a story, or cook his dinner, there would tears and questions.

Turning from the stricken face of my husband, I settled Noah opposite me. My throat tightened when he gave Adam a little wave and blew him a kiss.

'Come on, Ninja.' I reached for the oars. 'Time to go home.'

Chapter 47

Two months later

'Don't forget to make a wish,' I said, ready with my phone as Noah sucked in a deep breath, ready to blow out the candles on his cake. I snapped some photos as he blew, extinguishing the tiny flames.

'I wish dinosaurs would come back to life.'

'I don't think there's much chance of that one coming true,' Meredith murmured next to me, eyes dancing with humour.

I smiled. 'Especially as he said it out loud.'

Noah's friends gathered around him, their chatter filling the room. Jasmine peeled away to look at me with pleading eyes.

'Can I have a big slice, please?'

'Jazzy!' Meredith chided, giving an eyeroll. 'Anyone would think I didn't feed her. Though it does look delicious.'

'His grandma made it.' I took a photo of Noah scooping up a fingerful of chocolate icing.

'She couldn't come to the party?'

'Noah's going to hers tomorrow.'

Meredith pulled a sympathetic face. 'I suppose that's one benefit of being separated. The kids get to celebrate twice.'

Separated. Soon to be divorced. I'd become a statistic – part of a broken family. We were doing OK so far though, getting through it. Noah seemed relatively unscathed, thanks to Adam and me making superhuman efforts to keep things civil, though I know he missed their bedtime stories.

Adam was still at his mother's, as most of his savings had gone to Rachel and I hadn't decided whether to sell the house.

Jennifer had apologized over and over for Adam's behaviour, but finally gave up pleading with me to forgive him. Adam told her that we were better off apart, but I knew she didn't fully understand what had happened. How could she?

Dad broke into my thoughts. 'You went through a dinosaur phase at his age,' he said, once I'd sliced the cake and he'd helped me pass the paper plates around. 'You never went through the ballerina stage like a lot of girls.'

It was his way of trying to re-establish the bond between us. It was going to take time, but he was being patient. It helped that he was seeing more of Ruth, even referring to her as his girlfriend. She was here today, proving to be a natural with the children, organizing a game of pass-the-parcel, which had the children squealing with excitement.

Will and Sam were here too, currently chatting in the kitchen with Jo and her new partner, Daniel. Jo and I had been messaging more, and I was glad she'd accepted my invitation to visit before driving to Manchester to meet Daniel's parents.

Sam still had his dreadlocks, which Noah had found fascinating, but he'd scrubbed up well and – since working with Will on the boat – was back in touch with his parents.

'Sorry you never found out what happened to your sister,' he'd said, catching me in the hallway as I was bringing the cake through. 'S'pose it must have been an accident.'

A familiar knot tightened in my stomach; something unfinished. 'Don't worry about it, Sam.' I mustered a smile.

'Wouldn't have met *him* though, otherwise,' he said with a nod of his head, meaning Will.

My smile had been genuine. 'Neither would I.'

The party was winding down now, parents arriving to pick up their overexcited children. After I'd seen them off with party bags – Jasmine having to be practically dragged away by Meredith – and Jo and Daniel had left with promises to visit again, Will came through with a bottle of beer.

'That went well,' he said, looking completely at home. 'Took me back a few years. I used to love pass-the-parcel.'

Warmth flooded through me at the sight of him; this was his first visit since that awful day when Adam had tried to throttle him, though we'd spoken regularly on the phone. His presence was calming, but also set off a flutter in the pit of my stomach.

'Dad enjoyed himself.' I looked to where he was kneeling down, curved over the keyboard he'd bought Noah, elbows moving as he tinkled out a tune, while Noah clapped his hands. 'My grandpa's clever,' he said to Ruth, who nodded her agreement.

'He's so cute.' Will's elbow brushed mine as he reached for a paper plate and loaded it with crisps. 'I'm starving.'

'Driving long distances will do that to you.'

'Sam ate a couple of pasties on the way up. I don't know where he puts all the food he eats.' Will grinned as Sam came in from the kitchen, where he'd been chatting to Kristin, who'd stayed behind to help clear up. He was holding a can of cola and, not looking where he was going, stumbled on a piece of Lego and fell against Dad.

'Hey,' Dad grumbled, rubbing his shoulder as Sam reeled away, one hand raised in an apology. 'Watch where you're going.'

Sam froze, statue-like, his mouth falling open.

Noah giggled, the sound dying as he picked up on something in Sam's expression. 'Mummy?' He looked at me uncertainly.

'What's going on?' Will stared at me too, his puzzlement reflecting mine.

'It was you.' Sam's voice was a whisper, heard clearly in the pin-drop silence that had fallen. He wheeled around, meeting my gaze, pointing the cola can at my dad. 'It was him,' he repeated. 'Under the bridge.'

For a second, everything slowed down. Blood roared in my ears, drowning out everything but the sound of Will's voice, clear as a bell as he asked Sam, 'Are you sure?'

When Sam nodded, Dad pushed past him into the hallway as though he was about to be sick, Ruth following close behind.

Noah's eyes were on me, wide with bewilderment. 'Mummy?'

'Grandpa's not feeling very well.' My voice was light and high. 'Too much cake, I think.'

'I want a story from my new book.' Reacting to something he didn't understand, Noah rushed over to his heap of presents and plucked out *Dinosaurs in the Garden*.

'I'll read to him.' Will's hand rested briefly on my shoulder. 'Go and talk to your dad.'

'What's happening?' I turned to see Kristin, a tea towel in one hand, a mug in the other. 'Everything OK?'

'I have to talk to my dad.'

Sam had moved to the window, his face stark white against the darkness beyond, patting his pockets as if looking for cigarettes. 'I'm sorry,' he said, eyes glittering in the lamp light. 'I shouldn't have blurted it out. It was the shock. It's what he said to me that night, you know?'

'You're certain?' My voice was barely audible.

Sam scrunched up his face. 'You saw how he reacted, yeah?'

Moving past him with leaden limbs and a leaden weight in my chest, I found Dad collapsed on the bottom stair, hands clamped around his head.

'What was that all about?' Ruth hovered anxiously. 'He won't tell me.'

'I need to talk to him alone.'

'OK.' She nodded slowly, backing away. 'I'll leave you to it,' she said, eyes still on Dad. 'Call me later, Jon.'

When she'd retrieved her coat and bag and slipped out of the front door, I looked at him. 'Well?'

His gaze had a dislocated quality as if his mind was elsewhere. 'I'm so sorry, Jess.'

My heart lurched. I staggered against the wall and slid down it, trapped in a band of heat from the radiator. 'You were there that night.'

'That stupid boy.' Dad's voice was a growl. 'I should have kept my mouth shut.'

I forced back the tears threatening to fall. 'Tell me.'

He dropped his eyes like a child about to be scolded. The silence tightened, then, 'I didn't mean to push her. You have to believe me, Jess.'

His words hit me like bullets. 'You killed her.' I could barely project the words. 'Sam was right.'

'She was so surprised when I turned up,' he went on, as though I hadn't spoken. 'She was expecting *him*.' His lip curled, even after all this time. 'Lucian bloody West.'

'How?' It was a hollow whisper.

Dad's eyes flicked to mine and away. 'I left a message with the gallery, pretending to be him. I knew she wouldn't meet me otherwise.' The scale of deception made me want to vomit. 'I thought she might run away when she saw it was me, but curiosity got the better of her. She was drunk.' He gave the half-laugh I knew from old. 'I can't recall a time we talked when she was sober.'

'Why were you there, Dad?'

'I wanted to ask her why she was back.' He dragged in a breath, his face distorted. 'She started saying it was time you knew the truth about everything. I didn't realize until I saw the message on her phone exactly what she was talking about, but I knew she wanted to hurt you. I told her you didn't deserve it.'

'Jesus, Dad. You thought you were doing me a favour?'

He didn't respond, seeming lost in memory. 'She didn't like

that. Me putting your feelings first. All I got was a stream of abuse, about what a bastard I was, a liar, a cheat' – I thought briefly of Caroline – 'and so on and so on, telling me she'd seen what I was up to, that she knew all about my "other women". Again, his eyes flickered to mine, but it was as if he wasn't seeing me at all.

'I thought I'd been discreet,' he went on. 'She said she followed me one day, to some pub, and "how would Jess feel if she knew?"' It was a cruel impersonation of Rachel that brought a swell of fury to my throat. 'She threatened me. Said there was *so* much she could tell you, she'd even written it down. It was probably the drink talking. She was swaggering all over the place.'

'You should have left. At least made sure she got home safely.'

'She was so angry,' he continued, almost disbelieving. 'She said some awful things about …' He held me in his gaze for a moment, as if considering adding something. Then he lowered his head, kneading his brow with his fingertips. 'She knew Denny had been following her. I explained it was because I wanted to know how she was, but she wouldn't have it. Said she'd walked for hours some days, to mess with him.'

Blood rushed to my face. 'You can't blame her for that, Dad.'

'I tried to leave then, I really did. She came after me, slapped me hard around the face and I …' His breath caught, face twisting with pain. 'I pushed her, Jess. I never meant her to go in the water. There were no railings. She just went under.' His eyes were glassy, as though reliving the moment.

'And you did nothing to help?'

'I thought she would come up, and I would drag her out, but I was in shock.'

'So you thought you'd leave her there?'

'I know it was the wrong thing to do.' His voice was flat, as if his emotions had dried up. 'Do you think I haven't relived that moment a million times since? It never leaves me, Jess. I'll have to live with it for the rest of my life, but I didn't want to hurt you.'

'But you have, Dad.' Tears were falling fast. 'You killed my sister.'

276

From the living room, I heard Noah's laughter and Will's voice, in the kitchen a chink of glasses – life going on, but it would never be the same again. The two men I should have trusted most in the world had lied to me, to protect themselves.

'I'll never forgive you, Dad.' I got to my feet, insides trembling. 'Mum wouldn't have either.'

'Jess, please.' He held out a hand, his shoulders shaking. 'I want to be here, for you and Noah. Try to understand.'

'I should call the police right now.'

He froze, as if the possibility hadn't occurred to him.

'Does Denny know any of this?'

'God, no.' Distaste rippled over Dad's face. 'He thought I was on one of my fishing trips that night.'

I thought about that so-called trip, when I'd worried about him going off on his own. 'You would have got away with it if Sam hadn't seen you.'

He looked at me with hooded eyes. 'Would it have been such a bad thing? Wait,' he said, as I started to walk away. 'What good has it done, you knowing? Look at us!' I turned to see him on his feet, reaching for me. 'This is what I didn't want to happen. I don't want to lose you, Jess. You're all I have left, you and Noah.'

He sounded so much like Adam, I wondered for the first time whether I'd subconsciously chosen a husband that reminded me of my father. 'There's no coming back from what you've done.'

'It was an accident.' He spread his hands, voice imploring. 'I'm not a *murderer*.'

Again, the echo of Adam's words. At least my husband had been telling the truth.

'Are you going to turn me in?'

'You should turn yourself in.'

'I can't do that, Jess.' He shrugged, almost regretful. 'I want to be around for you and Noah.'

As if on cue, his grandson shot out of the living room and hurled himself at Dad. 'Will you do my bath time, Grandpa?'

'Sorry,' Will said, following. 'I couldn't stop him.'

Dad was already halfway upstairs behind Noah, who was shrieking with glee, high on birthday cake and being the centre of attention – how it should be. Could I really burst his family bubble any more than I already had? His father gone, then his grandfather. *Was it fair?*

Was it fair that Rachel was dead, and Dad had lied about it? He might not have killed her intentionally, but his hands had pushed her.

Will's arm wound around my shoulders. 'Was it him?'

I nodded, not trusting myself to speak.

His arms tightened around me. 'What are you going to do?'

Over his shoulder, I saw Kristin in the kitchen doorway. She must have heard everything. Her eyes were stormy, her expression taut. Something passed between us that I didn't understand. 'She's going to call the police.' Her voice was strong and decisive, as if she had pulled the words from my heart.

I broke away from Will, warm where his arms had been, drying my eyes with the heel of my hand. Upstairs, Dad roared like a bear and Noah yelped with giggles.

I reached for my bag and took out my phone.

Chapter 48

Whatever happens now, I don't regret what I did.

'I know I'm not yours,' Rachel said that night by the canal. 'I know Mum had an affair. I don't blame her, after what you'd been doing for years.'

Those were the words that came out of her mouth before that final push. Not yours. After everything I had done. I forgave Helen because I knew I deserved it. She had every right to get her own back. I willingly took on the baby and raised her as my own and Rachel had the nerve to say she wasn't mine. Well, I'm glad she wasn't. She was the result of her mother's desire for revenge with a man who came to fit a new bathroom window – a moment of madness, followed by a few happy years, and then nothing but trouble. Trouble that I have no doubt hastened her mother's death.

The truth is, I felt free, once the horror of Rachel sinking below the water had worn off. I was on edge for a while back home, until the police turned up. But they hadn't come to arrest me. Nothing suspicious, they said. Alcohol consumption.

Identifying her body … I could only think of Helen and how heartbroken she would have been. It was the first time I was grateful that she wasn't alive to witness the ongoing devastation her daughter brought to everything she touched.

Part of me longed to tell Jess she had nothing to fear but of course I couldn't and then she started digging about, playing detective, and I could only watch it play out and hope – if that's the right word – she would give up.

I'd been so relieved when Lucian turned out not to be Noah's father, but wished it wasn't Adam. I liked him, as much as I could like anyone my daughter married. I had Denny do some digging when they got together and his background was impeccable, no hint he was capable of cheating on Jess. Then again, I can hardly criticize. Maybe that was why I was willing to keep his secret. I know first-hand what men will do, the lengths they're willing to go to protect those they love. I wanted to protect my daughter.

She'll be fine without Adam. I'll always be there for her, and that chap who turned up at her house – Will – I can see where that might go, saw the way he looked at her. He took care of Rachel when she didn't deserve it, which speaks volumes about his character, and he ultimately led Jess to the truth about Adam, which I never would have divulged.

Rachel didn't deserve Noah, but Jess does. She's a natural mum, like her own mother was. For as long as I'm breathing, I won't let anything come between her and her son.

That's why I'm not going to tell her that Rachel wasn't mine. She would forgive her mother a fling, but knowing Rachel wasn't mine gives me a motive. She might not understand, and I can't have anything else driving a wedge between us.

She'll come round one day, I know she will. She's angry now, but she needs me more than she thinks. I can be patient. I'll wait as long as it takes for her to forgive me.

Chapter 49

Finally, Noah was asleep, worn out by the day's excitement. Kristin had taken over bath and bedtime duties before the police arrived, Dad jogging downstairs without looking at me to greet them with a guileless smile.

Once the officers had taken statements from me, Will, and Sam, while Dad sat silently at the dining table, they asked him to accompany them to the station. It was either go quietly or be arrested and he chose to go quietly, glancing at me over his shoulder as he left, shooting me a warm, bracing smile that filled me with dread.

The first thing I did when they'd gone was call Adam and tell him the truth. 'I'm so sorry I accused you,' I said, my feelings ricocheting between disbelief, anger, and grief – for Rachel, for the Dad I now suspected hadn't existed, and for Mum, because I wanted her to hold me and tell me I'd done the right thing.

'My God, Jess. I can't believe it.' Adam had reverted to his husband role. 'Do you want me to come over?'

'No … thanks, but I've got people here.'

Silence pulsed down the line. 'Thank you for letting me know,' he said quietly. 'I'll pick up Noah tomorrow lunchtime.' I didn't have it in me to discuss Noah's birthday with him.

I sat with Kristin, Will, and Sam, talking through everything that had happened as we tried to shape Dad's confession, his endless lies, into something that made sense, though we didn't come close. There was no excusing what he'd done.

All the while, Kristin held my hand and Will barely took his eyes off me, while Sam sporadically muttered, 'Shit, man. Couple of minutes earlier and I'd have seen it happen.'

'I'm so glad you're all here,' I said tearfully. 'And I'm sorry for getting you involved.'

'*You've* got nothing to apologize for,' Kristin said grimly.

When Sam went outside for a smoke, Will sat beside me on the sofa.

'It's hard to imagine now, but you'll get through this, Jess.'

Before I could speak my phone rang. I snatched it up. It was Dad, calling from home. He had denied everything, he told me.

'Sorry, Jess, but I can't go to jail. I wouldn't survive.'

His words barely penetrated the white noise in my mind. 'But my statement—'

'I know you want to punish me, Jess, but I can't do it.'

I hung up and burst into tears. The police called later to say that without a confession, or any evidence, there was no case to answer. Dad was a free man.

'Talk to him,' the officer said. 'Try to sort out your differences.'

It transpired Dad had made it sound as though what had happened was nothing more than a family feud, a vendetta against him, unjust accusations based on the difficult relationship he'd had with his younger daughter, coupled with a need for answers surrounding her death, which was nothing but a tragic accident.

'I hate him,' I wept on Kristin's shoulder. She, Will, and Sam were grim-faced with horrified disbelief.

'The bastard's got away with it,' Sam said, aiming a punch at the wall.

'He won't though.' I blew my nose, a steely resolve hardening inside me. 'He'll pay for what he's done.'

Kristin's eyes locked on mine. 'How?'

'He won't ever set eyes on Noah and me again.'

I slept like someone drugged that night, incapable of keeping my swollen eyes open. Kristin insisted on staying, promising to check on Noah, and I didn't have the energy to argue, glad of her steady presence in the spare room.

Will had driven back to London with a subdued Sam, once I'd assured them there was nothing more they could do.

'Thanks again for everything,' I'd said.

Will's face had been blank with exhaustion. He held me for a long moment, some of his warmth seeping into my bones. 'I'll call you tomorrow, OK?'

I'd nodded into his shoulder, too wrung-out to speak, then hugged an embarrassed Sam, whose arms remained stiffly by his sides.

'Safe journey,' I managed, holding back more tears until they'd gone.

Waking now, the fragments of a nightmare clinging, my lashes crusted with tears, I lay for a moment, my thoughts muddy and unfocused, a sour plunge in my stomach as I replayed yesterday's events; Noah's birthday, which should have been a happy day, sullied by what came after. But I wasn't going to let Dad ruin the rest of our lives. He'd been right about one thing, the day I found Rachel's phone among the belongings he'd wanted to destroy. We *did* deserve better.

Kristin was moving about downstairs, the smell of coffee drifting up.

I slipped out of bed and into Noah's room. He was still sleeping, breath puffing in and out, and I knelt by his bed for a while, hoping whatever came next wouldn't impact his innocence or happiness too much.

Finally, I straightened, leaving his door ajar as I left the room.

I showered quickly and dressed, humming to keep my mind empty.

In the bedroom, I took my phone off charge – I had a vague memory of Kristin plugging it in for me, before placing a glass of water on the bedside table, her cool hand on my forehead as she urged me to sleep – and turned it on. I wanted to look at the photos I'd taken of Noah before everything went wrong, smiling at one of him ripping open his presents, another of him wearing a sheet of wrapping paper as a pirate hat that Will had shaped for him.

There was a text message from Will. *Home safe. Thinking of you. Talk soon xx* Tears filled my eyes as I touched the screen. How odd, that comfort should come from a man I'd known for such a short time.

Spotting an email notification, I clicked on the app. Kristin was clattering in the kitchen, the sound of spoons in mugs, music playing quietly in the background.

I sat on the stairs and opened the message, heart somersaulting when I saw the message was from Rachel. How was that even possible? My eyes whipped to the subject line: HAPPY BIRTHDAY!! and down to the first paragraph. My breath high in my chest, I read:

Hi Jess.

I've scheduled this email to be delivered on your boy's birthday. After 6 p.m. Isn't that when parties finish? There will be a party, won't there? I think I remember my 6th. Too much ice cream, I was sick in the bath. Happy days.

Tears flooded my eyes. A message from Rachel, at last. A proper, chatty email – the sort I'd once dreamt of us exchanging.

Anyway, here's why I'm sending this, for my sins. I'm hoping I'll be far away by now if everything goes according to plan, so I won't have to deal with the fallout (I know, I know, I'm a bitch but read on).

Was she going to tell me about Adam? *Oh, Rachel, you already did.* Sniffing and wiping my eyes, I continued reading.

You won't want to hear this, but our dear father isn't all he seems (if you haven't worked it out by now, and I don't think you have). You remember his student, who came to the house? Well, she wasn't his only … whatever she was. Long story short, but I caught him once with a (grown-up) woman. I was skiving off school (big surprise) and saw them by the river kissing on a bench (vomit). It was obvious they'd known each other a while. She worked in the pub near the univer-sity. I know – what a cliché! I followed her there afterwards, found out her name and where she lived – not from her, I flirted with the barman, who got quite chatty. She looked like she'd been crying, which seems to be a theme where Daddy dearest is concerned. Anyway, he didn't know I knew about her, but I liked knowing he didn't know that I knew (if you get my drift). I suppose I can see now that it must have been difficult for him at times, Mum being ill and having to take care of her – he did love Mother, I'll give him that – though I used to see the way he stared at her friend Caroline. Tut, tut.

Anyway, when I came back to London, I remembered 'the other woman' and decided to look her up, see if she still lived there. I don't really know why. Something to do, I suppose. I was trying to stay on the good old straight and narrow for Lucian, after a rather poor start. I arrived drunk at the airport (never liked flying sober) and got myself a tiny bit arrested, spent the night in a cell. Still, it saved me looking for somewhere to stay.

Where was I? Oh yes, Dad's other woman. She did still live there, so I went to pay her a visit, only I didn't get to speak to her, which I'm glad about now. You'll never guess what, Jess! (Don't you hate it when people say that?) Spoiler alert: YOU HAVE A SISTER!!! (Capitals are necessary.) Well, a half-sister (I was going to say, 'another one', but you would find that weird, though I suppose it could mean I was only 'half' a sister to you – less than that, really).

I didn't handle it gracefully. I came out and told her the truth – turns out she had no clue – and where to find him if she wanted to (someone at the university told me he'd moved to the Lakes, big surprise – NOT!) but I warned her he wasn't worth it. Up to her. At least she has a choice. She was nice, actually. Her mum told her that her father – 'a music professor' – died soon after she was born and she wouldn't discuss him, so I don't think he knows about her. She looks a bit like you, that's how I knew for certain she was his daughter. If he does know, shame on him for not wanting anything to do with her. Her mother married and had a son, but she's a widow now. Anyway, what I wanted to say is, you should find your sister if she hasn't found you already. She's a much better person than I am. I think you'll like her. She lives with her mum in Finsbury Park and her name is Kristin Wells.

Good luck!

Rachel xx

Epilogue

Six months later

'Mum, come and look!' I joined Noah at the water's edge. 'It's a starfish.'

'So it is.' I crouched to admire its spiny skin and sunshine colours. 'Isn't it pretty?'

Noah poked it gently through the rippling water. 'Can I pick it up?'

'Best leave it alone,' I said with a smile. 'Let's go and tell Will about it.'

I trailed Noah up the sandy beach to the boatyard where Will worked, smiling as Noah began describing the starfish, and Will reeled back in comical surprise.

We lived in Fife now; a fishing village called Anstruther. I sold our house in Ulverston for less than the asking price, my share of the money stretching further in this part of Scotland. Home was a pretty three-bedroomed cottage called The Hideaway, with a view of the sea on a clear day, not far from the school where Noah had settled well.

He loved living close to the beach and, although he'd asked a lot about his Grandpa at first, he'd quickly become absorbed in his new life, helped by the recent addition to our family of a black and white kitten called Patch.

Jennifer visited often, and Adam – perhaps relieved that my father's betrayal had proved to be worse than his own – was on a mission to be the best father and ex-husband he could, making the four-hour drive every other weekend to spend time with his son while he looked for a place to live.

I hadn't seen or spoken to Dad since Noah's birthday. Ruth turned up at the house, a few days after his arrest, to beg me to make up with him.

'He misses you, Jess. Nothing can be bad enough that he deserves you cutting him off.' Something in my face must have convinced her. She didn't contact me again.

Denny turned up too, devastation etched on his craggy features, trying to mount a defence for Dad. 'You and Noah are his world, Jess. Your mum wouldn't want this.' I could have told him the truth, blown apart his friendship with Dad, but I didn't have it in me. His loyalties would always lie with Dad, even if he figured out the truth.

'You still coming for dinner tonight?' I asked Will, liking how content he was in the yard, the sea breeze ruffling his hair. He'd let Sam stay on the boat and used his savings to make the move to Scotland, buying up the old boatyard and renting a flat nearby.

'I never say no to a free meal.' Will's eyes held mine, and I wondered whether tonight I would invite him to stay over. When he'd suggested I move up here and make a fresh start, I hadn't hesitated. Our bond, forged under circumstances I could never have imagined, grew stronger every day, but we were taking things slowly.

'Hey,' said Kristin, as we arrived back at the cottage. On her afternoons off from the property agency in the village, she enjoyed indulging her new-found passion for baking. 'Victoria sponge,' she said, proudly holding up the tin.

'All for me,' Noah said, patting his belly.

There had been no question of Kristin not coming with us, once the truth came out.

'I wanted so much to tell you,' she'd cried when I showed her Rachel's email. 'I even tried a couple of times but couldn't go through with it.'

She'd moved to Ulverston – alone – determined to find me and confront Dad, but once there, had worried about the impact. Instead, she took the job at Cumbrian Cottages, deciding to get to know me first and maybe become my friend.

'And when I did, it became impossible to tell you the truth. I thought you'd hate me for keeping it from you. It was obvious how highly you thought of your dad, and I didn't want to ruin that by revealing he'd had an affair with my mum. It's not like she's carrying a torch for him. She couldn't understand why I'd moved so far from London.' It turned out that her mother still lived there, in the house in Finsbury Park where Kristin had grown up. 'And then … some of the things you told me about him.' Her tears had kept falling. 'I didn't want him to be my father,' she said baldly. 'He's not a good man.'

I'd respected her decision to not tell Dad he had another daughter. He didn't deserve her, she said. Plus, she didn't want to give him that kind of power; any reason to insinuate his way into her life. Like me, Kristin wanted nothing to do with him.

Now, I watched her moving around the kitchen and wondered why I hadn't spotted our resemblance sooner. The truth had been shocking, but strangely unsurprising – maybe because the day and preceding weeks had been so surreal that nothing could shake me up any more. Instead, I'd been overcome with gratitude that, once again, an unexpected gift had come my way, courtesy of Rachel.

'I only saw your sister once,' Kristin had told me, after we'd talked and cried. 'I think, at heart, she was a good person who cared about you.'

I still had ups and downs. Occasionally, the loss of my family felt visceral, and I struggled to get out of bed, but reminded myself

I *did* have family – I had Noah, and, through him, there would always be a link to Rachel and Mum. And now I had Kristin, one of the kindest, nicest people I'd ever met. *My half-sister*. I had Jennifer too, who couldn't switch off her maternal feelings, despite me no longer being her daughter-in-law. And, of course, I had Will. Families came in all shapes and sizes, and this was mine.

'Tell me a story, Mummy,' Noah said, once I'd persuaded him into the claw-footed bath in front of the window that overlooked the beach. He'd made a crown of bubbles in his hair, and my heart softened with love as I knelt by the bath.

'What kind of story?'

'A good one.'

I thought of the stories Dad and Adam had told themselves – and me – to justify their actions; stories that were lies. Lies had the power to destroy lives if they came out, and they had a way of snaking into the open.

My throat constricted as I studied my son's open face, the trust in his eyes. I wanted him to look at me like that, always.

No more lies.

'How about a true story?' I trailed my hand through the water. 'Something that really happened.'

'OK.' He nodded solemnly. 'Once upon a time …' he prompted.

I smiled. 'Six years ago, there lived a lovely young woman called Rachel—'

'Like Auntie Rachel!' he interrupted.

I swallowed. 'That's right.' I smoothed a hand over his cap of wet hair and cradled his cheek. 'Auntie Rachel carried a baby boy in her tummy for nine whole months, and when he was born, she gave him to her sister as a very special gift, to keep forever.' I paused, seeing the calculation take place in his eyes. 'The baby's name was Noah.'

He tilted his head. 'Noah, like me?'

My vision blurred through a haze of tears. 'Exactly like you, sweetheart.'

Ready for his questions, I rose to reach for a towel.

Through the window, someone walked along the beach, turning out of sight: a man; white hair, dark clothing, shoulders rounded. *Denny?*

My heart lurched, but when I looked again, he'd gone.

Acknowledgements

I would like to thank the amazing team at HQ Digital, especially my brilliant editor Belinda Toor for helping to make my book the best it could be, I'm so grateful. Thanks to Eldes Tran for her eagle-eyed copyedits, Loma Slater for her proofread, and to Audrey Linton for overseeing the process. Many thanks to Anna Sikorska for the amazing cover, and to everyone involved in marketing and promotion.

I'm in awe of the bloggers and reviewers who take time to spread the word and give lovely feedback, which makes all the hard work worthwhile – thank you each and every one, and to everyone who has bought and read my books.

As ever, thanks go to my lovely friend and co-writer Amanda Brittany for her support, and another big thank you to my friends and family who manage to stay interested and enjoy my stories!

I couldn't do any of it without my husband who has somehow survived this process twenty times. Once again, Tim, thank you from the bottom of my heart.

Keep reading for an excerpt from
And Then She Ran ...

She picked up
the baby in her arms...

AND THEN
SHE RAN

KAREN CLARKE

Chapter 1

Two days ago

'You can't take the baby, Grace.' Patrick's tone was pleading. 'I need her.'

'Please, just let us go.'

'I can't.' His tone hardened. 'I won't let you. It'll ruin everything.'

'If you don't, I'll go to the press.' My heart pounded. 'I'll tell them the truth.'

He froze, perhaps imagining the implications, what it would mean for his career. He came closer. For a moment, I thought he was going to hit me. I cringed as he punched the wall by my head. 'What am I supposed to say to people?'

I straightened my shoulders. 'You'll think of something,' I said, heart racing. 'You're good with words.'

He stared at me with something close to hatred. 'And if I let you go, you won't tell anyone?'

'I promise.' I kept my eyes on his. 'And you'll leave us alone?'

He was silent for a moment. 'Do I have a choice?'

I bundled Lily into her carrier, opened the door and ran.

Chapter 2

Now

I looked around the busy airport, heart drumming against my ribs. Despite the promise he'd made, I wasn't convinced that Patrick wouldn't come after me or have me followed.

The urge to keep checking hadn't left me since I boarded the plane in New York. When I wasn't feeding or pacifying Lily during the seven-hour flight, I was inspecting the other passengers in case Patrick had sneaked on board, or sent somebody to reclaim his eight-week-old daughter.

My chest tightened with worry, my hand rigid on Lily's back as I scanned the arrivals area once more, while a sea of people surged past. It was both familiar and strange being back in England – the first time since a fleeting visit to my mother's place in Berkshire four years ago. There was no one here to meet me. No one knew where I was. Patrick had probably guessed I'd return to the UK, but would have no idea where I was heading from Heathrow. I hadn't mentioned my aunt when we were exchanging potted life histories a year ago. He didn't know where she lived and I hadn't told him. Morag was a private person and I respected her wishes.

She'd only told my mother her new address in case of emergencies, though her sister was probably the last person Mum would turn to in a crisis, their long-standing rift unhealed.

Unaware of our noisy surroundings, Lily slept soundly at last in the ergonomic carrier Patrick had bought, designed to hold her against my chest like an embrace. Her cheeks were stained red, her long lashes spiky with tears as she nuzzled into me. I kissed the soft fuzz of her fine dark hair as I hoisted her gingham baby bag onto my shoulder. Grabbing the handle of my suitcase, I followed signs to the taxis, inhaling sharply as a blast of cold air greeted me outside. It was mid-March, but the temperature felt Baltic after the overheated journey and milder Manhattan weather I'd left behind.

I tugged out Lily's lemon-coloured blanket and draped it around her as she began to stir. 'Hush, hush,' I murmured, shivers of cold rippling through my cheap, zip-up jacket as I hurried to the first waiting taxi.

'S'cuse me, there's a queue.' A man stepped forward blocking my way. He had wiry grey hair and an aggrieved expression; the look of someone spoiling for a fight.

'Oh, I'm sorry.' Tears rushed to my eyes, anxiety spilling over. 'I didn't … I wasn't—'

'Leave her alone, Len. You can see she's got her hands full.'

A woman – probably his wife – gave a compassionate smile that creased her whole face. 'Take it, love. We're not in a hurry.'

Relief made me gush. 'Thank you, if you're sure? I need to get her home and settled. My husband's expecting us.' *Home.* I no longer had one.

'Shame he's not here to pick you up.' The man's hard gaze didn't soften as he jammed meaty hands in the pockets of his padded coat.

'Stop it, Len.' The woman rolled her eyes. They were large and glassy, like marbles. 'I remember what it was like with little ones, even if this one doesn't.'

The driver had got out of the taxi and was stowing my suitcase in the boot. He slammed it shut and returned to the driver's seat.

'Well … thank you,' I said to the woman, keeping my face averted, not wanting the pair to remember my face.

She was wearing a navy baseball hat, tortoiseshell glasses, no make-up. Plain, I suppose. Early thirties, hard to tell. Had a baby, but covered up. No idea what it looked like.

Lots of women with babies must pass through the airport every day. Maybe some of them were running away too, wearing a cheap disguise; reading glasses that slightly magnified everything; hair thrust into a generic baseball cap to disguise its length and colour; a baggy grey sweatshirt with shapeless jeans and jacket, all purchased at a Walmart on the way to the airport and changed into in the toilets, before I continued my journey in a different cab.

Patrick wouldn't recognise the dowdy, androgynous woman currently climbing awkwardly into the taxi. No one from my old life would.

Heart jumping, I sat back and settled Lily. She was falling towards sleep again, her rosebud mouth making little sucking noises. Love rose like a sickness. *This has to work.*

'Where to?'

I met the driver's disinterested gaze in the rear-view mirror, then took a last look through the window at the dreary grey afternoon, where the couple were now quietly arguing at the pavement's edge. 'Victoria Station, please.'

Once there, I'd buy a ticket and take a coach for the last leg of my trip; to my aunt's home in deepest Wales where, I prayed, no one would ever find us.

Chapter 3

It felt strange at first, being on the opposite side of the road. I kept catching my breath whenever a car drove past in the 'wrong' lane, but after feeding and changing Lily, glad of the empty seat on the coach beside me, I finally dozed, worn out from adrenaline and the flight. My body was still running on a different time zone, aware it was early afternoon in Manhattan.

It was seven-thirty and dark by the time we reached Fenbrith and rain was falling steadily. Lily awoke, blinking her round brown eyes – recently darkened from blue – as she looked about, her tiny fingers splayed out on my chest.

'Hello, little mouse.' I felt an ache in my lower back as I rose. 'Looks like we're here.'

The driver got out and dumped my case on the rain-slicked ground. 'OK?' he asked as I disembarked, as if compelled to question the silent woman he'd just driven for over five hours and two hundred miles.

I forced a bland smile, one hand cupping Lily's head as I summoned my steadiest voice. 'Yes, thank you. It's been a long day that's all. We'll be glad to get out of this weather.'

Long day. Weather. I was speaking a universal code.

'You and me both.' The driver nodded in tacit understanding. 'On holiday, are you?'

'Something like that.'

'Well, this time of year Snowdonia's not too busy so make the most of it.'

'I will.' *Every contact leaves a trace.* I realized afresh how hard it was to truly disappear, to become invisible. Especially somewhere like this, where a stranger was bound to stand out.

Patrick doesn't know where you are.

For a second, as the coach pulled away, I imagined him appearing behind me, saw the flash of anger in his night-dark eyes and felt the grip of his fingers on my shoulder. *You didn't really think I'd let you go, did you?*

I wheeled around, a tremor running through me. There was no one there, just Lily and me on the empty street.

The rain had eased, but Lily was growing restless, flexing against me, unhappy at being back in her carrier. It had been a couple of hours since her last feed, which I'd undertaken in a sleepy haze, thankful I'd stuck to my guns and continued to secretly breastfeed whenever I could, despite Patrick insisting I use formula or *at least pump and freeze*, as if I was a machine – or a cow. It was clear by then that fatherhood didn't suit him. Or maybe it was because Lily wasn't the son he'd longed for.

Shivering with cold, desperate to get my baby to warmth and safety, I moved closer to the pub I was standing outside; a low-roofed building with light spilling from diamond-paned windows. The Carpenter's Arms, according to the sign, which creaked in the breeze like something from a horror film. The pub where I'd arranged to meet Morag. As I bumped my suitcase into a sheltered porch in front of the door, I briefly considered phoning my mother to let her know I was in the country, but it was better she didn't know in the unlikely event that Patrick decided to call her. Then I remembered; she didn't have the same surname as me, had changed it after my father's death, which would make her hard to find. An image of Patrick rushed in again, his lip curled in anger. I squashed it down. The day was taking its toll. I needed to sleep properly, in a bed, and give myself time to adjust to my surroundings.

I hoped Morag was already waiting in the pub. She lived three miles from the village. I could hardly walk in the dark with a baby and a suitcase, and didn't want to attract attention by taking a local taxi – if there was such a thing in this tiny hamlet. It had the air of a place from a bygone era. I wouldn't have been surprised to see a pony and trap clatter past.

As Lily let out a thin wail, I reached for the worn brass knob on the door just as it swung inwards. A wave of beer-scented warmth, the chink of glasses and the sound of laughter hit me. A pungent aroma of food made my mouth water. *When had I last eaten?*

I stood back, a protective arm across Lily, and yanked my suitcase out of the way as a woman emerged, backlit by the brightness inside so I couldn't make out her features. She half-turned, starting at the sight of me lurking by the door.

As Lily began crying in earnest, a tired sound that squeezed my heart, the woman's eyes met mine. I was aware of her comforting scent; laundry powder overlaid with something earthy; the smell of a garden, a hint of rosemary, and when she spoke, I instantly recognized her voice: raspy with a hint of steel, her Welsh accent barely detectable.

'There you are,' she said. 'Why are you hiding out here?'

'Hey, Aunt Morag.' I heard my slight American intonation and knew I'd have to lose it. 'It's good to see you.'

She stared for a long moment, the silence punctuated by Lily's intermittent cries, then let the pub door close behind her.

'We'd better go.' She jerked her head at the tiny car park at the side of the pub. 'You'll catch your death out here.'

Dear Reader,

We hope you enjoyed reading this book. If you did, we'd be so appreciative if you left a review. It really helps us and the author to bring more books like this to you.

Here at HQ Digital we are dedicated to publishing fiction that will keep you turning the pages into the early hours. Don't want to miss a thing? To find out more about our books, promotions, discover exclusive content and enter competitions you can keep in touch in the following ways:

JOIN OUR COMMUNITY:

Sign up to our new email newsletter:
http://smarturl.it/SignUpHQ

Read our new blog www.hqstories.co.uk

🐦 https://twitter.com/HQStories

f www.facebook.com/HQStories

BUDDING WRITER?

We're also looking for authors to join the HQ Digital family!
Find out more here:

https://www.hqstories.co.uk/want-to-write-for-us/

Thanks for reading, from the HQ Digital team

If you enjoyed *My Sister's Child*, then why not try another gripping thriller from HQ Digital?